THE IRON ANGEL

D1051815

Also by Richard Poole:

Jewel and Thorn

The Brass Key

THE IRON ANGEL

THE THIRD BOOK OF LOWMOOR

RICHARD POOLE

SIMON AND SCHUSTER

For Will again
and Mark

SIMON AND SCHUSTER
First published in Great Britain in 2007 by Simon and Schuster UK Ltd,
A CBS COMPANY

This paperback edition published in 2008

Simon & Schuster UK Ltd
Africa House, 64-78 Kingsway, London WC2B 6AH.

This book is a work of fiction. Names, characters, places and incidents are either
the product of the author's imagination or are used fictitiously. Any resemblance
to actual people living or dead, events or locales is entirely coincidental.

A CIP catalogue record for this book is available from the British Library.

ISBN: 978-0-68987-551-9

1 3 5 7 9 10 8 6 4 2

Typeset in Garamond by M Rules
Printed and bound in Great Britain by
Cox & Wyman Ltd, Reading, Berks

www.simonsays.co.uk

CONTENTS

	Prologue: The Conspiracy	1
1	Into the Barrens	11
2	The Wren's Egg	28
3	Riggs and Wells	45
4	Secrets of the Foundry	60
5	Surprise Attack	76
6	The Crystal Vortex	94
7	Blue Rats, Blue Ratters	110
8	Cloak of Secrecy	129
9	The Great Nest	149
10	The Laboratory Eye	162
11	Ambushed	176
12	In the Mausoleum	191
13	The Church of the Iron Angel	205
14	A Storm in a Pulpit	225
15	Strange Rooms with Many Doors	238
16	Lizard and Butterfly	251
17	Fish and Flowers	262
18	Fire and Ice	275
19	Spine Wrench Jangles his Bell	287
20	Thorn Jack Gets Lucky	307
21	A Clash of Knives	319
22	About-face	332
23	Rites of Passage	345

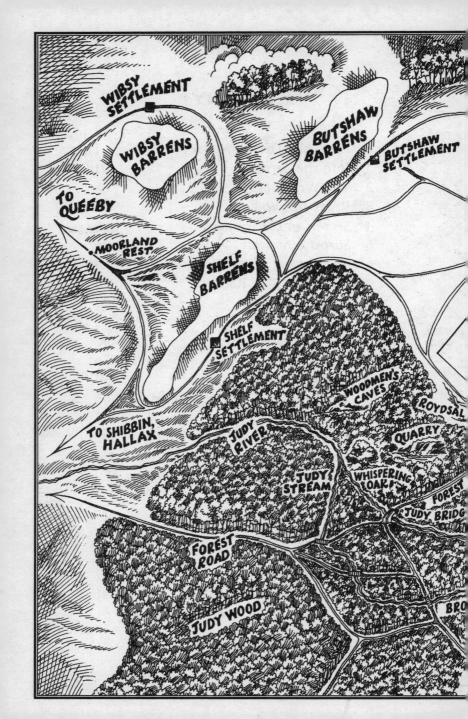

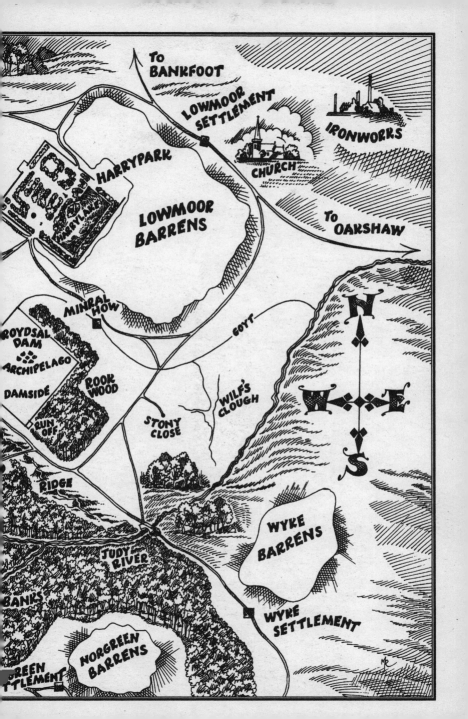

PROLOGUE
The Conspiracy

The stairs creaked as Racky Jagger went up to the second floor. The treads were scuffed and scratched by generations of feet, and a couple of steps had been inexpertly replaced. The banister wobbled under his hand: a good push and it might snap.

How like Querne to pick on a dump like this, he told himself. Her own hideout was richly furnished, but she harboured an alternative self that relished the low life and its sleazy haunts: decaying walls and roofs, crumbling ceilings and floors, and the furtive lives that were lived out between them. Well, this time she'd outdone herself: this tip stank of conspiracy.

He hadn't expected to find himself climbing these rickety stairs. He hadn't expected to emerge from the Barrens just where he did: Querne must have blazed a new through-route for him and the crystal he carried. He hadn't expected Oily Wells to be waiting with a saddle-rat for him and a verbal message from his mistress. Querne was in Lowmoor! He could draw only one conclusion: she was finally making her move, and he hadn't foreseen it. Distrust and curiosity struggled for mastery in his mind.

The landing offered a choice of battered doors, but only one was shut. On this he knocked.

After a time it opened and Spine Wrench appeared in the

gap. Spine owned the kind of face that once seen was never forgotten. He possessed a single bloodshot eye; ravelled skin skimmed the socket its partner might have occupied. He had a pendulous nose, a mouth that drooped at each corner and ears like knots of pink worms. Permanently shocked white hair sprouted from his skull. As he stood and stared at Racky, he leant so far to one side that he seemed about to topple over. The reason wasn't far to seek: his left leg was quite a bit shorter than his right. Not for the first time Racky wondered if Spine had been born with these grim deformities. If so, how had his mother reacted when the midwife held up to her what she'd laboured to bring forth? Had she cried out in horror?

Spine swayed but did not fall.

"Do I get to come in," said Racky, "or are you going to stand there all day admiring my pretty face?"

Spine grunted, stood back and motioned Racky inside. As Racky went by him, he could almost feel the hatred Spine emanated in waves. But it was of no consequence: Spine was no threat to him – not here at any rate.

The room was sparsely furnished. There was a small chest of drawers, a table and six chairs. Racky advanced to the table. Its top was notched with saw-cuts, as if once upon a time it had been used for carpentry. Three of the chairs were occupied: one by Querne, the others by men. Like Querne, the men were dressed in old and stained jackets and trews; but their well-fed faces and air of smooth self-confidence suggested that such clothes were not their usual garb.

This trio considered the new arrival as he swung his pack to the floor.

"Who's this?" said one of the men, directing the question at the Magian.

"Racky Jagger," she answered, "my close associate."

"Never heard of him," said the man. "How much does he know?"

"As of this moment, nothing."

"Not *that* close, then," quipped the man.

Querne rose to her feet. "Well, gentlemen, I think we're finished for today."

The two men exchanged glances, then also got up from their chairs.

"And good luck," added Querne.

The men nodded. Then, ignoring Racky, they filed out of the room. After them went Spine Wrench, and the door closed with a click.

The men might not know Racky, but Racky knew who they were: Tyler Mabbutt and Loman Slack, the richest men in Lowmoor. For some years they'd run Lowmoor foundry for Crane Rockett, but with the deaths of Rockett and Briar Spurr in the fire at Minral How, ownership of the enterprise had devolved on to them. They were an ambitious pair, having absorbed lessons in ruthlessness from the man whose place they'd taken. Oily Wells had told Racky that it was rumoured in the taverns it was they who'd set the fire that had put paid to their former boss.

Racky subsided into a chair and considered Querne. She looked exceptionally beautiful, as she invariably did when there were men to be impressed. But Racky knew that face. Behind it lurked the calculating brain of a venomous snake.

3

Racky said, "How did you get into the settlement, Querne? Changed your face?"

Querne smiled sweetly but said nothing.

"So, how will I recognise you outside these walls?" Racky persisted. "What alias are you using?"

"Moira Black," the Magian answered.

"The delectable Moira . . . I suppose I ought to be thankful that, here at least, you're wearing your own face."

"Fixed faces are so restricting. How on earth do you cope, being stuck with just one?"

"*You* were stuck with one, once."

"That was then; this is now. I'm not the person I was."

None of us is, thought Racky Jagger.

"Mabbutt and Slack," he said. "What were they doing here?"

"They want something, and think I can get it for them."

"And can you?"

"Of course."

"And *will* you?"

"In the short term. But then the situation will change."

What is she talking about? he wondered. What could Mabbutt and Slack want that they didn't already have? But that was a stupid question. Money and power were addictive: those who had them only ever wanted more. A better question would be: what was in this for Querne? The obvious answer was: revenge against Lowmoor, a revenge that he knew she'd been thinking about for years. But it was a simple answer, and few things were simple where Querne Rasp was concerned.

"Are you going to tell me what this is about?" he asked.

Querne smiled. She was enjoying this. "About a year ago, I approached Crane Rockett with a proposition. He liked the idea, and we reached an agreement. Mabbutt and Slack were then brought in: they were no less keen. Since that time, they've been working on various aspects of my plan. Rockett's death changed nothing; Mabbutt and Slack filled his place.

"The first phase of my plan is complete. It's time to move on to the second."

"Which is?" Racky prompted, as Querne had reckoned he would.

"To take control of Lowmoor."

Hello, thought Racky. Simple, brutal revenge isn't enough for this woman. She has to make a meal of it. "How will you take control?" he asked.

"The settlement will appear to come under serious attack. The Headman, the Council and the guards will be the targets. As soon as these are neutralised, Mabbutt and Slack will step in, using the foundrymen as enforcers, restoring order and confidence. The attack will be blamed on the settlement at Wyke – Lowmoor's long-time rival and a convenient scaperat. And so to phase three."

"Phase three?" queried Racky.

Querne's eyes glinted. "Within a fortnight, Mabbutt and Slack will move against Wyke, destroy its defences, quell its people and take control there."

"Just like that? Wyke's a powerful settlement."

"*Was*," corrected Querne. "I have the means to bring *any* settlement to heel in quick time – no matter how large or powerful."

Some associate *I* am, thought Racky bitterly. He hadn't a clue what "means" she meant. So he asked her – nicely.

"You'll see," the Magian replied.

There was a dreamy look in her eyes that Racky had seen there before, and it struck him forcibly that there was still more to this matter. But what? *Any settlement*, she'd said. Now he saw what that *more* was.

"There's a fourth phase, isn't there?"

Querne's eyes refocussed on him, and he read there that he was on the right track.

"You won't stop with Wyke, will you?"

"Clever Racky," said Querne. "You see further than anyone else. Mabbutt and Slack are useful tools, but they're no more than that. They're grasping, petty men who lack vision. *I* do not. The fourth phase of my plan is quite beyond their tiny minds." She paused. "Listen and learn. Under my personal direction, a new Lowmoor will arise – a centre of power undreamed of, the wonder and the terror of the world, the first empire of our age. I shall be its empress, and every man, woman and child will bow down before me."

"Empire?" Racky tested the alien word on his lips. Then another: "Empress?"

"An empress is a female ruler whose power is absolute; what she rules is an empire, a far-reaching, glorious realm. The terms are from the Dark Time."

Trawling with the yellow crystal through giant history, Querne had come across images of Catherine the Great. Catherine lived in gorgeous palaces and exercised the power of life and death over her subjects. Querne's imagination was pricked. Querne might be a fraction of the tsarina's size, but whatever Catherine could do . . .

The Magian smiled again. "*Querne the Great* . . . How do you like the sound of that?"

It depends, thought Racky.

"You're a genius, Querne," he said. "I hope there'll be a place for me in this new Lowmoor of yours."

"Of course there will, Racky. You are my right-hand man. You'll get no less than you deserve."

I bet I shall, he thought.

He said, "Mabbutt and Slack were here just now. Have you just given orders for phase two to begin?"

Querne's smile was sufficient answer.

All this time she had been standing. Now she sat down at the table. "You have the ruby stone," she said, "but not the green stone. Am I right?"

"Yes," Racky replied. He was used to such demonstrations of Querne's second sight. But he knew this faculty to be erratic, as unpredictable as a Syb's. "The green stone eluded me. This girl, Jewel Ranson, is clever. But then you know that, don't you?"

Querne's face darkened. Racky had just reminded her of something she'd tried to forget – not that she *could* forget it, of course – the confrontation between Jewel and herself at Harrypark in which Jewel had come off better.

"The girl was lucky," Querne said waspishly. "Next time she won't be."

"I don't doubt it," Racky said. "But now, with the ruby stone to add to the blue one I brought from the Spetches and the yellow one you had from before, you'll have three altogether. Aren't three enough for you?"

"Three? How can they be? I must have all five of them."

"Five?" said Racky with surprise. "I thought there were only four?"

"So did I, but there's a fifth. I've caught glimpses of it. And something tells me this fifth stone is the most powerful of them all."

"Do you know where it is?"

"Not yet . . . but in my bones I know for sure I soon shall. With the power of three crystals, I shall pinpoint where it lies. Then you shall fetch it for me."

"And leave the green stone to one side?"

"For the time being. But that too will come to me. I have seen it in my dreams."

Does that mean she saw me at the Barrens' edge, wondered Racky, waiting till Thorn and Jewel arrived so they could watch me disappear? It was painful to reflect that that action – a calculated piece of perfidy – might turn out to have served the Magian's darker purposes.

Whatever the truth, she didn't rebuke him. Letting her head fall back, Querne stared at the ceiling. Its grey was mottled with darker patches where rain had dripped through the roof-tiles.

"Five crystals . . ." she murmured and, holding up her hands, spread her fingers with their long, pearly nails, and looked at them. "Imagine," she said, half talking to herself, "to have all five of them here – at my fingertips . . ."

Even as she said this, a tremor of doubt passed through her frame. As yet her sense of the fifth crystal was tentative; even so, the fact that it was a formidable force could not be doubted. It lay on the horizon of her mind like a shadow, ambiguous, pulling her towards it, yet seeding her desire with needle-slivers of trepidation (never call it *fear*).

She emerged from her reverie to find Racky gazing at her. There was something in his eyes . . .

He doesn't trust me, she thought, and smiled inwardly. I wouldn't trust me if I were him. But he's mine. He'll never rouse himself to break the bond that ties us – *never*.

"Give me the crystal," she said.

1

INTO THE BARRENS

Thorn Jack and Jewel Ranson stood on the brink of Norgreen Barrens. They wore bulging rucksacks strapped to which were longbows and quivers that bristled with deadly arrows. Both seemed mesmerised by the wasteland. Livid and featureless like all examples of its kind, it stretched away in a gradual rise as far the eye could see. It made them feel even smaller than they were.

Little more than a day had passed since they'd stood at this same spot and watched as Racky Jagger lifted high above his head the ruby crystal he'd stolen from them. Then the stone had erupted, shooting out fiery beams of light, and Racky had vanished.

Today the sky was overcast, scummed with grubby smudges of clouds, and the smooth surface of the ground wore nothing of the sheen that Shelf Barrens had worn on a day fixed with sharp hooks in Jewel's memory. Norgreen Barrens looked empty of menace, but she knew that it was not – just as Thorn did at her side. At different times, different Barrens had nearly done for both of them. And now, after vowing that never again would she set foot in such a place, here she was on the point of doing that very thing. And why? In order to track Querne Rasp down.

I must be mad, she told herself for the umpteenth time. If these Barrens don't kill me, Querne most probably will.

Even so, mad or not, she had to do this thing. Whatever quirk of fate had made Jewel Ranson a Magian had elected her for this task: to turn away from it now would be an act of cowardice and a slap in the face of destiny.

But was it Thorn's destiny too? By what right was she dragging him with her to near-certain death?

Not that Thorn was being dragged: as soon as she'd announced her intention, he'd declared that he would come — as, of course, she'd known he would.

"Thorn, you've got to go back — *now!*"

There, she'd said it, though she hadn't wanted to; for, still worse than setting out to track down Querne, was setting out to do it alone.

But Thorn made no reply. He didn't even look at her. She might as well have imagined the words, rather than saying them out loud.

Then Thorn did turn towards her. "Are you scared, Jewel?" he asked.

"Yes," she admitted. "I know what Barrens can do to people."

"I'm scared too." But he was grinning.

"You don't look it," she observed.

"Men aren't supposed to look scared. But I'm quaking in my boots."

She raised an eyebrow. "Then we'd better get on with it."

Unslinging her pack, she took out the wrapped crystal, then put the pack back on. As he watched her, Thorn fingered the metal stock of the bow Roper Tuckett had given him. Thorn

12

might have stared long at the Barrens, but he'd been thinking of his sister. Haw had wanted to come with them, but he and Jewel had told her: no, this was too dangerous a quest. When they'd left Norgreen that morning, he'd half-expected her to follow, but she'd made no attempt to do so. Haw was in a deep sulk, she hadn't even said goodbye. That had hurt: he might never see her again . . .

They advanced towards the Barrens, then stepped out onto its surface. Under the soles of Thorn's boots the ground had a springy feel to it. It was a pleasure to walk upon. He counted off the paces: . . . seven, eight, nine, ten . . .

His heart was thudding in his chest and he felt a weakness in his knees. He tried to breathe evenly, to steady the trembling of his body. Sixteen years of dire warnings had told him not to do this. And here he was, doing it. Nineteen, twenty, twenty-one . . .

A yellow edge cut through the air, a knife-blade of radiance, and he blinked despite himself. Forty-two, forty-three . . . The air vibrated, coming alive. Splits and rents fractured its whole-ness, a brightness hard on the eyes.

Forty-nine, fifty. They halted. Fifty paces – the number they reckoned Racky had taken. Thorn moved behind Jewel, put his arms around her waist and clasped his hands.

Jewel unwrapped the green crystal and stuffed the cloth into a pocket. Holding the stone in both hands, she lifted it above her head. A light-splinter flashed in the air and struck a spark from the stone.

The crystal awoke. For a moment it glowed, then beams of light came jetting out of it, spraying in every direction. They were a fierce emerald, and Thorn was forced to close his eyes. But, even with his eyes closed, the world stayed eerily luminous. He pushed his face into Jewel's pack, blanking out the light; the coarse pack and the curve of her waist were his sole realities.

Jewel was barely aware of him. She and the stone were becoming one, a single mind, a single body. Crystal was flesh and flesh was crystal, and could she at this moment have stood outside herself, she'd have caught her breath at the sight of this strange transparent being – veins, sinews and bones transformed to leaf-green traceries.

All about her now, shot through with the crystal's radiance, leapt the shards and splinters of the Barrens' light-play. The atmosphere here, she sensed, was responsive to the crystal, to the make-up of the stone . . . She struggled to understand . . . The stone, without a doubt, was *organising* the light-play, which, losing its randomness, was forming some sort of order. Did the stone belong here, then? Was this strange region, the Barrens, its proper sphere of operation?

Abruptly, beneath her, the earth fell away. She looked down at her body, but there was no body there – only a swirl of particles, an endless glittering to-and-fro. But this curious dissolution didn't bother her in the least. I can still think, she thought. I think: therefore I exist. It was perfectly acceptable to be a seeing mind.

The process of ordering was drawing to an end. Whatever there was of her was floating above the surface of an ocean of shimmering light. Above her, the sky – if it *was* a sky – was a featureless grey, a nothingness devoid of height. In every

14

horizontal direction – ahead, behind, to left and right – the ocean stretched away until it was lost in its own distance. *Ocean* wasn't the right word, for it wasn't made of water. But in the absence of a better one, *ocean* would have to do. It possessed a curious double nature. At one moment it seemed to be made of bright waves in a gentle state of undulation, waves that appeared to move without achieving onward motion; at the next of rushing particles, trillions of bright pinheads.

It seemed to lack solidity. I could stick my fingers into it, she thought, if I wanted to – except I haven't any fingers!

But now she sensed something else: this ocean was alive. Not alive as she was alive – a person – but alive in some way. And something else: this ocean had suffered hurt. She sensed disruption, rents and fissures that had not healed themselves, portions torn away or lost, confused tracts of particles. Something had happened that had badly damaged it.

Now a phrase popped into her consciousness, as if a voice had spoken: *wave function*, it said. That was the proper name for the ocean. What was more – although she didn't understand how she knew – she realised with absolute certainty that this *wave function* was closely linked to the world in which she lived. It was the foundation on which everything depended – trees, stones, rivers, clouds and yes, people too. The damage it had sustained corresponded to the damage in the world. For, at some time in the past, a great disaster had occurred that had wiped away the giants, made Barrens of the settlements where they lived in large numbers, and somehow brought her own ill-fitting race of people here.

Brought her own race here ... The thought came like a

hammer-blow. Her people didn't belong here, they belonged somewhere else – *in another world entirely* . . .

So there *was* more than one world – as Thorn had speculated and she herself had doubted! Looking out across the ocean's seemingly endless shining expanse, it now came to her that if she travelled far enough in any given direction she would find herself in a region that was linked to a different world. A world slightly or hugely different from the world she'd grown up in. And beyond that region would lie another, beyond that another again. How many worlds might the ocean support? Ten, a hundred, a million? More than that? Too many to count? And somewhere, lost in the vast ocean, was the region that corresponded to the world in which her own small race had originated – till some disaster had snatched them up and dumped them down in the world she knew.

Perhaps, if she went looking, she could find that lost world.

But what if it, too, had been damaged in the disaster? It might be a whole lot smaller than the world that she knew. It might no longer be habitable.

Jewel steadied herself. Hold on to what you know. The temptation to go looking must be resisted. She wasn't responsible just for herself, she was responsible for Thorn, whom she'd left behind in the Barrens. And the business of the moment was Querne Rasp and the crystals. She had to find out where Racky Jagger had gone.

He had been here before her. In the undulating waves, she could sense traces of him, particles he had shed during his recent passage through.

Concentrating, she realised that these traces formed a trail.

There it went, trickling through the lifting and falling waves. She willed herself to follow it. Yet even as she did so, she couldn't be sure whether her mind or the trail itself was in motion. Am I moving or staying still? What a weird place this was!

There was something else too: for all his showmanship with the crystal, Racky hadn't created the trail; someone else had done that, for there were residues here of another person's passage through.

Residues she recognised: minute traces of Querne Rasp! Querne had passed through at some time – though "time" meant nothing here, as there was neither past nor future, only a strange, perpetual present.

The trail petered out in a sprinkling of Querne- and Racky-atoms.

Racky Jagger, where are you? she wondered. This is all very well, but I'm not getting anywhere . . .

As soon as she thought this, the strange realm dissolved away, receding from her like a dream, and she found herself back in the Barrens, her eyes misted with tears, solid ground beneath her feet and Thorn's arms about her waist. To her surprise she was still holding the crystal above her head, where it was raining out light. She fumbled the cloth out of her pocket and wrapped it round the stone. The crystal's radiance died. Scattered wings of light flickered and dashed above their heads.

"Thorn, are you all right?"

For three heartbeats there was silence; then she heard his voice saying, "Things are a bit blurred, but I'm fine. Has anything happened yet?"

"I'm not sure," she answered.

The spot on which they stood – was it the same one as before?

"Can you see the edge?" she asked. "My eyes are watering."

"I think so," he answered. "Yes, there it is!"

"Good. Take my hand and let's go."

Hand in hand they walked off the Barrens and found themselves in deep grass, quite unable to see what sort of land might lie ahead.

"This *isn't* where we were before," said Thorn decisively.

"You're right," Jewel agreed. "The question is, have we come out of the same Barrens at a different point, or have we come out of a different Barrens from the one we went into?"

"A different Barrens? Umm . . . We won't know the answer to that until we get somewhere." He beat at the tiresome, clustering stalks. "Always assuming there's a somewhere to get to in this."

"There'll be a somewhere, all right. You can bet Racky is somewhere, and I'm sure he came this way. Querne Rasp was here too."

"Querne? How can you know that?"

"Because I followed a sort of trail that she'd laid down for him."

"Followed a trail? But after we stopped we didn't *move* in there – did we?"

She grinned at his puzzlement. "We didn't seem to, but we did. I'll try to tell you what happened later. We should get moving for real."

"Which way? There's no trail. He must have come out of the Barrens to left or right of the spot we did."

"We'll just have to follow our noses, hope we hit a road or track. Better still, bump into someone who can tell us where we are."

She put the crystal back in her pack and they set off.

They pushed on through the dense grass till they hit a clump of bushes. The undergrowth here was impenetrable and they had to detour. Beetles crawled and flies buzzed. A hunting shrew, its tapered snout quivering, observed the humans from a clump of dandelions as they went by. But the sun's position and Jewel's senses kept them roughly to one direction. At length, hitting a shallow stream, they decided to take a rest.

Now they could compare what they'd experienced in the Barrens. Thorn had very little to report. He'd simply stood there holding on to Jewel's waist, his face thrust into her pack to protect his eyes from the bright light. His feet had never left the ground, he had no sense of shifting position, nor was he aware of any break in consciousness. Between shutting and opening his eyes, he thought no time at all had passed, that nothing had happened and the attempt to track Racky had failed.

Jewel's account of her experience completely stumped him. A shimmering ocean of particle-waves (she had to explain what an ocean was), this was the stuff of fantasy. Yet the change of land-scape outside the Barrens was solid proof of what she said. He knew enough of Jewel's gift to no longer be surprised by the fantastic things she told him. She could tell him the moon was dandelion-milk and he'd believe her.

And then she *did* tell him the moon was dandelion-milk. Or pretty much, for she told him of her discovery that this wave function, as she called it, underpinned not just the world they were in but countless other worlds.

"The things we see – objects – take on all sorts of shapes: some are big, some are small. Say, a wood, a hill, a dam; or a leaf, a pebble, a rat's tail. They all look different to us but at bottom they're the same, all the same basic stuff. And they – and we, too, we humans – all exist because of this ocean that isn't really an ocean." She gave him a look of frustration. "I'm sorry – I can't explain it, Thorn. I don't know enough, I haven't got the proper words."

He struggled to digest this. But then she said something that made complete sense to him: that the wave function had been damaged by some disaster in this world, a disaster that wiped out the giants and brought their own race here from a different world altogether.

"I knew it!" he exclaimed. "I *knew* we didn't belong here!"

Then something else occurred to him.

"All those worlds you sensed," he said, "was Heaven among them – and Hell?"

"I don't know. Perhaps. Maybe there are many Heavens and Hells, all different from one another." She got to her feet. "Come on. A world with Querne Rasp in it is more than enough for us to cope with, don't you think?"

The stream was a couple of inches deep. Taking off their boots, they waded through it and went on. Then, abruptly, they stumbled out of the bush-dotted grassland onto a road. It was well travelled, its bare surface hard-packed and marked with wheel-tracks.

The question was: which way now? They were about to toss a coin on the direction to take, when a distant rumble accompanied by a faint jingling came to their ears.

"Rat-carts!" Thorn exclaimed. "Now we can find out where we are."

There were three carts, two wagons and a carriage in the caravan, also a couple of rat-riders, one at the front, one at the rear. The jingling harnesses belonged to the two sleek rats pulling the handsome carriage that followed the lead rider.

Thorn hailed the rider, who came to a halt.

"I'm afraid we're lost," he said. "Can you tell us where we are?"

"Lost – how can you be lost?" The man was lean and tanned and was armed with a bow and quiver. A fresh leaf from a privet bush was stuck in his hatband.

"You'd be surprised," replied Thorn.

The man surveyed them suspiciously before answering. Perhaps he was inclined to make allowances for their youth.

"That way –" he pointed ahead "– is Lowmoor." He twisted in the saddle. "Back that way is Harrypark and the road to Butshaw and beyond. Where are you making for?"

"That depends," said Thorn. "Where are we nearest to?"

"Lowmoor," said the man.

Thorn and Jewel exchanged glances.

"Then that's where we're making for," Thorn told the rider.

"Well, if you speak nicely to Dicky Flipp – he's driving the wagon that's pulled by the roan – he might offer you a lift."

"Thanks for the suggestion," said Thorn.

The rider kicked his rat into motion and the caravan moved on.

Jewel thought she recognised the four people in the carriage from her visits to Rotten Pavilion – especially a woman with a sour face who eyed her disdainfully as the equipage rattled by.

"Are you Dicky Flipp?" shouted Thorn as the roan padded by.

"Whoa there!" commanded the wagoner and, jerking on the reins, brought the vehicle to a halt. His weathered, humorous face regarded them from under the cocked brim of a flat cap.

"Dicky by name, dickey by nature," he replied. "Who wants to know?"

"Thorn Jack and Jewel Ranson. We'd be grateful for a lift to Lowmoor, if you've room."

"Best get yourselves up here." He gestured to the seat beside him. "I wouldn't say no to a bit of company, like."

They got themselves up there. Thorn sat next to Dicky Flipp, with Jewel at the end. It was something of a squeeze, but the wagoner didn't seem to mind. Then the cart was in motion.

So, straightaway, was Dicky's mouth. He'd have talked, Jewel reckoned, the hind legs off a rat. It seemed a trait of wagoners – maybe the lonely lives they led. Where were they from? Where were they going? For what reason? For how long? Thorn proffered brief answers: Norgreen; Lowmoor; curiosity; couldn't say. Then, by way of deflecting the wagoner's curiosity, aimed some questions at him. Dicky, however, was happy to talk about himself, his work, his family and Lowmoor itself.

He appeared quite excessively proud of his settlement. His job, he said, had taken him to many other places, but none could match Lowmoor for size, wealth, and the industry and imagination of its inhabitants. It led the world in the most modern techniques with regard to building and metalworking, and the skill of its potters, weavers, jewellers and husbandmen were beyond compare. Its cooks cooked the tastiest meals, its ratmen bred the finest rats and its Ranters thought the most advanced thoughts. It was the only place to live.

That remains to be seen, thought Jewel.

"What about Norgreen?" protested Thorn.

"Norgreen?" Dicky shook with such violent laughter that he almost fell off the box. When he'd recovered, he said: "I've been there, and it's primitive – twenty years behind Lowmoor. You really ought to send people over to study what we've done. On second thoughts, don't – we don't want anybody stealing our ideas."

Thorn wasn't sure whether this was a joke or seriously meant. Remembering that Roper Tuckett had developed his flying machines independently of Lowmoor, he was on the point of challenging the notion of the settlement's superiority in all things when Jewel said, "I've also heard, Mr Flipp, that Lowmoor produces the greatest Magians."

"Magians? What Magians?"

"Isn't Querne Rasp from Lowmoor?"

Dicky, suddenly sober, eyed Jewel with calculation.

"Querne Rasp? What do you know of her?"

"I've heard a story or two."

"Such as?"

"Such as her picking out a killer from a line-up of suspects just by touching them on the forehead."

"Who told you that?"

"I really don't remember. Someone I met in an inn some-where?"

What a wonderful liar you are, Jewel, thought Thorn admir-ingly, turning his head to hide his grin.

"Well, that she did," the wagoner said, "though I wasn't there to see it. But we don't speak of her nowadays."

"You don't?" Jewel looked surprised. "But surely she's one of Lowmoor's greatest claims to fame?"

"That she isn't. She doesn't live in the settlement any more."

"I see. She found a better place to live," said Jewel mischie-vously.

"A better place? What better place? Not she," protested the wagoner. "She was banished. Driven out."

"Banished? I didn't know that. I don't suppose you know why?"

"Not know why? Of course I do. Listen: I'll soon show you what sort of a woman this Querne Rasp is."

"I'm all ears."

"I have a son. He's twenty-four now, but when the events I'm going to tell you of happened, he was eighteen, as was his best friend, Tyler Rimmer – and it's Tyler the story's about. Now Tyler was a fine young man of whom much was expected, and he fell in love with a girl and she with him. But Tyler had a rival called Lucas Wilks. Very good-looking was Lucas, but vain and arrogant with it: the sort who thinks he's God's gift to young women. Well, Lucas asked Tyler's girl more than once to come out with him, but she told him firmly: no, she wasn't interested. Lucas didn't like this, but instead of letting it drop he took to following the couple around with his mates and pestering them.

At last Tyler had had enough. There was a fight – a fair one according to my son, who was there – and Tyler bested Lucas. That's the end of it, Tyler thinks. But then, two nights later, Tyler gets clubbed on the back of the head in an alley. Not only that, but a rat-cart is driven over his legs and they're so badly smashed that both have to be amputated.

"Now Tyler testified that it was Lucas Wilks who clubbed him. He caught sight of him as he fell to the ground before he passed out. So Lucas was arrested by the Headman and put on trial. Now I expect you're wondering where Querne Rasp comes into this. Well, to everyone's astonishment she appeared before the Council to swear that Lucas couldn't have attacked Tyler because on the night in question he was at her house. It seems that he was, like, a favourite of hers. Now the Council had a choice: to believe Querne, who done them useful service in the past, or the poor lad knocking on death's door. It plumped for Tyler and banished Lucas for life.

"Querne wasn't pleased. She went to the Headman and demanded that the judgement be reconsidered. The Headman replied that the Council's decision was final. 'Are you calling me a liar?' Querne shouted by all accounts. 'No,' said the Headman. 'We believe you made an honest mistake over which night it was that Lucas was with you.' 'So now I'm an idiot!' Querne cried. But then, so I'm told, she went all cold and hard and said, in a voice that sent shivers down the spines of those who were there: 'I'll give you till tomorrow morning to reconsider your judgement. I advise you not to disappoint me.' And she flounced out of the room.

"Now the whole of Lowmoor was in awe of Querne Rasp –

25

which means afraid of her, too, like. But to allow one person to dictate to the Council – well, that's impossible. So later in the day the Headman, the Council and fifty archers – yes, fifty! – turned up at Querne's door and escorted her out of the settlement. She, too, was banished for life. And as she was led through the streets, people threw bits of rubbish and lumps of rotten food at her, and cursed her and called her all the foul names under the sun: you've never seen anything like it. That I *did* see. But then, as she was about to go through the gates, Querne looked back and shouted: 'Don't think you've seen the last of me! I'll be revenged on the pack of you if it takes me ten years.'"

"What happened to Tyler Rimmer?" asked Jewel.

"He died a week later. Very sad," said Dicky.

"I see. Where is Querne Rasp now?"

Dicky chuckled. "Lass, you're not the only one who'd like to know that! Truth is, nobody knows. Or if they do, nobody's saying. It's like she vanished into thin air. The Council, of course, took her threat seriously – still takes it seriously, though six years have gone by. Rumour has it that our agents are still trying to track her down. My own feeling is she's far away and has other fish to fry."

Thorn said, "Have you heard of a man called Racky Jagger?"

"No. Who's Racky Jagger?"

"Just someone we're looking for. We think he might be in Lowmoor."

"Well I can't help you there."

"Say you were looking for someone, Dicky – someone who wasn't keen to draw attention to himself . . . where would you start?"

"I wouldn't," said the wagoner.

"Why not?"

Dicky eyed Thorn thoughtfully.

"Listen, young man. While Lowmoor leads the world in all sorts of things, it isn't all sweetness and light. It has an under-side – the Belly."

"The Belly?" prompted Thorn.

"That's what it's called. It's a rundown area – houses, taverns, workshops, yards. All the riffraff, like, fetches up there. Respectable folk steer clear of it."

"So if you're looking for someone, the Belly's the place to go?"

"In a word, yes. But I wouldn't if I were you. They'll chew you up and spit you out."

Dicky whipped up his rat. The conversation lapsed. But while his last, colourful phrase still echoed in Thorn's mind, Lowmoor settlement hove into view.

2

THE WREN'S EGG

Deep-seated though his loyalties were to his home settlement, Thorn was forced to admit that Lowmoor was impressive. Its brick walls rose higher than Norgreen's wooden palisades, its gates were larger, cast in iron and handsomely ornamented, and everything about it looked to be on the grand scale. It had to be between three and four times the size of Norgreen. Neither of its gate-guards was under seven inches tall. They wore black trews, scarlet jerkins, black boots and black helmets, and carried stout iron pikes. What's more, they bristled with self-importance and were not about to let strangers in just like that.

When Dicky's wagon got to the gate it was waved to a halt, and Thorn and Jewel were questioned as to where they were from and their business in Lowmoor.

"Norgreen," said Thorn. "As for our business, I can't say we've any in particular. We've heard so much about the place – we thought we'd like to see it."

The guard pursed his lips, clearly less than impressed.

With a mischievous look on his face, Dicky Flipp chimed in, "They were asking about Querne Rasp. Seemed very interested in her."

"Were they now?" said the guard. He narrowed his eyes at

them, pondered for a few moments, then said, "Give me your bows, you two, and get down from that box."

"Our bows?" replied Thorn. "Is there a problem?"

"No problem. Normal procedure. If you satisfy Councillor Fairfax, you'll get your weapons back."

Thorn and Jewel handed over their bows and got down from the box.

Dicky Flipp grinned. "Enjoy your stay in Lowmoor!"

The cavalcade was motioned forward. Thorn and Jewel stood with the guard until it had passed, then the guard said, "Right. Come with me."

They went in through the open gate. On the left stood a brick guardhouse. Inside it, a third guard sat at a small table. When he and the gate-guard had exchanged a brief word, he got up and went out, presumably to take his colleague's place outside the gate.

"Right. This way," said the first guard.

As they walked through the streets, Thorn couldn't help but compare what he saw with what Norgreen had to offer. Sadly, the comparison did his home settlement no favours. For one thing, the streets seemed broader. There were more squares and open spaces where people could congregate. For another, a far greater proportion of the houses was brick-built than wooden, and many possessed two storeys and quite a few three. The part of the settlement they were passing through was predominantly residential, but besides the usual shops they passed several larger buildings – guildhalls or religious-meeting halls, perhaps.

At last the guard halted at a door and knocked. A ruddy-faced, white-haired man with deep-set blue eyes opened it. He surveyed Thorn and Jewel, then said to the guard: "Well now, Martin, what have you brought me today?"

"These young people, Councillor Fairfax, came in with some of our own folk. Seems they were asking after Querne Rasp."

"Indeed. I think you'd all better come in."

He took them into a sitting room and invited them to sit down. Martin left his pike and the two bows outside the door but remained standing, his face under its helmet unyieldingly stern.

Thorn decided to go on the offensive. "Is this how you treat visitors? Anyone would think we were common criminals."

"And *are* you, young man?" the Councillor asked him, unmoved.

"No, of course not," said Thorn.

"Then you've nothing to fear, have you?"

"So why are we here then?"

"Let's begin with your names, shall we?"

"My name is Thorn Jack. My friend's name is Jewel Ranson. We're both from Norgreen."

"Norgreen? You're a long way from home."

"We've heard a lot about Lowmoor. We had a fancy to see the place."

Councillor Fairfax laughed. "You'll have to do better than that. You've been enquiring about Querne Rasp. What is your interest in her?"

Thorn hesitated. It was Jewel who spoke up.

"Just that. Interest," she said. "Querne Rasp is a Magian, and neither of us has met one. They're very rare, as you know, and we've heard various stories about her. We were told she lived here. But the carter who gave us a lift said she was banished six years ago. He told us the whole tale. So it looks as though we won't get to meet her after all."

Councillor Fairfax sat back in his chair and said nothing for a time. His cool gaze gave nothing away: it was impossible to tell whether he thought what Jewel had said was the honest truth or a pack of lies. At last he said: "Lowmoor has a policy on vagrants. It is simplicity itself. We keep them out. Do you have money to pay for your stay?"

"We have money," Jewel said, and shook the money-bag on her belt.

"Very well. I will grant you entry to Lowmoor on one condition: that you take up accommodation in a place of my choosing. Is this acceptable to you?"

Thorn and Jewel glanced at one another. Then Thorn said, "You give us little alternative. We accept your condition."

"Good." Councillor Fairfax said to Martin, "Take them to Reeny Breaks. Tell Reeny I sent them."

"Of course, Councillor."

Councillor Fairfax stood, Thorn and Jewel followed, and the four left the room. There the Councillor picked up Thorn's bow and ran his finger along the shaft

"This is a fine weapon," he said, "as good as anything Lowmoor makes. May I ask who crafted it?"

"A friend," said Thorn.

"Then Norgreen may not be as far behind Lowmoor as we thought." The Councillor handed the bow to Thorn and considered the pair for the last time. "A word of warning. Stay out of trouble while you're here. I don't want to see you two in front of me again."

He waved a hand. They were dismissed.

The guard conducted them through the streets and rapped with the bird-headed knocker on the door of a brick-built two-storey house that was one of a block of five in a quiet neighbourhood. The door was opened by a slim, middle-aged woman with severe features and an almost lipless slit for a mouth. Her grey hair was gathered in a bun at the back of her head.

"Good afternoon, Mrs Breaks. Councillor Fairfax thought you might be able to find room for these young folks."

"Abner Fairfax, eh? Then find room I shall. Come in the two of you."

Thorn and Jewel followed Mrs Breaks into a sitting room that might just have been cleaned, so spotless were its surfaces. Perhaps it always looked this way. After subjecting the pair to silent scrutiny, the landlady said, "I trust you're not going to get into trouble while you're here."

"That's what Councillor Fairfax said," Jewel responded, "though I can't for the life of me see why he thinks we will. We're just visiting."

"Let's hope so. I take it you have the means to pay for rooms."

"If they're reasonably priced and answer our needs."

Mrs Breaks bridled. "I can assure you that my clients get value for money. No one complains."

I bet nobody dares, thought Jewel. She said. "Can we see some rooms, then?"

They followed Mrs Breaks upstairs. The guestrooms were austerely furnished, but spick and span. The landlady had a nose for dirt like Jewel's late father had a nose for a sale. But her prices weren't exorbitant and they declared themselves satisfied. Not that they had any choice.

Thorn was lying on his bed with his boots off, arms clasped behind his head when a gentle tap came at his door. He opened it: Jewel.

Thorn got back on the bed. Jewel sat down in the only chair.

She said in a low voice, "Have you ever had the feeling that someone's watching you?"

"You're right," he replied quietly. "If you look out of the window there's a man across the street. Councillor Fairfax is keeping an eye on us." Thorn grinned. "I don't think he trusts us."

Moving to the nearest wall, Jewel laid her palms against it and stood without speaking for a time. When she took them away, she said: "At least there are no spyholes in this room – or in mine."

"Good. Then we can talk if nothing more."

"Yes. Thorn – I'm convinced Racky's here. I can't sense him exactly, but I'm sure of it all the same."

"And Querne?"

"I can't sense her either, but something tells me she's here too."

"In disguise?" Thorn was aware that the Magian was able to change her appearance.

"After that story Dicky told us, I think she'd have to be.

33

Everyone here knows her face. She may have come with revenge in mind – against the Headman, the Council, who knows what's in her head? She probably has the ruby crystal. We'll have to tread carefully."

"These days I never get to tread any other way. But the man down there will follow us. And if we try to lose him, their suspicions will be confirmed."

"Then we won't do that – yet. Are you hungry, Thorn?"

"Jewel, how *did* you guess?"

She grinned. "Let's find a place to eat. Then we'll get rid of our tail and take a look at this famous Belly."

"Like, bellies first, Belly after?"

"Oh *very* funny, Thorn."

"Well, *I* thought it was," he said, with a look of mock-injury.

After consulting with Mrs Breaks on a place to eat, they left the house. Unwilling to leave her crystal behind, Jewel had it in a hip-pack. Their shadow tagged along, not troubling to pretend that he was other than what he was. Councillor Fairfax was reminding them they were here on sufferance. Put a foot wrong and they'd be out, double quick.

After checking out a couple of places their landlady approved, they settled on a tavern from whose sign a long-whiskered rat looked down imperiously. They seemed to have chosen well: early evening, but already the tavern was more than half full. Diners sat at stout wooden tables with pewter mugs in hand or at elbow, and the hum of conversation was spiced with frequent bursts of laughter. Around the panelled, dark-stained walls, high shelves carried brass pots and plates, and below them were portraits of racing rats and grinning jockeys. Dicky Flipp had mentioned that Lowmoor had a fine racecourse.

They took a vacant table and soon a waitress bustled up.

"Welcome to The Noble Rat!" she said. "Been here before?"

"It's our first time," said Thorn.

While the waitress listed the dishes that were available today, Jewel – who'd taken a seat with her back to a wall – noticed that the man who'd been tailing them had just followed them in. The room made a right angle where a pillar rose up from the corner of the bar to the ceiling, and the man had taken a stool on the far side of the counter in a position from which he could keep his quarry in view. You couldn't call him inconspicuous, for his left cheek sported a trio of hairy, whitish warts. Presently – with a concentration that bordered on the ferocious – he was examining the bottles ranged on the shelves behind the bar. Jewel and Thorn ordered food and drinks, and the waitress bustled off.

"No need to look now," said Jewel (for Thorn's back was to the man), "but our sticky friend has just come in."

"Probably came inside in case we slipped out through the back. I wonder if he's had his dinner."

The food was good but no different from the sort of thing they'd eaten elsewhere, so maybe Dicky's view of Lowmoor cooks was rose-tinted. Then, as Jewel was finishing her sweet, a wasp banded in black and yellow, no more than a quarter of an inch in length, alighted on her plate and began to crawl about, flexing its feelers as it went. "Watch out!" exclaimed Thorn, and looked round for something to clout the creature with.

"It's all right," Jewel assured him. "He's exactly what I want."

As Thorn watched – still concerned lest this interloper sting her – Jewel slid a hand up to the edge of the plate. After palpating her food, the wasp walked onto the girl's hand. Thorn drew in his breath, but Jewel seemed happy enough, and in a little while the wasp lifted off again.

"Watch what happens," said Jewel simply.

Thorn twisted round in his chair.

The wasp took a meandering course that brought it over the warty man's head. For a moment it hovered there unseen, then it shot down and landed on his hand, which clutched a mug.

With a loud yell the man sprang up.

"Bloody thing stung me!" he cried, outraged.

"Hey, that's nasty," said the barman. Then, along with the rest of the customers, he watched with sympathetic detachment as Warty subsided to the floor. He'd passed out with shock – as many people did when a bee or wasp stung them. People crowded around him.

"Time to go," announced Jewel.

As she paid and added a tip, she asked the waitress with a casual air in which direction the Belly lay.

"The Belly?" frowned the waitress. "You can't be meaning to go *there*?"

"Certainly not," replied Jewel. "We've been warned to keep away. We're asking where it is so we can be sure of avoiding the place."

"Thank goodness for that," said the woman, and told them how *not* to get to the Belly by the directest available route.

As they walked in the opposite direction to the recommended one, their surroundings began to change. Smart residential areas with shops and occasional taverns gave way to older houses that were not so well maintained, also poorer and cheaper shops. Passing tanneries and dye-houses, they entered a region of potteries and woodyards and brickyards stacked or heaped with raw, cut or manufactured materials. The next street was dingier still. It consisted of facing rows of dilapidated houses. Some had smashed boards and broken windows and looked empty of human life, but others were still inhabited, and lights gleamed on the inner side of grimy window-shades.

"This has got to be it," said Thorn. "Now we need a likely tavern."

The next street commenced as an imitation of the last. But further up one of the houses had burnt down, and blackened timbers stuck up from the ground like the forlorn, snapped-off ribs of an architectural skeleton. On what had been the living-room floor, a heat-twisted kettle pointed its forked spout at shards of broken pots and plates. Norgreen might have nothing to compare with Lowmoor's more impressive buildings, but it also had nothing to compare with Lowmoor's poorer ones, and it occurred to Thorn that rather different kinds of spirit might animate the inhabitants of the two settlements.

Clouds had drifted in as they'd walked and the light was fading now, but as they turned into the next street they caught sight of an inn sign three doors down. They walked on and halted beneath it. The sign hung motionless and askew, and showed a freckled egg on a nest.

"Is this what you mean by 'a likely tavern'?" asked Jewel.

Thorn grinned.

As they turned towards the doorway, a man shot out of it and fell flat on his face in the street.

"And don't come back tonight!"

A burly, black-bearded man loomed, filling the door-space. As Thorn and Jewel looked at him, he inspected his huge hands, then wiped them on his apron – which was none too clean to start with.

With a nod towards the sprawling man, "Filthy devil," he observed to Jewel and Thorn dispassionately. "Grease and grime from top to toe. There's no knowing where he's been."

"Looks to me as though he's just come out of your tavern," commented Thorn.

The burly man stared at Thorn, and for a moment Thorn wondered if he'd put his foot in it, but then the man erupted into a series of hoarse barks.

The drunk, meanwhile, had fought his way to his feet. It was no mean achievement. Turning towards his ejector, he took a lurching step forward, swayed perilously, threw out his hands to balance himself and just managed to stay upright. His hair hung down like the tails of a mop and there were rips in the knees of his trews.

"You'll be sorry for this, Mouse Kellett," he said in a voice as limp as a snowdrop's head.

"I'll be sorry for lots of things, but not for showing you the door. Go on, get home to your missus, and hope she doesn't take it into her noggin to give you a thumping." And turning on his heel, he went back into the tavern.

Thorn and Jewel followed him in.

A fug of heat and smoke met them as they entered the bar,

laced with the chatter of voices and the rattle of dominoes. The frowst of stale beer and sweaty bodies invaded their nostrils. The ceiling was low, the walls yellow and smoke-stained, and a couple of cheap, crude landscapes hung crookedly from nails.

The noise abruptly ceased as the regulars took in the appearance of these youthful new arrivals. The customers were mainly men, but there were women here too – three, as far as Jewel could see. Well, that's something she thought. But the women looked just as rough and ready as the men – as no doubt they had to be to hold their own in such a place. In the far corner, a bunch of young men were sizing her up, but she didn't allow her gaze to dwell on them.

Then the chatter started up again, as pub games and suspended conversations were resumed.

Behind the bar, Mouse Kellett was looking at them with humorous eyes.

"Two mugs of your best ale, if you please," requested Thorn.

"First time in Lowmoor?" enquired the landlord as he tapped off the beer from a flagon resting on a trestle.

"It is," said Thorn.

"Then it's all the more surprising you should find your way to The Wren's Egg."

"We were warned to stay out of the Belly. So we decided we had to see what it was we ought to avoid."

Mouse set the two pots on the bar and took Thorn's money.

"Actually," Thorn went on, "we're looking for someone."

"Is that right?" said Mouse.

Before Thorn could follow up, he was barged aside by a tall

man some years older than himself. Leaning on the bar, the man leered at Jewel.

"Hello, sweetie, haven't seen you here before."

She recognised him as one of the men who'd sized her up.

"I'm not a sweetie and you're right – you haven't seen me before," she replied.

The man turned to his friends and winked. "This little girl's got a sharp tongue!" He turned back to Jewel. "But I like a challenge," he said.

Thorn caught the man by the arm. "I'd be grateful if you'd take yourself off," he told him.

The man shook Thorn off. "Push off, kid," he said. "Little lady wants a real man, not a puffball like you."

"There's only one puffball here," said Thorn, "and it isn't me."

The man stared at him for a moment, then swung a fist at Thorn's face. But Thorn was expecting it and swayed away. Then, while the fellow was off-balance, he hit him twice decisively – first in the stomach, then on the chin, straightening his body as he delivered the uppercut. The man grunted and stepped back, treading on one of Jewel's feet, then sagged to the floor – not unconscious, but stunned.

A sudden silence had struck the bar. All eyes were locked on Thorn. The silence held for a long moment, then was broken by the scraping of chair legs. The three mates of the downed man had risen to their feet and were coming across the room with scowling faces and clenched fists.

That's torn it, thought Thorn. But a deep, no-nonsense voice rang out.

"That's enough. Back off, lads. One on one is fair enough.

Three on one is out of order." It was Mouse Kellett, and he meant it. He went on, "You three can stay and drink, but this chap –" he indicated the crumpled figure gasping on the floor "– has outstayed his welcome."

The three seemed disinclined to contest the landlord's will. Two hung back while one came forward and helped the fallen man to his feet. Moments later, the four of them were gone from the tavern.

The humorous smile was back on Mouse Kellett's face.

"I like a man who can look after himself," he told Thorn. "That fellow you put down is a nasty piece of work. Now, what do they call you?"

"Thorn Jack," said Thorn. "And this is Jewel Ranson."

"Well, Jewel Ranson," said Mouse, "you've got yourself a fine protector."

"She doesn't need a protector," said Thorn before Jewel could open her mouth. "But it was me he insulted, and I won't stand for that."

"Neither should you."

Now seemed like a good time to ask about Racky Jagger, but before Thorn could do so Mouse was called down the bar to refill some empty pots, and Thorn and Jewel were left to sip their drinks.

She smiled at him. "Hello, protector."

Thorn found himself blushing. "Look, I know you're perfectly capable of looking after yourself, but it wouldn't have been a good idea to reveal yourself here."

"No need to explain, Thorn," she said. "To be honest, I rather enjoyed your heroic defence of me."

Thorn was surprised, and said so.

"It would never do for me to become predictable, now, would it?"

I don't think you're ever going to be that, thought her companion.

Just as Mouse was taking payment for the last of a flurry of orders, a small man with thinning hair and bulging eyes came into the tavern.

"The usual, Ticker?" asked Mouse.

"Aye, Mouse," said the man.

As Mouse was drawing his beer, the new arrival looked with interest at Thorn and Jewel. Then, after a preliminary sip from his foaming mug, he joined a table of other drinkers and engaged his neighbours in conversation. Sideways glances at Thorn and Jewel suggested that the talk around the table was about recent events.

At last Thorn was able to attract the landlord's attention.

"We're trying to find someone," he said, "a man by the name of Racky Jagger."

"Are you now?" said Mouse Kellett.

"We were told he sometimes drinks here," lied Thorn.

"Oh aye? Who told you that?"

"A carter we met."

"And what was this carter's name?"

"I couldn't tell you. We didn't get to the point of telling each other our names."

Mouse said nothing for a time. Then, stepping along the bar, he lifted a hinged flap in the counter top and motioned to them.

"Go through to the back room," he said. "I'll be with you as soon as I can."

Thorn and Jewel pushed past a grubby drape that hung at the rear of the bar. Here, in front of a fireless hearth, an ancient woman in a rocking chair was rocking to and fro. She smiled toothlessly at them, then extended a hand to Jewel, who took hold of it.

"Hello," said Jewel, but the old lady simply continued to smile.

Thorn looked around the room. The walls were a nauseous pea-green. A worn couch and an armchair were alike uphol-stered in dark blue. Once this stuff had boasted a pattern, but constant use had rubbed it away. Drawers and cupboards hugged the walls, and on their surfaces lamps burned. To their left was a closed door and on the far side of the room an open-ing with another drape. One must surely lead to stairs since the building possessed two floors, the other presumably to a scullery. The customers of The Wren's Egg didn't come for wrens' eggs – nor any other sort of victuals, to judge by the tavern's facilities. Jewel wondered how the place had acquired its out-of-the-way name.

Now the drape swished behind them and Mouse Kellett came into the room. He stood facing them with his legs apart, big fists closing and opening as if squeezing something invisible.

"Listen carefully," he said. "You're only here in this room and not out of my pub already because I've taken a shine to you. People who come asking questions aren't welcome in the Belly. Folk here mind their own business and expect others to do the same. Loose tongues are bad for business. Now I don't know what you're after and I don't want to know, but if you'll take my advice you'll keep your mouths shut and get off back where you belong."

"So you can't help us?" said Thorn.

"Are you deaf, lad?" said Mouse.

There was a tingling silence.

Then Jewel said, "Your mother's a happy soul – despite the tragic life she's led."

"What do *you* know about my mother's life?" demanded Mouse.

"I know your father died of the sweats, that your only sister Elly was murdered in a street brawl, and that her killers were never caught."

"Anyone could have told you that."

"I also know that long ago when life was somewhat kinder, you and Elly had a pet mouse called Earwig."

Startled now, Mouse glanced from the girl to the old woman – still smiling her beatific smile – and back again. Then, "Are you a Syb?" he asked.

Jewel met the landlord's gaze unperturbed. "Now who's asking questions?" she coolly retorted.

RIGGS AND WELLS

Jewel and Thorn did not leave The Wren's Egg straightaway. Collecting their drinks from the bar counter, they moved to a corner table from where they could survey the various comings and goings and talk quietly.

"The landlord," Thorn began, speaking in a low voice, "do you think he knows Racky?"

"I'm sure he does," said Jewel. "I also think he knows Racky's here in Lowmoor. But I doubt he knows where he's staying. What's more, I suspect that he doesn't want to know."

"So we're stuck . . . back where we started."

"Not quite. Your fight caused a stir, and there's nothing like a stir to get people talking – about us, I mean. Let's sit tight for a bit. As Rainy's father said to me once, you never know when a tasty fish is going to bite."

So they sat tight. And after a time a fish did bite. The little man with the bulging eyes got up from his table, sidled over and sat down.

"Evening," he said.

Jewel and Thorn returned the greeting.

"First trip to the Belly?" asked the man.

"It is," answered Thorn.

"From out-of-settlement, are you?"

45

"We are."

"Fancied a spot of lowlife, eh?"

"Not exactly," said Thorn. "This place looks like taverns pretty much everywhere, I'd say."

"The Belly's much maligned. Those of us who live here wouldn't live anywhere else in the world." The man took a swig of ale. "Let me introduce myself. My name's Ticker Riggs."

Thorn shook a clammy hand.

"Pleased to meet you, Mr Riggs. My name's Thorn Jack. My friend here's Jewel Ranson."

Ticker Riggs nodded at Jewel. Perhaps he didn't think the slim girl of much account. At any rate, he directed his next words at Thorn.

"You're capable of taking care of yourself, so I hear."

Thorn smiled, but said nothing.

"I see that you're a man of few words," said Ticker Riggs.

"Actions speak louder than words," said Thorn.

"True. Even so, words can be pretty weighty things."

"That's true too."

Ticker regarded them slyly. "Now I'm not the kind who listens in to other folks' conversations, but I happened to overhear you utter two particular words."

"Oh? What words were they?"

"Racky Jagger."

Ticker paused. Thorn decided to say nothing; let the man go on, if he would. And, soon enough, he did.

"Now that's a name that isn't spoken idly in these parts."

"Oh? Why is that?"

Ticker chuckled. "Come now, Mr Jack, don't take me for a

fool. I'm sure you know as well as I do that when *that* name is mentioned, another has a habit of cropping up."

"Does it? *What* name?"

Leaning towards Thorn, Ticker whispered in his ear.

"Now that," Ticker resumed, "is a very dangerous name, very dangerous indeed."

"So we gather," said Thorn. "But the person who goes by it is, I understand, long since gone from Lowmoor and no longer welcome here, so I don't see why you mention it."

"I'm relieved to hear you say so. So it's only Mr Jagger that you're interested in?"

"Yes. We're keen to meet him."

"May I ask why?"

"You may. But you won't get an answer."

Ticker Riggs chuckled. "You're a close one, Mr Jack. But close is no bad thing to be nowadays. We live in tricky times."

"So I've noticed. People are all too easily tricked out of their lives."

"Ah! You're a thinking man, as well as a man of action." Ticker leaned forward. "Now, it just so happens I'm in a position to help you."

"You mean you know where Racky is?"

"I do. But this sort of information, as I'm sure you appreciate, isn't the sort as comes cheap."

Thorn glanced at Jewel, who gave a little nod.

"Let's talk money," said Thorn.

Ticker's eyes gleamed. Then he looked furtively about.

"Not here," he said, "my place. You two, leave now. Wait for me at the near end of the street."

And with that he got up and went back to his former seat.

Thorn and Jewel finished their drinks and left the tavern. As they walked to the end of the street, Thorn said, "I don't trust this Riggs."

"Neither do I," said Jewel. "But he's the only lead we've got. Let's play along for now."

Time passed. Then Ticker Riggs came out of The Wren's Egg. Casting furtive looks behind him, he made haste towards them.

"Right. Come with me," he said.

Ticker Riggs walked quickly, almost scurrying along, body bent, head down as if sniffing out the spoor of some vanished animal. Thorn and Jewel hurried after him through shadow-infested ginnels and smelly alleyways.

They emerged into a street of single-storey wooden houses that remained standing by the simple expedient of leaning on one another. Here Ticker halted at a door whose wooden panels were cracked and warped, its green paint peeling. He rapped six times on the door. Nothing happened. He rapped again.

This time there came the sound of bolts being withdrawn, and the door was drawn back to reveal a thin, worn woman dressed in a grey dress and pink shawl. Her clothes had seen better days. Ticker gave her a cuff.

"Damn it, Mary, are you deaf?"

"You know I am, Ticker." Mary's voice was a hurt whine.

"Make yourself scarce, woman. I've important business tonight."

"Yes, Ticker," said Mary, and took herself off to another room.

Turning to Thorn and Jewel, Ticker waved them inside and shut the door.

Dingy and dank and cold, meanly furnished and lit by a couple of weak oil-lamps, Ticker Riggs's living room was less inviting than a stall in a rattery. Motioning Thorn and Jewel towards a bald brown settee, Ticker plonked himself down in an armchair of similar vintage. Jewel removed her pack and set it down by her feet.

"Now we can talk freely," Ticker declared.

The talk was of money, but when Ticker demanded half in advance, Thorn told him no.

"I don't trust you," he said. "You'll get the money when we're sure Racky is where you think he is."

"I said I'd lead you to him," said Ticker. "Isn't that good enough for you?"

"No."

"So that's how you want to play it, is it? Well, we'll see about that." And he shouted "Now!"

Four men burst into the room with knives in their fists. They were muscular and mean.

Ticker set this up back in the tavern, thought Thorn.

He looked towards Jewel, who gave her head a slight shake. Quickly surrounding the couch, the men stood glaring down at them.

"What's going on here?" said Thorn. "I thought we were doing business."

"We are," said Ticker Riggs. "*You're* about to offer me *all* the money you have, and *I'm* about to accept it. Then you're going to answer some questions. After that . . ." He grinned unpleasantly.

"That sounds one-sided, to say the least."

"Who cares how many sides it's got?"

"*I* do, for one. Who are you working for, Riggs?"

"*Mr* Riggs, to you."

Ticker's gaze dropped towards the floor. He'd just seen Jewel pull her pack a little closer to her leg.

"What's in the bag?" Ticker asked.

"Nothing," Jewel replied.

Ticker chuckled. "Pull the other one. You've kept that bag close since I first saw you in the Egg. I think it's time you opened it."

"Open it yourself."

Ticker considered this invitation, then turned to one of his men, "Fetch that bag here."

The man picked the bag up and tossed it to Ticker. He was slow to react and it struck him in the chest.

"I said *fetch* not *throw!*" he cried, but his accomplice had already turned his broad back on him. The thug's face was expressionless.

Swallowing his indignation, Ticker set the pack down on the floor, unfastened the straps and peered inside. Then he plunged his hands in and brought out the wrapped crystal.

"What's this?" he asked.

"Nothing," Jewel replied.

Ticker's lip curled. "You need a good beating, girl."

"Like the ones you give Mary? I'd like to see you try."

Ticker laughed, as if to say: *You will, soon enough.* Then, placing the package on his knees, he threw off the wrappings and stared at the dark-green stone.

"What's this?" he asked again.

"What does it look like?" said Jewel.

At this point, Ticker decided to take a closer look at the stone. But he'd barely got hold of it when it emitted a green flash. With a cry of pain and surprise Ticker threw it away from him. The stone landed on the floor, rolled between the booted feet of two of the men with knives and came to a halt at Jewel's feet. Snatching it up, she thrust it towards the nearest man. A beam of energy leapt from the stone and struck the man with such force that he was thrown through the air. But even before he hit the floor, Jewel was on her feet and swinging the crystal towards the next man.

It was over within moments. The four thugs lay unconscious. Wisps of smoke rose from blackened patches on their jerkins and there was a smell of singed flesh. Thorn had shut his eyes to reduce the impact of the dazzle, but when he opened them his vision was tinted green with afterburn.

"You all right, Thorn?" asked Jewel.

"I'm fine! That was smart," he replied.

"I have my moments," she said.

Jewel walked forward and stood over Ticker Riggs. The crystal's light had died to a glow, but Ticker had the look of a man whose prospects have suddenly taken a serious turn for the worse. He'd shrunk into his chair and appeared to be doing his best to squeeze his body into the crack between back and seat. He'd made some progress, but nowhere near enough. Now he held up a trembling hand, as if to ward off a fresh explosion of energy from the stone.

"No," he whimpered, "please, no . . ."

51

"Don't you like my crystal, Ticker?"

"Put it away – *please* . . ."

"Not yet. I've got some questions for you. Now listen Ticker, my stone always knows when someone's telling me lies. So if you want to find out what it does when that happens, lie to me."

Ticker blenched. "What – what do you want to know?"

"Do you *really* know where Racky Jagger is?"

"No . . . Though I did hear he's been seen in the settlement."

"Who told you that?"

"A mate at The Wren's Egg. He's pally with one of the gate-guards who saw Racky arrive."

Jewel paused, to digest this meagre piece of information. It sounded like a dead end.

"So," she continued, trying a different tack, "why did you decoy me here?"

"To get your money."

"Is that the only reason?"

"Er, no. I'm a nose."

Evidently Ticker meant something different from the organ in his face. "A nose? What do you mean?"

"An informant, like. I keep my ears and eyes open. Anything interesting I hear down here in the Belly, I pass it on."

"And who do you pass it on to?"

"I – I can't tell you that."

"Oh come on, Ticker, you're a very brave man. I've seen how brave you are – smacking that vicious wife of yours. A man as brave as you will have no trouble telling me." Jewel leant forwards and thrust the stone in Ticker's face. It tossed out a shower of sparks. Ticker yelped and shrank another size. "*Will you, you little worm?*"

"No, no! Oily – his name's Oily Wells."

"Oily Wells? Who's he?"

"Oily's a gofer for the big men at the foundry."

"The foundry? I thought it belonged to Crane Rockett?"

"It did, but he's dead, and there are new bosses now."

"Who are the new bosses?"

"Tyler Mabbutt and Loman Slack."

The names meant nothing to Jewel and Thorn.

"The foundry . . . is that where these beauties are from?" Jewel waved a hand at the men slumbering on the floor.

"That's right. I got a message out to Oily while you were in the back room."

"Right bag of tricks, aren't you, Ticker?"

"Erm, no, not really . . ."

"Don't be modest now. So . . . this Oily – where does he live?"

"Not far from here."

"Right. Take us there. We'd like to meet this Mr Wells."

Ticker looked aghast. "Take you to Oily's place? He's not going to like that."

"*I* won't like it if you don't. Now, get up out of that chair."

Ticker struggled to his feet. "This is the end for me," he groaned.

"My heart bleeds for you," said Jewel.

Soon they were walking again. The gloom was deepening now and the streets seemed almost empty. Ticker went in front, with

Jewel right behind him. She'd put the crystal back in her pack, sure he wouldn't try to run. Whatever fight he'd had in him had long since leaked away.

"Ticker, I've a question for you," said Thorn. "A man with three warts on his cheek who follows people – can you tell me his name?"

"That's Warty Chapman," said Ticker. "Everybody knows Warty. He's a Council nose, works for Abner Fairfax. Fairfax likes to think he has his finger on the pulse."

"And has he?" asked Thorn.

"I couldn't say. My own finger's not on it, Mr Jack."

That seemed undeniable.

Whoever or whatever this Oily Wells was, he was clearly better off than Ticker Riggs, for the street he lived in was almost respectable. Oily's house had two storeys and was built of red brick, but still contrived to look run-down and neglected.

The door boasted an iron knocker. Ticker took hold of it and rapped. Thorn and Jewel pressed themselves up against the wall, one on either side of the door.

After a time a voice said testily, "Who is it?"

"It's Ticker Riggs, Mr Wells."

"Ticker? What the hell are you doing here?"

"I've got to speak to you, Mr Wells."

"Push off, Ticker. I told you never to come here."

"I know . . . but I had to. I've got important information that the bosses will want to hear."

"The bosses?" There was a brief pause, then Oily said, "All right – but this had better be good. If it isn't, I'm going to fry your skinny backside."

Bolts were shot back inside. Almost before the door had opened, Thorn had shoved Ticker aside. Throwing himself through the gap, he charged heavily into Oily, who went sprawling on his back with a cry of surprise.

Jewel prodded Ticker inside and the door was re-bolted. They were in a narrow hallway.

"Get up," commanded Thorn.

Oily made no move to comply. He seemed content to lie on the floor, propping his body on his elbows. His red-rimmed eyes moved from Thorn to Jewel, then back again. That he was thinking was obvious, also that he was thinking fast.

Physically, Oily didn't look much cop. Thorn had bounced him pretty hard, but a good push, he now thought, would have had the same result. With his dark-bagged eyes, bony nose, sparse hair and sparrow shanks, Oily made Ticker Riggs look a picture of health and strength.

"Friends of yours, Ticker?" he asked.

"No way, Mr Wells," said Ticker, trying to sound apologetic. "They forced me into this."

"A couple of kids? What happened to the men I sent? Weren't four of them enough?"

"Erm, no . . ."

Oily looked at his captors with what might have been a calculating respect, then got up off the floor and took them into his living room.

It was crammed with assorted jumble that might – both from the look of it and from the prevailing smell – have been liberated that morning from some junkyard or tip. A couple of ancient armchairs, upholstery ripped and sprouting fluff, fought to hold off a surge of rickety cabinets and tables, their wood chipped and scored, inside or on top of which cracked vases and battered knick-knacks vied for scraps of living-space. In one corner of the room stood a stuffed racing rat, identifiable by the owner's mark branded on its head. Dun fur moth-eaten, tail squirming like a worm, it reared up on its hind legs, showing few signs now of its former pedigree.

Oily deposited himself in one of the armchairs, raising a puff of dust in the process. Ticker hesitated, then dropped into the other armchair. Jewel and Thorn remained standing.

"What do you want?" Oily asked.

"We're looking for Racky Jagger," said Thorn. "We believe he's in Lowmoor and you know where."

Oily considered this.

"Tell him, Ticker," prompted Thorn.

Ticker said hurriedly, "Best answer their questions, Mr Wells. They may look no more than kids, but they've got this weird stone . . ." He hooked a thumb towards Jewel. "This girl here used it on the foundrymen. Believe me, it's something that you don't want to see."

"A weird stone?" said Oily, scepticism in his voice. His eyes darted around in their sockets as he calculated the odds on Ticker's statement being true. At length he licked his lips and said, "Well, it would take something special to put four foundrymen down . . . Racky's in Lowmoor, but I can't tell you where for the simple reason I don't know."

Jewel considered this. He's telling the truth, she thought. "And Querne Rasp," she asked. "Is *she* here too?"

"That she is." Oily produced a hoarse laugh. "But you may as well try to catch the wind as catch *her* – weird stone or no weird stone."

"Is she using a disguise?"

"Naturally. Querne has as many names as Querne has faces."

"What alias is she using?"

"Moira Black."

It was the alias Querne had used when they'd met at Rotten Pavilion. Jewel pictured the gaming room and how, for a brief moment, the Magian's mask had slipped to reveal her true face beneath.

"What's she doing in Lowmoor?"

"Better ask her that. She wouldn't tell a nobody like me what her game is."

"I never supposed she would. But I think you might have an idea."

"Ideas are ten a penny. Any fool can have one."

"So what's yours?"

"I think she's come for revenge. And I think she'll get it, too."

"Will she? Against who?"

"Those who kicked her out of Lowmoor. Those who joined in humiliating her when she left."

"That sounds like a lot of people."

"It *is* a lot of people. Pretty much half the settlement."

"So how do you revenge yourself against so many people?"

"You tell me – you're the clever one."

"Ticker says you're a gofer for the new foundry bosses. What's their interest in Querne Rasp?"

"You'll have to ask them that. They don't—"

"—tell nobodies what their game is," finished Jewel.

"You've got it," said Oily.

"I'm a quick learner, Mr Wells. And what I've learnt about you I don't much like."

"Sorry to hear it, but I'm too set in my ways to change."

"I doubt whether you've made much of an effort," put in Thorn.

Oily laughed. Was he relishing the exchange? "You're right, I haven't," he admitted. "In fact, when you come down to it, I'm not a nice person. I lie, I cheat, I steal. But somebody had to be me, and I got stuck with the job, so what can I do?"

A shaft of insight struck through Jewel. "Racky and Querne were here, weren't they – I mean *here in this house?*"

Oily hesitated, then said, "Yes, yesterday afternoon."

"What about Mabbutt and Slack? Were they here too?"

"They met with Querne in my upstairs room. Had a confab, they did. But I wasn't present."

"And you didn't listen at the door?"

"With Querne Rasp inside? Do you think I've a death wish?"

Jewel didn't suppose he had. Number One would always count for most with Oily Wells.

Oily added, "Anyway, Spine Wrench was there, watching his mistress's back."

Hmm, thought Jewel. "When did Querne and Racky leave?"

"They stayed here overnight – went off this afternoon."

"And you don't know where they've gone?"

"Haven't a clue. Cross my heart. Told you, girl, I'm not a party to their plans."

"How – if you need to – do you make contact with them?"

"I don't. They contact me."

Jewel fell silent. She could think of no more questions.

"Let's go," she said to Thorn. "We're not going to learn anything more from these two."

"What shall we do with them?" he asked.

She considered Riggs and Wells. "Nothing," she said. "But if either of them crosses our path again, they'll regret it."

They left the house.

4

SECRETS OF THE FOUNDRY

Concealed in the murk that seemed to cling to a house wall, Thorn and Jewel peered across a broad patch of waste ground at the gates of Lowmoor foundry. Constructed of metal bars, it reminded them of the gates that had defended Minral How. Just inside stood a guardhouse; light glimmered in the window.

The foundry had been built in the northernmost part of the settlement. The shapes of buildings and chimneys bulked blackly against the lighter glooms of the darkening sky. To the rear of the works lay the settlement's outer wall. Here, on the inside, the foundry was protected by a high, taut fence, its mesh topped off with barbed wire.

Now, for the first time that evening, the clouds broke apart. In the gap appeared the bright, upper horn of a voyaging moon. A movement on the far side of this fence now caught Thorn's eye. A man was patrolling its length. He was armed with a pike.

"See the guard?" whispered Thorn. "They seem keen to keep people out."

"Safety-consciousness?" said Jewel. "Or have they something to hide?"

"Time to find out," said Thorn.

Cloud shrouded the moon again. Taking advantage of the

darkness, Jewel and Thorn crept away and went west, sticking close to the buildings there. They neither met nor saw anyone. When they'd put a decent distance between themselves and the foundry gate, they slipped across to the fence. For the second time that evening, Jewel unpacked the crystal and held it against the fence. Strands glowed red, gently hissing as she worked to melt them. When a sufficient number were severed, Thorn pulled the netting apart and they squeezed through the gap. But no sooner had Thorn drawn the edges together again than they heard the crunch of footsteps.

"Over there!" whispered Jewel.

Moving a few paces sideways, they crouched down in the lee of a heap of wire coils.

As the footsteps came closer, the moon lifted its upper arc above a cloud, and when the patrolman emerged from behind the piled coils he was plainly visible. Like his colleague, he carried a pike. The patrolmen walked on a few paces then stopped. The tang of melted iron remained on the still air. Could the man smell it? He came towards the fence. Jewel and Thorn shrank back into their pool of deep shadow, and the patrolman passed by at a distance of no more than a foot. But now he stopped, sniffed, knelt to peer at the base of the fence, then began to finger the mesh.

"What in Hell's name . . . !" he murmured.

Thorn leapt at him and clapped a hand to his mouth. Still clutching his pike, the guard fell sideways with Thorn on top of him. Then Jewel too was there, reaching out for the guard's forehead. Moments later, he went limp.

They dragged him under the lee of the coils.

"He'll sleep the night through," said Jewel.

"Fine," said Thorn, "but we're going to have to move fast. They'll miss him before too long."

Quickly Jewel repacked the crystal, then they slipped across to the wall of the nearest building. It was solidly built of brick and had been constructed with its rear to the fence. It had long, rectangular windows, but all were protected by iron grids and had drapes on the inside that concealed the building's contents from view. Quietly Thorn and Jewel went along to the first corner. Thorn took a peep around it, but the coast seemed clear so they hurried down the side.

As they reached the next corner, the moon ducked out of sight again, obscuring the identity of the heaps and stacks of materials that dotted the large yard beyond.

Grateful for the darkness, Jewel and Thorn advanced along the front of the building to the first of two doors. This was a large double affair and padlocked. A second, further down, was a smaller door that featured a keyhole. Jewel tricked the lock and they went in, closing the door after them.

"We need some light," said Thorn.

"No problem," she replied.

Out came the crystal again: it was proving invaluable. Its gentle glow revealed that the building was a storeroom for the basic products of the works: domestic utensils and cutlery; hammers, axes and boxes of nails; knives, pike-heads and arrowheads.

They emerged into the yard to find the moon riding triumphantly in an open patch of sky. The clouds were ragged and looked to be clearing. Bad news for night-prowlers but, sighting no patrolman, Jewel and Thorn set off to cross the yard, flitting from one dark heap to another – charcoal, probably, for the foundry's furnaces. Beyond these heaps were two rows of rat-carts, their shafts resting on the ground. The carts in the first row were empty; in the second they were loaded with scraps of metal scavenged from across the countryside. From such relics of the giant world were fashioned the articles and implements that humans depended on.

Ahead stood a large brick building with a tall chimney. Its doors stood open to the night air and a glow came from within. Thorn and Jewel hunkered down by the rear wheel of the last cart: a figure had moved in the glow. A patrolman stood there, outlined with his pike against the ruddy light beyond. As Thorn and Jewel watched, a second guard appeared from around the corner of the building.

The two exchanged greetings; then, "Have you seen Tommy?" asked the first. "He ought to have come past by now."

"No . . . Better go look for him," said the other. "You walk his round – I'll check back at the gate. And watch yourself."

When they'd gone, Jewel said, "Let's take a look inside the foundry. I'd like to know what they're working on at this time of night."

They crossed the space to the open door and, slipping inside, moved quickly towards the glow. Squeezing between two stacks of moulds, they came to a halt. Ahead, across the open floor, a couple of foundrymen were walking sideways across the floor away from a huge glowing brick furnace part-sunk in the ground. Each held the end of a long pole, the centre of which expanded to form a cup. The contents of the cup glittered and steamed. Halting, the men began to pour a stream of molten iron into the round hole of an inch-square mould. The mould was one of a row. It was impossible to tell what shape the casting would take.

Jewel and Thorn pulled back.

"I'm no wiser," she whispered. "We need to find finished examples of the product they're working on."

They scouted round for a time, but found nothing unusual.

No patrolman stood at the door, and they put the foundry behind them.

Parallel to the foundry building lay a brick-sided dam. Here and there moonlight polished its black surface to a silver-soft sheen, but at regular intervals this was creased into a frown by a flow of faint ripples. When the two young people reached the dam's far end, they were able to see why: water was fed in here by a beck. This they crossed by a little bridge, and went on to the squat building that lay on its further side. The twin of the storeroom they'd already explored, it had barred and draped windows, but a big square board had been nailed to its double door. On a glossy white background a red circle boldly stood out.

"Meaning *Danger*?" offered Thorn.

"Or *Keep Out*?" suggested Jewel. "Either way, this building's special, and I want to know why."

She tricked the lock.

They found themselves in a large storeroom or warehouse. Out came the crystal again. Split-level flooring allowed rat-carts to be reversed up to a dock for loading, and the dock was equipped with block and tackle for raising and lowering heavy items. A flight of steps took them up onto the dock, and they moved deeper into the building.

The larger part of the warehouse was given over to a host of small carts, their wheels chocked to prevent them rolling about. On the first carts lay iron balls – three or four to each. The balls came in two sizes. Thorn hefted one of the smaller balls, then set it back on its heap.

"Heavy," he told Jewel. "Solid iron, I'd say."

On the other carts were objects the like of which neither he nor Jewel had seen before. They came in two related types. The larger type comprised a kind of iron tube or cylinder mounted on a solid, four-wheeled wooden base. The upraised snout of the tube gaped blackly; the other end was closed by a hinged circular cap – presently clamped shut. A small hole appeared in the top of the tube at this lower end. The tube of the second, smaller type was both shorter and broader.

"What on earth are they?" asked Thorn.

Jewel's answer was to kneel beside the nearest of the larger mechanisms. Laying her hands on it, she closed her eyes and opened her mind.

"They're weapons," she said at last.

"Weapons?" echoed Thorn.

"Yes – modelled on some that existed long ago in the Dark Time. They're called *cannon*. But I don't see . . ."

She straightened up and looked around. Away to their right, a portion of the warehouse had been partitioned off. On the door was a smaller version of the emblem they'd seen outside.

"Let's take a look in there," she said.

The door was locked, but quickly yielded to Jewel's wiles, and in they went. The room contained several stout tables, and on these stood small barrels and a scattering of tools. Picking up a crowbar, Thorn prised the lid off one of the barrels. It was filled with grey-black grit. Placing a pinch on the palm of her hand, Jewel lifted it up to her nose and cautiously sniffed.

For a time she said nothing, simply staring at the grit. Then she turned to Thorn and said, "Everything makes sense to me now. The name of this stuff is *gunpowder*. If you set fire to it, it explodes. Use a fair amount and the effect will be devastating. But you can also use smaller amounts to fire the cannon. You set a charge in the hole at the lower end of the barrel, load one of those iron balls and touch off the charge with a burning taper. The ball shoots out and will travel a fair distance to its target. In this way you could attack a settlement without risking the lives of your own men. Imagine using ten cannon against Wyke or Norgreen – they'd surrender in no time."

Thorn tried to picture such a thing, but his imagination failed. "But how—" he began.

"Querne Rasp. She must have seen these things through a crystal. Actually, they're pretty primitive. I'm sure the giants invented much more destructive things, but our culture isn't advanced enough to reproduce them. Still, the gunpowder and cannon are bad enough. I see now why Querne formed an alliance with Crane Rockett, and after him Mabbutt and Slack. She wants revenge against Lowmoor: she tells them how to make gunpowder. She can kill whoever she likes in virtual secrecy with the stuff. Lay a substantial charge and a trail of powder to it, set fire to the trail from a safe distance and watch the results. But the cannon are something else . . . You wouldn't need cannon to take control of Lowmoor. They suggest bigger ambitions."

"Bigger ambitions?"

"Don't you see, Thorn?" Jewel's eyes gleamed coldly in the light of the crystal. "She'll start by getting rid of the men who banished her from the settlement – the Headman, the Councillors. Or rather, Mabbutt and Slack will, because they'll do the dirty work. And then where? Butshaw, Shelf, Wyke, Harrypark – Norgreen too? She'll make slaves of everyone."

"But why?" questioned Thorn. "What have the people there done to her?"

"Nothing at all, would be my guess. But the Querne Rasps of the world don't need to justify their actions. They do things because they can. Look at the Spetches, or Deacon Brace, or the men who attacked us on Roydsal Dam. And none of them were Magians . . . This gunpowder's ready for use. If men – foundrymen like the thugs that Oily sent to Ticker's house – have been trained to use it, Querne could strike at any time. And she's here in Lowmoor."

Realisation gripped Thorn. "You mean – to set the plan in motion? To kill the Councillors?"

"Yes – I'm sure of it! And she's going to do it soon!"

"Soon? How soon? Tonight?"

"It's possible. Tonight – tomorrow . . ."

"We've got to stop her." He stared at the gunpowder. "Can we blow this stuff up – take out the building and the cannon?"

"Nice idea. Except that the explosion would be so massive

that it would probably take out a good chunk of Lowmoor and set fire to the rest of the place."

"*That* devastating . . . What else can we do, then? Go to the Headman?"

"We don't know where he lives – or who he is, for that matter. But we know Abner Fairfax."

"Fairfax . . . Will he believe us?"

"He will if we bring him here and show him what we've found. He must surely have the authority to inspect this place."

"Then we'd better get moving."

Thorn listened at the storeroom door. The moon hung in a clear sky and the night seemed tranquil enough. But no sooner had Jewel and Thorn moved off than noise broke out behind them. Next moment, men with burning brands appeared around the corner. Some were armed with pikes, others with bows and arrows.

"There they are!"

"Run!" cried Thorn.

They took to their heels. An arrow hissed past Thorn's ear and buried itself in a rat-cart.

They sprinted between the fuel-heaps, using them as makeshift cover. Feet came racing after them. Then Jewel and Thorn were across the yard; their boots clattered on the bridge. They ran down the side of the dam, jinking from side to side to make arrow-shots difficult. A couple of shafts flew over their heads and disappeared into the water. They were nearing the end of the dam when a second group of armed men appeared in front of them, holding high their brands. A couple were armed with bows, the rest with pikes.

"Stop right there or we shoot!" Bows were raised to back the command.

But Jewel and Thorn had already stopped: they could go neither forward nor back; on their left was the foundry wall, on their right the dam.

The dam . . . In its end wall, perhaps five feet from where they stood, was the mouth of an arched tunnel – a culvert – into which water sluggishly flowed. In the flickering light of the brands, Thorn saw that there was an inch or two of clearance between the underside of the arch at its highest point and the water surface.

"The culvert!" whispered Thorn. "We've got to dive and swim for it!"

Jewel did not hesitate. She broke into a run and threw herself forward in a dive. Thorn was at her heels and hit the water moments after.

Taken by surprise, the foundrymen gazed with disbelief at the broken surface, black but gleaming where its ripples caught the torchlight.

Then, "Fire!" came the order, and a couple of shafts pierced the water. The trespassers did not reappear.

Jewel swam on, conscious of her dragging clothing and the hippack containing the crystal. Around stretched cold, liquid night. She couldn't tell how deep she was, nor what direction she was taking: could only trust, if she swam straight, that she'd end up at the mouth of the culvert. She'd taken a deep breath before diving; with luck it would get her there. Her right hand brushed something – mud. She'd hit bottom, and now adjusted, swimming upwards a little. As she did so, her right hand, reaching the outermost point of its sideways arc, fleetingly touched other fingers. An eerie moment; then reassurance came. Thorn was there though she couldn't see him; he'd caught up with her.

Thorn too felt the touch. Jewel was at his side! He felt a wild exhilaration. This was a madcap escapade, but it was what he was born for: the knife-edge, the unknown. He swam strongly but carefully, stretching out at each stroke in case the dam wall, not the culvert, lay directly ahead. Jewel, he was sure, would be doing exactly the same. His breath was good for a while yet.

Hampered by her pack, Jewel was starting to labour. If only she could surface! But that would only be possible when they were safely out of view. It wouldn't be too clever to take an arrow in the back. She forced stroke to follow stroke, straining her eyes against the murk, groping forward with each thrust, eager for a touch of the dam wall.

Then her chest brushed some obstacle. She felt about beneath her and found a ledge of brick or stone. Ah, she knew what this was! The culvert wasn't an archway, it was a circular hole: what she'd encountered was its lower lip. And now a hand touched her side: Thorn was here too. Their hands met and briefly clasped; then, together, they kicked forwards and upwards.

As Jewel broke surface, she kept her head down. But Thorn, who'd come up faster, had forgotten the low archway, and his skull banged into the brickwork.

"Ow!" he exclaimed, and instead of air got a mouthful of black water, some of which went down his throat before he could spit it out.

"Whose idea was this?" he complained, coughing and treading water.

"Yours, I seem to remember." Jewel was concentrating on getting air back into her lungs. The air smelt dank, but better dank air than none.

On three sides was pitch darkness. On the fourth, a crescent of deep grey with its flat edge facing downwards mildly alleviated the darkness.

Thorn rubbed the top of his head. "Will your crystal work in here? We could do with a spot of light."

"Of course. But first we need to go deeper into this tunnel. We don't want those men back there to see we've got a light."

He agreed, so they swam slowly on into the darkness, testing out the height of the roof as they went. It was clammy and clotted with moss that squelched when their heads pressed against it, but it neither dipped nor rose, and they hadn't gone far when Thorn announced that he could touch bottom with his feet. The floor of the culvert was sloping upwards. Soon they could stand up. The roof came down to within an inch of Thorn's head. The water was chest-high. Thorn helped Jewel unstrap her pack, held it for her while she got the crystal out, then slung it around his own waist. The stone was enough for her to manage.

She woke it to gentle life, and it showed them a stretch of the tunnel, colouring the brickwork a rusty green and making the black water shine with an unearthly opalescence.

"You look like a half-drowned rat!" she told him.

"As long as I'm only *half*-drowned . . ."

Side by side, they began to wade down the tunnel. The

moss grew long here and let down thin slimy strands that, when Thorn sought to brush them aside, clung lovingly to his arms.

Jewel halted. "Thorn!"

A foot or so ahead, a pair of eyes was watching them from the surface of the water. But, as the two humans returned the stare, more of the creature's head appeared: it was a frog. Its slotlike mouth opened and closed. Then, swivelling about, it swam quickly off with powerful thrusts of its webbed feet.

They went on. The water level dropped further: first to waist-height, then to knee-height. Yet the culvert's dimensions remained the same. Similar thoughts were passing through Thorn's and Jewel's heads. Where did it go? Would there be a way out at the end? And if there was, would more foundrymen be waiting for them there?

The tunnel bent left. Rounding the bend, they saw before them a metal ladder. Its lowest rung just cleared the water; above, it disappeared into a circular shaft in the tunnel roof.

"An access point," murmured Thorn. "Put the light out, Jewel."

She doused the light and they stood beneath the mouth of the hole, looking up. There was nothing but blackness up there.

"I'll climb up – take a look," said Thorn.

And, as quietly as he could, he set his feet on the ladder. Water ran and dripped from his legs. He felt cold. Oh for dry clothes! he thought.

He began to climb, but the ladder was short. He'd counted only fifteen rungs when his further progress was blocked. He felt around above his head . . . a round manhole cover. He was on the point of giving it a good shove when a scraping noise came from above. An animal, perhaps? Human feet?

But the next sound was different: the scrape of metal against metal. With dismay, he recognised it for what it was: men were working to prise open the cover.

He set off back down, descending as quickly as he could, but was only halfway when he heard the cover lifted away. Wrapping his arms around the ladder, he slid the last few steps and only narrowly avoided falling back into the water.

"There are men up there!" he hissed, pulling Jewel away from beneath the access shaft.

Next moment a light appeared above.

"They're down there!" shouted a voice. "Look! The water's disturbed!"

Already Jewel and Thorn were moving away down the tunnel. The crystal warmed into a glow. They splashed on round another bend. Would the guards come after them? Thorn beat off strands of moss. Filthy, sticky stuff . . . Once again the culvert curved.

Beyond the bend the water deepened. Within a dozen steps they were wading waist-deep. Then the crystal's glow revealed what lay ahead again.

Twenty more paces, and they stopped. The tunnel had opened into a chamber. In the chamber lay a pool. In the far chamber wall a second arched culvert took away the overflow. But where the culvert that led from the dam had offered swimmers a reasonable clearance, this one had virtually none: only the tiniest of gaps appeared between the water surface and the underside of the archway.

It's impossible, thought Thorn.

"We'll have to turn and fight," he said.

But when Jewel made no reply, Thorn turned to look at her.

Waist-deep in water, hands dangling in the flow, the girl was staring out at nothing. But Thorn had seen that look before. She's gone out of herself, he thought. But why here? Why now?

Voices echoed down the tunnel. Men with lights and weapons were approaching. He and Jewel would be standing targets. Thorn made to seize Jewel's arm, but at the last moment held back. Something in her very remoteness dissuaded him. She did nothing without a reason . . .

The voices were growing louder, and along with them came splashing sounds as they battled through the water.

Jewel – come back, come back! he urged.

She opened her eyes and smiled at him. In the stone's green glow, they seemed shot through with uncanny gleams.

"We can swim through!" she said.

"Swim through?"

"Come on!" Then she was wading through the pool, the crystal held before her. Thorn pushed on in her wake.

"We need the crystal to light the way. How will you swim and hold on to it?"

"Leave that to me. Take a deep breath!"

He glanced round. Light showed from around the bend in the tunnel. The foundrymen were almost upon them.

But here was the archway. Jewel tossed the crystal into the water a little ahead. It sank from sight and the current carried it under the archway. Next moment the girl followed, ducking under and striking out.

Thorn sucked in air and kicked away after her.

Churning up the water, armed with a mixture of pikes and bows, men came splashing into the chamber.

But the fugitives were not to be seen.

5

SURPRISE ATTACK

Had the frog that had swum away lingered in the second culvert, it would have beheld a magical sight. First, a green glow moving onwards through the water; then the object producing the glow – a crystal, all bright veins and sinews; after the crystal a swimming girl, her dark hair streaming out; and last a young man, his features fierce with determination. Whenever the girl touched the stone with her outstretched fingertips, it would spurt away from her like a thing possessed.

But the frog was long gone. Instead, a creature with a crested head, short legs and a long, whippy tail came snaking smoothly past, and Thorn almost took a second gulp of water as its shining eyes loomed eerily out of the dark. But the newt wasn't interested in him; then it, too, was gone.

A little further and Jewel was kicking upwards, the crystal clutched between her hands. Thorn followed, and broke surface.

They trod water, gratefully sucking in breaths of clean night air, an island of light in a world of darkness and silence. The moon was swaddled in cloud again, and they might have been alone at the silent end of the world, the dry earth drowned and lost.

"*That* way," said Jewel pointing. Turning onto her back, she kicked out, holding the still-glowing crystal above the water-surface.

Thorn swam beside her and they soon reached the bank, where they climbed out and squelched their way miserably up a gentle, muddy slope.

"What was it you said about a drowned rat?" said Thorn.

"Make it two drowned rats," said Jewel, and shivered. "We need to get out of these wet clothes."

"By the look of it we're outside the settlement."

"Yes. But we can't be far from the wall."

Straining his eyes against the dark, Thorn thought he could perceive a dark mass low against the sky. "Is that it over there?"

"I think you're right."

They moved off towards the dark mass, picking their way among stones, knots of grass and clumps of wild flowers, their soggy clothing slopping against their bodies as they walked.

It was indeed the wall, and running along below it was a well-trodden path. They debated briefly which direction to take, then set off down the track. After a time, this brought them to a small stone building. It possessed two barred windows and a stub of a chimney. Its door was padlocked, but the padlock yielded to Jewel's subtle probings and in they went.

This was clearly no home from home, but neither was it unwelcoming. It contained four chairs, a table and a cot. By the fire-grate was a heap of kindling; flint and tinder lay on a shelf beside a couple of oil-lamps and a full container of fuel, and on the cot was a stack of blankets, coarse but thick. Thorn and Jewel were in luck.

In a little while they had a fire going, had stripped off their wet clothes (Thorn delicately turning his back on Jewel as she undressed) and, wrapped in blankets, were busy drying their garments – and Jewel her long hair – at the fire. This was a tiresomely slow process, but a necessary one: catching a cold held little appeal for either of them. Meanwhile, conscious that night was passing and time precious, they discussed what they'd say to Abner Fairfax when they saw him.

But events took a twist. Jewel was fully dressed again and Thorn had one arm inside his jerkin when the door was thrown open and a uniformed man burst in. Behind him came others, their pikes levelled threateningly.

"Who are you?" demanded the first man, who seemed in authority.

"We might ask you the same question," Thorn replied evenly.

The man appraised them for a moment. Then he said sternly: "I am Master of Guards. You have broken into a guardroom and have no business to be here. Your light was seen and reported to me. Now I will ask you again: who are you?"

"My name is Thorn Jack. My companion's name is Jewel Ranson. Coming along in the dark, we fell into a pool and came in here to get dry."

"A likely story," replied the Master of Guards. "What are you doing, creeping about in the night near the settlement?"

"We weren't creeping," replied Thorn. "Believe it or not, we were just about to set off for the gate."

"Only spies and subversives move about at such a time. I demand to know what you were doing."

"I've told you." Thorn glanced at Jewel, who gave an encouraging nod. He went on, "Jewel and I have urgent information for Councillor Fairfax. And when I say 'urgent', that's exactly what I mean. We have knowledge of a plot against the Headman and Council. You'll best serve your settlement if you take us to Fairfax. *Now.*"

The forthrightness of this statement took the Master of Guards by surprise. But then his features hardened again. "A plot? What plot?"

"That's for Councillor Fairfax's ears."

"What do you know of the Councillor?"

"We were brought – that is, we *met* him today. Or maybe now it's yesterday."

The Master had caught Thorn's slip of the tongue. "You were brought before him?" he said.

"Er, just as a matter of course, when we arrived."

The Master of Guards considered his youthful captives in silence. There was something here, but what it was he couldn't tell. To be honest, this pair didn't look like spies, but they didn't look innocent, either. These days, it was wise not to judge by appearances. The lad was certainly lying, or was dealing in half-truths, and the Master hadn't risen to his position by dint of making hasty decisions that he later came to regret. And waking a Councillor in the middle of the night was no light matter . . .

"Right," he said. "You two will come along with us."

Jewel took a step towards her pack, which was resting on the floor.

"Don't touch that!" ordered the Master.

Jewel halted. The Master came forward, picked the pack up and tested it for weight.

"What's in here?" he demanded.

"A magic crystal," Jewel replied, keeping a perfectly straight face.

The Master of Guards smiled. The girl had offered him the fantasy answer of a child, yet she didn't look like a child. Well, he'd check the bag out later, when he'd got these two to base.

"Right," he commanded, "you two, *out*. And *don't* try to escape: you'll get pikes in your backs." He turned to the men behind him. "Escort formation," he ordered.

The Master extinguished the lamps they'd lit and re-padlocked the door, leaving the fire the pair had lit to burn out in its own time. The six guards had formed up around their prisoners. Four carried pikes; two bore flaming torches. They looked tough and vigilant. Then the Master of Guards barked out an order and the detachment moved off.

"You've *got* to take us to Councillor Fairfax," Thorn repeated urgently. "Lives could depend on it."

"Thorn's right," said Jewel. "What, after all, have you got to lose?"

The Master of Guards considered that he had plenty to lose and did not reply. He, his captives and four of his men were back in Lowmoor in a room at Guard Headquarters. He'd questioned the young people again, but Jewel and Thorn had refused to say any more than they'd already said. He was feeling frustrated and beginning to entertain thoughts of harsher methods of interrogation.

Turning to the girl's pack, he began to unfasten the straps.

"I wouldn't do that, if I were you," said Jewel evenly.

"You're not me," said the Master.

"That's true – but don't say I didn't warn you."

There seemed to be nothing in the pack but something roughly circular wrapped up in a cloth. The Master pulled the bundle out and began to unpeel the wrappings. As he did so, his right hand came in contact with the object they contained. There was a bright green flash and he let out an undignified yell and dropped the thing on the table. It was a large chunk of crystal and dark green in colour. His hand bore an angry scorch-mark.

"What is it?" he demanded.

"I told you – a magic crystal. And as you've just found out the hard way, it's no use to you. I suggest you give it back to me."

"Whatever it is, it's dangerous. It would be better off destroyed."

"Pikes and bows and arrows are dangerous things, Master of Guards, but I see no sign that you want to destroy *them*."

"You're an impudent girl."

"So people keep telling me. But you only say that because you've lost the argument. Does your hand hurt?"

"No."

"I think it does. May I touch it?"

"For what reason?"

"I can heal your hurt."

"Nonsense!"

"How do you know it's nonsense? What are you afraid of?

Losing your precious dignity? Or are you simply afraid of me?"

The Master of Guards glanced around the circle of his men. Their faces wore the professional blankness they always did in his presence. I'm starting to look a fool, he thought. If I can't cope with this girl, I may as well resign my post.

"Very well, then," he said. "Let's see what you can do."

Jewel took his hand in hers, then stood looking into his face. The Master of Guards was a tough fellow, the most skilful pikeman around, but he found the stare of this chit of a girl almost unnerving. Nevertheless he held it and the burning sensation in his hand began to ebb. When it had gone entirely, the girl let go of his hand. The skin was pinkly normal. He rubbed it in disbelief.

"What are you?" he asked. "A Syb?"

Jewel smiled teasingly. "Just a chit of a girl," she said. "Now, will you take us to Councillor Fairfax? Or at least give him our message and let him make up his own mind whether to listen to us or not?"

Abner Fairfax wasn't exactly pleased to be rousted out of his cosy bed in the middle of the night: but if the Master of Guards thought the occasion warranted it, it was the Councillor's duty to listen. Even so, Fairfax could not have anticipated the nature of what the Master had to tell him.

"A plot – against the Council?" he exclaimed.

"Yes. And they say they'll give the details to no one but you."

"It doesn't seem very likely . . . those two are little more than children. Still, I'd better come and see them."

And as they walked through the lamplit streets of the better part of the settlement, the Master of Guards told the Councillor about the strange stone and the way the girl had cured the burn.

"That was what decided me to come and see you," he finished. "This girl is no ordinary girl."

"So it would seem," the Councillor mused.

Once arrived at Guard Headquarters, he dismissed the four guards and spoke to Jewel and Thorn with only the Master of Guards present. The teenagers cut their story to the bone, dwelling only on their discovery and the huge threat it posed.

"This is a very tall story," Fairfax observed when they'd finished. "Why on earth should I swallow it?"

"Because as one of the Council members who took the decision to banish Querne – not to mention the fact that you're in charge of security here – *you* are a prime target," said Jewel. "Ignore our warning at your peril."

"Gunpowder . . . cannon . . . cannonballs . . . I've never heard of these things."

"Only because they don't exist in our world – or rather didn't, till Querne reinvented them. But many things existed in the past that don't exist now – as the artefacts that settlements keep in their Treasuries clearly prove. Who knows what secrets the giants knew that we've yet to rediscover?"

Like the Master of Guards before him, Councillor Fairfax had to recognise the strength of her argument.

"You've told us what you found at the foundry," he said, "but you didn't say how you got in or got out. There's a strong fence round the place, the installation is well-patrolled, and you were found outside the settlement."

"We have our methods," said Thorn evasively, "just as you

have yours. The foundry patrol cornered us, but we escaped through a culvert. That's how we came to be outside the walls and soaked to the skin."

There's much here they're not telling me, the Councillor thought.

He said, "This crystal of yours . . . What is it? Where is it from? What does it do?"

"If I could answer those questions," said Jewel, "I'd be wiser than I am."

"You're too modest, Jewel Ranson. You're clearly wise beyond your years. And, if you're telling the truth, no ordinary person could have achieved what you've achieved – with or without the help of your stone. You also cured the Master's hand. Are you a Magian?"

Jewel returned his stare coolly and offered no reply.

The Councillor leant back in his chair, clasped his hands behind his head and directed his gaze at the ceiling. It was blank and powerless to suggest how he should act. Yet he had to make a decision.

The silence lengthened. At last he motioned to the Master of Guards, and the two men left the room, leaving the crystal on the table. For some reason, the stone seemed to have slipped the Councillor's mind.

"Do you believe their story, Master?" he asked outside in the corridor.

"I honestly don't know," replied the Master of Guards. "It may be the truth, but it may also be an attempt to lead us into a trap."

"Yes – that had occurred to me. But if all this is simply

designed to lead us into a trap, it's a cumbersome and elaborate way of going about things. And far from certain of success. It's been rumoured for some time that Mabbutt and Slack are up to something, but they're careful and they're clever and they have ways of intimidating people: my best attempts to nail them down have been thwarted up to now. As you know they tried for election to the Council and were rejected, and they're not the sort that takes rejection lying down. No, I think these young folk are telling us the truth, or as much of it as they under- stand – fantastic as it seems. Now, there can't be more than thirty men in the foundry's entire workforce and it's the middle of the night. If we take a strong force, we should be able to over- come them."

The Master of Guards rubbed his chin. "If all thirty are there, it's a lot to take on. The most I can deploy is twenty men."

"But our men are trained fighters. And I can't see Mabbutt and Slack having their whole workforce out . . . If we fail to act on this warning, generations yet unborn may—"

Fast on one another's heels sounded a series of explosions – one, two, three, four. The walls of the corridor shook and cracks appeared in the ceiling. Puffs of dust appeared from nowhere. The two men stood stock-still, wild-eyed, stunned, seemingly caught in a stoppage of time. Then, as Fairfax lifted a hand to sketch the beginnings of a gesture, a second round of explosions began. But neither man heard it, for now a shower of bricks came crashing through the wall as if the obstruction hadn't been there, and they were killed instantly. Then the ceiling fell in, crushing their already mangled bodies beneath its timbers.

Had Thorn and Jewel stayed where they were when their

questioners left the room, they too would have died. But all of a sudden Jewel snatched up her pack, shoved the crystal into it and shouted to Thorn, "Under the table! Quick!"

He didn't stop to ask for reasons. The table she meant stood against a side wall; it was ugly but serviceable, with a thick top and stout legs. Jewel and Thorn were halfway towards it when the explosions began. The first four charges must have been set on other sides of the building, for they were able to scramble under the table and get their hands over their ears before the second round erupted. But the room they were in was a target this time, and with a terrific *BANG*! the wall flew apart. Bricks hurtled across the room, smashing down the opposite wall, and the ceiling collapsed at an angle. Beams came crashing to the floor, followed by items of furniture from the room directly above. Debris thumped on the tabletop, but the table held firm. Dust billowed around Jewel and Thorn, making them cough and pull out kerchiefs to cover their mouths and noses. Then the rain of debris ceased, to be succeeded by an eerie silence.

"Gunpowder?" hazarded Thorn – and found that he could barely hear the sound of his own voice. His head felt as if it had been stuffed with bog-cotton.

Jewel nodded. "We got here too late."

Flames flickered across the floor. Thorn clutched Jewel's arm. "Fire! Oil from the lamps! We've got to get out of here!"

They crawled out from under the table. Through the drifting dust they saw a ragged hole in the end wall. Their eyes stung by dust, they made their way across the room, clambering over obstacles or squeezing under beams. Behind them, the fire was quickly taking firm hold, but the hungry young flames at least afforded some light. Now came the sound of more explosions, but this time some way off – the conspirators must be attacking other targets in the settlement. The whole operation had been meticulously planned.

Those parts of the roof that hadn't so far collapsed were a tee-tering shambles, and as Jewel and Thorn scrambled over the tumbled bricks, several tiles came crashing down only inches away from them. Then they were clear of what had once been Guard Headquarters and hurrying down a side street. The moon slipped out from cloud cover; under its wan light settlers were emerging from their houses in various states of dress and undress, rubbing sleep from their eyes. Some cast suspicious looks at Jewel and Thorn as they went by, but no one tried to stop them, and after a time they slowed to a walk.

"Councillor Fairfax and the Master of Guards are dead," Jewel told Thorn. "I sensed it after the attack. And by the sound it, Mabbutt and Slack have attacked the homes of the other Councillors. By now they may all be dead."

"They beat us to it," said Thorn grimly. "After they saw us in the foundry, they decided to strike tonight. They were taking no chances on us escaping and warning the Council."

"Yes – but I suspect they were planning to attack tonight in any case. If all the Councillors and most of the guards are dead, the settlement will be left like a boat without a rudder. Mabbutt and Slack will take over, using the foundrymen as enforcers. We've got to get out of Lowmoor before they gain complete control – grab a breathing-space to rethink our approach to finding Querne."

"I wonder if Querne knew that we were in Guard Headquarters? If we weren't spotted getting away, she may think we've been killed."

"That's possible, but I wouldn't bank on it."

"So we collect our gear and run?"

"Got any better ideas?"

Everywhere in the moonlit streets, people clustered by doorways, excited and fearful, chattering in little groups.

When Jewel and Thorn arrived at Reeny Breaks's house, they found their landlady in the street with a couple of neighbours.

"Where have you two been?" she demanded. "You never came back last night."

"We were unavoidably detained," answered Thorn.

"Wait till Councillor Fairfax gets to hear about this."

"He already has," said Thorn.

The landlady's mouth fell open.

As Thorn and Jewel went into the house, another round of detonations occurred.

"Oh my God!" cried one of the neighbours. "It's the end of the world!"

The end of *one* world, thought Jewel, but the start of another: the world according to Querne Rasp.

Pushing aside their tiredness, Thorn and Jewel gathered their gear and walked out of the door.

"Where are you going?" demanded Reeny Breaks, as her short-term guests went by.

"Damned if I know," answered Thorn.

The landlady glared after them.

But Thorn's words were only too true. "By the way, where *are* we going?" he asked Jewel as they hurried along.

"I don't know – too tired to think. Out of this place, that's all."

Turning a corner, they saw a crowd ahead. It had gathered around a house. Or what was left of a house – a chimneystack and part of a wall with a shattered window in the middle. The rest of the structure had collapsed. The houses to left and right of it had sustained severe damage, and the most of the others in the street had had their windows blown in. Men were working among the ruins to shift beams and bricks, but in the absence of hoists to shift the heavier material, this was difficult, slow work.

Jewel and Thorn halted at the edge of the crowd.

"Whose house is this?" Jewel asked a bystander.

"Don't you know?" replied the woman. "It's the Headman's. He and his wife are under there – and their son and daughter too. It's absolutely terrible. I live just up the street. There were these massive bangs . . . All my windows shattered. But at least I'm alive. What could have caused the explosions? What's the world coming to?"

Just then a cry went up.

"They've found someone!" exclaimed the woman.

The crowd surged forward. Jewel and Thorn went with it.

Two men emerged from the ruins carrying a limp body which they laid gently on the earth.

The woman they'd spoken to clutched the arm of a tall man. "Who is it?" she asked.

"The little girl," replied the man. "Looks to me like she's dead."

Then he spotted Jewel and Thorn. "Who are you two?" he asked suspiciously.

"We were just passing," Thorn replied, and turned away.

But the man gripped his arm. "Hold on there," he said. "I've never seen you before. Exactly who are you?"

Jewel grasped the man's arm and looked him straight in the eye. "We're just visitors," she said.

"Visitors . . ." the man repeated. "Visitors, of course . . ." And he let go of Thorn.

As Jewel and Thorn moved away, similar thoughts ran through their minds. Killing guards was one thing, killing children something else. Querne was utterly pitiless. And anyone who stood in her way would get the same treatment.

I was right, thought Jewel, Querne has to be stopped.

But how?

As Thorn and Jewel walked off down the street, a male figure with the brim of his cap pulled low over his eyes and a scarf wound round his neck so that it obscured his chin and mouth, shoved through the crowd to get a closer view of the body. He stood for a time taking in the pathetic sight, then swung on his heel and elbowed his way clear of the throng.

As if to follow Thorn and Jewel, he took a dozen steps in the direction in which they'd gone. Then he stopped, irresolute and isolated in the street, as if paralysed by the impact of what he'd just seen.

All customary order, it now seemed, had broken down. The streets were in a ferment, with people scurrying here and there on obscure expeditions. Few of those swapping the latest rumours in huddled groups paid much attention to a couple of passing teenagers. Spotting a torchlit detachment of pikemen marching towards them, Jewel and Thorn slipped into an alley, but the pikemen — grim-faced and plainly full of purpose — went by without throwing so much as a glance in their direction. There were six men in the group, and though they weren't in guards' uniforms they all wore the same clothing — black jerkins, trews and boots; probably a detachment of foundrymen. Already Mabbutt and Slack were taking a grip on the settlement. And somewhere in the middle of this upheaval was Querne Rasp, a deadly long-fingered spider in total control of her web.

Jewel and Thorn came to the open ground that lay between the outermost buildings and Lowmoor's eastern gate. On either side of it, secure inside glass cases mounted on posts, oil-lamps burnt. In the light of one, a stout single pikeman stood on watch, dressed in the same black outfit as the detachment they'd earlier seen. No guards proper were in sight, nor was anyone else about: the uproar in the settlement hadn't — yet — prompted anything in the way of panic departures.

"What if he's under orders to let no one leave?" said Thorn.

"Then we'll have to persuade him to change his mind, won't we?"

"Odd, that very same thought had crossed *my* mind."

They went towards the gate. The pikeman barred their way.

"No one's to leave tonight," he said.

"Surely you can make an exception for us," said Thorn.

"No exceptions," said the man.

"Not even if we offered you an inducement?" said Thorn.

"You trying to bribe me?"

"*Bribe* has a nasty ring. I prefer the word *encourage*."

The pikeman hesitated. "And what form would this encouragement take?"

"Hard cash. We're keen to leave."

"Just how keen, would you say?"

Thorn named a sum.

"In my view, that's only half keen," the man said. "Double it, and you're on."

"That's a lot of money," said Thorn.

"Take it or leave it," said the guard. "Or should I say: Take it *and* leave?" He chuckled at his own wit.

"All right," Thorn agreed, then threw a shifty look around.

Seeing this, the guard said, "Best do this inside the guardhouse." Then, with a glance at Jewel, he added, "*You* can stay out here."

In the guardhouse, Thorn began to count money out on the table. The pikeman stood with the butt of his weapon resting on the ground, its spike pointing at the ceiling. But when Thorn reached the agreed sum, the pikeman kicked him in the leg. Thorn fell on the floor.

"You little vermin," hissed the man. "Now get out and get back where you came from – you and your tart."

"But – our money!" complained Thorn.

"I'm keeping that. Let it be a lesson to you. And if I see you here again . . ."

While the threat hung in the air, Thorn made to get to his feet. His first effort ended in failure, his leg buckling beneath him. Gritting his teeth he tried again, but he'd only half risen when he threw himself at the pikeman and butted him in the stomach. The force of his rush threw the man against the wall, which his head met with a crack. With Thorn on top of him, the pikeman slid to the floor. He was out for the count.

Thorn got to his feet and scooped his money off the table.

"So you managed to persuade him," said Jewel when he came out.

"Naturally," Thorn replied. "I'm a persuasive sort of fellow."

He unbarred the gate. But, no sooner had Jewel and Thorn made their departure from Lowmoor, than a figure appeared from an alley and crossed the open ground at a trot. He glanced into the guardhouse.

"Idiot!" he said to the recumbent pikeman.

Then, pulling back the same half of the gate that Thorn had opened, he took off his cap and applied an eye to the crack. Black dark was all he saw.

6

THE CRYSTAL VORTEX

Jewel awoke abruptly. She lay warm in her sleeping bag, above her head the tent roof. It was daylight outside. Across the tent, Thorn lay huddled up, still deeply asleep.

Something had woken her . . . but what?

Her eyes wandered to her pack, which lay close to her side, and at once she knew the cause. Drawing out the wrapped crystal, she unrolled it from its cloth.

She hadn't laid a finger on it, but it was emitting a rhythmic pulse. There it came regularly on a steady count of five – a lingering heartbeat of light. Something had woken the stone, and the stone had in turn woken its mistress . . .

As Jewel looked at the crystal, a shiver of fear passed through her like a fast ripple through water. But in the aftermath of the shiver there came a surge of expectancy. Deliberately denying herself any time for second thoughts, she gripped the crystal with both hands. Green light flared, blinding, consuming her body, the tent, the world...

Then died back to a steady glow. Still, it seemed, she had the crystal fast in her hands, for she could clearly feel its heat and the slow pulse of its fiery heart. Yet she couldn't see her hands, she could see only the stone. It hovered in front of her, riding on the empty air. And Jewel herself, where was she? Present and not present, it seemed, for when she looked down for her body she saw nothing but darkness.

The crystal hovered in nothingness, a void as black as the space between stars.

Then it was moving, floating away. She felt it tug at her mind. Obediently, she followed.

The darkness was retreating. A passageway defined itself, then, leading upwards, a staircase. The crystal drifted up the staircase, down a landing and came to a door. The door was shut, and there the crystal halted. Jewel stopped beside it, waiting for it to move again. But the crystal didn't move, and now Jewel understood that having brought her thus far, it would take her no further: the next move was for her alone to take. So, willing herself into motion, she moved towards the door, passing soundlessly through the wood as if it – or she herself – were no more than an illusion.

In the room she paused, hovering. A woman stood with her back to the door, chestnut hair silky and flowing. She wore a well-cut black jerkin, a scarlet skirt that dropped a little way below her knees and black knee-length hide boots. Her left hand rested on her hip, her right – fingers and thumb splayed – was dramatically raised. In mid-air a little above her hand three glittering crystals hung, forming a neat triangle: one bluebell-blue, one ruby-red, the third amber-yellow. They were all of a size.

The woman closed her fist and made a snapping sound with her fingers. The three crystals began to revolve. They moved slowly at first, so that their forms remained distinct. Then they began to gather speed until they lost definition, their colours merging together. The air in the room was pulled with them until it too churned and swirled sympathetically. The crystal triangle was a wheel, a whirling, soundless vortex with, at its hub, vacancy, a kernel of nothingness. The whole room seemed to vibrate and specks of dust came drifting down from the ceiling.

The woman sank into a chair set a little to one side, her arms at rest in her lap. Now that her body was partly turned towards Jewel, the girl was able to recognise her: it was Querne Rasp – who else? – wearing (for now) her own face. But Querne's eyes were closed, and Jewel realised that the Magian had gone out of herself. And Jewel knew where Querne had gone: into the vortex at the heart of the crystal.

But why? As soon as this question floated into Jewel's thoughts, she knew she had to know the answer. She willed herself to move again, but had gone only halfway towards the crystal vortex when she felt seized by a force that was more powerful than herself, drawn swiftly the rest of the way and sucked into the dark well at the heart of the turbulence.

Caught up its fast spin, she was dizzyingly whirled: now crushed, now stretched until she felt her mind would explode.

But abruptly the motion ceased, the world tilted and stilled.

Her giddiness drained from her. Things began to come into focus.

She was a disembodied eye drifting above a landscape. She passed over a wind-stirred meadow with occasional clumps of trees, but this soon gave way to moorland dotted with yellow-flowered gorse bushes and other scrubby growths. Down to her right she saw a survival from the Dark Time – a church with a tall spire topped off with a cross. It stood in a churchyard packed with gravestones and blackened tombs and statues, much of the stonework overgrown. Then came more rugged moorland, through whose surface domes of rock broke like the humped backs of a surfacing school of grey-skinned earth-monsters.

Now she was floating towards a dam or large pond. Brick-sided, giant-built, it looked deep at one side but fairly shallow at the other, where green rushes sprang from its stagnant waters. Beyond lay a jumble of buildings made of brick and tin-plating in various states of decay. A couple of tall stone chimneys jutted out of the general mess.

The nearest building was long and high-walled. Its window-spaces gaped. Much of its roof had collapsed, leaving behind the metal skeleton that had held it in place. Only a few of the rectangular plates that had kept out the rain still survived. Below them she glimpsed a shambles: pieces of fallen roofing and massive, derelict machines.

The building that abutted it was rather better preserved and boasted a tall, tubular tower of blackened stone.

These and other structures surrounded a large yard in which products in a wide range of shapes and sizes were stacked or stored: massy iron girders; steel rods and plates, coils of wire of different thickness. Unrestrained, grass and weeds had gained holds in the heaps and stacks: mosses and wild flowers grew there, and long-stemmed feathery grasses waved their heads in the mild breeze.

Somewhere in the middle of all this, looking oddly out of place, sat a tidy stone-built house. One-storey, square, with a short, stubby chimney, it had two windows on the side that she could see and a door in the end from which the weather had stripped the paint. The roof was tiled with red shingles, but many of these had loosened and slipped to leave gaps here and there. In some, tufts of grass nested, and even wild flowers.

Without warning, she found herself dropping towards the roof. If at this moment she'd had a mouth and a throat, she might have cried out, but having neither she was unable to utter a sound.

She passed without sensation through a patch of roof-tiles and dropped towards the floor, halting abruptly some three feet above it.

Somewhere, not too distant, she sensed another human presence. It was no more than a tang, a scent trailing on the air, but it could be nothing else.

Querne Rasp . . . Querne too was here. But the Magian's spirit was invisible. As mine, it now occurred to Jewel, must also be.

Then she saw them —

Rats! Rats of all sizes, big and small, with butting heads. A nest of them. No — not one nest, many nests, made of scraps of torn cloth that, Jewel supposed, would make for a comfortable place to sleep if you happened to be a rat. The creatures were normal but for one thing: their fur was blue-tinged, a deep blue verging on violet, and it gleamed where it caught the light. As if they sensed her presence, some of the rats had turned their heads to look in Jewel's direction, yet they seemed uncertain too, as if they couldn't trust their senses, and the girl realised that they were looking straight *through* her. They can't see me, she thought. I'm invisible to them, just as Querne is to me . . .

Why is she here? Jewel wondered.

Simple, came the answer: she's looking for something.

Which means that I must look too, though I don't know for what . . .

She willed herself to move and cross the nest-ridden floor. A few of the rats twisted their necks to stare up as she passed over, noses twitching, whiskers alert.

Jewel searched methodically, moving in straight lines across the room from wall to wall. More than half the space had been covered when all at once she was seized by an odd persuasion of *attunement* – as if some organ had been sensitised by a not-too-far-off presence.

She made a dart towards the floor. Directly beneath, half a dozen young rats jumped up and scampered away. Now she was floating only inches above the floor. And there, nestling among the rags and twists of cloth was a black stone.

At first sight it looked ordinary enough. But as Jewel stared at it a shaft of light, piercing one of the many gaps in the roof, struck its surface. The stone sparkled, throwing bright slivers through the lance of the sunbeam. It was a crystal, not a stone, and now, transfigured, it appeared more purple than black – a profound and potent purple.

As Jewel contemplated the crystal, a powerful sense of its significance formed in her mind. It was larger than the other crystals and more powerful. At the same time, there was something unnerving about it, a sharp edge of menace. It would be no small thing to try to wield this grim stone. Even as she felt strongly drawn towards it, she felt a deep reluctance to grasp hold of it.

Just as well that grasping anything was presently out of the question. But she was going to have to grasp it, for if Querne beat her to it . . . *For this was the crystal that belonged at the hub of the vortex!*

At the centre of the star! The star, not the triangle – for there were five crystals in all, her green stone making the fifth.

But now a soft voice sounded, as if the words had been spoken deep inside Jewel's head.

"Girl," it said, "you'll never live to hold this crystal in your hands!"

Mocking laughter followed, a ringing like a silvery bell. The mocking laughter of Querne Rasp . . .

The icy tones broke the spell. Jewel's vision was fading now: the black crystal, the rumpled nest, the blue rats . . . all were fading. The double search had achieved its end.

A thin mist enshrouded the girl. Slowly she became aware of her hands and the green stone she still held. There it was, the telltale pulse now dimming at its heart. Around her, the grey walls of the tent materialised – and there, hands tucked under his head, watching her, Thorn Jack.

Then her crystal seemed to twitch, and into her mind came a word she'd never heard spoken in her world.

Quincell . . .

So *that's* its name, she thought, the name of the other crystals too . . . Then, straightaway: But what on earth are *quincells*?

"Quincell." She spoke tentatively, testing the strange syllables

100

that had carried to her from another world. Her voice sounded rusty, as if it hadn't been used for an age.

"What did you say?" asked Thorn.

"Quincell," she repeated, more confidently this time, and pointed to the stone, which had now ceased to pulse and was its usual dullish green. "That's what these crystals are called. Don't ask me what the name means, I haven't got a clue. But there are five of them in all. There's this one that I took from the Puckfloss sisters on Nettle Island. Querne Rasp has three: a blue stone, an amber stone and the ruby stone you stole from Wyke." She paused.

"And the fifth one?" pressed Thorn.

"The crystal woke me: it was pulsing. I went out of myself and saw Querne Rasp with her crystals. She was wielding all three. The green crystal belongs with them: it got drawn towards the others because of some natural sympathy. Then Querne went out of herself and I was drawn after her through this vortex in the air created by the spinning crystals. She was looking for the fifth crystal and she found it. And so did I. It's black, though it shines purple when it catches the light."

"This black crystal, where is it?"

"In a Dark Time ironworks, a total ruin of a place. There can't be many hereabouts, so it must be the one Luke Gill was exploring when he was blinded. I remember Rainy saying it's on the far side of Lowmoor."

"The far side from Harrypark?" exclaimed Thorn excitedly. "That's the eastern side – the side we're on now!"

"Yes. The ironworks lies somewhere beyond a Dark Time church. Thorn, I know now what it is we have to do: we must get to this crystal before Querne Rasp does. It looks bigger than the others and I think it's the most powerful. If Querne gets hold of it, there's no knowing what she might do . . . Her powers will be enhanced far beyond what they are now – even with the three crystals she has. But it's not going to be easy. For one thing, she knows *I* know where the black crystal is." Jewel paused, then added, "She may even have planned it so I'd be drawn after her . . ."

She fell silent. Thorn watched her. It was clear that she was brooding on what she'd just said.

"And the other thing?" he finally prompted.

Jewel roused herself, smiled ruefully and told him of the blue rats – a whole building full, nest upon nest, too many to count. And the black crystal, lying slap bang in the middle of them . . .

"Wild rats!" Thorn pulled a face. "If there's one thing I hate . . ."

"I'm not too keen on them myself, but there's nothing else for it. Let's have some breakfast and get going. The morning's well advanced. It can't be far from midday."

They'd made camp beneath a blackthorn off to one side of the Oakshaw road, but still weren't far from Lowmoor. Now, as they sat eating, they each kept an eye on the road. What they wanted was a traveller they could ask directions of. But no traveller had appeared by the time they'd broken their fast, so they packed up their gear and peered up and down the road.

"Someone's coming," said Jewel, pointing back towards Lowmoor.

Sure enough, someone was – a solitary walker. In due course, his outline – with its telltale, flat-crowned, broad-brimmed hat – defined him as a Ranter. He carried a stout ash-plant and wore a pack upon his back and, as he came up to them, Jewel saw a well-built, full-bellied man in his forties. His full lips were offset by a jutting crag of a nose, and his grey hair was drawn back and tied in a tuft with a black ribbon. Black was very much his colour: the shade of his knee-length coat, shirt, knee breeches, stockings and shoes, and – needless to say – his tall clerical hat.

"Well, blow me down . . ." murmured Thorn.

"Do you know him?" asked Jewel.

"Don't I just!" he returned.

The Ranter's eyes were fixed on them. His face now lit up.

"Bless my soul!" he exclaimed. "Thorn Jack, as I'm alive!"

"Manningham!" cried Thorn, and next moment the two were locked in a manly embrace.

When the embrace ended, Thorn was the first to speak.

"So you survived your journey," he said.

"Thanks to you," replied the Ranter. "*And*, I'm pleased to report, it was a most satisfactory mission. I made converts to the faith. Hallax, one may say, is half civilised these days."

Thorn turned to Jewel. "Jewel, this is Manningham Sparks, the Ranter I met in Judy Wood when I was journeying with Racky. Manningham, this is my very good friend, Jewel Ranson."

The Ranter bowed. "Delighted to meet you, Jewel Ranson. Any friend of Thorn's, as they say . . . Did you know he saved my life?"

"No, he never told me that." Jewel shot a look of surprise at

Thorn. He'd mentioned a Ranter who'd impressed him, but he hadn't said a word about saving the man's life.

"That's Thorn all over," said Sparks. "Full of natural modesty. He's a fellow in a thousand. But what on earth are you doing here?"

"Hoping to meet someone who can give us directions," said Thorn.

"Directions to where? Lowmoor?"

"Not Lowmoor – we've come from there. To the Dark Time ironworks. We think it may not be far from here."

"The ironworks? Why in Heaven's name would you want to go there?"

"I think it would be best if we didn't tell you that," said Jewel. "It's knowledge, I'm afraid, that could be dangerous, Reverend Sparks."

"Please call me Manningham, Miss Ranson. But *dangerous*? How so?"

Jewel and Thorn exchanged glances. "Last night," she volunteered, "the two of us barely escaped from Lowmoor with our lives. Have you just come from there?"

"Yes. But not willingly. I was expelled . . . yes, me, a devoted man of the cloth! Can you conceive of the indignity? But it seems that foreigners – that's anyone not born in the settlement – are being rounded up and questioned. A Ranter, I'm more conspicuous than most, so I was the first to be kicked out. I fear for the future of Lowmoor. The Headman and his Council have in a fell swoop been murdered, as have most of the guards. A group led by the foundry's owners has taken provisional control, and today, I suspect, in an emergency ballot, will have its position confirmed by a majority of the settlers. Fear rules the settlement, fear of unknown enemies, and in such a situation lives all at once become cheap."

Thorn said gravely, "Would it surprise you, Manningham, that those responsible for the murders you've mentioned are the ones who've taken over?"

The Ranter looked grim. "It ought to, but it doesn't. The Devil wears a face of friendship the better to take a grip on your soul."

"The Devil in this case," said Jewel, "happens to have a woman's face: her name is Querne Rasp. But time's pressing. We must get on our way. Can you give us the help we need?"

"Something tells me what you're doing is important, and God's work. I can do better than direct you – I'll *take* you where you want to go."

"That's not necessary," said Thorn, thinking the Ranter's presence might be something of a burden. "Directions will be enough."

"Will they? What do you know about the ironworks?"

"Well, we know there are rats there – rats with blue fur."

"What else?"

"What else is there to know?"

"Let's get moving. I'll tell you as we walk."

The three set off down the road.

"My mission," said Manningham Sparks, "takes me to many strange places. The ironworks is one. You see, the rats aren't the only tribe that happens to live there: there's also a tribe of humans."

"Humans?" exclaimed Jewel, who couldn't imagine anybody

wanting to live near wild rats – and *those* rats in particular. "They must be mad."

"Perhaps they are. Either way, they're a law unto themselves. And they're as human as you and me. They call themselves the Blue Ratters. They're the rats' sworn enemies. It's a long-standing – well, *feud*, I suppose, if you can accept that a feud might be fought between humans and animals. This feud has lasted for at least two generations, so long that none of the Ratters now can tell you just why and when it started. But it's enough for them that it did, and their war against the rats is their chief purpose in life and their reason for existing. So much so, that if they ever managed to wipe the creatures out, I don't know what they'd do with themselves. Maybe become wanderers, scouring the land for other savage breeds to fight."

Thorn looked at Jewel, to find her eyes already on him.

"Perhaps they'll agree to help us," he said.

"I rather doubt it," said the Ranter. "They're jealously protective of what they see as their territory – the ironworks and the land about it – and they don't take kindly to people who encroach on it. Though few outsiders who've seen a blue rat live to describe the beast."

"It seems you did," Jewel said.

The Ranter chuckled. "I'm a special case," he said. "I know the best ways in and out. The Ratters are highly superstitious. They believe in God and the Devil – God being on their side, of course, and the Devil on the rats' – and as I'm the only man of the cloth prepared to go anywhere near them, they're happy for me to visit them and deliver the odd sermon. It makes them feel good and reinforces their sense of mission. I suspect that when I'm not around they indulge in some rather primitive practices, but I can't do much about something that I have no knowledge of."

Thorn thought this attitude, for Manningham, surprisingly head-in-the-sand. He said, "What about Jewel and me, then? What d'you think they'll make of us?"

"Who knows?" replied the Ranter teasingly. "But so long as you're with me, they're not likely *absolutely* to shoot you out of hand."

"Meaning they'll only shoot us *half* out of hand?"

The Ranter laughed boisterously. "*Half* out of hand! That's very good, Thorn. But no," he added soberly, "the Ratters aren't in the habit of doing *anything* by halves."

They hadn't been walking long when Manningham Sparks turned east. There was a track of sorts here, complete with the marks of cartwheels, but it looked little-used, and if the terrain hereabouts hadn't been so desolate it would surely have long since been obliterated by growth. But as a guide it was service-able and it wound among patches of purple heather and spiky gorse, dipping and rising as it went.

After a time, away to the right, Jewel spotted a Dark Time church. Its body was dark and bulky, its tall steeple topped off by a cross. Without a doubt it was the church she'd seen that morning through the crystal. On her travels with her father she'd sighted churches before. They survived in remote spots, visited only by those intrepid people (as they no doubt imag-ined themselves; to her they were nothing but scavengers) who were obsessed with the search for transportable artefacts. Never had she come close to such an edifice, however.

"That church," she said to Thorn, "I'm sure it's the one I saw in my vision."

"*That* church," the Ranter volunteered, "happens to be where I was going when I bumped into you two . . . *Is* where I'm going when you're safely delivered."

"A Dark Time church!" The exclamation came from Thorn.

"Why not? If humans can live in giant mansions, they can live in churches too."

"So, who lives there?" Thorn asked.

"A sect that goes by the name of the Church of the Iron Angel. *Church*, indeed! That's a laugh. It's a cult, a law unto itself. They're as unholy a crew as you could never wish to meet."

"An unholy *religious* group?"

The Ranter harrumphed. "Yes! It's no great contradiction. Religion comes in all shapes and forms – all shapes and *mis*-shapes. Take a visionary, inspiring, power-hungry leader, a plausible myth, a bunch of gullible misfits and a remarkable – though to my mind demonic – effigy, and you've got the Church of the Iron Angel."

"If you think the Church unholy, why do you go there?" Jewel asked.

"I'm good friends with one of the members – Fleck Dewhurst, a ratman. I hope to get him to leave before the cult goes too far."

"Goes too far?" questioned Thorn.

"Yes. But it's a depressing subject, and I'd rather not talk about it. It has nothing to do with you two, in whom the sap of life drives in a contrary direction. Anyway, you'll never have cause to go any nearer that godforsaken place than you are to it now."

The Ranter fell silent. His face had clouded over. He plodded dourly on, cloaked in his own gloomy musings.

It's not like Manningham, thought Thorn, not to say what's in his mind. The Church of the Iron Angel must be sinister indeed . . .

7

BLUE RATS, BLUE RATTERS

As they followed the print of wheel-tracks threading the narrow, green-dark passage at the base of the ivy-clogged trunks of a tangle of bushes, Manningham Sparks half whispered, "I hate coming through here. But one way into the ironworks is as dangerous as another, and this happens to be the quickest."

Thorn didn't much care for their choice of route either. He and Jewel held their bows loose in their hands, arrows nocked. You never knew, the Ranter had told them, when a blue rat – or a Blue Ratter – might suddenly pop up. It was best to be prepared.

Half a dozen big beetles armoured in blue-black shells ambled away as they advanced, and delicate-limbed spiders watched them pass, motionless. Well, insects Thorn could handle.

Moments later, from somewhere ahead, came a shrill cry of alarm. A second followed on its heels.

"Someone's in trouble!" Thorn exclaimed. "Come on!" And he broke into a run.

"Erm . . ." began Manningham Sparks, but Thorn and Jewel were past him already, loping away and threatening to leave him behind. Clutching the brim of his hat and casting nervous glances about, the Ranter hurried after them.

Clear of the bush-clump, the track described a slow curve to the right through thick grass, then delivered them onto the edge of a squarish, man-made reservoir (a fraction of the size of Roydsal Dam) that Jewel straightaway recognised as the one she'd flown over in her vision. There, on the far side, grew the tall rushes she'd seen.

More cries sounded ahead. She followed Thorn along the dam's edge, their boot-soles slapping urgently on the grey ground. Hard as rock (though it wasn't rock, being some giant-made substance they'd encountered often before), it was cracked and split in places where weeds had gained a footing. On their right was a red-brick wall, on their left a row of high metal railings. Or what was left of them. Once, upright and proud, they'd marched along the dam's edge, installed there no doubt to prevent workers from tumbling in. Now they were heavily corroded; many had rusted through and fallen, some into the water, some onto the dam's edge, and where these lay across their way Thorn and Jewel leapt over them. Manningham puffed along well to the rear, feeling every year of his age and every ounce of his weight, and wishing he were ten years younger (better still, twenty).

The wall was coming to an end. There was a gap of some four feet before a second building began, built of identical red bricks. Reaching the corner, Thorn swerved around it, then pulled up short. Jewel halted at his side.

Blue rats – five of the creatures! They crouched in a rough semicircle, eyeing the girl and boy they'd backed up against the far wall of this dead-end recess, no more than six feet away. The two humans, their faces grim, neither more than thirteen years, each held a barbed pike, ready to fight for their lives. But they were hopelessly overmatched: at any moment the rats would attack.

Except that Thorn and Jewel's arrival had complicated the situation.

The nearest rat, a formidable beast with the sleek, blue-black fur that marked its kind out as unique, twisted its neck and looked back. Sighting Jewel and Thorn, it turned to face them – as did the two rats to its immediate left and right. But the central rat was clearly the leader. It came padding slowly towards them, followed by the other two. Three feet off it halted and, rearing up on its hind legs and pawing at the air, gave a savage snarl. A string of spittle hung down from the yellowed teeth of its upper jaw, one of which, Jewel saw, was broken off at the root.

Jewel's bowstring twanged. As the arrow flew at the rat, the creature dropped back on all fours. But the shaft, instead of zipping over its head as it must have expected, dipped sharply and buried itself in the animal's right eye.

The rat took a half step forward, as if to shrug off the hit, then slumped to the ground and lay still. The creatures to right and left uttered high-pitched squeaks of outrage, then together came bounding forward. Thorn fired, striking one animal in the cheek but failing to stop it. Meanwhile Jewel, barely troubling to take aim, had fired again. Her rat was almost on her when the second shaft struck it full on the nose. The wounded animal shrieked, sheered off and went scampering away.

Thorn's was made of stronger stuff. It leapt and bore him to

112

the ground, knocking the air out of his lungs and pinning him with its front legs. But as it opened its mouth to close its jaws around his head, Manningham Sparks hove into view and jabbed at the rat's flank with an ancient two-inch nail that he'd picked up nearby. The animal squealed with pain and half turned from its chosen victim. This gave Thorn the chance he needed: pulling his knife from its sheath, he drove it up into the rat's throat. The beast made a gurgling noise and lurched away from Thorn, knocking the Ranter to the ground. But still he clutched his nail, and the rat, evidently deciding that the odds were stacked against it, began to drag itself away, blood oozing from its wounds.

Jewel, who now had nocked a third arrow, glanced towards the retreating creature but, even as she dismissed the idea of shooting at it, the animal collapsed, its head lolling. Jewel switched her attention to the young people at the end of the recess.

While she and Thorn were absorbed in their own defensive action, the two remaining rats had attacked. They'd come off worst, however. Young the two humans might be; cowardly they were not. Of the two remaining rats, one lay on the ground with the boy standing over it, his pike ready to jab again if it gave so much as a twitch. Watched by the girl, the other rat was making off, dragging along with it a pike whose point was embedded in its neck. As Jewel thought about firing, the rat reached the corner and disappeared from view.

The battle was over. Three of the rats were dead or dying, two had escaped with nasty wounds. Thorn, on his feet now, was bruised, but otherwise fine. No one else was even scratched.

The two parties walked towards one another, meeting by the fallen rat with the arrow through its eye.

Taking this detail in, the boy produced a wry smile.

"Fancy stuff," he said. "Or was it a lucky shot?"

"A lucky shot," said Jewel.

"Don't believe it," said Thorn. "Nothing my friend does can be put down to luck."

"Whatever you say," said the girl. "Lucky for us you turned up just when you did. If you hadn't, we'd be rats'-meat."

Manningham Sparks said, "What are the two of you doing here? You don't look more than twelve to me. Aren't children of your age forbidden to wander off alone?"

"We're not children," said the boy in an aggrieved-surly tone, "and we weren't 'wandering off'. We came to look at the goldenfish."

"Goldenfish?" put in Thorn, who'd never heard of any such creature.

"In the dam," explained the Ranter. "Been in there since the Dark Time."

Half admiringly the girl said: "Lock has never been much good at doing as he's told."

"Looks like he's not the only one." The Ranter frowned at the lad. "I know you," he said. "You're Lockwood Rime, the Blue Ratter Headman's son. Isn't that right?"

"That's me," the boy confirmed. "But my friends call me Lock."

"You ought to know better," said Manningham Sparks. "You should be setting an example, not dicing with death. And what's *your* name?" he asked the girl.

"Tessy Briggs, Ranter Sparks."

"So you know who I am, Tessy?"

"Doesn't everybody?"

"I very much doubt it," said the Ranter.

"She means everybody here, in the works," said Lock, his tone of voice implying that the Ranter was none too bright.

Thorn looked hard at the lad, who stared arrogantly back at him, his hand gripping his pike, whose butt rested on the ground. Lock might be insolent, but he was a tough customer – tougher, Thorn reckoned, than he himself had been at twelve. But then, if you were raised to fight rats, you'd need to be.

A shout now sounded from behind them. Looking back, Thorn, Jewel and the Ranter saw a group of adults jogging toward them, six of them: four men and two women. They wore waistcoats and trews made from tanned rat-hide. Their arms were bare from the shoulder down. Some were armed with bows, some with pikes; all carried knives in sheaths that almost reached their knees. On all six faces, stretching from the inner corner of each eye to the outer point of their jawbone, was a bright stripe of blue dye. The women looked just as lean and dangerous as the men. The six took in the scene of carnage and, from their stern expressions, found little comfort in it.

"Ranter Sparks," greeted a tall man, his arms sculpted with sinew, his face tanned and narrow-eyed.

"Hello, Critch," replied the Ranter. "These are my friends: Jewel Ranson and Thorn Jack. Jewel and Thorn, meet Critch Barraclough."

"I'm glad to know you," said the Blue Ratter, shaking hands with Jewel and Thorn. "We sighted a rat slinking off and feared the worst, but by the look of things here you two can take care of yourselves. The tribe is in your debt. But as for *you* two –" he turned to confront Tessy and Lock "– you're damned lucky to be alive. What the hell do you think you're doing coming out here by yourselves? You've put not only your own lives but other people's at risk. There are two more parties out looking for you. Tessy, your mother's beside herself. And as for you, Lock, you ought to know better. You're the Headman's son, you ought to set an example."

"But it's *boring* in the refuge," Lock complained bitterly. "There's nothing to do but work. I can fight like any sixteener: why can't I go on patrol?"

"I'm not going to argue with you. That's Bran's – your father's – job." Critch turned to the Ranter. "You know Bran, Reverend Sparks, and right now, he's as angry as I've ever seen him be. It's not the first time Lock has done this sort of thing. He hasn't yet grasped the simple truth that it's better to be bored than it is to be dead."

"Being bored *is* being dead," said the unrepentant Lock.

"You've a lot to learn," said the Ranter.

"I can't wait for you to teach me," said Lock scornfully. "Do you always fight with rusty nails?"

Only now did Manningham realise he was still gripping the blood-smeared nail. He threw it to the ground, where it made a ringing sound, then inspected his hands, which were orange with iron-rust. "Necessity is the mother of invention," he said, and went to pick up his ash-plant.

"What does that mean?" asked Lock, clearly implying *not a lot*.

"That's enough, Lock," said Critch Barraclough. "You should respect Ranter Sparks. How many rats were there, Tessy?"

"Five," answered the girl. "Three are dead, two escaped — injured, but they escaped."

"Then it's time we moved from here." He shot a look of regret at the carcasses of the dead rats. "Pity to leave this lot behind: there's good meat and hide here. But maybe we can send a foraging party out later."

Interesting, thought Thorn. Racky had told him that in some settlements he'd visited — far from Norgreen — rats were bred for consumption, but never before today had Thorn encountered first-hand evidence of the practice of eating rat. Well, live and learn.

Critch Barraclough issued some brief orders and the party formed up. He and two of the other Ratters went in front, then came Tessy and Lock, then Thorn, Jewel and Manningham Sparks. The remaining Ratters brought up the rear.

They set off at a gentle trot — gentle perhaps because of the Ranter, who was clearly uncomfortable with any speed of foot-travel faster than walking. They went on down between the dam's edge and the red-brick building, then turned right along the frontage of the latter. Opposite the brick building was a long shedlike structure, but its roof had long since fallen in, baring a gridwork of struts, and all its windows were smashed. Only jagged shards of glass now stuck out of their battered frames. The space between the two buildings might once have been a broad road, but had long since become a playground for rampant vegetation. Clumps of fireweed flourished here, its tall woody stalks towering above the travelling party; a bank of convolvulus threw out sculpted blossoms of eye-blinding whiteness, each cup big enough to accommodate a human head.

Beyond the end of the brick building another one began. Warily, the party crossed the intervening space then trotted on, hugging the wall – a tactic, Thorn assumed, that reduced the number of directions from which possible attack might come. The shed ran on opposite them.

The red-brick building came to an end. Beyond it stood a much smaller building with a wooden door and a small window. The Blue Ratters' refuge was an unexceptional structure, no more than a hovel to a giant. But in front of it stretched a large rectangular area on which not a single blade of grass had taken root. The reason for this was obvious as the party ran on to it, and the sound changed that their twenty-two boot-soles made: the surface was a single massive plate of sheet metal, which clearly had survived the passing years with some aplomb.

Beside Jewel, the plump Ranter was red-faced and panting, and his features registered relief as the party slowed to a walk. Between the wall and the edge of the steel plate rose a thick column of metal. Throwing her head back, Jewel peered up and saw that at the top it bulbed out into a ponderous circular head. Edging across to it, she ran her hand along the base of the column as the party went by. The metal was cool and smooth, and into her mind jumped a strange word – *scales* – to be followed by another – *weighbridge*. An image formed in her mind. Ah, now she understood! Here the mechanised vehicles that the giants used for transporting the ironworks' products would be weighed as they left or arrived. She smiled wryly. What an abyss separated present and past!

Ahead, in front of the door of the refuge, two sentries stood on watch. The open space that fronted the structure clearly worked to its advantage: it would afford warning of attack, and providing the building's walls and flooring were kept rat-proof, the tribe would be safe inside.

Salutes were now exchanged between Critch Barraclough and the sentries; then Critch stepped between them. Jewel and Thorn were familiar with the door-within-a-door arrangement in adapted Dark Time structures. This one was different, however, in the respect that it was a double-door – obviously so more people could go in or out at any time. Let into each half was a square of clear glass.

Throwing open the right-hand door, Critch Barraclough motioned that the party should go inside.

In the Dark Time, this building had been one single room. Looking upward, Jewel and Thorn could see, some ten feet above their heads, the spiderwebbed rafters that held up the roof-slates: the roof appeared intact. But at ground level, parallel to the outer wall of the building at a distance of some two feet, a wooden partition ten inches high ran laterally from left to right, making this first space long and narrow.

On the left was a carpenter's shop. Tools hung on pegs, all in apple-pie order, and Thorn noticed a couple of double-handed saws. Also here were benches, lathes for turning wood and, beyond, wood itself, tidily stacked in a variety of shapes and sizes.

On the right, three rat-carts were parked with their rear ends close to the wall; their shafts slanted down to rest their rounded ends on the ground. Beyond lay a rattery. A series of wooden stalls had been built against the outer wall, each with a door and an observation window. Opposite stood tables and shelves equipped with the typical gear of a tack room. So, thought Jewel, at least the Blue Ratters don't have it in for *all* rats . . .

The party now passed through a broad gap in the partition, and the newcomers were faced with more evidence of the tribe's industry and love of order.

The room was an armoury. To the right stood racks of pikes and knives, unstrung bows and arrows. On the left were work-benches strewn with tools, raw materials of leather, metal or wood, and finished and half-finished weapons. Beyond, partially sunk into the floor like the one in Lowmoor foundry, was a large pot-bellied furnace, and Thorn noticed anvils and whet-stones for sharpening blades and pike-points. A couple of men were working here, and just at this moment an aproned, leather-masked smith drew a heated blade out of the fire with a pair of long tongs and began to beat it out on the anvil with rhythmic clangs of his hammer.

Now, passing through the second cross-partition, Jewel and Thorn found themselves in a third area. On one side were three long tables where the tribe must gather for meals; there might be eighty or ninety chairs. The legs of a fourth, smaller table were shorter than the other three, and its benches lower — designed presumably for the younger members of the tribe. Beyond the tables, the space was foreshortened by another wooden wall in which a double-door was set; through that a kitchen might lie, but as of now its secrets remained concealed.

Away down on the other side of the room was a space that reminded Thorn of Norgreen's Council room – except that there you wouldn't have found a circle of rat-heads, cured, stuffed and mounted on poles, their jaws bared in fierce snarls. Battle-trophies, he supposed, grim reminders of a war that was far from over. In the midst of the rat-heads, three men had been sitting in conference when the party came in. Now they rose from their chairs and started across the room.

Already Critch Barraclough had brought his group to a halt. "Party dismissed," he announced.

The five warriors departed through a door in the far partition.

Jewel studied the faces of the young Blue Ratters. Tessy appeared distinctly nervous. Lock was staring at the ground with a sullen expression on his face.

The three men came up to them. Two were white-haired elders. The third was middle-aged, but looked of undiminished powers. His iron-grey hair was swept back and fell to his broad shoulders. His arms were bare and muscular. The resemblance between him and young Lock was strong: if the lad survived to middle age, he would be something like this.

The Headman halted and stood for a time without speaking, letting his keen gaze pass from Manningham Sparks (to whom he gave a slight nod) to Jewel and Thorn, then to Tessy and last of all to Lock. Refusing to meet his father's gaze, Lock kept his eyes sulkily fixed on the floor.

At last Branwell Rime spoke. "So you found them, Critch. Where?"

Critch Barracough told him, then added what he knew of the fight with the blue rats. Introducing Jewel and Thorn, he said that if they and the Ranter hadn't appeared when they did, Tessy and Lock would almost certainly be dead.

When Critch's story was told, the Headman began by commending the bravery of the outsiders, expressing the tribe's – and his personal – gratitude to them and said that the Blue Ratters were honoured to have them as guests in their house. Then, turning to Tessy and Lock, he sternly upbraided them for foolhardiness, sentenced each of them to a month's duty at the latrines, and finished by curtly dismissing them to their quarters.

When the youngsters had gone, he introduced Jewel and Thorn to the two elders, then invited all present to take a glass of wine with him. When the group had settled itself within the circle of rats' heads, and the two elders had furnished everyone with a glass of wine, he asked Jewel and Thorn what had brought them to the ironworks.

"For visitors," he said, "as you can easily imagine, are few and far between here – with the exception of Reverend Sparks, for whom, as he knows, there's always a welcome within these walls. And never more so than today. Fighting rats with a rusty nail! This, Manningham, is a new side to your character: one I knew nothing of."

"To be honest, Bran," said the Ranter, who seemed at ease with the Headman, "I knew nothing of it myself."

The Headman laughed. "We never know what we're made of till we're tested by events."

"So it would seem."

Turning to Jewel and Thorn, the Headman asked where they were from.

"Norgreen," said Thorn.

"You're a long way from home. So what brings you here?"

It was Jewel who answered. "We're looking for a stone, Headman: to be exact, a black crystal."

"A black crystal? I never heard of such a thing. Why should you seek it here?"

"Because here is where it is — in a building in the ironworks."

"How can you possibly know this?"

Jewel hesitated, so Thorn stepped into the breach. "My friend, Headman, is a Magian, though she's too modest to say so. She saw the crystal in a vision. To speak plainly, this crystal is no ordinary stone. It has remarkable properties, though these may only be exploited by a Magian. But another Magian knows of it, and it's vital we get hold of it before our rival does."

The Headman scrutinised Jewel with a fresh intensity. "Magians . . ." he said, "I've heard tell of such beings. But you look ordinary enough."

Jewel made no reply.

The Headman spoke again. "May I know the name of this rival?"

"Why not?" she answered. "Her name is Querne Rasp."

The Headman looked grave. "Querne Rasp . . . I know this name. She's dangerous, I'm told."

"More dangerous," said Jewel, "than all the blue rats in the world."

The Headman didn't smile. "Then her powers must be awesome. And is she too coming here?"

"I think it more than likely. In the past she's set a man called Racky Jagger to hunt out crystals for her, but this one poses such problems that I expect her to come herself. And what's more, Querne has a personal score to settle with me."

The Headman thoughtfully stroked his chin. He didn't like what he was hearing. "Are you certain of the whereabouts of this stone?" he asked.

"Yes." Jewel described the building that she'd visited in her vision.

The Headman looked more troubled still. "You've just described the Great Nest . . . We've never dared attack it. A hundred and fifty warriors couldn't be guaranteed to succeed, and we have less than half that number. And far too many would fall to make the venture worth the risk."

One of the elders now spoke for the first time. "Querne Rasp," he said, "she's twice your age, isn't she?"

"Twice my age and more," said Jewel.

"Then she will possess twice your power. Do you deny that?"

Jewel could see well enough which way the elder was going. Should she brazen it out, or should she opt for honesty? "I can't deny," she replied, "that Querne is more powerful than me. She's also utterly ruthless, and if she finds out that you've lent me any assistance, the consequences could turn out to be unpleasant for your tribe."

The old man sat back and the Headman picked up the point.

"Your honesty, Jewel Ranson, does you credit," he said. "But even if I were minded to pander to Querne Rasp – which I'm not – honour would demand otherwise. You and your companions have saved the lives of two of this tribe, and we are bound to honour that action, even to the extent of risking our lives on your behalf."

"That's good to know," said Jewel, "but I don't want your tribe to risk a single life for me. I'll go alone to get the crystal — first thing tomorrow morning. I want to be gone from here by the time Querne arrives."

The Blue Ratters greeted this confident statement with disbelief. Even Thorn looked sceptical.

"What you propose is impossible," the Headman said emphatically. "The rats will tear you to pieces as soon as they catch your scent."

Jewel smiled. "Perhaps they will," she conceded. "And then again, perhaps they won't."

She and Thorn were sitting with their backs to the direction from which they'd entered the area, and now, as approaching footsteps sounded behind them, Branwell Rime glanced past them, then rose to his feet. Seeing the elders follow suit, the Ranter and Jewel and Thorn also got up from their chairs and turned to face the new arrival.

Astonishment showed on Thorn's face. Walking languidly towards them was someone he'd never dreamt he'd ever see again.

"Mu—" he began, then choked off the rest of the word and threw a quick glance at the Headman. But Branwell Rime only had eyes for the person joining them.

"Briar my dear," he said, "come and meet our visitors."

Briar Spurr halted and surveyed the Headman's guests. Her face gave nothing away as her gaze passed over them, even though to Thorn it seemed to dwell for a moment on him. He of course couldn't take his tranced eyes off her. As far as facial appearance went, his mother seemed little different from the way she'd looked at Minral How. So, he thought, she must have escaped the house before the fire went sweeping through it . . . She had the same chiselled features, blue eyes and purple lips, the same thick tresses of hair, long, lustrous and midnight-black. But the pink lounging gown that she'd worn at Minral How was unthinkable here – as was the crimson nail-paint and the dark eyeglasses she'd affected in that place. Instead she was clad in a hide jacket, metal-studded and thong-tied, and matching hide trews. This outfit gave her a martial air, enhancing her formidableness, and it was easy enough to imagine her drawing a bow in combat. Her beauty with its cool, imperious aura remained untouched: beauty whose power reduced men to fools and worshippers. Was Branwell Rime her latest victim? It rather looked that way.

The Headman launched into a round of introductions, but when he made to pass from the Ranter to Jewel and Thorn, Briar cut him short.

"We three have met before," she announced.

"You have?" said Branwell. "Where?"

"In Harrypark," she replied. "I was with Crane then. Jewel and I had an enjoyable tussle in the gaming room. What a surprise to meet you again – and here, of all places." And Briar extended a limp hand first to Jewel, then to Thorn.

But if anyone had ever looked less than surprised, it was Briar. As Thorn grasped his mother's fingers and held them for a moment, he thought: This is mad – I'm shaking hands with my own mother . . .

Only two things were wrong with what Briar had just said. First, Thorn had not been with Jewel at Harrypark. Second, the three of them had met more recently. Well, if his mother preferred not to mention the momentous events that had happened at Minral How, he'd go along with that – at least until he could manage to get to talk to her alone.

Jewel, however, didn't feel quite so accommodating. "It's a long way from Harrypark to the ironworks," she said, "and I'm not just thinking of distance. You've gone from the lap of luxury to austerity itself. This is quite the last place I'd have expected to meet you."

"Then you don't know me," said Briar.

"So it seems," replied Jewel with a mischievous smile. "I had you down as a person who rather liked her creature comforts. Anyone would think you were trying to hide yourself away."

"Think what you like," said Briar coldly. "Creature comforts can get boring."

"Well, perhaps this isn't the first time you've changed your life," said Jewel.

"Maybe not, but change is the essence of life, don't you think?"

Whatever Jewel thought, however, she didn't get to say, for Briar had had enough of this teasing little exchange. Giving the girl no time to reply, she turned to the Headman and said, "Bran, I gather that your son is in disgrace. But he refuses to talk about it, so you must tell me what happened."

"Gladly," said Branwell Rime. "But our guests must be tired."

A brief discussion followed between the Headman and his

Councillors, the upshot of which was that the tribe's honoured guests would each be assigned a sleeping cubicle.

The party broke up. As Thorn walked off with the others, he wondered what the chances were of getting to speak to Briar privately before dinner time.

8

CLOAK OF SECRECY

Well, thought Racky Jagger, now I know why people plump for living in the Belly: the powers-that-be pay little attention to you here. Lowlifes don't revolt – they're too busy surviving to have time for ideals.

He was returning from a walk through the streets of Lowmoor. It had taken half as long again as he would have expected it to take normally. But it wasn't a normal day: the settlement was effectively under martial law. Passing through the better parts, he'd been stopped several times at checkpoints by armed, black-uniformed foundrymen and subjected to questioning. Had he not been able to give them a password that guaranteed his safe conduct, he suspected he'd have been beaten up and imprisoned – or worse – simply for being not Lowmoor-born.

But his walk – as well as proving informative on the state of the place under the new regime – had given him time to think. Hurried on by the sight of the Headman's daughter crushed in the house collapse, his personal crisis, so long threatened, had at last arrived; he just *had* to make up his mind about where his deepest loyalties lay.

Here, in a quiet backwater, stood the house that the Magian had picked as her base after leaving Oily Wells. Hitched to a hook set into the wall was a sleek saddle-rat. So – Querne had a visitor! Racky's curiosity was pricked. Quietly he unlocked the door and went in.

Voices came drifting from the sitting room at the rear of the house. Racky paused. One of the voices had to be Querne's – but who was with her? Just the one man, by the sound of it, and it wasn't Spine Wrench, who Racky knew was out buying food. Racky moved silently to the door of the sitting room and began to listen.

". . . But are you absolutely sure the time has come?" said the male voice.

"The time has come. You knew in your heart that it was near: you've spoken of it often enough." Querne's voice was smooth with complacency. "Anyway, have you ever known me wrong about a prophecy?"

"No, of course not . . . but now it's here . . ."

"Now it's here its implications horrify you? Why? It's no more than you've believed to be necessary all along."

Ah! Racky had it now – the man was Higgins Makepeace! Now what the hell was the Grand Ranter doing here in Lowmoor? He very rarely quitted his Church. Racky had long suspected that Querne and Makepeace were mixed up together, but he'd never before had first-hand evidence that they met.

"That's true. But now it's staring me in the face . . . so many lives . . ." The Ranter sounded doubtful still.

"What is a brief life against the promised eternity? Less than a snap of finger and thumb."

There was a pause before the Grand Ranter said: "What

about you, Querne? What you're up to in Lowmoor — it hardly looks like the policy of someone who expects the world—"

"Doesn't it?" Querne cut in, denying Racky the satisfaction of hearing what it was she believed the world was about to do. "I'm having fun while the going's good — dancing, you might say, on the brink of the void."

"It's an odd kind of fun."

"So is yours, Higgins."

"It's quite the opposite of fun."

What on earth, Racky wondered, are these two talking about?

All at once, Querne became stern. "Higgins, haven't I guided you from the first day we met? Wasn't it me who saw the potential in the Iron Angel, me who encouraged and inspired you? Where would you and your Church have been had it not been for the myths I dreamt up for you? You would have had no Church, no following, no power. Your powers of eloquence would have remained unrealised. You'd still be a vagabond, a thief and scrounger, instead of a man of consequence."

"And my soul would still be clean," said Makepeace half accusingly.

Querne laughed. "Your soul was never clean," she declared.

"Maybe not, but I was never a murderer till I met you."

"Listen Higgins," countered Querne. "Had murder not been in you, you would never have acted it out. All I did was free your spirit, give you the courage of your convictions, show you how to seize the moment."

Murder! thought Racky. Higgins Makepeace a murderer! That such a righteous exterior should cloak such a secret . . .

131

The man was a fine hypocrite! Racky had never trusted the fellow, but it had never crossed his mind that Makepeace might have descended to murder.

To Querne, of course, killing was just another means to an end. Look at Lowmoor right now, he thought: the place is sick with it, all of Querne's conjuring. And if I stick with her much longer, I'll be sucked further in – smeared with the blood of innocents. I must leave her, leave her now . . .

He slipped away and let himself out of the house. But he'd taken no more than half a dozen paces when he stopped. He stood for a moment, debating with himself, then turned back and re-entered the house. This time, however, he entered noisily, banging the door shut after him.

"Racky? Is that you?" Querne called.

"Yes, I'm back," he replied, and went into the sitting room.

"Makepeace!" he exclaimed, feigning surprise at the man's presence. "What brings you to Lowmoor?"

"Visits to members of my flock," the Grand Ranter answered smartly.

"Is that so?" commented Racky. "It looks to me rather as though it's Querne you're visiting."

"I could hardly ignore her."

"No? I'm surprised you knew where to find her."

"Spine Wrench keeps me informed."

"Ah, Wrench – what a treasure that man is."

Makepeace frowned. "Well, I must be off – got to get back to my Church."

"Goodbye, Higgins," said Querne, "and remember: great things are never achieved where there is doubt and indecision."

"How very true," said the Grand Ranter. "I shall not forget your words. Goodbye then, Querne."

His gaze lingered on the Magian, and to Racky's eyes he seemed reluctant to tear himself away. But at last, with a curt nod to Racky, the Grand Ranter picked his hat up from the tabletop on which it reposed. Then, with a flourish of his black travelling cloak, he was gone.

"What did *he* want?" Racky asked.

"Encouragement? Inspiration? What do men ever want from women?"

"Love chiefly, I'd have thought."

Querne trilled with amusement. "Poor Racky, what a romantic you are — a quite incurable case!" Then her face became serious. "But we too must be off."

"We too? Off where?"

"To the Dark Time ironworks that lies to the east of here."

"The ruined ironworks? Why there?"

"It's where the fifth crystal is — in a building full of rats."

"Rats? *Blue* rats, you mean?"

"Yes, blue rats I mean. Which is why I'm going myself rather than simply sending you. And there's a further complication. Jewel Ranson also knows of the crystal's whereabouts. She's on her way to get it now."

"Jewel? Thorn will be with her."

"You know your son better than I. But don't worry — I'm not expecting you to fight rats for me. You'll be there to watch my back, keep an eye out for the Ratters. So — let's get ourselves ready to travel, then pick up our mounts from the rattery."

Just as well I came back, Racky told himself grimly as he

followed the Magian up the stairs. Thorn too at the ironworks! There was more at stake in the game than Querne Rasp's lovely back.

Like those of Thorn and Manningham Sparks, Jewel's cubicle was a small partitioned space. It held a cot, a chair, a cupboard and a little square table. Soon after she'd moved in, a knock had come at the door and a couple of children had entered bringing a bowl of water, a green towel and a rough cake of soap.

Jewel had washed thoroughly. Now she sat on the cot, giving her hair an occasional rub. It would have been an understatement to say she was preoccupied. Her thoughts ran on a single subject: how to get the black crystal from the house of the blue rats.

As it happened, she had an idea. But as yet it was no more than that: whether she could turn it into a reality – well, that remained to be seen.

Or in this case, she thought with a secret smile, *not* to be seen. For she was mulling over a stratagem employed by Querne Rasp when the two had talked at the bar in Rotten Pavilion's gaming room. The room had been busy, with people coming and going about them, but nobody had paid the pair the slightest bit of attention. It was as if the two women had been enclosed in a cocoon: no one sought to talk to them or tried to invade their space. Yet when Querne addressed the barman, he responded immediately.

Querne had called it her "cloak of silence". Though undetectable, it had been real – Jewel was quite sure of that. But how had the trick been done? Effortlessly, it seemed, for Querne had been doing several other things at the time, masking her face as Moira Black and talking relaxedly to Jewel. It struck the girl again how fiendishly clever this Magian was. How could Jewel hope to match her? Nevertheless she had to try.

She laid the towel aside and began combing out her hair. The action calmed her, and went well with thinking. So how *had* Querne done it? Had she invaded the minds of people who came close to her, blanking out a particular area of their perception? Such an approach might possibly work with a single subject, even two – but in a crowd? It would surely be too difficult, even for Querne.

Jewel leant back in her chair and stared up at the wooden ceiling, absently tapping the end of her nose with the comb. Could Querne have discovered the secret of invisibility? Well, for one thing Jewel herself had been included inside the cloak. And for another, she herself could see Querne at all times. Maybe, she thought, Magians can't be invisible to Magians; their perceptions are more sensitive than those of ordinary people . . . Even so, Jewel doubted that even Magians could bring off such a tremendous feat as invisibility. Their powers were rooted in real mental-physical processes.

She tried a different angle of thought. How is it, anyway, that you see this thing or that? If it's night and pitch-dark, you won't be able to see a person standing a foot away – though you'd see them perfectly clearly with the benefit of daylight. Or indistinctly with lamplight. So the key to seeing is *light*. Light, Jewel knew from her experience with the crystal, was a flow of particles. Could Querne somehow have exerted an influence on those tiny particles? Projected some kind of impulse that affected the space around her, deflecting – or better still *confus-ing* – light-beams so that, although she was close to people, they didn't notice her?

This seemed a more promising idea. Summoning now considerable powers of concentration, she focussed on the immediate region around her body, refining her senses until she picked up the light-particles endlessly streaming towards her. Then, flexing a till-now sleeping component of her gift, she projected a counterforce to deflect the bright atoms. The effect was odd, to say the least. Around her, a kind of dead zone came into being: outlines became indefinite, colours appeared blurred, the world seemed dulled, half alive.

It was difficult at first for her to hold the impulse steady, to maintain its intensity, but the more she persevered, the easier it became, and after some time she found she could do other things while holding it there – like combing her hair, putting her boots on, walking around the little room. Her confidence grew till she felt ready to test her cloak. She needed an unsuspecting subject . . .

A knock sounded at the door, but it was less a knock than a tap, as if the sound had been smothered, had travelled a distance much greater than a foot.

Jewel made no response, and the tapping came again. Then a voice called "Jewel?" – the sounds half stifled and slurred.

It was Thorn. Jewel waited. There was no lock on the door and now, tentatively, the handle was depressed and the door pushed open. Thorn's head appeared around its edge. Briefly he surveyed the room, frowned and withdrew, closing the door behind him. It was clear that he hadn't seen her.

So far so good. Now for a more demanding exposure.

Quitting the room, Jewel set off down the corridor. She'd memorised the route by which she and others had been brought, and went along confidently. Turning a corner, she saw one of the Ratters no more than a dozen steps away. He was striding purposefully down the centre of the passage, and his trajectory would inevitably cause them to collide. But rather than take herself out of his way, Jewel continued as she was. The man moved to one side and they passed with space to spare: yet he'd given not the slightest indication that he'd seen her. He'd simply altered course, as if responding to the prompting of some obscure inner sense.

Jewel grinned. This was fun.

She now emerged into the area that was split into dining room and Council room. Here a couple of young tribespeople were busy laying tables. Neither even so much as glanced in her direction. She halted for a time. More Ratters went by without registering her presence.

Good, she thought, I can deceive human beings. But now she had to submit herself to the crucial test. Still holding the impulse in place, she set off again, directing her steps towards the central break in the partition. She crossed the armoury, went through the second partition, turned left past the rat-carts and entered the rattery.

Chance now played its part in advancing her plan. Here, in accordance with standard practice, each rat occupied its separate, enclosed stall. And there was the ratman, mucking out a stall with its gate half open.

As he spaded dry knots of droppings into a wheelbarrow, he

talked quietly to the resident rat – loosely tethered by its collar to a wall-ring. Chatting like this was common practice among ratmen, and she'd done it herself with Ranson and Daughter's cart-rats; like ratmen, she was convinced that the sound of human speech firmed up the bond between humans and the animals in their care. And in this case the rat – a piebald doe with a foreshortened tail – gave every appearance of taking in the ratman's chatter. She was standing perfectly still with her head slightly cocked, eyes fixed on the ratman as, electing to take a break, he now leant on his shovel.

Jewel walked straight into the stall and took up a position to one side of the gate. The ratman gave no sign that he'd seen Jewel come in, but that was by the by: it was the rat that Jewel was interested in. Would she smell the girl? If she did, Jewel's cloak would be proved incomplete. But the rat's posture remained unchanged; still she stood with her head on one side, apparently mesmerised by the lilt of the ratman's voice. Raising her arms above her head, Jewel waved them vigorously. The piebald failed to react.

Resting his shovel on his barrow, the ratman now picked up the shafts, so Jewel slipped out of the stall. She watched the ratman latch the gate and move on to the next stall. Hinges squeaked as he threw open the gate. Again he left it ajar and Jewel was able to walk straight in after him.

The occupant was a sturdy buck with a dark-brown hide.

The ratman hailed him. "Thomas! Time to spruce you up a bit!" And set to work shovelling dung.

The buck eyed him for a time, then allowed his gaze to wander. For a moment, it lingered on Jewel as she lounged by the gate, and she wondered if somehow Thomas had sensed her; but now his gaze passed on, and he dropped his head to sniff at the mixed heap in the ratman's barrow.

Jewel hung on a little, then decided to call a halt. Her experiment was a success. Thank you, Querne Rasp, she thought: don't ever tell me I can't learn from you. Except that, it now struck her, *cloak of silence* seemed inapt as a description of the effect. *Cloak of secrecy* would be better. And that's what I'll call it, she thought.

She went out of the stall, then on an impulse dispelled the cloak and gave the gate a push. The hinges squeaked as it swung away, and the ratman and his animal looked up and stared at her.

"Yes, lass?" prompted the ratman. "Anything I can do for you?"

"Er, I'm looking for the Ranter . . . You must know him – Reverend Sparks. He wouldn't be here by any chance?"

The ratman guffawed. "*Here*, missy? What an idea! Not till the Reverend takes up preaching God to rats will you find him here! Try the dinner table – that's more his sort of place!"

Jewel smiled. "Thank you for the advice. I'll do that."

Once outside the rattery, she perched on a flatbed cart. It was as good a spot as any to do some uninterrupted thinking.

Thorn had fully expected to find Jewel in her room. Damn! Where could the girl be? There was no way of knowing. He'd reckoned on getting Jewel to pinpoint Briar's quarters by way of a routine exercise of her Magian's special skills, and – once they got to her door – divining whether or not Briar was alone. Now he'd have to come up with an alternative plan of action.

139

He wandered off down the corridor, not paying much attention to the various turns he took. By the time he came to a sense of his surroundings, he was lost.

He was debating which way to go when a young man of his own age appeared from around a corner. Perhaps seeing uncertainty etched on Thorn's face, he stopped.

"Hello," he said in a friendly manner. "You must be Thorn Jack. I've been hearing about you."

"Yes, that's me," said Thorn.

"Great thing you did today! How I wish that *I*'d been there! Somehow I always seem to miss out on the action. But what are you doing down here – looking for the latrines, are you?"

"Um, yes, that's right," said Thorn.

"Then they're just back where I came from. But be warned: Lock's in there and, what's more, he's in a foul temper! See you around, Thorn Jack!"

And off the young man went.

The latrines, thought Thorn wearily. What use are they to me?

At which point he realised they were exactly what he needed. Funny how things work out . . .

He set off up the corridor. Now, Lockwood Rime or Tessy Briggs? – assuming Tessy was there as well, serving out her punishment. Tessy, I think, he decided: she seemed likely to prove the more amenable of the two.

He came out into an open space, on the far side of which was a wooden wall with two doors. One was marked with a male symbol, the other with a female one. He crossed to the women's door and knocked. After a time the door opened to reveal Tessy

Briggs. She held a long-handled mop and looked at him with surprise.

"Thorn Jack!" she exclaimed. "But what are you—"

"I need your help, Tessy. Come out of there and talk to me." He grinned. "But for both our sakes, leave that ferocious weapon behind."

She gave him an odd look. "What—?" Then, tumbling to his meaning, answered his grin with a giggle. "Oh, the mop!" She glanced round, as if expecting the Headman to come bounding out of concealment. Then, when no one bounded from any-where, "All right," she agreed and, ridding herself of the mop, shut the latrine door behind her. "But you'd better make it quick."

"I can't promise to do that. Look, you owe me a favour, Tessy. I want you to take me to Briar Spurr's quarters."

"Briar Spurr's? Why?"

"That's my business," he replied.

"But if someone in authority sees me, I'll be in for it."

"No you won't, because I'll claim responsibility. I'll explain that I got lost and twisted your arm to help me out – which is no more than the truth."

Thorn's confidence must have impressed her, for Tessy now fell in with his wishes. They went swiftly down corridors, pass-ing a couple of tribespeople who shot questioning looks at them but didn't stop to challenge them, until finally they arrived at a door.

"This is Briar's door," said Tessy. "The Headman's is the next one along the passageway."

"Right, thanks for your help," said Thorn. "Now, you'd better get back."

Disappointment showed in her face, but she did as she was bid.

Thorn listened at the door. He could hear nothing but silence. If Branwell Rime was inside with his mother, the pair were keeping quiet. But Thorn was past caution now. Boldly he knocked at the door.

"Who is it?" asked a voice.

"It's me, Thorn," he replied, keeping his voice as low as he could.

"Go away, Thorn," said the voice. "I don't want to talk to you."

"But *I* want to talk to *you*." He tried the door. It was locked. "And I'm going to do it if I have to smash this door down to get in. Do you want me to make a scene? Much better to open up."

There was a pause. She's thinking it over, he thought. Come on Mother, unlock the door.

Then she did, and in he went.

Briar's quarters were as plain and uncompromising as her garb. Her room was twice as big as Thorn's, but its furnishings were similar. Simple and functional, they entirely lacked the elegance that had marked the home she'd shared with Crane Rockett. The only significant difference between this room and Thorn's was the large double bed. But that merely confirmed his assumption that she and Branwell Rime were lovers. Lock's mother, he guessed, was dead, perhaps a victim of the blue rats. A factor in the lad's disgruntlement? Well, he's not the only one who's disgruntled, thought Thorn.

Briar neither sat down nor invited Thorn to do so. Instead

142

she stood facing him, the pair tense as old rivals on the verge of a wrestling bout.

"Hello, Mother," said Thorn.

Briar did not reply.

"Your turn to speak, Mother," he pressed.

"What would you have me say?" she asked.

"You could say, 'Hello, son. How nice it is to see you again'."

"I told you last time we met: I'm *not* your mother, Thorn."

The finality of her words seemed to block any possibility of progress in the discussion. But Thorn had been here before, and this time he was determined not to walk away from her.

He said, "Not my mother? But you are — and you're Haw's mother too. That's why you gave me the brass key when you might have turned your back on us. Aren't you going to ask if I got your daughter away from the Spetch twins?"

Briar took a few moments to ponder the relevance or otherwise of this matter to her life, past and present. "Well — did you?" she conceded.

"No, as it happens; I messed up. Jewel rescued her — singlehanded. Haw is safe in Norgreen. As for the twins, they're both dead."

Briar smiled knowingly. "Of course they are. That girl's a Magian, isn't she?"

"Yes, she is."

"Lucky for you — at least till now. But Magians are dangerous people. I wouldn't trust her, if I were you."

"Listen who's talking!" There was disdain in Thorn's voice. "When it comes to trust, Mother, *you* are in no position to lecture anyone."

Briar did not reply. For a time, neither spoke. The air crackled with tension. When, inevitably, the sparring resumed, Thorn was the first to jab.

"Mother, why won't you admit you're Berry Jack?"

"Berry Jack is dead. She died a long time ago."

Hello, thought Thorn: she's acknowledged the name at last. *Now* I'm getting somewhere . . .

"No she didn't," he contradicted. "She's standing right in front of me. You are Berry Jack and Berry Jack is my mother."

At that moment a great weariness came into Briar's face. "Very well, have it your own way. I *was* Berry Jack – once, a long time ago . . . but I'm not Berry now and I shall never be her again."

"Why not? What's to stop you?"

"I was never much of a mother when I *was* a mother, Thorn, and it's too late to start again."

"I don't see why."

"Of course you don't. You're not me, and you're not a woman."

Thorn weighed his options briefly: should he press the issue further or should he try a different tack? A different tack, he decided.

"Now that you've answered my first question, answer this one, if you will. Tell me who my father is."

Briar reacted with surprise. "Your father?" she said, as if repeating the word made the question seem absurd.

"Racky Jagger says he's my father – not Davis Jack, the man you married. So, Mother, which of them is it?"

Where on Briar's face weariness had shown, there now was

pain, and her son experienced a perverse surge of triumph. He thought: I'm forcing her to face things she buried years ago.

Briar thought for quite some time before producing a reply. "Please – don't ask me this, Thorn – not for my sake, for yours. No earthly good can come of it."

"It's too late to talk about good. But it's not too late to tell the truth. And that's all I want from you."

"Very well, I'll tell you the truth. The truth is: I don't know."

"You don't know?" Thorn was scandalised. "How can you not know?"

Briar turned her eyes away. "There are some things a mother shouldn't talk about with a son."

"But you're not much of a mother, and as a son I scarcely rate."

"My God, Thorn, you really know how to twist the knife. Where did you learn such vicious tricks?"

"I had pretty good teachers. Now, answer the question, *Mother*."

"Very well. Back then, in the time before I married Davis and Racky left Norgreen, both were my lovers. Neither knew about the other. Each believed himself the only man in my life. I found myself pregnant shortly after Racky had gone. I *had* to marry Davis – there was no alternative."

There was a pause. Then Thorn said, "Would you have married Racky if you'd had to choose between them?"

"Perhaps . . . How can I know? The question never arose. Davis and Racky were so different. Davis was gentle and considerate. Racky was passionate, unpredictable. Davis was like a quiet stream; Racky a river in spate. Davis charmed me; Racky swept me away . . . What more can I say?"

Thorn thought she'd said quite a lot; he was out of his depth now. He would need time to balance, in imagination's private place, the attractions of gentleness against the claims of turbulence. For he still had questions to ask, and if he didn't ask them now, he might not get another chance.

He'd been forceful up to this point; his next question emerged more tentatively. He said, "After my father's death, why didn't you and Racky marry? Not straightaway, I mean — but after a suitable interval."

As Briar averted her gaze again, her hair fell across one eye. "The possibility never arose."

She was lying, he was sure. He sensed the existence of a secret, a last mental barricade he had to break through if he was to have any chance of understanding everything.

"I don't believe you," he said. "You forget I've talked to Racky. I know how he feels about you — he's in love with you even now. I don't believe he wouldn't have asked you to marry him back then."

Briar straightened, tossing her stray locks away from her face in the gesture that had fixed itself in his mind in early childhood, the one memory he'd retained when the rest of her physical attributes had faded away.

"Well he didn't," she insisted.

"Don't lie to me!" he cried.

"The truth will hurt," she said quietly. "You don't want it, believe me."

"How do you know what I want?"

She looked at him steadily. "Very well," she said, in a cold, punitive voice: "You asked for it, here it comes. Racky *did* propose to me – three months after Davis was killed. I turned him down."

"And?" he urged her. "*And*?"

"He wanted to know why, so I told him, didn't I?"

"Told him what?"

"I told him I'd no intention of marrying a murderer."

Thorn was stunned. "A murderer?" he breathed, the sounds alien in his mouth.

"Don't you get it, Thorn Jack – or Thorn Jagger, if that's your name? The arrow that killed Davis came from Racky Jagger's bow . . . the arrow whose fletching no one could identify. Racky was always a good shot. He wanted Davis out of the way so he could marry me himself. But I knew what he'd done and I wasn't having any."

Thorn was stricken. His mind, which had been so clear, was now in a state of chaos. Briar produced a warped chuckle, a she-demon's icy snicker.

"Why do you think I left Norgreen? I couldn't bear the place any longer. Couldn't bear Racky watching me every time I left the house. Couldn't bear the bitter memories that assailed me in the streets. And, most of all, I couldn't bear my own self. For who but me had brought down this woe upon my head?

"So, now you know everything, how do you like it, son of mine? When one of your fathers murdered the other, he as good as killed me too. You think me beautiful, don't you Thorn, you and countless other men? But I'm hollow, a kind of ghost, the spectre that won't abandon the feast though it's got no stomach for food."

She fell silent at last. Thorn moistened dry lips.

"How – how can you be sure that you're right about all this? Did Racky admit the killing to you?"

"Not in so many words. But I read the truth in his eyes. Hadn't he told me often enough that he'd do anything for me? *Anything* included killing, I finally came to see. So I took myself off, without a word to anyone. I travelled to Wyke, then to Lowmoor, and came at last to Harrypark, where I met Crane Rockett. I was a hollow woman and Crane was a hollow man. Who else should I take up with? Till *you* turned up, son of mine, and sounded the death-knell for Crane. Strange how events come full-circle – how fate loves to play with us, to have the last laugh! And now here we both are, and it's happening again. I wonder . . . will this be the last act? And if so, for whom?"

9

THE GREAT NEST

Early next morning, Thorn stood outside the doorway of the Blue Ratters' refuge and watched Jewel walk away and disappear from sight. Rejecting the Headman's offer to send a detachment of warriors with her – if not all the way to the Great Nest, then to a spot from which they could keep the approach to the building under surveillance – she'd insisted on going alone, saying it had to be this way, that this would be safer both for her and for the Blue Ratters themselves. Her confidence had left the Headman nonplussed.

A hand descended on Thorn's shoulder.

"A remarkable lass," observed Manningham Sparks gravely.

"That she is," Thorn agreed.

"I've prayed long and hard for her. She's in God's hands now. Well, I too must be off."

One half of the Ranter's brain had urged him to stick around to see the outcome of Jewel's venture, but the other half had urged his prompt departure. His planned visit to the Church of the Iron Angel was late by a day, and he was chary of further delay: there's no knowing, he told himself, when matters there will reach crisis point. But crisis point was inevitable and he had a hunch as to when it would arrive; so, with a wry salute to Thorn (they had already said goodbye), the Ranter was on his

149

way, flanked by a squad of warriors who'd see him safely clear of the place. Soon they too had vanished from sight, and Thorn was alone but for the door-guards and an overactive mind.

Two subjects wrestled for his attention. One was Jewel and the peril into which she was walking. Thorn had wanted to go with her, but she'd made him promise not to pursue her on any account. This was no less than he'd expected. Ever since, during the crossing of Roydsal Dam, she'd lost Rainy, Jewel had been unwilling to expose her friends to dangers which she, as a Magian, had special ways of combating – as last night she'd said she had, for she'd tested out a new defence to use against the rats, and had a definite plan of action. Even so . . . Thorn fingered his bow, which was hooked over his shoulder along with a packed quiver of arrows. Ought he to break his promise (given with the utmost reluctance) and follow her anyway? Should he slip away from the refuge?

He worried the question for a time, then his mind changed course, re-engaging with what he'd learnt from his mother the day before. Right through the meal he'd eaten that evening (or, rather, had toyed with, for he'd left his appetite behind – along with a bleeding chunk of his already ravaged innocence – when he parted from her), and later as he'd lain sleepless and baffled in his cot, he'd butted at the brick wall Briar had built across his mind.

Probability: Racky Jagger had murdered Davis Jack.
Possibility: Racky Jagger was his father.
Possibility: His father was a murderer.
Possibility: Davis Jack was his father.
Possibility: Racky Jagger had murdered his father.

Was that a logical ordering? Well, however he ordered it, he would never know the truth: *that* had buckled and faded from sight like one of those smoke rings the Spetch twins had been expert at blowing. Briar had driven a fresh spike into her son's heart, and he'd no alternative but to find a way of living with it.

Again his mind switched tracks, returning to Jewel. He knew where the Great Nest was and how to find his way there, having listened as one of the tribesmen briefed Jewel earlier. It would not be hard to follow her footsteps . . . He stood motionless, gazing at the pale sky above the ironworks, as if hoping to find a sign there that would tell him what to do.

Only when she was out of sight of the refuge did Jewel halt so she could summon into being her precious cloak of secrecy. When once again she got going, she moved at the heart of the now familiar dead zone. Beyond the ring-fence of her mobile cocoon, the colours of grasses and plants and, further off, of the decaying structures of this Dark Time installation, seemed half sucked out. Fine: as long as the world looked like this and not like its proper self, she'd be happy — *more* than happy.

The Blue Ratter who'd briefed her on the layout of the buildings had been lucid and concise. Jewel navigated from corner to corner, from wall to wall, daring open spaces only when she had to. Ancient, rust-clogged machines and tarnished stacks of factory products reared above the weeds and grasses. She paused and craned her neck to look up at a chimney. The massive, stone-block structure appeared to shoot up from the ground like a stupendous blackened cannon, its fiendish barrel bolt upright, ready to blow holes in the sky.

She'd no sooner set off again than a scuffling noise in the undergrowth stopped her dead in her tracks. A blue rat emerged – nose, head, body, tail – to stand sniffing and peering about. Its bright gaze passed over her, but the rat gave no sign that it had registered her presence. It's not here by chance, she thought: it's a scout on its rounds, doing just as humans do in the interests of security.

After a few moments' pause, the creature moved off again. Jewel took a deep breath. It was a small victory for her chosen mode of defence, but the big test was still to come.

She went on, and didn't stop till she came in sight of the Great Nest. Then, in the lee of one of several silvery cylinders, she stood and studied the building. It resembled nothing so much as a small-scale house: small to a giant, of course. It was around half the size again of Rotten Pavilion but – unlike Harrypark's gambling-house – was topped off with a chimney pot. In front of it was a small clearing and across this space blue rats were purposefully trotting, coming or going on ratty business. As they passed one another, they would raise their muzzles and sniff, as if performing a salute – or did rat recognise rat by the way each comrade smelt? Jewel did a quick count, and made the number to be a dozen. This raised a grin on her face. The One and the Twelve, she thought. And this time *I* get to be Punch!

Then her features stiffened again. There'd be many more than a dozen rats inside the Great Nest. And, once in, she wouldn't be hanging about to count them.

Right, she thought, this is it. Out she walked into the open. The building's wooden door had once been painted bright green. Most of the paint had peeled off, and what few patches remained were bleached to ghosts of the door's former glory. The rats were going in and out through a hole in one corner — much as the twins had at Roydsal, and Crane and Briar at Minral How. But blue rats weren't carpenters; they had gnawed their way in and, as Jewel neared the hole, she saw on the wood the grooves their teeth had inflicted.

To the right of the hole, an enormous rat stood on guard — bigger still than the rat she'd shot through the eye the previous day, and quite the biggest she'd ever seen. The harshness of his hide told her he had to be a buck. His eyes blazed with an aggression barely contained. His ragged right ear attested his battle-worthiness. As the other animals passed, they raised their muzzles in deference; but this arrogant sentinel made no answering salute.

There could be no turning back. Nipping smartly into the gap between two returning rats, Jewel moved towards the door, tense inside her frail shell. But, like the scout she'd met, the guard betrayed not the least sign of sensing her. As she ducked to go through the gap, a rat making its departure passed no more than an inch away — but didn't even hesitate as it went shuffling past.

She was inside the Great Nest.

Thorn stood on the extreme edge of the factory weighing-plate, gazing in the direction that Jewel had taken. Time was dragging painfully, yet no great amount could have passed since she'd disappeared from sight. Had she reached the Great Nest? Was she inside right now? He nibbled his lip, hoping —

against his sceptical self – that the Ranter's prayers would count for *some*thing.

A far-off movement caught his eye. Had someone or something there disturbed that knot of all-heal? Yes – for now the flower stems parted and a man's head and shoulders dipped briefly into view. He gestured at Thorn, then drew back into cover.

Distant though he was, the man was unmistakable.

Racky Jagger! Here, now! The manifestation was startling. That Racky was here was one thing; that he should try to contact Thorn . . . Was Querne Rasp then here too? And if so, where? Was Racky up to his old tricks?

Thorn threw a glance back at the two door-guards. Neither one, he realised, had seen what he'd seen. They stared stonily ahead.

Taking no time to ponder the consequences of his action, Thorn stepped off the weighing-plate and hurried away down the track. He'd taken less than twenty steps when a voice called after him, but he only quickened his pace. The door-guards, he knew, weren't allowed to quit their posts. Reaching the point where he thought Racky had popped into view, he scanned the greenery. Was Racky playing hide and seek? Then Thorn spotted, amongst the stalks, his would-be father's bald head and sun-weathered face.

"In here, Thorn," Racky hissed. "Come on – there's no time to lose!"

"What do you want?" demanded Thorn. He'd been betrayed enough already.

But, sticking out a hand, Racky grabbed Thorn's arm and

hauled him into cover. A musty, herby aroma assailed Thorn's nose. He snatched his arm free.

"What are you doing here, Racky?"

"Your girlfriend, Jewel – don't want to see her dead, do you?"

"Dead? Of course not—"

"Then you'd better follow me! Querne's here, in the iron-works. She's going to ambush Jewel. She believes Jewel will use the green crystal to get the black one. She'll wait till Jewel comes out of the rat's nest, then she'll kill her and take both of the stones – unless we step in and do something to stop her."

"*We* . . . ? I don't understand . . . You're Querne's right-hand man!"

Racky's lips curled: here came his old sardonic grin. "I was," he replied, "but I've finally come to my senses. I've switched allegiances. Querne doesn't know that, she thinks I'm watching her back. Still, you can never be sure with Querne – she always says she knows people's minds better than they do."

Perhaps she does, Thorn thought, but she's made a mistake. For Jewel had chosen to leave her crystal at the refuge. This because then, if Querne turned up, only one stone would be at risk. Logic had argued that Jewel ought to arm herself with the green crystal: if she had to fight the rats, what better weapon did she have? But this, she thought, was how Querne would expect her to think. So she'd taken the less logical course and left the stone behind. All this Thorn knew because Jewel had told him. But there was no way in the world that he was going to confide in Racky.

They were pushing through plant stems. Thorn clutched his bow to his chest in order to stop the string snagging. Pollen, shaken free from blossoms, dusted their heads and clothing. Racky sneezed.

Thorn abruptly came to a halt. "Racky, why should I trust you? Why the sudden change of mind? Why shouldn't this be just another of your traps?"

Racky too stopped and, turning round, stared at Thorn. When at length he began to speak, he spoke unusually slowly, leaving a pregnant pause between one sentence and the next.

"Because my life, in recent weeks, has come to seem worthless to me? Because Querne is out of control and plans to terrorise the world? Because I've got to break the hold she's long had over me? And because you are my son and I've done you a terrible wrong?"

Racky's speech rang with the force of reasons long contemplated. Is he genuine? wondered Thorn. Can he really have changed? The speech had a prepared quality, as if Racky had anticipated having to make it.

Thorn held back from a response.

Racky whipped out his knife. Thorn recoiled instinctively, but saw the man offer the weapon to him, handle foremost.

"Take it," Racky commanded. "I betrayed you at Whispering Oak. I betrayed you at Roydsal. I don't deserve to live. Take your revenge – cut my throat."

Thorn stared at the knife, then plucked it out of Racky's hand. Racky threw back his head, baring his throat for the cut.

Thorn said, haltingly, "Did you kill my father, Racky? Did you kill Davis Jack?"

The answer came straight back. "Yes, I killed Davis Jack. He took what was rightfully mine. For years, for what it's worth, I've regretted killing him. What I did back then was wrong. But Davis Jack wasn't your father. *I'm* your father, Thorn."

Thorn took a step forward and slowly raised the knife. His mind was a tumult of emotions.

"Do it, Thorn, do it quick. Who in the world will miss me?"

Racky was staring at a spray of blossom inches from his head. Each flower had eight petals neatly arranged in pairs. They were blindingly white. Mouse-ear chickweed, he thought. But why is it called that? The insides of a mouse's ears are pink . . .

The blade crept towards Racky's neck. The skin there was creased and weathered, and each wrinkle imprinted itself on Thorn's memory with a dreamlike vividness.

What if Racky killed my father and I allow him to live?

What if Racky *is* my father, and I kill him? What then?

The conundrum again. It was beyond Thorn to solve. The blade trembled in his hand, its point pricking Racky's flesh. A thread of blood ran into his shirt. But he remained motionless.

Thorn let drop his knife-arm.

"Take it back," he told Racky, offering him the knife. "More than enough blood has been shed in my family."

Racky looked at him strangely, then gave a double nod. Taking back the knife, Racky slid it into its sheath.

"Come on, Thorn," he said. "There isn't a moment to lose."

Never in her life had Jewel seen so many rats. The biggest rattery she'd visited was nothing to the Great Nest. Ratteries were orderly places. Each animal had its own stall – except for suckling does, which were never parted from their litters. Here there were no stalls. As for order – if such there was – it took a very different form.

She paused to take stock and get her bearings in the place. The rats' home was a single room. Light came in through its grimy windows and gaps in its roof-slates. On one side, defended by a tiled and raised hearth, was a fireplace that boasted a flame-reddened iron grate. On the other side were a desk and a chair. A second chair stood at an angle a little distance away. The desk's upper portion, set snug against the wall, was honeycombed with drawers and open-fronted compartments. These the rats had colonised; a few were crawling around up there, and from time to time a bewhiskered snout would protrude above a shelf and eyes look down on the teeming scene.

Kittens bounded and skipped, chasing one another's tails. Several groups held mock-battles, squeaking with madcap glee as they tumbled, wrestled and rolled. While Jewel took in her surroundings, one creature detached itself from a squirm of playmates and shot up the leg of the nearest chair. The others untangled themselves and followed, and soon the pack was romping on the high wooden seat.

Every rat's fur gleamed blue-violet in the light. Nowhere else had Jewel seen pelts of such an unnatural shade. Perhaps, she thought, it's something the rats picked up from the locality – some deposit from the metals here, in the water or what they eat.

But she had her bearings now, and she set her legs in motion.

Rats were criss-crossing the space directly in front of her, but Jewel made not the slightest effort to steer clear of them. She trod a line as straight as a die; if any rats were in her way, she simply walked straight at them – when they would shift to one side, not even glancing in her direction, as if responding to a prompting from so deep inside themselves that they were unconscious of its existence. Beyond this space the nests began, and through these she now must steer. Here the rats were mostly does, a fair few of them suckling young and, seeing the numbers involved, Jewel was struck with the futility of the Blue Ratters' mission. However many beasts they killed, there would always be more. Where was the point of what they did? Better to build one's life, she thought, around creating rather than killing. At the same time, she knew that it would be pointless to tell them so: their attitude to life was utterly alien to her own.

But then she thought: Who am *I* to judge? Didn't I dedicate my *own* life to killing – and didn't I kill? And not rats but humans?

She smiled inwardly. The Spetch twins *had* been rats, for all their two-leggedness, and she – Jewel Ranson – had extermi-nated them . . .

Jewel moved deeper into the nests. The floor was scattered with scraps of cloth, hay, thin gnawings of wood and other pliant materials that made for warmth and comfort. In one nest a doe was asleep; her buck lay beside her, keeping a watch on his young. Further on, a kitten was licking the fur of an acquiescent sibling. The practice seemed unremarkable, but Jewel knew what it meant: grooming was a peaceful way of asserting dom-inance. A little further, and Jewel recoiled as a doe raised her bloody muzzle from the torn rags of a kitten. Her jaws moved rhythmically. Monstrous? No . . . Jewel had heard of such a practice, though not till today had she witnessed it. The doe's behaviour was an example of the way that nature worked: unsentimentally, starkly, economically. The baby had been born dead or too sickly to survive. The mother was simply cleansing her nest.

Surely, Jewel thought, I've got to be getting near the spot where I saw the black crystal.

It had been nestling among some ragged twists of cloth and other rubbish.

She went down on one knee and laid a hand on the floor. Aware of the need to maintain her defences, she wondered if she'd be able, without losing control of the cloak, also to sense the whereabouts of the stone. This required nothing less than the splitting of her consciousness, but when she tried dividing her mind she found it not too difficult. Her brain seemed to separate into two equal areas – left brain, right brain. The organ might have been waiting for her to make use of this function.

Within moments, she'd succeeded in pinpointing the crystal's position.

Jewel straightened and set off again. Skirting a couple of nests – one vacant, one occupied by a suckling doe, she came to a third in which a female lay in a half doze, her muzzle laid flat on the nesting material. She was well on in pregnancy. No more than a couple of inches away, the black crystal peeped from a fold in a rip of yellow cloth.

Sorry, Mrs Rat, but it's time to shift yourself.

And so, as Jewel moved towards her, the doe did – crawling forward until the girl's way was clear. But, like the other rats, she betrayed no sign that she'd detected the human presence.

Jewel poked at the cloth, laying the crystal completely bare. It was half as big again as the green stone she had – not much smaller than her head. It lay motionless, somnolent, but as she stood gazing down she was struck by the oddest persuasion. The stone was aware of her: it had lain waiting for her, lain waiting a long time. The air seemed charged with expectancy, as of some imminent event. But, as she slipped her pack off her shoulders, put it down beside the crystal and unfastened the straps, she thought: Nothing's going to happen. I'll stow the crystal away and get back to the refuge.

Then she realised that she hadn't brought a cloth to wrap the stone. She'd have to damp it mentally. Projecting a counterforce through her fingers, she stooped and got her hands around it.

But, as she lifted it up, the crystal brushed her efforts aside. Blazing out purple-violet, it enveloped the girl and sucked her into its dark heart.

10

THE LABORATORY EYE

The darkness began to flicker. At first the flickering was too rapid to make sense, but when its speed began to abate, Jewel grasped that what she was seeing was a sequence of images. The sequence continued to slow, and now she saw that the images were all the same image – as if a single picture was whizzing past her, over and over again.

Still the images slowed . . . and, at long last, stopped.

A kind of disembodied eye, Jewel was floating close to the ceiling of a room in a Dark Time house. Three of its walls were covered with shelves, and the shelves held nothing but books. Books – the most mysterious of Dark Time artefacts. On a table were more books, and piles of white paper, some marked with columns of letters, numbers and symbols. Sticklike writing implements stuck up from a pottery holder.

Two men sat at ease in black-upholstered armchairs. The younger was in his twenties. He was slim and clean-shaven and had short, frizzy hair. His skin was so dark as to be almost black. His companion was much older, and white-skinned like Jewel; the hair on top of his head was thinning, but he wore a thick beard with more grey in it than brown, and spectacles with tinted lenses.

She'd seen parts of a giant skeleton, but that had been a

lifeless thing, and in comparison with herself the size of the men was almost a shock. The one-time masters of this world . . . how much at ease they seemed in their skins.

Both men held bulbous glasses, the glass incised with intricate patterns. The young man now emptied his and set it down on a small table.

"All right, James," he said. "I'm with you so far. It's true as you say that I'm the one physicist in the department who believes in the many-worlds hypothesis, rather than paying it lip-service. But I still don't understand why it's me you've brought here tonight. I've barely got my Ph.D. I've only published one paper. What profile do I have? Who, except my former teachers, has even heard of me?"

"Don't belittle yourself, Christian! You're the most intelligent person in that whole benighted department; I'm convinced you'll do great things. You're young, but that's a positive qualification. You're as yet uncompromised. You don't belong to a clique, you're uncontaminated by the politics that bedevil relations there and which, as you know, prompted my sudden departure. Your mind is open and objective. And, last but not least, you're the only former colleague for whom I don't feel utter contempt." James rose from his chair. "Shall we go down to the lab?"

Christian smiled wryly. "Well, after that vote of confidence . . ."

The two men left the room. Jewel drifted after them. She was slow to reach the door, which closed just as she got there, but she passed easily through the wood and continued to follow them. The men went down a corridor to a door at its end. This

James unlocked with a key he took from his pocket. Inside the door, he pressed a number of switches on the wall. Light sprang into being below, revealing a flight of stone stairs. James began to descend. Christian followed and Jewel floated along in his wake.

At the bottom of the stairs, brick walls painted white enclosed a stone-flagged area. On several worktables lay a clutter of tools and equipment and an assortment of gadgets from the small to the sizable. Three of the room's four walls were lined with shelved rows of identical flattish, rectangular panels mounted on metal stands and narrow, upright, also identical black boxes, the two forms alternating. There must have been more than a hundred of each, crowding shoulder to shoulder, spewing out wires and cables that here and there were gathered into bundles that ran across the floor to a black box that stood on the central table. The frame of each panel contained a space of luminous blue marked with a couple of black words that Jewel couldn't read.

Christian whistled. "So this is your quantum computer! Very impressive, James. It knocks the department's set-up into a cocked hat. The hardware alone must have cost you a small fortune. How on earth could you afford it on a lecturer's salary?"

"I couldn't, of course. But, along with the house, I had a legacy from my father. I ploughed most of it into this."

Christian moved to the central table and stood gazing at the black box to which the cables ran. It was perhaps eighteen inches high, twenty across and twenty deep. On the front were letters and markings, a couple of buttons and several rectangular areas that to Jewel resembled the fronts of tiny drawers —

except that if they were drawers, they didn't have handles in the middle. A little way below them, a small oval eye showed a bright green light.

"This is the daddy, I take it," said Christian.

"Yes," said James. "This is the heart of the thing. I call it the Mayfield Machine. It's going to revolutionise the whole of physics!"

"It looks innocuous enough."

"True," James replied, "but it's a wolf in sheep's clothing. I keep its teeth in this container."

Beside the Mayfield Machine lay a square, flattish box. James removed the lid and stepped aside so that Christian could take in its contents.

The base of the container was moulded out of metal. In it, four matching pockets surrounded a larger fifth. Each contained one of the crystals with which Jewel was familiar. How small they now seemed! In a giant's hand they'd be no bigger than a child's marbles. So this was where they'd come from . . . but how had they got into Jewel's world?

Unless her world *was* this world . . .

Christian was puzzled. "What on earth are these?" he asked. "They look like knuckles of quartz: the pretty rocks kids buy in geology exhibitions."

"So they do," said James. "As it happens, their colouring is neither here nor there – it amused me to colour them. I call them quincells." He stressed the word on the first of its syllables. "The term's an acronym: QUantum INformation CELL. You're familiar, of course, with what people call – in hand-me-down language – computer chips. Well, these are quantum chips, the only ones in existence. They're artificial – I developed them myself through experiments with silicates." He gestured to Christian. "Go on, touch one," he invited: "one of the outer four."

Christian stuck a finger out towards the ruby crystal. As he made contact with it, there came a scarlet flash of light and he pulled back with a little cry.

"Hey! The little beggar gave me a shock!"

James was amused. "Quincells," he said, in his best lecturing voice, "are extremely sensitive: a bit like sea anemones – though they don't do curling up! This is because each one contains a micro energy-cell. They react to any energy-source they come in contact with. A touch is enough to get a response out of them. They'd interact with human minds too, if they got the chance. I'm a firm believer, like Bohm, that consciousness is rooted in quantum mechanical features. Ideal would be a person with some form of enhanced mental power, like ESP or telekinesis. The capabilities of such a mind working in tandem with one or more quincells would be staggering – though, of course, that person would have to be careful not to overload himself."

"Fascinating," said Christian.

"As you're well aware," James went on, "the Holy Grail of quantum computing was to find a way of using optics to combine solid states with semi-conductor systems. Well, my quincells are the result. They talk to one another, exchanging photons continuously."

"How many qubits are they capable of processing?"

James smiled. "To be honest, I don't know. Ten to the nth?"

This number meant nothing to Jewel, but it was obvious that

James was impressed by it. "So, what program are you intending to run tonight?" he now said.

"The ultimate program!" James pronounced with a thrill.

"Ultimate program? What do you mean?"

"I mean one that, given time, will deliver nothing less than a total description of reality."

"Total?" Christian was fumbling. "You mean – not just our *own* universe – but the *multi*verse?"

"That's *exactly* what I mean! What is our entire biosphere, including ourselves, our culture, all our ideas and all our knowledge, but *information* – a kind of self-generated, on-running computer program? DNA – information encoded so it can pass itself on – is only the most obvious instance; nature evolved it. In the multiverse, of course, the biosphere is replicated over and over again, sometimes with only minor changes, sometimes with enormous ones. In some worlds *Homo sap* exists, in others the poor sap doesn't, or maybe self-conscious life appears in different forms."

He paused to consider the effect his words were having on his guest. Christian was staring at the quincells in their box.

James went on, "Now, the banks of PCs you see lining the walls have been programmed with a mass of information about our local biosphere – the only one of many-worlds our minds can experience. When I run the program, the PCs feed information to the five quincells. A continual exchange takes place among them at subatomic level. Now, the master quincell – the bigger black one you see in the centre there – behaves rather like the observer in a quantum experiment who collapses possibility into classical reality – this realm we see, smell, touch. That is, it identifies points of bifurcation or trifurcation – those points at which reality splits to produce the many versions of the world that we call the multiverse. The results are then fed back to other PCs which act as memory banks: from these, slices of reality can later be reconstituted and experienced virtually."

Christian said, "Fine. But –" he pointed to four identical machines further along the bench "– what do these printers do?"

"Ah, the printers. Well, as the black quincell processes the variants the others feed through it, it takes what you might call *snapshots* of them. These snapshots are then translated into a mathematical language that I myself devised. Selections – titbits if you like – will be printed out for our delectation while the program runs."

"This is weird," said Christian. "I feel like the narrator in Wells's *Time Machine* – on the point of witnessing one of the great moments in science."

James chuckled modestly. "Not that bad an analogy. Since time and space are a single entity, in a way quantum computation's a kind of time travel – or as near as we can get to it at this stage in our science. So – shall we begin?"

"By all means," said Christian.

To the right of the computer stood a flattish rectangular panel similar to those that lined the walls. It too was presently blue and marked with a couple of black words. Jewel drifted closer to hover a little way above the men's heads. Now she could see, after the second word, a short winking vertical line. A word popped into her mind: *cursor.* The panel was called a *monitor,* the lit area on it *screen.* She found she also knew the name for the board set below it: *keyboard*, and the square or rec-tangular buttons mounted on it in serried ranks, each marked with one or more letters or symbols, were therefore *keys*. James pressed one with a finger and, within moments, rows of curious symbols began to run across the screen from left to right. I'm looking, Jewel thought, at a man that Roper Tuckett would call an experimentalist. One far in advance of Roper, yes, but fired by the same zeal. And Roper would give his wisdom teeth for the bird's-eye view I've got . . .

James now pressed a button high on the front of the black box: a compartment slid out. In it were five pockets. Donning a pair of white gloves, James transferred the crystals from their box to this compartment, then closed it again. A button set above the last one produced a second, narrower drawer. Into it went a leaf-thin, silvery disk; then this drawer too was closed.

James tapped away at the keyboard; with each strike, fresh letters and symbols jumped onto the screen. The black box began to hum.

"The experiment begins!" James announced resonantly.

All around the walls, the computer screens had come alive with flickering lines of symbols. James paid them no heed. His attention remained on the lone monitor. The printers remained inactive.

"Did you test-run the program?" Christian enquired.

"Yes – but I factored a time-block in. It ran for exactly five minutes – long enough to check that the quincells were inter-acting, but not long enough to see any results coming through. Today there's no time-block. Unless something goes wrong –

which, barring some blow-out in the national grid, won't happen – I'll let the program run."

At last there came a series of clicks and, one after the others, the printers went into action.

"Just over eight minutes – not bad at all," said James.

He and Christian moved along the table to the printers. Sheets of lined white paper came scrolling out of their jaws, covered with all manner of symbols. Each printer would buzz for a time, then briefly fall quiet. When around two feet of paper had emerged from the foremost machine, James tore a section off and began eagerly to scan it.

"Ah! Here's something that should interest you, Christian. In this world, let's call it World A, Britain has just elected a black President – apparently the first ever."

"*President* – not Prime Minister?"

"That's what I said."

"So we're a republic . . . What's his name?"

"*Her* name, actually. It's Primrose Morton. Maybe somewhere a parallel Christian is raising a glass to her."

"A whole bottle, I don't doubt . . . as long, that is, as I got born there . . ."

James tore a sheet off the next machine in the line.

"World B . . . Terrorists have flown a jumbo jet into the Kremlin, killing the Soviet President and his closest advisers . . . Doesn't sound as though the Berlin Wall came down in *his* world."

"Sounds like pure fiction to me."

James was paper-tearing again.

"If you think *that* sounds like fiction, listen to this, young man. In World C the American War of Independence was won by Great Britain, and America remains a British colony ruled by the house of Hanover – still a going concern."

Christian chuckled. "That's not fiction, it's out-and-out fantasy."

"There you have the multiverse – a endless supply of novel plots!"

Time passed. James interpreted more printouts for Christian. Each successive world, it seemed, was more fantastic than the last, but as most of what James said meant little or nothing to Jewel, she started to get a little bored . . . till the moment James stiffened and held a hand up in the air. He was listening intently. Christian listened too.

With the ticking of the four printers and the hum of the master computer, the room was awash with sound.

"Hear what I hear?" asked James.

"The computer," said Christian. "It sounds different – harsher."

"Just what I thought."

James returned to the monitor and studied the stream of symbols hurrying across the screen. He frowned.

"Something wrong?" asked Christian.

"I don't know . . . Some of this stuff is beyond me. There are symbols here I didn't invent, don't understand . . ."

"That's impossible. Programs can only contain what programmers have programmed in."

"Precisely . . ." James studied the screen for a time, then turned to Christian with a strange look on his face. "Do you know what this looks like to me?" he said. "A virus!"

"But surely, your system's isolated, isn't it?"

"Yes . . . and no." A strange gleam had appeared in the experimentalist's eyes. "Yes, because it's hardwired to nothing outside this room. No, because no quantum system is ever isolated."

"So what you're saying is . . . the computer's experiencing a form of interference?"

"Yes, Christian . . . But 'virus' is the wrong word for this – it's our old friend *entanglement*."

"But for entanglement to occur, the quantum effect must be real – not notional as you supposed. Your system is interacting with something outside itself."

"That's right." James seemed stunned by the novelty of the idea. "I didn't anticipate this . . ."

Symbols now were whizzing across the monitor and wall screens, as if crazy to get from one side of them to the other. The printers chattered madly, spewing out streams of paper. James watched as if mesmerised, fascinated by the way his brainchild was misbehaving.

Jewel's attention, however, was drawn away from the monitor. Something strange was happening to the black box. Its surfaces seemed to shimmer, as if the particles of which the metal was made were vibrating. The casing appeared to be modulating from black to dark grey . . . As the girl watched, faint coloured lights became visible inside. As the casing grew ever lighter in shade, the lights strengthened. Now James and Christian were staring at it too. It was becoming transparent. Inside the see-through shell, the machine's innards showed as silver-pale suggestions. But the five vivid nuggets that were

James Mayfield's quincells blazed out like a star: its points yellow, red, blue and green, its heart a brilliant purple. A continual flow of rainbow-coloured threads linked the crystals in a kind of light-web. But as the two men watched, entranced, something else began happening.

The star started to rotate.

"My God!" James exclaimed. "The quincells are *moving!* But that's impossible!"

Christian peered at the computer. Impossible or not, the movement was happening. In fact the quincells were speeding up. The four outer points, at first separate, had merged to create what looked like nothing so much as a coloured wheel.

"They're spinning!" he declared.

"Amazing!" said James. "This is beyond my wildest dreams."

"With that darker stone at the centre," Christian hazarded, "it rather resembles a vortex!"

"A vortex," James murmured. "By God, Christian, you're right!"

He turned to the monitor. The rush of symbols had stilled. He bent over the screen.

"What does it say?" demanded Christian impatiently.

"The black quincell seems to have locked on to one particular world. I can't make sense of all this stuff, but from what I *can* read, World X's version of Earth is much smaller than our planet. So is the human race. It's virtually illiterate and technologically backward. Humans ride around on rats. But here's an interesting point, some have PSI abilities. That could explain why the quincells have homed in on this world."

"And if our hypothesis is correct, this world really exists!"

A flash of mauve light pulled the two men's eyes back to the black box. It was a mere shadow now. But the rapidly spinning quincells seemed to vibrate with life.

And, to Christian's eyes, with ever-growing menace.

"James, don't you think you ought to shut the program down?"

The inventor ignored him. He was staring at his creations. The vortex now was tossing out coloured sparks as it spun. Only when Christian seized his friend's arm and tugged at it did James wake up, like a man emerging from a trance.

"*Think*, James. Vortices. What is it they do? They suck things in, isn't that right? And this is a *quantum* vortex. That implies a corresponding vortex at the entangled end!"

"A double-ended vortex, sucking and spewing at both ends . . ." James seemed stunned by the proposition. "But that could have the effect of a mini black hole!"

Urgently, Christian said, "You've got to shut it down, James!"

"Shut it down? Well yes, perhaps you're right – I don't want to damage the hardware."

He hesitated, then, moving to the monitor, tapped a number of keys.

Nothing happened. The set of symbols remained fixed, as if locked in position.

James frowned. Again he tapped a sequence of keys. Again nothing happened. Then he was battering the keyboard, going at it like a madman. A key snapped off and jumped up, hitting him on the nose.

"It's not responding!" he cried.

The ghostly box rose slowly from the tabletop and hovered in mid-air. No longer spitting sparks, the centre of the vortex glowed purple-black, dilating like a malignant eye.

"What's happening?" yelled Christian.

"I don't know . . . The quincells have properties I didn't bargain for. God knows what's going to happen!"

But Jewel knew – knew also that nothing could prevent it.

Moments later, the future arrived.

The quincells flared up, an exploding rainbow. A fraction of time after came a fearsome detonation.

Jewel was hurled into space. With blackness came silence.

11

AMBUSHED

Stars appeared on the blackness, tiny winking points of light. They grew larger until they were no longer points but splashes; then the splashes in turn expanded, reaching out and merging; soon there were more of them than of the original blackness. The light softened, and out of its uniform shading pale patches of colour began to define themselves. The patches took on the look of things. The solid world was arranging itself. But there, at the dead centre of Jewel's field of vision, a small clot of blackness persisted stubbornly.

The crystal, she realised. Still she held it in her hands. But the violet radiance at its heart was extinguished now: it was just a lump of rock.

Just a lump of rock that had devastated a world.

No – *two* worlds.

And it was quite heavy, too.

Jewel glanced about her. Surely blue rats would have arrived in droves by now, attracted by the disturbance, eager for something to attack.

But nothing seemed to have altered. The doe lay stretched out in the spot to which she'd moved. Her head was turned away from Jewel. As for the cloak of secrecy, it was active as before. Like no time at all had passed.

And it hasn't, she realised. *Whatever happened to me, happened outside of time. The crystal plucked me out of time and now it's dropped me back in again.*

She held the last piece now – she could complete the picture puzzle. The crystal had shown her the disaster that had damaged the wave function which underpinned the many-worlds. No God was responsible – just a man, a single giant who had overreached himself: James Mayfield, whose experiment had gone disastrously wrong. *Entanglement*: that was the word the two men had used. When the vortex exploded, it had mixed up two worlds – sucking clean whole regions of Mayfield's home world, sweeping away the giant race and who knew what other animals above a certain size (though not fish – for how could she forget the great pike!). At the same time it had sucked Jewel's kind out of *their* world – a world they'd perfectly fitted – and dumped them down here among the tatters of the earlier civilisation. And after that? Even if at first her people had remembered their origins (something she rather doubted; had their memories been wiped clean by the shock of the transition?), they'd quickly forgotten them – perhaps as an alternative to losing their minds. As for the five crystals, the explosion had scattered them through the Lowmoor area – somewhere within which James Mayfield must have lived. Five crystals, scattered and useless – except, that is, to Magians, beings uniquely suited to bonding with the stones. Thorn would be wide-eyed when she told him what she knew.

But first things first: now she had the black crystal, she must get back to the refuge.

Tucking the crystal into her pack, she set off back through the nests. The rats ignored her as before and, this time, she ignored them. She had full confidence in the cloak, which she now wore as easily as one might an extra skin. Reaching the stretch of clear floor, she struck out across it. As before, rats trotted to and fro, steering neatly around her. At the entrance hole she tagged on to a couple about to leave. Moments later, she was outside. The guard buck was still there. His glistening eyes passed over the moving rats and right through Jewel herself.

I'm empty air to him, she thought.

She went towards the clutch of cylinders she'd used earlier as cover. Would – before she reached it – the blue-furred sentinel wake to her presence, come bounding after her and sink his teeth into her neck?

A silly fancy. Reaching the cylinder she'd used for cover, she rounded it. Good! But she wasn't safe yet; she had to keep the cloak in place.

The sun was up now. She moved from shade to sunlight, then back into shade again. In a narrow defile amongst a strew of pocky bricks, two rats loomed round a corner. There would be no room to pass! But, as Jewel was on the point of turning round to hurry back, the rats pre-empted her action. As if prompted by a sudden change of mind they wheeled about; a last tail flicked out of view.

At the end of the defile, Jewel peered beyond the bricks. Already the rats had disappeared. She went on. Here was the last brick in the scattering. She turned a corner—

—and felt a blow to the back of her head that knocked her

sprawling to the ground and dissipated her cloak. As she lay in the dirt, hovering on the verge of unconsciousness, she became aware of a figure down on one knee at her side. A blurred face swam into her vision; but it wasn't so blurred as to be beyond recognition.

"There are times," said Querne Rasp, her voice sweet with satisfaction, "when the crudest methods serve a Magian best." She let a stone drop from her hand.

"You – you –" was all Jewel could get out.

"Save your breath, little girl. Oh dear, Miss Jewel Ranson . . . Why didn't you accept my honest offer at Harrypark? I would have shared the world with you. But that owl was too much. If there's one thing I hate, it's going swimming fully clothed.

"But enough about me, let's talk about you. What do they say – live and learn? I'd say you're learning right now, but as for living, I fear you've come to the end of that. You're going to be rats'-meat, Jewel."

Hands picked at the straps of her pack, which was lifted away.

Querne chuckled. "By the way, that cloak of yours. You did well there. You're a quick learner, Jewel. But though it fooled a nest of rats, it didn't fool me. Did I tell you before that it was me who invented cloaks?"

Summoning what little strength she had at her disposal, Jewel willed herself to crook a finger at Querne; perhaps she could fire a charge . . .

Querne slapped her on the hand; she felt a burning sensation . . .

"Naughty, naughty!" said Querne, and laughed a cold, tinkling laugh.

Jewel's eyes were watering; she blinked away tears. Then saw that Querne was dangling something silvery near her face.

"Can you see it?" her enemy asked.

"*Whis?*" said Jewel hoarsely, then tried again. "Whistle?"

"Very good. But it's different from the one your friend summoned the pike with. This whistle summons rats. Like to test it out, would you?"

Jewel said nothing. Querne's chuckle sounded again.

"What's up, Jewel Ranson? Lost your spirit of adventure?" She shrugged. "It rather looks as though I'll have to do it myself."

Querne put the whistle to her lips and blew on it. No sound emerged. But then it won't, thought Jewel vaguely. It's not for human ears.

Querne straightened up, strapped Jewel's pack on her hip and stood looking down at the girl.

"Well, toodle-oo! I must be off. Things to do. I'd say, 'Enjoy your dinner!' except I rather doubt you will, being the eaten not the eater!"

Then she was gone.

Jewel willed herself to roll over onto her side. Her body refused. It was a limp, pathetic hulk. As for the cloak of secrecy, it was beyond her to remake it. Her mind began to drift. Soon blue rats would arrive . . . She tried not to think of them . . . of their eyes, their spittled tongues, their bottomless hunger, their teeth . . . She tried not to think of them . . .

A sound impinged on her ears, the scuffle of rats' feet on

180

earth. Why can't I pass out? she wondered. Then at least I'd know nothing . . . But still, maddeningly, she went on floating just above the lake-surface of oblivion.

The scrabble of feet was close now. She shut her eyes tight like a child frightened in the dark . . .

Rancid breath blew in her nose. They'd arrived. Querne Rasp had beaten her. This was the end.

Racky pushed out of the vegetation, Thorn right behind him. Then the pair stopped dead. Less than three feet away and close to a jumble of old bricks, Jewel lay motionless on the ground. Next moment, two rats emerged from a channel between the bricks.

They had eyes only for Jewel. They sniffed at her body, as if assessing its suitability for consumption.

Thorn was first to aim and fire. The rats were fearfully close to Jewel, but there was no alternative. Thorn's arrow flew true and struck the first rat in the neck. Racky's shaft thudded into the second rat's hindquarters.

Squeals erupted from the pair. Turning away from Jewel, they scurried away among the bricks.

Thorn and Racky ran to Jewel. Thorn lifted her upper body, cradling her head in his arms. Her eyes were open, he saw, and she smiled vaguely at him.

"Rats . . ." she murmured. "Querne . . . whistle . . ."

Thorn turned to Racky.

"Querne was here – she did this. It was she who summoned the rats. More will be coming. We've got to run."

"Let me take her," said Racky. "Watch my back as we retreat."

Thorn relinquished Jewel to Racky and reached for an arrow from his quiver. But as he was nocking his bow, a massive rat burst into view and, putting its head down, slammed full tilt into him. The bow flew from Thorn's grasp, he shot backwards through the air and hit the ground with an impact that shocked the breath from his body.

The great rat straddled him. Its pupils glittered like black gems, its facial fur stood erect and now it cranked up its jaws to sink its teeth into his head.

But the bite never came. Squealing in fury, the rat abruptly wheeled away; then, crazily, began to spin round in circles. Struggling to his feet, Thorn saw to his astonishment Racky perched on its back. With one fist he gripped a tuft of fur; the other held his knife, and with this he stabbed the maddened beast over and over again.

In order to mount this attack, Racky had had no option but to lay Jewel back on the ground. She was in danger, Thorn saw, of being trampled by the rat. He ran forward and scooped her up. None too soon: the rat's cable of a tail whipped by him in the air and he felt the wind of its passing.

Still Racky clung to the rat. It squealed in pain and indignation. Then, throwing itself to the ground, it rolled over on top of the man. His ribcage gave way with a sickening bone-crack. Then, having rolled one way, the rat rolled back again, crushing the man a second time.

Racky lay on his back, face, arms and clothing bespattered with rat's blood. Thorn willed him to rise, but all Racky could do was lift one feeble hand. The rat got drunkenly to its feet. Its blue fur was matted with gore. Its right ear, severely torn in some previous encounter, hung down like a tattered flag. It took an unsteady step towards its erstwhile rider, then stood swaying uncertainly. Laying Jewel down again, Thorn picked up his bow, plucked an arrow from his quiver, moved to point-blank range and shot the beast through the eye.

With its one good eye, the rat squinnied at the human for a time as if to say, "I'm invincible. Haven't you heard? I can't believe you've done this." Then its legs buckled beneath it and it subsided on the ground with an unheroic sigh.

There was a shout behind Thorn. Twisting, he saw a party of Ratters making towards him. There were a dozen in the group. Branwell Rime was at their head; just behind came Briar Spurr. In leather fighting strip, she looked fiercely beautiful and alive to her fingertips.

In an instant the Headman sized the situation up.

"Deploy!" he barked out.

The Ratters fanned out in defensive formation. Bows nocked, they now covered the approaches from the brick-heap.

"What happened?" demanded Rime.

"Jewel's hurt," replied Thorn, unwilling to mention Querne Rasp. "We were attacked by rats. Racky – that's the man there – jumped on the big one's back. But it rolled over on top of him."

"Then, whoever he is, he's a dead man," said Rime. He waved a hand at the rat. "I know this beast: it's killed at least one of our people. But the girl: how is she?"

Jewel had rolled onto her side. "Help me up," she now said. "I feel groggy, but I'll live."

"Live, will you?" Rime exclaimed. He examined her scalp

with its caked blood. "By the look of the blow you've had, you should be no longer for this world."

Jewel grinned lopsidedly. "I'm not so easy to kill."

Three blue rats came bounding out of the gaps between the bricks. A salvo of arrows met them. Two of the animals fell dead; the other — stuck with arrows like a mobile pin-cushion — went hobbling off.

"We've got to get out of here," said Thorn, "before more rats arrive."

"Wait," said Jewel.

Though she felt good for nothing, she knelt beside Racky and laid her hands on his body. After a while she looked up at Thorn. "There's nothing I can do. He's much too badly hurt."

Briar pushed the girl aside. Racky's eyes were closed, but when — to Thorn's surprise — his mother stroked Racky's cheek, he opened them and looked at her.

"Berry Waters . . ." he said quietly. "What is this – a dream?"

"Hello, Racky," she replied.

"So you talk, too," he said.

"Hang on, Racky. We'll soon have you out of here."

Racky produced a croaky chuckle.

"Not alive you won't, Berry. I've no feeling in my legs. Meaning: my back's broke." He paused for breath, then went on, "Time has been kind to you, Berry, kinder than to me. Did you bribe it or, like everyone else, was it in love with you?" He grinned wryly. "Look at me: I'm a wreck." He stopped again, painfully dragging air into his lungs. Then his eyes went cold. "Why did you marry Davis Jack? You betrayed me, Berry. You should have married no one but me."

Briar regarded him steadily. "Why did you leave Norgreen, Racky? You should never have gone away."

Racky laughed again. "It's just like old times. I ask a question, you answer with one. Does nothing ever change?"

"Some things do," Briar murmured. As Thorn knelt by Racky's side, he saw tears in his mother's eyes.

Racky looked up at Thorn. "Goodbye, Thorn," he said. "We fought well, didn't we – today as the other days? Try to remember me for the good things I did, not the bad." He sucked in breath again. "And listen: if you love that girl of yours, stick to her. Don't go messing things up like me and your mother did."

Slowly his eyes closed.

Thorn grasped Racky's hand. It was cold, cold.

"Goodbye, Racky," he said. Then, responding to a prompting whose logic eluded him, "*Father*," he added.

Racky managed a faint smile.

Jewel hunkered down beside Thorn. "Racky," she demanded, "Querne Rasp: where can I find her?"

Racky's lips moved slightly but no words came from them.

Jewel placed her fingertips on the dying man's forehead. "Racky, this is important. You've got to answer me. *Querne: where can I find her?*"

Racky's eyes opened again and slowly focussed on the girl.

"Querne . . . bolt hole . . ." he said, then drifted away again.

"*Where?*" Jewel pressed him. "*Where?*"

"Church . . . Angel . . ." His voice was barely a murmur now. "Door . . . north aisle . . ." Racky's eyes now fixed on Thorn. His lips continued to move, but no audible sounds emerged.

"Racky, what is it?" asked Thorn.

"Pock – pock –" muttered Racky.

"Pocket? You want me to take something out of your pocket – is *that* it?"

Faintly, Racky gave a nod.

Thorn started to pat the pockets of Racky's jerkin one by one. "This pocket? This one?" he urged.

Third time lucky: another nod. Plunging his hand into the pocket, Thorn drew out a metal case three times as long as it was broad, its length the width of his hand. Its edges and corners were rounded off, and in one end a button was set, squarish and red, that its holder could press with his thumb.

"What is it?" demanded Thorn. "Is there something inside it?"

Vaguely Racky shook his head. Again he attempted to form words, but the only sounds that emerged from his lips were "I – I".

His eyes closed. Then, when Thorn and Jewel imagined he'd spoken his last words on Earth, his lips parted and he whispered, softly but perfectly audibly, "Down into Hell . . ."

Air came sighing from his chest in the gentlest of exhalations.

"He's gone," said Jewel to Thorn.

The young man moistened his lips.

The Headman, who was watching, said nothing for a time. What had passed between Racky and Briar might well have given him food for thought. But the man on the ground could not be a rival to anyone. Rime touched Thorn on the shoulder.

"Come on, we've got to move."

Thorn got to his feet. Already the object Racky had given him felt warm against his palm. It was lightweight; probably hollow. He pressed the button a few times, but even when he held it down nothing seemed to happen. Oh, well. Most likely it was some artefact, dating from the Dark Time, Racky had picked up on his travels, and useless now (though why Racky had given him this instead of the locket containing his mother's hair, Thorn could not have said). He stuffed it into a deep pocket.

Branwell Rime deputed two of the Blue Ratters to carry Racky. Dead comrades were abandoned only in desperate situations and this man, though unknown to him, rated as one such. In double quick time the party formed up and moved off.

Thorn travelled alongside Jewel, casting anxious glances at her. She was pale, but didn't complain. Once more, the Magian's rapid healing powers were serving her well. He'd seen, of course, that her pack had gone, so she couldn't have the crystal. What had occurred in the Great Nest? Had Querne taken the black stone? From the way Jewel had gone about questioning Racky, it looked that way. And now his old guide was dead. After betrayal on betrayal, he gave his life for me, thought Thorn. The great cynic, the unbeliever, the man who wore Punch's head . . . He surprised me at the last . . .

Thorn looked up at the stone chimney pointing its finger at the sky. The height above it was blue and clear, not a cloud to threaten the sun. Racky Jagger, thought Thorn: I never fathomed him while I knew him and maybe now I never will — however long I get to live.

As soon as they got back to the refuge, Jewel drew Thorn to one side.

"I've got to talk to you," she said.

But only when the two were alone in her cubicle did she speak.

"Querne has the black crystal," she said, then gave him a full account of what had happened, including her vision in the Great Nest and the conclusions she'd drawn from it.

Thorn listened calmly, showing not the least surprise. Inside, he felt, not so much excitement as a sense of completion. Here at last was the key that unlocked the final door upon the mystery of this world.

"My guess," Jewel finished, "is that Barrens are linked together like the threads of a spider's web – which is why, using the crystal, we could travel from one to another."

He nodded. "That makes sense. All of it does – or it would if my brain was big enough to hold it all. I don't think, if get the chance, I'll tell Manningham the truth. Human beings as information – and a giant, not God, responsible for the disaster? He'll never believe that." He paused, then went on, "Those shapes we saw in the Barrens: what do you think they were?"

"A sort of residue," she answered. "Traces, printed in the air, of the giants and the buildings that once existed there. Ghosts, if you like. The moving columns I saw the day I crossed Shelf Barrens with my father were the legs of people: they were simply walking about. As for the creature that jumped through me – I think it must have been some kind of pet animal. Small in giant terms, but a monster in ours. Its kind must have been wiped away along with the giants. But we're going to have to talk about all this another time. Thorn, we've got to go after Querne. She has four quincells now, including the most powerful one that's at the heart of the vortex effect. It's no longer just a question of what she'll do to Norgreen and the other settlements with the knowledge she gets from the crystals: if she tries to wield all four together she may lose control, just like this man Mayfield did, and cause a second disaster. She could destroy all that we know, simply wipe our race out as Mayfield wiped out the giants. This world may not be perfect, but it's the only one we've got."

Thorn pursed his lips. "I see that . . . but can you be sure? If she summons up the vortex, it might reverse the effect and put us back where we belong."

"I'm sorry to have to say this, but I very much doubt it. Think how damaged this world was when the vortex exploded: how damaged was ours? It might no longer be habitable. What's more, even if the giants got transported to our world, and even if somehow they've managed to survive there, I can't see any reason for the quincells to target them like they targeted us. They don't have Sybs or Magians, people with special abilities to attract their attention. And will one of the giants have put together another Mayfield Machine? I can't see it. As for Querne, something tells me that, as yet, she doesn't know the crystals brought disaster on the world. I think the crystals react to what they find in those who touch them. Like when Elphin touched my crystal in Harrypark and had her opening. Even if Querne wields the black crystal on its own, there's no guarantee that she'll see what I saw. I'm not Querne and she isn't me."

Thorn looked glum at this. Jewel was right. But it was no good hankering after what was impossible. After a time he said, "If I leave here right away, I'll miss Racky's burial. But I think I can trust my mother to oversee that. Racky, I'm sure, would be keen for me to do the right thing."

"I'm sure he would," Jewel agreed.

"Right," he said. "Let's grab our gear, say a quick round of goodbyes and be on our way."

12

IN THE MAUSOLEUM

When Thorn told Branwell Rime that he and Jewel had to leave, the Headman detailed an escort to take them clear of the ironworks. The first leg of their journey passed uneventfully. Not a rat was sighted.

Briar Spurr was one of the party. When they were through the shrubbery on the far side of the walled dam, it was time for mother and son to face one another again.

"Goodbye, Thorn," Briar said.

"Goodbye, Mother," Thorn replied.

Then, to his surprise, his mother opened her arms to him. Only for a moment did Thorn hesitate; then his own arms were round her, and mother and son embraced.

As they disengaged, Briar said, "Will you come back and see me, Thorn? I've no plans to leave this place."

"I'll be back," he promised her. "To see you – and Racky's grave."

She nodded. Then, with a brief exchange of waves, Thorn and Jewel were gone.

How different, Thorn thought, as the distance between him and his mother grew, was this second farewell from their parting at Minral How after Briar had unexpectedly handed over the brass key. She struck him as changed: no longer unbending, no longer coldly self-enclosed. More — yes, this was the word he wanted — *vulnerable*.

I may have lost two fathers, but I've got my mother back.

Then, in a chill wash of reality, came the thought: I may never see her again. Querne Rasp might see to that . . .

And Briar, fighting the blue rats . . . just how long would *she* survive in that deadly environment? And what on earth did his mother expect to gain by staying there? What could be more futile than the life she'd now embraced? Didn't rats have as much right to exist as humans did? There in the ruined ironworks they weren't threatening anyone; they were minding their own business. Why should humans make it *their* business to make war on them? Surely there were better things to do with your life.

But those better things Briar had thrown away, along with the softer, more yielding name she'd been given at birth. Only in one respect, thought Thorn, has she acknowledged the past and the claims it has on her: and that's me. She's as difficult to make out as Racky always was.

It was Jewel who caught sight of the tip of the church spire. There, capping it, was the telltale cross she'd first seen in her vision. Spotting a track that looked as though it would take them to the church, they turned along it. As the spire grew in size, Jewel and Thorn seemed to shrink, swallowed up by the taller patches of grass through which they walked. Thorn thought back to the disaster that had deprived his kind of its home world. I shall never feel other than an alien in this land . . .

The giant building had survived the years' toll pretty well. Here and there, on the roof and on the planes of the steeple, grey slates had split and parted company with their brethren; stretches of guttering had fallen, and tough grasses and plants had colonised crannies and holes. But the majority of the stained-glass windows appeared intact, the stonework looked as solid as ever, and the spire, rising above the west end of the church, jabbed at the blue vault of Heaven, a symbol of spiritual yearnings that had outlived the race of people who'd conceived and erected it.

Jewel and Thorn had a plan of action. Introduce themselves as friends of Manningham Sparks and get inside. Gain time by expressing interest in joining the cult. Locate the door Racky had mentioned. Slip away as soon as they could, go through the door and then, well, down into Hell – as Racky, dramatic in his dying as in his living, had ominously described whatever lay underground.

High, spike-topped iron railings had once enclosed the churchyard. Whole stretches of these had collapsed, to be swallowed by grass and wild flowers, but remnants still stood here and there – stood or leant, ready to fall. Long denied paint, they were extravagantly eroded. Many uprights had rusted through, and what was left jagged downwards or jabbed upwards, forlornly pointing to where the absent parts of their limbs had once appeared. Beyond, trees and bushes lifted themselves to various heights and, above the lowest growths, the tips of stone statues and monuments could be seen.

As Jewel and Thorn neared the railings, these stone objects were lost to sight. The track led into thick scrub, then to a break in the fencing; and they were in the churchyard.

Ground level was an entanglement, a carnival of green. Ivy and other creepers clawed at the scattered, blackened tombstones as if they'd like nothing better than to drag them to earth. Ivy's suckered, springy stems had conquered some of the slabs, clothing the stone with spade-bladed, darkly-lacquered leaves.

There was barely a trail here – or the travellers had mislaid it. They fought through a patch of scabious, its air-blue blossoms bobbing on slender stems, and a clutch of winged beetles backed in shiny olive plates shot up all around them, buzzing and fussing like a flock of angry gems. Next came a fallen gravestone. As Jewel glanced across its surface, her heart leapt in her breast. But it was only a scab-skinned toad that squatted there. It had no interest in these humans; its green eyes blinked dreamily in their distended attics.

Beyond the gravestone rose a rail-fenced tomb. Inside rust-peeled railings, a huge headstone stuck up from the ground. Sculpted with sprays of leaves and flowers and podgy, stubby-winged infants, it was topped by a man's head. His flowing tresses were intact, but time had not been kind to him: it had gnawed off his nose.

The church wall loomed ever nearer, beetling over them with all the menace of a barrier built across the end of the world. They stepped out at last onto a paved, well-kept pathway. Someone here, at least, was winning the battle against the weeds.

But which way to go? As they debated this question, a man came hurrying into view. He closed on them, and Jewel and Thorn saw he was young – early twenties, at a guess. He had sparse, flyaway hair, a frog-trap instead of a mouth, and a nose and ears purloined from a face not his own. Except that it *was* his own, of course. He stumbled to a halt, breathing heavily, and gasped, "Have you seen Manningham Sparks?"

Jewel and Thorn exchanged glances. Then Thorn said, "Why do you ask?"

Only now did it seem to strike the man that he hadn't the least idea who these two youngsters were. "Manningham's a friend of mine. I'm worried about him," he explained.

He seems genuine, thought Thorn. Then something clicked in his mind. "Are you the ratman – Fleck Something?"

"Fleck Dewhurst, that's me. But how—"

Jewel cut him short. "Manningham mentioned your name. He's our friend too. We last saw him early this morning. Why are you worried about him?"

"I've just been told at the church that Warty Chapman's looking for him. Warty has three unsavoury types in tow. Lowmoor bruisers – ironworkers probably. Manningham went for a walk. If they've grabbed hold of him . . ."

"Right. Which way would he go?"

"I've a pretty good idea. I've walked with him a couple of times. He usually goes the same way."

Thorn unshouldered his bow. "What are we waiting for, then?"

But Fleck was still sizing them up. Jewel saw what he was thinking: that if it came to a pitched battle against Warty and three thugs, he and a couple of teenagers wouldn't stand a chance.

"You don't have to worry about us," she reassured him. "Thorn and I can take care of ourselves."

"And anyway," added Thorn, who'd also read the ratman's look, "exactly how were *you* going to tackle four of them?"

Plainly Fleck hadn't given much thought to this question. Correction: no thought at all.

"Erm . . . um . . ." he vacillated.

"*Which way?*" demanded Thorn.

"Follow me," said the ratman, and set off at a trot.

The path hugged the church wall, cornering when the wall cornered, but several yards beyond the corner Fleck stepped off the pathway and struck out along a scarcely-marked trail through the undergrowth.

"See that angel?" He waved a hand.

Yes, Jewel and Thorn saw her.

"Manningham loves that angel. She's the reason he comes this way. Says she reminds him of his mother."

The angel posed on a pedestal on the far side of a gravestone whose inscription was scribbled over by bright-yellow lichen. She had to be fully seven feet tall. Wings sprouted from her shoulders, but she still contrived to be dressed in an ankle-length shift. Eyes closed, her face beatified by a half-smile, she held her hands steepled in prayer. To her rear, as dark as she was bright, stood a mausoleum — a grime-encrusted, windowless house of the dead with a central door. Yews crowded this grim building, overhanging its pitched roof of cracked and mossed grey slates, lending the scene an air of doom-laden menace. So contorted were the yews it was impossible to say just how many trees there were. Perhaps there was only one, and it had ramified and spread with a view to claiming this region of the church-yard as its own.

The trail became a corridor: vegetation had been trampled down or pushed to one side: a rabbit run? It was more of a tunnel, in fact, since some way above the three humans, dandelions bent their sleepy heads towards one another, as if attempting to kiss.

Thorn drew an arrow from his quiver, quickly nocked it and, holding the weapon at his waist, followed Fleck down the tunnel. Jewel brought up the rear. Dense greenery closed round them, hiding the angel from view.

They advanced carefully, but nothing could stop the stalks on which they trod from squelching or crackling. It was hot in here, too; the world seemed locked in an afternoon drowse. Till, without warning, something burst out of cover. Jewel jerked backwards, raising a hand to fend it off as the creature zoomed towards her face. At the last moment it sheered off and went fluttering away, a wingtip dusting her hair.

"Did you see it?" she whispered, shaken. "It had a skull on its body . . ."

Thorn grinned. "A death moth. Harmless. This *is* a churchyard!"

"Humph!" muttered Jewel, unimpressed by his lack of sympathy, and on they all went.

Jewel, her senses sharpened by her encounter, kept a lookout for more moths, but no more of the creatures popped up to startle her. The atmosphere of drowsy heatedness resumed its sway. This is a day, she thought, for lying about, sunning yourself and dreaming, not for stalking villains through a Dark Time burial ground.

Now, on their right, appeared a featureless wall – the edge of a block of whitish stone some eight inches in height and a couple of feet in length. This was one side of the angel's pedestal, for, looking up, they could see the figure's elbow and the downward curve of a wing, both projecting beyond the stone. The track made a turn at the corner of the block, and the stone continued on their right until, perhaps halfway along, the track meandered off to the left.

A shadow fell over them. They must be close to the mausoleum that stood to the rear of the angel. And yes, there – rearing above a mess of vegetation – were its soot-blackened stones.

They twisted and turned with the track, then came out into the open. The area fronting the mausoleum was paved with flagstones, and in the crevices between them tufts of wiry grass and knots of daisies stuck up. The building's designer, thought Thorn, must have been half in love with death. Above the heavy stone lintel protruded a matching pair of corbels, and on these sat leering gargoyles, their malevolent faces half animal, half human. The thick posts that upheld the lintel were carved alternately with lizards and symbols. The symbols meant nothing to him. The ironbound door that had closed off this vault now sagged askew from a single hinge, and there was nothing to stop the curious from venturing inside.

The atmosphere here seemed burdened and ominous – as taut as the half-drawn string of Thorn's bow. He became aware of his every breath; the beating of his heart hung on the brink of audibility – as if, with only a slight increase of intensity, that organ might start to boom.

There came a scream from the mausoleum, muffled somewhat by the vault.

"It's Manningham," whispered Thorn. "They must be torturing him."

Jewel nodded. "That kind man . . ." Her facial skin seemed to tighten, ageing her by five years. She turned to Fleck. "*You:* stay here, out of sight."

Fleck looked at her wide-eyed. "But—" he began.

"You heard what I said."

"Erm, right you are," he faltered. The girl's eyes were cold as ice, her voice as hard as diamond. All at once, she near frightened the pants off of him.

He watched his two companions go padding across the flagstones and pause in the lee of the broken door. As Thorn unslung his pack in order to free himself for action, "Wait," Jewel said. "You've got a coil of rope in there?"

"Yes, why?"

"Give it to me, Thorn."

When the rope was in her hands, she said sternly, "I'm ready."

Right at that moment, voices came to their ears. One was shouting.

"How many more times must I tell you? I don't know where they went. And if I did I wouldn't tell you. I'm a man of the cloth. I've lived by my word and I shall die by my word."

"You old fool," said a harsh voice. "If dying's your fancy, you've found exactly the right man."

"I didn't," said Manningham boldly. "It was you that found me."

Sounds of a brutally-slapped face: once, twice, a third time. Then a third voice broke in – a voice they'd once heard in a Lowmoor tavern. It was nervous to say the least.

199

"Look here, Raven," Warty Chapman faltered, "I do believe he doesn't know. He's a man of some reputation."

"Reputation?" said the harsh-voiced Raven. "Reputation? His reputation with me is that of an idiot. This maundering, blubber-gutted, knock-kneed black-hatter knows exactly where they are, and I swear by his God I'll have the truth out of him if I have to hack the fat toes off his feet one by one."

"That's what you think," muttered Thorn.

Stepping round the edge of the door, he took half a dozen steps, planted his feet, aimed and fired. Jewel, at his shoulder, took in the scene inside the vault. Some four feet away, his arms and legs bound, Manningham Sparks lay on the floor. Two of the men held him down. A third knelt at his side, a thin knife in his hand. Warty Chapman stood nearby, looking distinctly uncomfortable. But even as Jewel registered this, the man with the knife fell back, Thorn's arrow protruding from his ear.

The three remaining men gaped at the fallen Raven, then turned towards the door.

"It's them!" shouted Warty.

Then the other two men were on their feet and running towards them, bellowing curses and pulling knives from their belts. Thorn let fly with a second arrow, but the man at whom he'd fired side-stepped, the arrow missed him and, coming to ground, went skidding along the stone floor.

There was no time for a third shot. Thorn dropped his bow and drew his knife.

The men were less than a foot away when Jewel threw the rope. Coiled when it left her hand, it unwound as it flew. The men were almost shoulder to shoulder when the rope struck them and wrapped itself round their necks. Tightening like a flying snake, it yanked each towards the other. Their heads met with a sharp crack and they collapsed in a heap, knives clattering to the stone. Dazed but still conscious, they pulled at the rope in an attempt to free themselves, but the efforts of one merely caused the other to gasp. As coil added itself to coil, their gasps turned to gurgles and then to sounds of choking.

Jewel stood over them, eyes glittering balefully, a girl become a demon, watching their final, pitiful scrabblings.

"They're strangling," Thorn said, appalled.

"You shot Raven," she retorted. "Anything you can do . . ."

Four scrabbling hands went limp. The men's eyes bulged in their sockets, starred red where veins had burst.

Jewel looked towards Warty Chapman. The late Abner Fairfax's unconvincing nose was edging along, back to the wall – no doubt in hope to get past them, reach the doorway and flee. Abject terror was in his eyes.

Jewel walked towards him. Warty shrank against the wall.

"No, please . . . please," he wailed, "I didn't want to come after you, but my new masters made me. And hurting Sparks was Raven's idea."

Jewel pointed a finger at the bridge of Warty's nose.

"Your new masters?" she asked.

"Mabbutt and Slack," he gabbled. "The old Council's dead or disbanded. Mabbutt and Slack are running things."

"So you've switched allegiances – easy as winking. Yes?"

Warty was sweating profusely. He nodded in reply. Jewel jabbed his brow with her fingertip. Warty screamed.

"Let him go," said a voice.

Keeping her hand high, Jewel glanced over her shoulder.

Manningham Sparks had rolled onto his side and was looking at her. His face was streaked with blood.

"Let him go," he said again. "Chapman's not an evil man."

"Not all those who do evil things are evil men."

"Please, Jewel Ranson, spare Chapman for my sake."

Jewel gazed at her captive and wrinkled her nose. The stench of fear that came off him was worse than a dung-heap.

"I think you know me now," she said. "If you cross me again I *will* kill you. Be sure of that."

One again she touched his head and once again Warty screamed. Then she let her hand drop.

Shaking, gibbering and tearful, Warty slid to the floor. A vivid red spot burnt on the pink skin of his forehead. He might have been trying to express his heartfelt thanks, but Jewel already was walking away. Reaching the helpless Ranter's side, she knelt down beside him and touched a finger to the cords that bound his wrists. It was the selfsame finger that had tormented Warty Chapman. The cord parted, its threads burnt clean through. Then she freed his legs. Manningham made to sit up.

"Lie still," she said harshly. "I'll tend to your wounds."

The Ranter did as he was bid, his eyes searching her face. Thorn stood by, saying nothing.

His voice trembling in the vault, Manningham Sparks said to Jewel, "You're a Magian, aren't you? No one but a Magian could do the things you do."

Jewel did not reply. Deep in the vault's gloomy recesses, shelf on shelf of stone coffins cradled the skeletons of giants – white bones amid the dust . . . In the air hung the must-laden perfume of decay. Jewel's hands moved over the Ranter, closing the wounds Raven had made.

"Why do you kill?" he asked. "You have the power of healing in you."

Still Jewel said nothing. The Ranter tried again. "Don't you know God hates human pain and those who inflict pain?"

"If God made the world, God made pain," she replied. "But right now it isn't God that's healing your wounds."

"Yes it is," retorted the preacher, his voice stronger now. "The person that's healing me is the God within you."

Jewel laughed. "If I've got God inside me, then the Devil's in there with Him!"

Manningham, shocked, opened his mouth to say something, then thought better of it. A little later he said quietly, "I shall pray for you."

Jewel made no reply.

When they'd helped him to his feet, he ran his hands down his body, touching the scars of his wounds with a sense of wonder.

"I'm grateful to you both," he said. "Thorn, this is the second time you've come to my rescue."

Thorn smiled. "Let's hope there isn't a third. But it was our fault, Manningham, you found yourself in this fix. You should have told them where we were."

"I couldn't do that," said the Ranter. "God was watching me. What would He have thought?"

"What indeed?" said Jewel.

Manningham said, "How did you know where I was?"

203

"Fleck Dewhurst's outside. We happened to meet in the churchyard. He was worried about you."

"He's a good lad, is Fleck."

"Listen, Manningham," said Jewel, sounding more her normal self now, "Fleck's waiting outside. Not a word to him or anyone else about my being a Magian. Better still, swear him to secrecy about what happened here."

"Of course, if that's what you want."

"That's what I want – what *we* want," Jewel corrected, to take in Thorn. "And it's not all we want." She smiled sweetly at the preacher.

"Only ask, and it shall be given. But what are you doing here? This is the last place I'd have expected to see you."

"Yesterday *we* didn't expect to fetch up here either. Still, here we are. Listen, Ranter Sparks: we need to get inside the church. It could be a matter of life and death – many lives, many deaths. Will you help us to do that?"

"A matter of life and death? Are you serious?"

"We are –" this from Thorn "– but don't ask us to explain."

"How very mysterious," said the Reverend Manningham Sparks. "What exciting lives you live. Well, you can count on me. Tell me what you want me to do."

13

THE CHURCH OF THE
IRON ANGEL

"Manningham?" said Fleck as soon as the Ranter emerged from the mausoleum. "You all right?"

"Never better," answered Sparks, clapping the ratman on the back.

"But you screamed," Fleck objected.

Were those smears of blood that he could see on Manningham's face? He shot enquiring looks first at Jewel, then at Thorn, but the pair remained silent.

Warty Chapman had been ordered to stay in the vault until they'd gone, then to clear out of the churchyard and not come back again – ever. He'd been happy to comply.

"I don't get it," Fleck persisted. "Where are Chapman and his thugs?"

"Taking a well-earned rest," said the Ranter, with an arch look at Jewel, surprising the girl by this flash of black humour. "Fleck, it would be best if you forgot all about them. Also if you kept away from this place after today. Just forget the vault exists."

"Forget it?" queried the ratman, as if he couldn't believe his ears.

"That's what Ranter Sparks said," Jewel chimed in. "And it's very good advice. This is a bad place, Fleck, and bad things happen in bad places."

"Er, right," Fleck agreed. He couldn't fault her reasoning.

"Now that's settled, let's be off." And putting an arm round Fleck's shoulders, the Ranter propelled the ratman across the flagstones towards the track.

Fleck glanced back at the mausoleum. He was reluctant to leave the scene, but something told him opposing Jewel would be a very bad idea. Moments later the four of them were threading the tunnel through the greenery.

"So, Fleck," puffed the Ranter, as he deftly eased his bulk around the spiky fronds of a thistle, "you've met my friends Thorn and Jewel?" He might have been picking up the threads of an agreeable conversation that had suffered nothing more than a brief, trivial interruption.

"Well, yes, but I can't say we've been properly introduced."

"How irregular. Still, you know their names now, so you can bypass the handshakes. Let me tell you why they're here. Mr Jack and Miss Ranson are keen to meet Higgins Makepeace and hear the Grand Ranter preach. His fame and that of the Iron Angel have spread far and wide, and Jewel and Thorn are giving serious consideration to joining the Church."

"Is that right?" Fleck Dewhurst sounded less than convinced.

"So they say, and who am I to cast doubts on their commitment?"

Manningham, thought Jewel, would have made a fine hypocrite if his calling hadn't driven him in a different direction.

"Yes," she said; then, injecting into her voice what she hoped didn't sound like a wholly fake enthusiasm, went on, "Thorn and I are both deeply interested in religion, and the Church of the Iron Angel may be just what we're looking for. Manningham tells us you're a valued member of the group here, so who better than you to introduce us to your leader? Just for a short visit, at first, so we can get the feel of things."

Valued member of the group? More like its general drudge, thought Fleck, and suspected that the girl was soft-soaping him. But she and Thorn had got his friend out of a hole; so he thought he ought to give her the benefit of the doubt. "Fair enough," he replied. "I can't see anything wrong with that." Implying, perhaps, that *seeing* was one thing, and *knowing* was something else. If Jewel and Thorn had a secret reason for coming here, it was beyond his fathoming.

The paved path they'd trodden earlier took them along the church walls and past Fleck's rattery. It was a fairly small structure, with only three resident adults and a litter of four kittens, but Fleck explained that a large part of his job was tending the carriage-rats and saddle-rats that brought non-resident cultists to the church for services. As it happened, he added, a meeting had been arranged for the following afternoon, when the cult's resident members would be swelled by many followers who lived in settlements. It promised to be a momentous assembly — perhaps the most important in the history of the sect. Grand Ranter Makepeace (Fleck spoke his leader's name with respect) was also preaching later today, but this would be a small-scale, more intimate gathering, a sort of limbering-up for the main event.

The side entry into the church, a weather-bleached oak door, was set in a stone-flagged porch. A child might have squeezed through the gap that yawned between door and floor, but a door of human dimensions had been hung in one corner. Fleck lifted the latch and they entered.

Just inside at a table sat a young man with a spotty face and eyebrows so faint as to be almost non-existent. He cast suspicious looks at them, his hand hovering close to a bell-pull that, if he gave it a tug, would doubtless summon reinforcements. On seeing Fleck and the Ranter, however, he let his hand drop.

Fleck gestured at Jewel and Thorn.

"Friends of the Reverend," he explained. "They're thinking of joining us."

The young man nodded gravely, as if this was no more than the Church's due. "Go on through," he said. He didn't move from his chair.

"This room is the vestibule," Fleck informed the newcomers, as they did as they were invited.

A pointed archway lay ahead, its great door wedged open – as it must always have been, for had it originally been shut no human could have opened it. Passing under the archway, Jewel and Thorn were drenched in diagonal shafts of rainbow light. Massive and high above them, the windows of the church were made of countless pieces of glass of every imaginable colour. Each mote of dust irradiated in the sun's spears seemed to sparkle like a separate and joyful living being, and Thorn was almost persuaded that if he reached out a hand he could grab a rich fistful of these bright particles.

As the four floated along, bodies rinsed in brilliance, Fleck explained that this part of the church was the south transept.

"There's a transept on each side. They're like stubby little arms on the main body of the church: *that*'s known as the nave."

Jewel looked at the ratman with a newfound respect. *Nave, transept, vestibule* . . . these were terms unknown to her. "How come you know such wonderful, ancient words, Mr Dewhurst?"

"Please call me Fleck, Miss Ranson."

"All right – but you must call me Jewel," she replied.

Fleck blushed. "Well Miss, er Jewel, I've this friend . . . He can read books, he knows lots of things, things that belonged to the Dark Time, things even Grand Ranter Makepeace doesn't know. The pity is, my friend doesn't believe in God, he's – I've got to say it – a heathen. But I live in hope that one day he'll come to see the light . . . And there's no light like the light you get in here," he added, waving a primrose-yellow, then lilac arm in the dust-glitter.

"What's your friend's name?" asked Jewel.

"Racky Jagger," Fleck replied.

Racky! thought Thorn. Even in death he's still alive . . . alive in Fleck, alive in me – alive for sure in my mother . . .

His eyes sought out Jewel's, and they exchanged muted signals. It seemed the wrong time to tell Fleck that Racky was dead.

They passed into the nave where their eyes, drawn by a double row of mottled pillars, were snatched aloft towards the vaulting: there, arching, riblike beams met at the angle of the roof-ridge. Jewel and Thorn stopped as one. So stirred were their hearts by the splendour of the sight that, for a time, neither could speak. They felt humbled, like children drawn for the first time into a realm of adult ritual beyond their experience.

Manningham Sparks stood by, smiling.

"Tremendous, isn't it?" said Fleck, his voice dipping like an oar-blade into the liquid silence. "I know exactly what you're feeling – I've felt it many times myself, though never quite as strongly as on the day I first saw it. I thought then there was nothing on earth so wonderful as this place, and nothing has happened since to make me change my mind. The giants knew how to shake your soul, and here's the proof."

Thorn and Jewel looked about them, confronted everywhere with mysterious structures. On the left, Thorn saw banks of brown seating extending across the nave. They were broken midway by an aisle. The far end of the building seemed an awfully long way off: how many giants might have gathered here to pray?

On the right, Jewel was gazing up at a massive wooden structure.

"What's that, Fleck?" she asked.

"That's the pulpit. Racky says it's where the giants' minister – their Ranter – stood to preach. Steps lead up from the other side. From up there he'd be able to look down on the congregation. When we go on a bit further, you'll see a human-sized pulpit Grand Ranter Makepeace uses. It was modelled on that big one."

Leaving the pulpit behind, they started across the broad space that separated the rows of brown seating from the rectangular area to their right – obviously the business end of the church ("The chancel," helpful Fleck supplied). Set in the far wall of this area was a huge arched window of coloured glass. This was symmetrically divided into sections of different sizes. The smaller ones held abstract patterns, but the larger ones showed human figures engaged in significant encounters. In one scene a tall figure possessed of golden hair and folded wings (another angel, presumably) was addressing a crowd of bemused people and pointing out beyond the frame. On another a pale, bearded figure sagged from a wooden cross, nails through his hands and feet, a ring of thorns on his head and a bloodstained gash in his side. Presumably these pictures had meant something to the giants. Now they were incomprehensible. Below the window stood a huge wooden table ("That's the altar"); on it a pair of tall candlesticks, their metal blackened with age, flanked an ornate brass cross, again with a figure dangling from it. Cross and candlesticks were strung together with cobwebs.

On the left-hand side of the space were three brown rows of seats, the rearmost high-backed and set flush against the wall. The opposite wall was dominated by a huge inverted chevron composed of close-set honey-gold tubes of varying thicknesses.

Abruptly, from the coloured window, sound and movement came. There must, Thorn thought, be a hole there somewhere, for a fat grey bird now came flapping away from it, wings strenuously working. As the bird passed over the humans, three heads turned in unison to trace its erratic flight. The bird rose, soaring almost to the height of the roof-ridge, but as it moved further away it shrank in size and was lost to sight.

"A dove," Fleck pronounced. "They roost on ledges and cornices and crap on everything. Ranter Makepeace has tried to poison them, but they're pretty wily creatures and, as you see, they're still here. There are bats in the steeple, too – but they only come out at night."

They moved on, and Jewel and Thorn now turned their attentions to the more human-sized arrangements midway across the church. Here, set out in a semicircle, were several rows of chairs – enough to accommodate perhaps sixty people. Here too was the pulpit to which the ratman had referred. Viewed elsewhere, it might, thought Thorn, have been a quite impressive structure, but the original they'd passed still bulked formidably in his mind, and this imitation struck him as almost pathetically small.

Not so, however, the object a little way behind the pulpit.

The trio drew level with it and stopped. Fleck stood without speaking, observing Jewel and Thorn as they considered what might be supposed to have brought them to the church.

The Iron Angel was a mere three feet tall – around six times Thorn's height. In a church of giant dimensions, it – he? – might have amounted to a negligible presence. But such was not the case. Neither Jewel nor Thorn could drag their eyes away – even though the thing appalled them.

Later, thinking about the impact that the Angel made on her, Jewel would come to the conclusion that although the church was majestic in its size, decoration and architecture, these very qualities gave it an air of remoteness, a quality of otherness. By contrast, the effigy, standing down here on the floor – where you might, if you were so minded, reach out and touch it (though neither she nor Thorn did) – had seemed to speak directly to her. To speak – or to cry out. For the Angel was a creation of torn and tortured metal. True, it suggested nothing so much as a human shape, but no such human as it might be thought to portray had ever lived or could live. It had a body and a head, two arms and two legs (if you were minded to interpret those shapes with some freedom), but at the same time it was made of rents and spikes and jagged edges. Inhuman in a different way were the scalloped flanges of iron that spread out from its shoulders like a pair of ungainly wings.

All these things were there to be seen. But what people remembered most when, in the effigy's absence, they pictured the Angel, was the look upon its face. Quite how its face expressed what it expressed no one could say, for those bent and twisted strips and plates of metal ought not to have been capable of expressing anything. Yet they spoke, and eloquently. This was a face that pitiless torture had failed to drain of pity. Its slack mouth and distorted, hollowed-out eye-sockets still managed to seem beseeching, as if imploring the viewer to weep not only for this winged and outcast being in its torment, but for a world which permitted such suffering to exist.

As Jewel and Thorn gazed, they heard the sound of footsteps. Turning, they saw a group of people hastening towards them. At their head, his mane of white hair streaming behind him, was a man whose face seemed chiselled out of a chunk of pale stone.

He halted inches away, and his retinue of four – three young men and one woman, none more than three or four years older than Thorn – drew up smartly behind him.

"Ranter Sparks," said Higgins Makepeace, "you are, as always, welcome here . . . though I could wish that you were with us as much in spirit as in body."

Manningham said, "God, as you know, has my spirit in his keeping: it isn't mine to dispose of."

"Quite so, quite so."

Then came a period of silence as the Grand Ranter's eyes dwelt in succession on Jewel and Thorn.

And what eyes! Deep-sunk between a jutting brow and prominent cheekbones, they seemed to burn with blue fire.

Higgins Makepeace, Thorn realised, was staring at his shoulder. My bow, he thought, made of the same stuff as the Angel . . . Fleck of course had noticed it, and he'd said nothing about it, but perhaps the Grand Ranter disapproved of weapons – especially in his church.

Fleck Dewhurst began to speak. "Grand Ranter, these two young people—"

But Higgins Makepeace cut him short. "I know what brings them here, Fleck."

I hope you don't, thought Thorn.

Sweeping an arm towards the effigy, the Grand Ranter declared, "*He* has brought you here! Am I not right? *Am I not right?*"

His voice could have punched nails into stone.

Thorn said, "Well, yes, I suppose so. Him – and you, Grand Ranter."

"Him and me . . . But I – I am merely the servant of the Word. I am nothing. I am *less* than nothing. But he – he is *everything.*"

This ringing declaration seemed to vibrate through the dust that drifted in the atmosphere.

"You worship him then?" said Jewel.

The Grand Ranter laughed – a laugh that might have shrivelled a leaf. "How little, child, you understand!" He paused, then went on, "But how could you understand? Understanding begins here. That is what you have come for. Am I not right? *Am I not right?*"

"Yes," Jewel answered, feeling browbeaten already but willing to play along. "Yes – you are right."

Higgins Makepeace smiled, a smile of fierce benevolence, a smile cut from a wintry crag.

He's mad, Jewel thought. But he's an impressive madman.

The Grand Ranter said, "Where are you from? What are your names?"

"We're from Norgreen," said Thorn. "My name is Thorn Jack. My friend's name is Jewel Ranson."

Higgins Makepeace swivelled to face his four disciples. "Behold, my friends, how far word of us spreads!"

There came a chorus of approval from the four followers.

"Norgreen!" repeated Makepeace with obvious satisfaction. "You are the first to come to us from that particular settlement."

"The Iron Angel," said Thorn, "is a name on every settler's lips."

This was such a blatant lie that for a moment Thorn himself thought: Damn! I've gone too far – he's bound to see right through me!

Makepeace smiled indulgently.

"What you have to understand is that the Iron Angel, wonderful as he is, is an image, a thing of earth – a representation, in fact. What he represents is an idea, a truth, a *way*. *Those* are the things that matter. Likewise, these bodies in which our divine spirits are clad are no more than passing rags. It is our *souls* that are eternal."

"How right you are," said Thorn. "That's exactly what we wanted to hear, isn't it Jewel?"

Jewel thought Thorn was laying it on a bit thick. She said, "Your words are inspiring, Grand Ranter. But tell me, please, who made the Iron Angel? How did he come to exist?"

"I will tell you what I tell all those who come to my Church. Some five years ago, I had no inkling of the role that God had — in His infinite wisdom and mercy — ordained for me. At such a low point was my life that I will readily confess to you I seriously considered putting an end to myself. Then one rainy, windswept night, desperately seeking shelter and at the end of my tether, I happened to stumble upon this church. The outer door — which was then just as you see it is today — was ajar, and in I came. There was a full moon that night, though I'd seen precious little of it, but as I stumbled in the darkness, the moon came out from behind the clouds and fired its beams through the windows, kindly lighting my way. So I came on, past the great pulpit, looking for a spot to lay my head. The moonlight suddenly disappeared, a patch of cloud must have covered the moon, and I stood for a time in pitch-darkness. Then the light was back again, but it was a very curious light. The church at large was massive and dark. Only a single area, this very space on which we stand, was lit, and with an almost unearthly glow. It revealed the strangest sight I'd clapped eyes on in my life.

"Here stood the Iron Angel, bathed in a pastel radiance. He was enclosed in scaffolding, and in the scaffolding were plank floors linked together by ladders. And down on the ground were heaps of metal – the raw materials of his making – and scattered on tables were various tools. I came towards the Angel, and then, through the scaffolding, his face looked down on me. And in that moment a shock went through me and my life was transformed. I knew what this pitiful vision meant. I knew he was waiting here for me – yes, for *me*! – to speak for him. *I was the chosen one!*"

The last sentence was uttered with a thrill. Then Higgins Makepeace paused and scrutinised Jewel and Thorn, doubtless to gauge the impression his story was making on them. Seemingly content with what he saw, he went on.

"Just then I heard a groan. Turning away from the Iron Angel, I noticed an armchair set on the far side of the table. Slumped in it was a man. Walking up to him I saw that a knife lay on the floor by his feet. His arms drooped over the arms of the chair, and his hands were red with blood. Blood had run from his slashed wrists and dripped to form puddles on the floor. His eyes were closed. Surely he must be dead. I reached out and touched his cheek. His eyes opened and he looked at me.

"'So, you have come,' he said.

"'Yes, I have come,' I replied. 'But why – why have you done this?'

"He smiled vaguely. 'It was ordained. My work is finished, and so am I. I am flying with my Angel. It is sweet, so very sweet . . .'

"At that moment I realised that *Angel* was the name of the sculpture and that this man had created it. Suddenly, with a strength that took me utterly by surprise, his bloodstained hand gripped my arm. His eyes burnt with a feverish light.

"'Have you seen him?' he asked.

"'Yes,' I said, understanding perfectly, 'I've seen him.'

"'And do you understand?'

"'Yes,' I said, 'I understand.'

"This assurance quietened him. His grip on my arm relaxed. He said, 'It was ordained that you would come. You are the chosen one. Bury me in the churchyard.'

"'What is your name?' I asked.

"But in that instant his head slumped sideways: he was dead. I reached up and closed his eyes. Next morning I buried his body. And so began my Rantership. And so it continues to this day."

The conclusion of this story was greeted by murmurs of approval from the four followers. But if what the Grand Ranter had said had answered one question, it had posed many others.

Thorn said, "But what was it you saw when you first looked on the Angel? What had his maker seen? What did he mean by flying with the Angel?"

Higgins Makepeace smiled. "You ask many questions, Thorn Jack, and I shall not answer them now. But I am to preach this afternoon and, to those who have ears to listen, all will be made plain. Then you shall hear the necessary truths that rule our world, and your thirst shall be quenched." He paused. "In the meantime, come with us, and observe how we live."

"We were hoping," said Jewel, "to have a look round the church. Neither of us has ever seen such a building before."

"Nor will you see its like elsewhere. God preserved this edifice for one purpose and one only, and that purpose is the Church of the Iron Angel. As for looking around, you may, and my friends will be glad to escort you."

His eyes bored into Jewel.

I see, she thought: we're not to be trusted. And if we're sur-rounded by cult members, we shan't be able to slip away. Not just yet, at any rate . . .

"That will suit us fine," she said.

"Good. Now, come this way."

And turning on his heel, he set off in the direction from which he'd first come. Fleck Dewhurst gave Thorn and Jewel a goodbye wave, then walked away towards the door. The four followers formed up around the new arrivals and off the seven of them went, dutifully treading in the Grand Ranter's wake.

He led them into the far transept, as Fleck had taught them to call it, and through a door within a door set in an arched opening.

This room, back in the Dark Time, must have been where giant Ranters prepared themselves for services. Here stood an ancient table and a glass-fronted cupboard in which a variety of ceremonial objects stood patiently on shelves, as if waiting for their owners to return and put them to work. They included large, tarnished cups with ear-shaped handles, a stack of metal dishes and a smallish crucifix. A picture – painted presumably on a religious theme – had once brightened one wall, but rot and insects over time had played merry hell with it and all that now remained was the frame, still on its hook, from which a few sad tatters of material straggled down.

At floor level, however, the room told a different story, a story of human dimensions. Off to one side stood a trio of long tables. One was in the process of being set for a meal by a couple of cult members. Beyond, at the edge of the room, cooking was in progress: over a fire in a stone hearth constructed beneath a soot-blackened chimney flue original to the church a couple of metal pots were set, one of which a middle-aged woman was stirring with a long-handled spoon. Grey smoke drifted up and disappeared into the flue. In Thorn's eyes, the whole set-up formed a curious variation on the Blue Ratters' refuge.

The Grand Ranter paused by the half-laid table and looked on with approval as the work continued. Then he motioned to two of those who still encircled Jewel and Thorn.

"Thomas . . . Josy . . . show our guests where they can leave their packs. Then show them around, will you? They will be joining us for our meal and, after that, attending the preaching."

"Yes, Grand Ranter," replied the pair, as if in a single breath.

"And you, Ranter Sparks, I take it you will also be there?"

"I wouldn't miss it for anything," Manningham said with a straight face.

Higgins Makepeace frowned, then turned and strode off. The two unnamed disciples followed, as if tied to him by rope.

"I'll see you later," Manningham now said to Jewel and Thorn. "Enjoy your sight-seeing tour."

And he too moved away.

Thomas and Josy had similar soft features, not handsome, but not ugly. They looked somehow unfinished, as if life so far had slipped by without marking them. An air of serenity seemed to play about their heads.

They're brother and sister, Jewel saw: but no, they're not twins. Thomas was the older; perhaps eighteen or nineteen.

Their similarity, she thought, went beyond physical likeness: it stemmed partly from their beliefs, from the way that they lived.

Thomas announced, "You can put your packs in the dormitories."

"I think," said Jewel firmly, "we'd like to keep them with us for now – until we decide if we're going to stay."

To be separated from their packs would pose an unwanted problem when the chance came to slip away.

"As you wish," Thomas replied. If he disapproved of what Jewel had just said, he didn't show it.

"But," said Jewel brightly, "we'd love to see the dormitories."

"This way, then," Thomas replied.

The dormitories were separated from the dining room and kitchen by wooden partitions. There was one for the men and one for the women. Each contained two rows of beds, some neatly made, others stripped bare. Identical cupboards filled the spaces between the bed-heads.

"Everything you see was made in our workshop," Josy explained as the four stood in the doorway of the men's dormitory.

"How nice!" exclaimed Jewel with an enthusiasm that belied her true feelings. The life of regimentation this drab room implied would be deadly to her spirit. How could people live like this?

"*Niceness* isn't something that's important to us," said Josy with mild sternness, as if correcting an errant child. "Beauty, pleasure, sensation – the world outside is full of distractions. We have a higher purpose here. We nourish the purity of the soul."

"Yes," Thomas agreed. "We have cast off frivolous things and live from day to day in the truth. Until the great day comes when we shall all fly free."

Their manner of speech, thought Thorn, had an oddly mechanical quality, as if they'd learnt a set of phrases and were repeating them dutifully. And there was that word *fly* again.

"What is the 'great day'?" he asked. "How will you all 'fly free'?"

"Our leader will preach this afternoon. He will make many things clear."

"I can hardly wait," said Thorn.

He was unable to keep a note of irony out of his voice, but neither Thomas nor Josy gave any sign of noticing.

"How long have you been here?" Jewel asked Josy.

"Since I was born."

"How can that be? The Grand Ranter said—"

"That his Rantership began only five years ago? That is true. You must understand that we in this Church are *reborns* – reborn in the truth of the Iron Angel, our prophet. I was nothing till I came here, I did not exist."

"But you must have had a life before that," Jewel objected; "a mother, a father – you must have lived in a settlement?"

"Perhaps." Josy's face was blank. "I do not remember."

Jewel didn't believe the woman. But in this place, it seemed, one truth – if such it was – wiped out all others.

"Come," said Thomas. "We shall show you our workshop."

The workshop lay beyond the dormitory. It was surprisingly well equipped. There were tool-benches and hand-driven lathes for turning wood. Finished items stood in the corner – chairs and stools, cupboards and tables, wooden bowls and various oddments.

"Our needs are few," said Thomas. "We despise money, which is a corrupter of the soul, but it is necessary to live. We trade with nearby settlements."

Thorn was inspecting the finished products. They seemed solid and well made.

"How did you learn to make these things?"

"The second person to join our leader was a master carpenter. He has passed on his skill."

"That was lucky," said Thorn.

"Luck?" said Thomas sharply. "Luck played no part in it. His coming was God's will."

Just then they heard a bell.

"The midday meal is about to begin. We must all wash our hands."

While Thomas conducted Thorn to the men's washroom, Josy took Jewel to the women's. The sexes, it seemed, were segregated except when it came to manual work. Jewel wondered if marriage was allowed, and asked Josy.

"Between members of our Church who live in the settlements, yes; but not within our community. Members of our community who wish to marry must leave. It is a question of purity."

Jewel wondered if sex-thoughts popped into Josy's head. Glancing sideways at the woman, she guessed that if they did, they'd be rigorously suppressed: Josy's mind was a garden in which only the ideas the Grand Ranter planted there were allowed to grow and flower.

Jewel and Thorn were assigned chairs between Thomas and Josy. They unshouldered their packs and set them on the stone floor. Before they all sat down to eat, the Grand Ranter, at the table's head, said a prayer in a voice that sliced through the silence like an axe:

"Let us remember that God provides what we eat, and give thanks to Him."

Voices repeated the prayer word for word. Then everybody sat. Thorn counted those present. Aside from himself, Jewel, Manningham Sparks and the Grand Ranter, there were fifteen cultists: eight men and seven women. Manningham was sitting at the other end of the table. Fleck Dewhurst was absent.

The meal was soup and cornbread. The bread was good but the soup bland. Thorn stirred the chunks of vegetable suspended in the liquid, then looked about for salt, but could see none on the table. Perhaps salt was impure. The meal passed in total silence. When Thorn had finished his portion, Thomas was only halfway through his. He gave the appearance of pondering every spoonful he took, as if within it lay the key to some profound spiritual matter and, if he chewed away mentally, mouthful after mouthful, he'd bite through it in the end.

So this is the Church of the Iron Angel, thought Thorn: carpentry and tasteless soup and getting preached at all the time. If I lived here, I'd soon be screaming with boredom. He glanced at Jewel, who looked back expressionlessly. She too had finished her soup. She thinks the same as me, he thought. The sooner we get out of here, the happier I'll be.

14

A STORM IN A PULPIT

"I'm worried about you, Jewel."

The girl looked at Thorn in surprise. "Don't be," she told her friend.

"But I am," persisted Thorn.

The meal was over, and the pair sat waiting for Thomas to reappear. Higgins Makepeace had called Thomas out of the room after the meal. From not too far away, Josy and the other cultists who'd escorted them that morning made no attempt to disguise the fact that they were keeping a close watch on the new arrivals. Well, let them, thought Jewel. Trouble was, she was getting a touch anxious herself: now Querne had the black crystal, what might the Magian be up to? Time was passing. But Thorn, it seemed, had more immediate things on his mind.

He said quietly, "I can't get what happened in the mausoleum out of my mind."

It was the first time the pair had been able to talk since saving the Ranter.

"I can't see why," Jewel said.

"The way you killed those men . . . it seemed – well, so ruthless . . ."

"You killed a man too. I don't remember *you* holding back."

"That's true," Thorn admitted, "but . . ."

"But what?"

"That was different."

"Not for those three men. Dead is dead however you play it."

Play it? "Maybe it is, but—"

"Look Thorn, they deserved to die. And their deaths came far quicker than the Reverend's would have done, if they'd been allowed to have their way."

This too was true, Thorn recognised. Jewel was outmanoeuvring him. Nevertheless, he tried again.

"I'm just worried that you're changing . . . well, too fast, and—"

"Of course I'm changing, Thorn. It's known in the trade as growing up. And, in case you hadn't noticed, so are you – in a big way. How many men have *you* killed since you first left Norgreen?"

This blunt question rocked Thorn. He tried to conjure a ready number, only to find he didn't have one. God! He'd have to think back, start to count them on his fingers . . .

"See what I mean? You don't know." Jewel was smiling. And somewhere in that smile – perhaps in the corners of her mouth? – lurked something dark and unsettling.

But Thomas now came up to them, closing off the exchange.

"We don't have time right now to show you around," he announced. "The preaching's about to begin. We must go and take our seats."

The four cultists formed up around them.

Jewel thought: With a few flashes of my crystal I could knock these nuisances out! She was sorely tempted, but too many other folk were close by to make this feasible. Fleck had spoken of a small-scale and intimate event, but the cultists' numbers had more than doubled since the meal. There'd probably be a scuffle, people might get badly hurt and she might get separated from Thorn.

"This way," Thomas intoned.

The six walked out into the transept. Thorn took in the stained-glass window dominating the north wall. It showed the same bearded man with flowing hair who hung on the cross, but in much pleasanter circumstances. Clad in a rope-belted garment coloured the blue of sunny skies, he was sitting on a rock talking to three wide-eyed children. Also in the picture was a strange four-legged animal with a white coat and a stubby tail. With his right hand the man was patting the animal on the head. Like the children, it listened intently, seemingly able to understand the speaker's every word.

How different this man is from the Iron Angel, thought Thorn. He tried to imagine what the Angel, if his tongueless mouth could speak, would have to say to little children, but no words suggested themselves. And what would the giants who in the Dark Time attended this church have made of the thing that now held pride of place here?

They emerged from the transept and began to cross the aisle that ran down the north wall of the nave. Right, thought Jewel, let's take the rat by the ears.

"That door there," she said, halting and pointing to where, halfway down the aisle, a large wooden door was set into the side wall. "Where does it lead?"

"I couldn't tell you," Thomas replied, with an almost practised lack of interest. "It's kept locked and it's out of bounds, so naturally we disregard it."

Naturally, thought Jewel . . . Some curiosity *you've* got.

But that was the door Racky Jagger had meant, she was certain. Beyond it lay the entrance to Querne Rasp's lair. And now it struck her with equal certainly that neither Thomas nor Josy nor any other resident cultist had a clue that Querne was here . . . The great church clutched its secret to its heart.

But Higgins Makepeace? He knew. Oh yes, Makepeace knew. He'd been here five years . . . If Fleck knew Racky, so must he . . . Up here, Makepeace thundered out his half-baked doctrines, while below Querne Rasp schemed her murderous, vengeful schemes. Were the two linked in some way?

Jewel's brow furrowed. What she and Thorn needed was the chance to slip away. And since the cultists weren't going to permit it, she herself would somehow have to bring about that chance.

Create a diversion, she thought. She began to think, *hard*.

Thorn looked down at the stone slab whose surface he was treading. Tramping feet had part-obliterated the signs engraved upon it. Away to his right rose the first of many rows of rigid seats, all executed in the same dark unprepossessing wood. The people who'd filled them had – like the members of the Church of the Iron Angel – believed in God. But not the same god, he thought . . .

A bell began to toll. They seemed fond of bells here.

"We must take our seats," said Josy. "Soon the preaching will begin."

Many folk were already seated in the chairs that faced the pulpit. Others were taking their seats, and there was a buzz of conversation. The resident members of the cult occupied places in the first and second rows, but their mouths were clamped shut, their eyes fixed on the floor. Perhaps forty cultists in all were here today. Higgins Makepeace was not to be seen.

Jewel broke away from her escort. She went up to the pulpit and began to caress the polished wood.

Thomas hurried after her.

"You shouldn't touch it," he said.

"Oh? Are pulpits out of bounds too?"

"Well, no, but—"

"There's no harm then, is there?" she answered, not taking her hand away. "It's so beautiful. Who made it?"

"I – er – our master craftsman. Look—"

"I must tell your master craftsman what a fine job he did. Is that him there?"

She pointed with her free hand at a bald man in the front row whose beard was streaked with grey. He seemed deep in meditation.

"Yes, that's him, but look, we really ought to sit down."

"Of course – if you say so."

Jewel gave the pulpit one last, lingering caress, then they rejoined the others, who were yet to take their seats. Thorn pointed to a figure sitting in the back row.

"There's Manningham. Let's join him."

He waved, and the black-clad Ranter returned the salute.

"I don't –" began Thomas, but Thorn and Jewel were off already "– think the Grand Ranter would approve . . ." He stood for a moment irresolute, cast a helpless look about him, then hurried after the errant pair. The rest of the escort followed them.

By the time they caught up, Thorn and Jewel had dumped their packs behind their chairs and were taking seats next to Manningham. The Ranter had been sitting at the far end of the back row, but seeing the young people approach, he'd moved along to make room for them. So now Thorn and Jewel sat at the end of the row. They smiled pleasantly at Thomas as he arrived, closely followed by the others. Thomas, perhaps, had had a somewhat different seating arrangement in mind, but now he and his companions had no option but to occupy the seats directly in front of Thorn and Jewel. From here, during the preaching, he and Josy took it in turns to keep a watch on their guests.

Again the invisible bell tolled, and now the hum of voices stilled. In a silence fizzing with expectation, the Grand Ranter strode to the pulpit, his grey mane majestic, his ankle-length cloak of solemn black billowing behind him. Without a glance at those assembled, he ascended the pulpit, his steps loud in the silence.

Then, from a height more than twice that of a man, Higgins Makepeace subjected his quivering congregation to scrutiny. His chiselled features and hollow cheeks gave him the look of a man hungry if not for food, then for truth as, one by one, his lance of a gaze skewered those gazing up at him. When his eyes fell upon Thorn, it seemed to the young man as if the Grand Ranter were weighing up the worthiness of his soul and was finding it lacking.

At last Makepeace spoke. "Welcome, friends. Once again we are gathered before the image of our Angel. Let us begin with a short prayer." He closed his eyes and bowed his head.

The congregation rose to its feet and everyone bowed their heads – everyone, that is, except for Thorn, Jewel and Manningham Sparks, who continued to stare at the figure in the pulpit.

Reverently, the Grand Ranter intoned, "God, powerful and wise beyond human understanding, He who loves those who love Him and punishes those who deny Him, look kindly on our Church. Bless our attempt to live as You would have us live and destroy those who oppose us. In the future that You, in Your infinite grace, have promised, give us faith and courage to do Your most dread bidding, catch us up in Your strong arms and let us fly with You forever. Let it be so."

"Let it be so," his followers murmured, and sat down again.

Your most dread bidding, thought Thorn. What can he mean? And there's that word *fly* again . . .

Higgins Makepeace surveyed his flock, then began to speak again.

"Tomorrow is to the day the fifth anniversary of my coming to this Church – the fifth anniversary of the revelation of the Angel. Tomorrow the die shall be cast; tomorrow all shall be made plain; tomorrow those who truly believe shall be granted what is closest to their hearts – immortality!"

With that last, thrilling word, a great murmur went up and shouts broke out. Makepeace smiled indulgently, then held up his arms to quell the voices.

"Listen: I shall tell you how it was, how it is, and how in time to come it shall be.

"Here on Earth, in that age we rightly call the Dark Time – for truly it *was* dark – there lived a race of men and women who were God's chosen people. If you doubt that to be so, look at the pictures in this church, immortalised in glass so we may see and understand. There is beauty, nobility, light in every countenance. This race of beings was many times our size and our strength, so that one man's weakest finger could raise from the ground a weight greater than any two men here could lift with four hands. They built great settlements and houses, they built churches, roads and bridges, dams to hold water, and extensive pleasure grounds.

"But such great work did they do that as time went by they let slip from their hearts and minds the bounty and goodness of Him who had made them capable of it. The maggot of pride gnawed at them till, in their growing delusion, they began openly to boast that no one but their own mortal selves had made them great. They forgot God and His holy word, neglected His churches, ignored His ministers and fell into evil ways, worshipping money and trivial things and pursuing the sins of the flesh. Swallowed by fiery-eyed demons of greed and vanity, they descended deeper and deeper into abandonment and corruption till they preyed on one another like the horned black slugs that creep and crawl in dirt and slime."

The Grand Ranter paused and looked with piercing eyes at his flock.

"High in Heaven, God saw everything, for He cannot help but see. In His deep distress – for never doubt that He loved this race beyond all other things – He took counsel with himself, asking how He could deflect them from the evil that enmired them.

"Then He thought: surely if I send a messenger to them, they will heed him, give over their evil ways and return to purity and truth.

"So He called to Him his most beloved and beautiful angel, and charged him to go down to Earth and walk among the people, spreading the true word of God and calling men and women out of darkness into light. And the angel went down and walked among the people and did his master's bidding, preaching the true word and calling men forth out of the slime.

"But men mocked him and ignored him till the angel grew despondent, unable to make headway against the stubbornness of this race. And at last, feeling that all other avenues were closed to his feet, he strode into the greatest room in the greatest building where this people's wisest Councillors sat to make and unmake laws. And he began to harangue them, telling them how they had fallen below God's expectations, listing their sins and calling with all the eloquence and all the passion that he had at his command for a return to truth and virtue.

"But the Councillors thought him mad. They called in their enforcers who – no more than thugs and bullies – took the angel into an alley where they began to kick and beat him. The angel did not resist them and, saying nothing, continued to look upon them with eyes of pity and of love. But this infuriated the servants of the Councillors even more, so they took him up and nailed him on a high cross of wood."

Turning, Makepeace swung an arm towards the many-coloured window where the bearded figure hung. "There you behold him. Soon the angel lay dead. Then God, who sees all things, sharing every joy and pain, was exceedingly wrathful that His dearly beloved angel should be humiliated, tormented, and cruelly done to death. And He saw, with dismay and the utmost bitterness, that this race was beyond redemption.

"So, rising up in His wrath, He smote the settlements of men, blasting them out of existence. So the Barrens were created, places of illusion where ghosts drift in the air, ghosts that drive into madness any human who wanders there. And God winnowed the souls of men. The many evil ones He damned to eternal torment in Hell, the few good ones He sent to eternal bliss in Heaven.

"Then God considered what more to do. His sadness ran deep, but springs of hope still flowed in Him. And at last He determined to make humanity afresh.

"But (He said to Himself) this time I shall make them small so they will never forget their smallness. And I will set them down in the blasted landscape of my first creation, in order that they may learn and keep to the paths of righteousness. And so it came about that our race appeared on Earth."

He halted, and the silence seemed to throb like a living heart.

"All this," he went on in a quiet but telling voice, "was revealed to me, your humble servant and oracle, five years ago come tomorrow, when for the first time I set foot inside this church. Why, you may ask, did this revelation occur then? Why should it not have been vouchsafed to humans long before? Why should it not have been delayed to a day far distant in the future?"

The Grand Ranter paused to let his questions reverberate. Once again his eyes passed over the faces of his listeners. "Only search for the answer within yourselves and you will find it. Once before, God sent a message to humankind. It came by an angel, a winged being of flesh and blood. Then, five years ago, He sent a second message – except that this time his messenger was iron, not flesh and blood."

The Grand Ranter paused. Then, in a sweeping, dramatic gesture, he swung round again, this time pointing a lean finger at the Iron Angel.

"There he stands! For God had determined that this second angel should be beyond the harming of men. And this time his message was for only a chosen few. That meaning is simple: it is this. Human beings have fallen prey to the same errors as before. Turning blind eyes to the warnings that lie about us everywhere – the Barrens, the broken walls, the scattered ruins of fine houses – humanity has again embraced ignorance and sin. The tide of evil is rising, greed, anger and murderousness, and this time you can be sure that it will swallow the whole world. Only one certain road to salvation is left to us – the road of sacrifice symbolised by our effigy."

The Grand Ranter paused, as if to savour the effect that his rhetoric was having.

Manningham Sparks turned to Thorn and whispered in his ear. "Impressive, Higgins, isn't he? And dangerously persuasive. But it's blasphemous nonsense from start to finish. *Grand Ranter* he calls himself – but it's a fake title, self-appointed, not one conferred by his peers in a proper Church, as mine was."

The Grand Ranter began again. "You are the righteous ones, you are the ones who have seen the light. And if, when the final test comes – and come it will tomorrow, for I feel it in my bones and in the sinews of my limbs – if when it comes you have the courage of your convictions, He will catch up in his arms and take you flying through the heavens – even as He caught up the man who made the Iron Angel and whose death it was my privilege to witness on this spot."

Higgins Makepeace flung his arms up in a dramatic gesture, but at that very moment there came an ominous splintering sound. For a long moment the Grand Ranter remained locked in his pose, consternation on his face; then he dropped out of sight. His upraised hands were the last of him to disappear. In the crash that followed, the pulpit rattled and rocked as if contemptuously swatted by God's invisible hand.

The congregation leapt to its feet in an excited babble of voices. First to respond positively were the resident cult members sitting in the front row. As one they swarmed towards the pulpit. A little more slowly away were Thomas, Josy and the other pair in front of Jewel and Thorn, but then they too were hastening towards their lost leader, their charges forgotten.

"Woodworm!" Jewel shook her head, but was unable to smother her grin. "Those little beasties get everywhere! Time to go, I think."

"Bye, Manningham!" said Thorn.

Then he and Jewel had snatched up their packs and were sprinting away.

"Hey! Where—" exclaimed the Ranter.

He swung back to take in the chaos in front of him. No one there had eyes for anything but the disaster-smitten pulpit and its fallen occupant.

Making up his mind, Manningham got himself to the end of the row and set off after Jewel and Thorn at a lumberingly undignified and unRanterlike canter.

Jewel and Thorn had disappeared round the corner of the pews into the north aisle long before he got there himself. Rounding the bend, panting already, he saw them far ahead. As he chugged along in their wake, the pair stopped by a side door. What on earth were they up to? That door, surely, was kept locked.

Sucking in air, he laboured along. As he neared them, Jewel drew the palm of her hand back from the wood close to the lock, grasped the handle and pushed the door open.

"Where are you going?" the Ranter cried.

"Inside," said Jewel simply.

"Inside?"

"Goodbye, Manningham," said Thorn. "Don't tell people where we went. And see you when we see you."

And now they were through the door, slamming it in the Ranter's face as he lurched to a halt. He seized hold of the handle, but the door refused to budge. It was locked again.

Neither Jewel nor Thorn had been holding a key . . .

But then, thought the Ranter, a Magian wouldn't need a key.

He hadn't the least notion what might lie behind the door. But, as he stood there recovering his breath, he remembered a time some months before when he'd unexpectedly bumped into Racky in the church. The Ranter hadn't been aware that Racky was anywhere in the building: he'd jokingly asked if Racky had just walked through a wall.

God in Heaven! Manningham now thought: perhaps he had.

15

STRANGE ROOMS WITH
MANY DOORS

"Poor Manningham," said Thorn as Jewel turned away from the door. "I feel we've treated him shabbily."

"It can't be helped," she answered briskly. "We couldn't afford to hang around."

"He's the nicest Ranter I've met."

"*Niceness isn't something that's important to me*," said Jewel, looking down her nose at him and speaking with mock-solemnity.

Thorn looked at her and laughed.

"Well, I like him too," said Jewel. "He knows a monster when he sees one, and that's what Higgins Makepeace is."

"Yes," agreed Thorn. "I wonder what he means by 'the road of sacrifice'?"

"I don't know. I don't like the sound of it. Still, we've other things to think about."

"What did you do to the pulpit?"

"Weakened the planks in the floor. I'm surprised they lasted as long as they did."

"At least it shut Makepeace up."

"Not for long, I suspect. He didn't have far to fall. I doubt he's broken any bones."

"Pity he didn't land on his head."

"That's one trick I couldn't manage. Come on, let's get moving."

The room they found themselves in was stone-flagged, high-ceilinged and bare of furniture or adornment. An arched window, tall, narrow and plainly glazed, let in the sunlight. Jewel and Thorn crossed to where a large rectangular opening yawned in the floor. A flight of massive stone steps led down into darkness. They were thick with dust. How many years might it be since giant feet had trodden them?

"What did Racky say?" said Thorn. "'Down into Hell'? But we can't use these steps."

"No. There must be another way."

They turned to survey the room. After a time, Jewel pointed: "Over there, in the far corner, there's something sticking up."

"Yes, I see it. Let's take a look."

They crossed the room.

What her sharp eyes had caught sight of was a small table with a couple of oil-lamps on top, also a tin that looked to contain flint and tinder. Beyond the table was a circular wooden guardrail upheld by vertical iron struts. Inside it, a spiral stairway plunged into blackness.

"Down into Hell," murmured Thorn.

"Or something worse," said Jewel wryly.

All at once she felt a reluctance to venture down these stairs. Who knew what traps Querne had set for unwanted visitors? Below, all was enemy ground, territory unknown: Querne's advantage would be huge. How could Jewel – a raw Magian – and Thorn – brave as he was – hope to stop Querne from doing whatever it was she planned to do? Twice Jewel and she had met, and twice Querne had prevailed. When the two had faced one another on the bridge in Harrypark, only the owl's intervention had saved Jewel from disaster. There'd be no owls underground. And then there had been the ambush in the ironworks, when Jewel, ignominiously taken by surprise, had been rendered helpless. Querne doesn't care, Jewel thought, what methods she uses to gain her ends: after what happened at Harrypark, no holds are barred – it's her or me. My only advantage is that Querne must think me dead. But whether this was enough to carry Jewel through to the end – well, that remained to be seen. Useless to think her single crystal could oppose Querne's four. It would be futile to go up against Querne without a plan . . . but what plan could Jewel concoct when the circumstances of the final confrontation between them (if indeed she and Thorn managed to get that far) were impossible to predict?

Impossible to predict . . . But she was a Magian, wasn't she, with a gift of sight . . . sporadic and ungovernable as its manifestations were. Mightn't that count for something? She needed to think, *think*—

Thorn touched her arm and Jewel jumped back into the present. "Worried?" Thorn asked.

"You a mind-reader?" she said.

Thorn grinned. "Mind-reading I leave to you."

Jewel thought: Thorn's quite attractive when he grins; and returned his smile. Gradually their smiles faded, but still they gazed at one another. Neither said anything.

This was the moment when these two might have exchanged their first kiss. But something held them back. Was it the tender seriousness each one read in the other's face? Was it their sense of the perils they faced and the uncertainty of the outcome? Well, something held them apart.

It was Jewel who turned away. "We need some light," she said.

"Well, there are lamps here," said Thorn. He examined them. "They've been used before. They look all right to me."

"Then light one," Jewel said. "I'll use the crystal if I have to, but not otherwise."

Thorn lit an oil-lamp. Lifting a section of the guardrail, which was hinged, Jewel motioned him through and they started down the steps, with Thorn leading.

The stairway dropped through a hole bored in the flag-stone. Then what had been a floor became the ceiling above their heads, and they found themselves descending into a room of unknown dimensions. The stairway hugged a wall, to which it was bolted at intervals; apart from that, all was dark. Round and round the pair went, their boots clattering on metal, trying their best to ignore the wallowing space; for all that stood between them and a fall that must be fatal was a handrail that angled down the stair at waist-height. When they'd gone some way, they halted and craned upwards. The hole through which they'd descended had shrunk to a tiny round of faint light.

"This staircase!" said Thorn. "Querne's power is awesome."

"Awesome, and still growing. She probably had only one crystal when she bored that hole in the roof, fashioned this stairway. But she did a superb job. Her power to shape matter is nothing short of terrific. No wonder she believes she can rule the whole world."

"Have my ears gone wonky, or is that admiration I hear?"

"Credit where credit's due."

They started off again. Round and round they went, concentrating so as not to miss their footing. At last, with relief, they stepped off the staircase onto a floor that seemed made of solid rock.

"It's no good," Jewel admitted. "I'm going to have to use the crystal."

It lit up a Dark Time chamber perhaps eight feet in height. Its walls were smooth and grey and there were six of them in all, each identical to the rest. At the midpoint of each wall was a wooden giant-sized door. Set in the corner of the nearest was a door of human dimensions. Away across the room, the lowest steps of the giant stair, enclosed in a vertical sleeve of stone, were visible through an arched entryway.

They walked to the nearest door.

Thorn said: "I bet it's locked. Still, *you* could open it."

"I wonder . . . Why don't *you* try opening it?"

"Me?" Thorn shrugged. "All right."

The door proved to be unlocked. On its far side was light. Studding ceiling, walls and floor were starry nuggets that glowed yellow. Only one person could have scattered these gems here: Querne Rasp.

In dimensions and shape, this second room was the twin of the one they'd left, with the same six, uniform walls made of some grey material, and the same six giant doors at the midpoint of each wall. Only in lacking staircases did it differ from the first room.

Thorn crossed to the nearest gem-light, squatted and rubbed it with a finger. It was smooth like glass and coloured his skin gold.

"Now what?" he said.

"Now we try another door – that one opposite, I think."

This door, like the last, had a human entrance in the corner. Probably all of them had. The third room, like the last, was lit by scattered lights and had a roof of flagstones. But, barring the straight stretch of wall they'd entered through, its walls were made of rock. Its shape suggested a badly mistreated circle – beaten in here, stretched out there. And, so far as they could see, it possessed just the one door – the door they'd entered through.

"Let's go back," Jewel said.

They returned to the second room. Four untried doors remained.

"Which one?" said Thorn.

"This one," said Jewel, indicating the first door on the left.

It boasted a human entryway; on they went through it. The fourth room was lit by gem-lights. Some four times bigger than the third room had been, it was irregular in shape: more a cavern than a room. It had two stretches of straight wall – the one through which they'd come, and a second angling away on its immediate right. Midway along was a giant door with a human door set in the corner. The rest of the walls had the cragginess of a natural formation.

"I think, Thorn, we can dispense with the lamp," said Jewel.

While he blew the lamp out and set it on the ground, she extinguished the crystal and returned it to her pack.

"Right," she said: "Let's walk around the walls, see if we come on anything new." She pointed. "We'll start with that stretch of straight wall."

Beyond the door fixed in this wall, they found another room complete with six walls and six doors: the twin of the second room they'd seen.

"Do we go in?" asked Thorn.

"No. Carry on," answered Jewel.

Thorn shut the door and they continued on round the edge of the rugged cavern. Soon enough they did indeed happen on something new: a human-sized door set directly into the rock. Querne Rasp's doing? – it had to be. Opening it, they found a tunnel lit with gem-lights. They went down it to the end; here lay a matching door. Beyond it was the biggest cavern they'd so far come across. Over to the right, a stretch of giant-made wall complete with door thrust out into the cave. Walking in a little way, they saw beyond it another straight stretch with a big door halfway down.

But, turning on their heels, they went back down the tunnel and continued round the cavern they'd begun to explore. Neatly positioned in rocky nooks, they came on two further Querne-made doors which both opened onto tunnels. The first led to a cavern many times longer than it was broad. Its extremities lay so far off that, despite the presence of gem-lights, they lay shrouded in gloom. The cavern might or might not contain doors of human dimensions; only a search would answer that question, but they didn't go inside. The second tunnel gave access to a small cavern-room not unlike the first irregular room they'd happened on. They saw no doors from where they stood, either giant or human.

Completing their walk round the rugged cavern, they stopped at the door that led back to the second six-sided room.

"Right," said Jewel. "Let's put our heads together. What do you make of it all?"

"Well, to begin with, there are some six-sided rooms the giants made; then there are caves with rough walls that look as though they were always here. The church was built over them. How far they extend, how many there are, it's impossible to guess. To be honest, I'm flummoxed. It's like a maze down here. I can't get my head around it."

"There's nothing wrong with your head, Thorn. A *maze* is exactly what it is – or, better, a labyrinth. Querne has hidden herself away in an underground labyrinth." She paused. "My guess is, from what we've seen, that around the room we arrived in lie six other six-sided rooms, each opening off one of the central room's walls. These seven rooms form something like what bee-men call a honeycomb shape. Beyond *them* lie irregular caverns, some with doors made by Querne, some with none – dead ends, in fact. And somewhere in amongst them is the bee-mistress herself . . ."

Jewel saw Thorn frown, but she herself felt only excitement. The game had defined itself. A labyrinth was a challenge: a thing to test herself against, a thing to be relished. In matching herself against Querne's creation, she'd be matching herself against Querne.

Thorn said, "Then there's no telling just how big this labyrinth might be."

"No . . . but even Querne's enhanced powers must have limits."

"We could blunder about for ever . . . Why not try using your own powers to pinpoint her hiding-place?"

Now why hadn't Jewel thought of that? "Good idea. Let's sit down."

They took off their packs, sat on the floor and drank from their water bottles. Then Jewel laid the palms of her hands on the floor and shut her eyes. She sat like that for quite some time.

When her eyes opened at last, she looked at Thorn and shook her head.

"It's no good. Stone's more difficult than wood. I can't get far at all. But my guess about the central honeycomb was correct."

She glanced at her hands.

"Look at my hands . . . they're filthy. The floor here is thick with dust."

Thorn considered her hands and pointed out across the floor.

"Yes. And look — we've left a trail of footprints behind."

Jewel looked and saw footprints leading away to the right and coming back from the left.

"Now why didn't *I* notice that?"

"Why should you have? I only noticed them while you were concentrating."

Jewel's forehead puckered. "I don't remember leaving footprints in the six-sided rooms . . ."

"Let's check."

They went through the door.

Jewel was right. The floor of this six-sided room was perfectly clean. Jewel led the way across it to the door that led to the small cavern with no other visible exit. There, just inside, was a scrabble of footmarks where they'd stood to look around. So this floor was dusty too!

Jewel said: "Do you realise what this means?"

"I think so. If all the cave-rooms are dusty, and if someone – Racky or Querne came this way—"

"Or Querne's servant, Spine Wrench . . . Then," Jewel finished, "there may be a trail of footprints all the way to her lair!"

"In which case, all we have to do to find her is follow them!"

"*When* we find them. *If* we find them. That could take some time. We might have to look through many doors."

"*How* many?"

"Picture the honeycomb. Around the innermost room with six walls are six others. Each room has six giant doors. Some lead to more six-sided rooms, the rest open on caves with doors of our size, or none. How many giant doors that open on caverns must we check?"

Thorn shut his eyes, but for the life of him he couldn't picture the seven rooms with their many doors. His brain didn't work that way.

"It's no good," he confessed. "I can't picture anything beyond the middle room."

"No, it's difficult," she conceded. "Well, by my reckoning there are eighteen doors to be checked. We've already gone through two, which leaves sixteen more. We'll have to work our way round the outer ring of rooms."

Thorn looked glum. "Sixteen more? That could take ages."

"It could. Still, we might get lucky. Let's begin."

They *did* get lucky. They got unbelievably lucky. They went on to the next door, and when they glanced inside they saw, tracking away, a neat set of prints made by boots a little bigger than the pair Thorn was wearing. Racky's or Wrench's, they had to be.

Excitement gripped them and they hugged one another.

"Now who's brilliant?" said Thorn.

"*We* are," answered Jewel. "Cross your fingers *all* the caverns are as dusty as this one."

Thorn disengaged himself. "But what," he said, "if the prints were made to lead us straight into a trap?"

"It's possible," Jewel agreed. "Trouble is, I don't see any alternative to following them."

They set off. The cavern they were in bent away to the left, sloping gradually downwards. Its scattering of gem-lights made the footprints easy to follow. Ignoring the giant door that lay to their left, the prints described a curve, tracking close to the left-hand wall.

The prints took them to a human door at the cavern's far end. Like the other Querne-made doors, it opened into a tunnel bored through rock. Beyond lay a small cave. Once again, the footprints proved easy enough to follow. Once again, the floor sloped, taking them deeper into the earth.

They came to two identical doors set fairly close together. The footprints led to the left-hand door. Through it they went, and along the passageway to the door that lay at its end.

Surprise awaited in the next cavern. There were gem-lights in the floor, but none in the ceiling or walls. The cavern gaped like a mouth; but teeth, tongue – any features it might possess were lost in blackness. And even the floor lights didn't cover the whole area but led off in three streams: one to the left, one to the right and the third straight ahead.

As they stood there, a sense of the magnitude of this cavern, its massive undisclosed hollowness, crept in upon them both, bringing with it a fresh uneasiness.

Which, thought Jewel, is exactly why Querne left it like this. Probably all these caverns were as dark as this to begin with. Is this where the trickery starts?

Thorn pointed ahead.

"At least we can see the footprints."

Tracking the middle light-trail, they vanished into the heart of the darkness.

Unshouldering her pack, Jewel extracted the green crystal from its wrappings. Anxious to conserve her energies, she coaxed it into a glow just sufficient to surround the pair of them with a nimbus of light. Beyond it, the make-up of the cavern remained unseen.

"Right, let's go," she said.

They moved off again. It might have been the spoor of a wraith they were tracking as it flitted this way and that.

Abruptly, out of nowhere, came a *rush-swish* of wings. Jewel ducked instinctively as something shot by overhead, so close she felt the beaten air of their passage on her face. There was a crack as the crystal fell from her hand, rolled away and went out. Thorn had dodged to one side – off the light-stream into the dark. From that direction came a thump.

"Thorn!" she called. "Are you all right?"

Now she heard a scuffling sound.

"Er, I think so. Fell over and banged my elbow."

Thorn re-emerged onto the trail, rubbing his arm.

"Bumped into a rock," he explained.

"Where's your bow, Thorn? You had it over your shoulder," said Jewel.

"So I did. Must have dropped it."

She grinned. "Like I did the crystal. Hang on while I locate it."

She went down on one knee and set her palm to the ground. Ah, the crystal lay that way . . .

Soon she had it back. It seemed undamaged, and she got it glowing again. By its light they searched for Thorn's bow and found it by the rock he'd banged against.

"Why do I bother?" he asked himself, as he hooked the bow over his shoulder. "This, against a Magian, will be just as much use as a cloth cap against an axe."

Jewel stared up at the rock, which disappeared into the gloom above their heads, then laid a hand on it.

"It's a pillar," she declared. "Probably one of many that support the ceiling." She turned to Thorn. "Was that a colony of bats that flew by?"

"Yes," answered Thorn. "Don't ask me why I ducked – they wouldn't have bumped into us."

They got going again. The light-trail and its dusty footprints started to bend away to the right.

Then, out of the darkness, a small door materialised.

16

LIZARD AND BUTTERFLY

The next cavern was different again. For one thing, the lights were back on every rock-surface. But what they lit was different. Roof and floor were uneven, and down from the ceiling here and there hung showers of stony needles. Up from the floor, as if striving to meet them but not yet managing to touch, rose clusters of answering spikes.

"What are they?" asked Thorn.

"I don't know," Jewel replied.

One route led into the room and disappeared among the clusters, but the footprints, less obvious on the rocky floor but still discernible, hugged the wall. Thorn and Jewel set off to follow them, treading carefully lest they trip. At one point the prints, forced by a rock-fall to loop away from the wall, took them into and through the midst of a copse of stony towers. A series of ridges like the webbing that connects a frog's fingers linked the trunks of the spikes at their base, and Thorn and Jewel had to scramble up and over a number of these, their boots fighting for purchase on the slippery surface: for water, dripping from the tips of the downward-pointing spikes, struck the upthrusting tips below them and ran down to the floor.

As Jewel's hands slipped over the rock, a word slipped into her mind: *stalagmites* . . . So that's their name, she thought.

The footprint trail had disappeared, but scuffmarks on the rock said they were on the right track.

Their hands damp and benumbed, their limbs bruised, they came to a door. At the end of the tunnel that lay beyond it, another surprise awaited them.

Light and colour assaulted their eyes. Here, in an underground cavern where they had no business to be, summer colours rioted. The colours belonged to blossoms and the blossoms to flowers that sprouted – so it seemed – directly out of the surfaces of the walls and rock formations. The flowers came in all shapes and sizes. Near at hand on delicate stems sprang sprays of white bells half the size of Jewel's head. Away to their left, down from the wall in an extravagant gush of spade-shaped leaves, hung heavy circular purple blossoms, bulging petal-clusters that must have been eight inches across.

The air was warm and humid; water dripped from the walls and ran trickling down the rocks. There were no footprints here, but there was only the one path. It unwound among mossy rocks that lifted high above their heads. Rounding one craggy outcrop crowded with countless yellow stars, they came on a pool into which water dripped and where a dozen lily pads floated, complete with white, cuplike blooms. Beetles with shiny blue backs paddled across the limpid surface, and waterboatmen on stiltlike legs sculled busily about. Then the air was filled with movement: a flock of black-and-yellow butterflies came fluttering into the clearing. As if unable to make up their minds, they wove a cloud of erratic patterns, jinking and jittering in the air before settling on the lily pads or the never-before-seen flowers that drooped crimson, blue or orange above the mirror of the pool.

Jewel caught Thorn's arm.

"There!" she whispered. "Can you see it? Some sort of lizard, I think . . ."

He followed her pointing finger. A strange creature was sitting on the moss-bed of a rock, so still you might have thought it had been carved from emerald. It was the same green as the moss and had an attentive, crested head in which a moony, lidless eye gleamed, utterly motionless. As Thorn made out its snaky tail, one of the butterflies happened to land a few inches away. Even as the butterfly was folding shut its vivid wings, the lizard unleashed from its mouth a long, whiplike coil and snatched up the butterfly. But so large was the butterfly that it wouldn't fit in the lizard's craw: a flange of iridescent wing was left sticking out. The lizard swivelled its head to one side and silently gulped; more of the wing was sucked in, and beneath the reptile's jaw a sag of skin wobbled about.

"Ugh! It's horrible!" Jewel cried.

"Rather the butterfly than me," was Thorn's heartless reply.

They moved on, passing flowers you might imagine in a dream but never encounter in the real world. White toadstools like small tables with red-spotted caps had colonised several rocky shelves. Further along was a weird fungus like a gigantic scarlet tongue, its surface spongy and glabrous.

"Imagine lying on that," said Thorn. "How comfy it would be!"

"I'd rather not," said Jewel. "The way things are here, I wouldn't be surprised if it took it into its horrible fungusy brain to swallow me!"

"That reminds me," said Thorn. "What with all this walking, I'm starting to feel peckish. How about stopping for a bite to eat?"

"All right," said Jewel.

They found a ledge of rock, took off their packs and sat down. As they nibbled on some oatcakes they'd brought with them from Norgreen (could it really be less than three days before? – it felt like an age), a number of multi-hued butterflies with black-pupilled, eyelike markings flew jerkily over their heads.

How long, Jewel wondered, have we been down here? Is it evening up above? Normal time, it seemed, was suspended in this world . . . *Querne's* world, she told herself, that's at once more and less than the world we've left behind . . . What else will we come across before we get out of here? Not for the first time, a sense of foreboding darkened her mind, and she saw again the lizard with the butterfly jammed in its mouth.

The cave of blossoms seemed the most extensive they'd penetrated so far. At last, however, their winding path delivered them to a door almost lost amid a tangle of creepers that put forth skeins of turquoise flowers.

Once again, in the next cavern, Querne Rasp sprang a surprise.

No darkness with bats, no spiky rocks, no flowers and fungi and flitting insects.

No: an underground lake.

And there at the shore, as if it had been waiting for them, a boat.

Jewel and Thorn stood and stared. The cavern was broad; its

rocky floor sloped down to meet gently lapping water. A wooden jetty, mounted on piles, ran out into blue-black water. And there, at its end, lay the boat.

But the height and depth of the cave and the size of the lake, they couldn't tell. For, just beyond the boat, a wall of mist rose from the water, filling and clouding the air and hiding the roof. It seemed to sluggishly roll and curl, yet kept its distance from the shore, leaving the boat floating in a pocket of clear space.

Jewel and Thorn glanced at each other, but did not speak. Then, side by side, they walked down to the lake and stepped out on to the jetty.

It was Thorn who pointed out the first oddity.

"Look! The boat – it isn't moored!"

The boat rode at the jetty's end, but was not attached to it. There was nothing to which to moor: not a ring or a bollard in sight. Yet the boat remained stationary, open to boarding.

"Well," said Thorn hesitantly, reminded of the sailing boat they'd stolen from Nettle Island, "do we board her or don't we?"

"If we don't, we must go back. I can't see any other way of getting across this cavern."

"Perhaps there's a route around it – one we haven't discovered yet." But even to Thorn himself, his suggestion lacked conviction.

"Very likely," Jewel agreed. "I can't see Querne not giving herself a choice of ways through. But right now I can't see any alternative to the boat. We'll lose time if we go back. I like this mist no more than you, but if Racky came this way he must have crossed in this boat."

"OK. Let's go on board and look around."

Thorn stepped over the gunwale and into the boat. It was smaller than the sailing boat they'd stolen on Roydsal Dam, but three times the size of the rowing boat he and Racky Jagger had taken up Judy River. Positioned amidships were four seats, two in front, two behind. Jewel joined him and together they looked around.

The girl said: "Tell me, Thorn: does anything about this boat strike you as strange?"

"Yes," he replied. "It has a mast but no sail, and neither rowlocks nor oars . . ."

"So . . . how do we make it move?"

He clutched her arm. "We don't. Look!"

Puffs of mist like blown smoke were creeping over the prow.

It's closing in! Jewel thought, then realised that it wasn't the mist that was shifting, it was the boat nosing away from the jetty – and with no means of propulsion and no visible desti-nation.

"Can you stop this thing?" asked Thorn.

"I could try," she replied. "But even if I could, what would be the point of it? We'd never get to find out where it's taking us, would we? We may as well sit down."

So sit down they did, setting their packs in front of their feet.

The mist now encircled the boat and, up above their heads, at a height of around three feet, joined to form a canopy that hid the cavern roof from sight. But although, below that height, wisps encroached over the gunwales, they drifted no further inboard. The mist, like a well-trained cart-rat, knew its proper place.

Time passed.

Due to the many twists and turns of their path through the labyrinth – not to mention the spiral stairway – Thorn had long since forfeited all sense of direction. He began to wonder where they were, in relation to the church and the churchyard up above. Given the cragginess of the ceilings of the recent caverns they'd come through, together with the fact that they were deeper underground, it seemed likely they'd moved out from under the floor of the church and were now below the surface of the surrounding countryside. Jewel, he became aware, was gazing down at her pack. Abruptly reaching forward, she began to undo the straps. Then she pulled out her crystal, swathed in its cloth, and unwrapped it.

"Jewel," he began—

But already an emerald spark had kindled at the quincell's heart. Jewel offered no reply. Then the stone flashed out green, blinding Thorn in the process and irradiating the mist, and he threw himself sideways onto the decking, banging his right knee, and clamped his hands over his eyes.

Had the quincell called to Jewel or had the girl awakened it? However it was, she felt herself drawn towards its core, into its vivid leaf-light. As on earlier occasions, her bodily shell dropped away, leaving her floating as lightly as a tuft of thistledown. The blackness turned to a dark blue, the dark blue to lighter shade. She was up in the sky again. There was not a breath of wind. Away on the horizon stretched a pale skein of cloud. Below, the earth resolved itself, and there beneath her lay a church. Not any church, she thought, but one particular church. That steeple with its cross, that overgrown churchyard, that neatly kept path . . . this was the building they'd so recently left behind. But why should the quincell show her the church? She drifted down towards it and passed directly through the roof.

She hovered above the great nave. There were the stained-glass windows, there the ranks of nut-brown seating, there the altar with its candlesticks and discoloured crucifix . . . What time was she in – the present, or some past before the coming of Querne Rasp or the creation of the Angel? Then her attention was drawn by something that answered the question for her.

She dropped lower and hovered again.

Directly below was the Iron Angel with, close to it, a gantry. The gantry had platforms at different levels with ladders linking them to the ground, and on the uppermost platform two men were standing, their eyes fixed on the tortured writhings of the grim effigy.

One man Jewel recognised; the identity of the other wasn't difficult to guess. And now a conversation began.

"It's magnificent," said the first man, clapping the other on the back, "it's an absolute masterpiece. Utter beauty and ultimate pain – it's everything I could have wished for, the perfect symbol and inspiration for the Church we shall establish. The Church of the Iron Angel! Soon people will flock to us and a new era will begin!"

But it seemed that the speaker's companion didn't share his enthusiasm, for he now turned on the first man a face etched with misgiving.

"It may be what *you* wanted, Higgins, but it isn't what *I* envisaged. Don't you see it's all wrong? The vision I had six months ago – it's come out all . . . *distorted*. There's pity in it, yes, but where's the beauty I intended, where's the sense of serenity? *This* thing I've made —" he gestured "— it's an abomination."

Higgins Makepeace looked taken aback. "Come now, Stephen," he said coaxingly, "surely you exaggerate. Why not give the Angel a day or two to settle down in your mind – then you'll see it's perfect."

"*No*, Higgins!" Stephen declared, "I shall *never* change my mind – never, no matter how long I live with it! This isn't something I've just realised now I've got to the end, it's a feeling that's been growing in me for days – nay, for weeks. I should have stopped work long ago, I should have destroyed this – *perversion*, this lump of obscenity, I should have started again. It was *you* – your belief that drove me on in spite of myself. And now I *shall* start again. I shall take it all apart, it can't go on standing here, desecrating the house of God—"

Higgins looked horrified. "But you can't do that, Stephen – the plans we made, our grand scheme—"

"I can, and I will. And it was never *our* scheme – it was *your* scheme, *your* brainchild. Well, that's worthless too. You and I, Higgins, we have to turn away from the past, we have to start again from scratch."

"Start from scratch . . . ?" Higgins repeated, staring at Stephen as if at a man who'd gone mad.

But the Angel's creator's gaze had moved back to his creation. Stepping forward, he gripped the railing than ran around the edge of the scaffolding at waist-height. He'd said all he meant to say; his decision was final.

His companion stood without moving. Silence vibrated in

the dusty space. Enclosed by the sheer stupendousness of the edifice, the two tiny men seemed like a pair of precocious ants. Then, with a quick, decisive movement, Higgins drew his knife from its sheath and stabbed Stephen in the neck.

The wounded man emitted a cry and swung away from Higgins, but the Grand-Ranter-to-be stabbed his victim again and again.

Stephen lurched away, teetered, made a grab at the rail but missed, then toppled over it. He hit the floor like a sack of grain carelessly tossed from a rat-cart, and lay without moving.

Higgins stood above him, looking down at the still body. Then the tension of the moment squeezed a few words out of him.

"You fool, Stephen," he muttered. "Did you really think to rob me of the glory that was promised?"

He stood for a little while longer, then moved to the top of the first ladder and began to descend.

Higgins Makepeace, thought Jewel, you're a murderer and a liar. What would your followers do, I wonder, if they knew the truth of things? Leave you alone to rot beside your metal monstrosity?

Why, she wondered, had the quincell chosen to play this scene for her? Was there something about Makepeace it wanted to draw to her attention – something beyond the simple human interest of the event? Was it something, perhaps, about the Iron Angel? Or was she on the wrong track: had the crystal simply picked up on the fact that the Grand Ranter and his doings were factors fresh in her mind? Perhaps, she thought, I ought to take this opportunity to explore the church a little more . . .

Just then she felt a sharp tug. Next moment, she was drawn back up towards the roof, through the vaulting, and into the sky. The blue darkened into black . . .

A hand was on her arm. Jewel opened her eyes. Thorn . . .

Her friend stood by her side. There was excitement in his face. The quincell was in her hands, at its nub a dying glow.

"Jewel?" he said, "Jewel?"

"Thorn?" Her voice sounded a little rusty. Yet she couldn't have been gone for very long, could she?

"Jewel, I had to wake you. Look! The mist!"

Sluggishly, Jewel took in her surroundings. She'd forgotten where she was: in a boat on a lake in a mist-ridden cave somewhere in Querne's labyrinth. But something was different . . .

Ah! That was why Thorn had brought her back! The mist was clearing.

I've something to tell him, she thought. But the truth about Higgins Makepeace could wait.

17

FISH AND FLOWERS

Out beyond the prow of the boat, the mist had thinned. Now, instead of resembling a mass of piled-up, whitish pillows, it curled and twisted in skeins and wisps, a far more skittish customer. Through these drifts and swirls, darker-coloured streaks and patches could be glimpsed. The walls of the cavern.

As the mist continued to thin, the patches grew larger until the contours of the rock beyond began to define themselves. At last the boat passed out of the mist-bank: all that remained beyond the prow were a few ravelled shreds, the sad last gasps of once all-conquering clouds.

Up ahead and to port and starboard the black surface of the lake stretched to nearing shores. Above, for the first time, the roof was also visible. This cavern was many times bigger than the others they'd explored. Its walls rose sheer out of the water, a mass of tumbling bluffs and buttresses and ribbed columns. High above the boat, the rocky ceiling weightily hung, spangled – like the walls – with the gem-lights that they'd seen so often before. They must be deep in the earth.

Thorn got to his feet.

"I wonder if this lake has any fish in it?" he murmured.

As if to answer his question, the water was suddenly scissored open off the starboard bow and several silvery fishes came shooting through the air. Or were they flying? For the creatures had wings which skimmed the water surface before they dived out of sight. Once again they leapt, aiming directly at the boat and splashing down not far away. Surely the end of the display: but no! Bursting out a third time, they came whizzing over the bow. Four made it safely across to touch down in the lake, but the fifth had misjudged its jump and landed on the planking of the deck with a soggy thump. Thorn and Jewel hurried forward. The fish lay on its underside, wings outspread, regarding them (or so it seemed) with expectant eyes. It was perhaps three inches long, and the semi-translucent membranes of its winglike fins seemed shot through with pastel tints.

Jewel stroked the fish with a finger, but it didn't flap about. "Can we get him back into the water?"

"Him?" questioned Thorn.

"He's a male," Jewel replied.

"Well, he'd make a nice dinner. Quite a few dinners, in fact."

"Don't be like that," she said. "He's much too handsome to eat."

"Only kidding," he replied.

"Were you?"

Thorn grinned.

One on each side of the fish, they squatted, got their arms under his body, and lifted. He wasn't light, but neither was he as heavy as he looked. Together they edged towards the port bow, staggered the last few steps and tipped the fish over the side. Water fountained into their faces.

Thorn sniffed his damp sleeves. "Ugh! I stink of fish!"

"Me too," said Jewel. "Still, not to worry. You've done your good deed for the day."

"If another one arrives, it'll be his last flight."

But none did. Evidently the fish had had sufficient exercise, or had taken Thorn's warning to their cold-blooded hearts, for none showed its head again.

The boat moved slowly towards the shore.

At this end, squeezed in by the narrowing cavern walls, the lake ran up into an inlet. Here was a jetty identical to that from which the boat had sailed.

The vessel approached it in a curve and came to a halt side-on, pointing back towards the lake. Shouldering their gear, Jewel and Thorn disembarked, walked along the jetty and began to climb a slope much like the one they'd left on the opposite bank. For up ahead, in the right-hand flank of an arrowhead recess in the rock, a door was invitingly set.

Their boots scraped as they climbed. Jewel yawned audibly.

"I'm tired," she announced. "It's got to be night-time up above. How about finding somewhere to sleep?"

"OK," Thorn agreed. "But the ground's pretty rough here. Shall we try the next cave?"

Wearily she nodded agreement.

Soon they reached the door. Like the others they'd encountered, it was unsecured by a lock. Thorn pushed it open, glanced through and gave vent to an exclamation.

The cavern was low-ceilinged and scintillated with colour and light. The light came from the usual source, the colour from hundreds – or was it perhaps thousands? – of precious stones. Rubies, diamonds, emeralds, opals and a host of other varieties neither Thorn nor Jewel could name glittered from walls and roof and studded in profusion the crags that jutted up from the floor. The cave was a mass of grottos — attractive nooks and mysterious crannies.

"It's like a treasure-house," murmured Thorn.

"Except," countered Jewel, "that Querne has no need of one. She told me so herself. This labyrinth is her playground — a sort of present to herself. Compensation, perhaps, for her banishment from Lowmoor?"

"Try asking her when you see her!" Thorn cocked his head. "What's that?"

They listened.

"Running water?" suggested Jewel.

"Sounds like it . . . Let's find out. This way, I reckon."

Before she could reply, he took off up a slope of rock, boots crunching on carbuncles of blue stone as he went. Jewel stood watching. She'd be damned if she was going to go after him just yet. At the top of the slope, he turned and waved, then dropped out of sight as he went down the far side. Jewel waited patiently. Then his voice came, muffled by the intervening crags: "Over here, Jewel — it's perfect!"

This had better be good, she thought. If I don't lie down soon I shall fall down anyway.

"Coming!" she called.

She laboured up the slope and stood panting at the top.

She wasn't surprised she was so tired. It had been a long, eventful day. Her little trip with the green quincell had used up the last of her energy.

Descending the downslope, she slipped and went sliding

down the rock, jarring her back, scraping her legs and grazing a hand on the protuberances of the uncut gems. At the bottom she fetched up in a heap and lay gasping and feeling sorry for herself. Could this be the same girl who'd managed to rout the Spetch twins? Who'd got the black crystal out of the Great Nest (before losing it)? She felt like a discarded rag.

But the tinkle of water sounded very close now.

Thorn appeared from around a rock. He'd dumped his pack and bow. A look of concern appeared on his face.

"Jewel – are you all right?"

"I, umm, slipped." She grinned weakly. "Just scratched myself a bit. I'm so tired, Thorn . . ."

"Food and rest, that's what you need."

He helped her to her feet.

"Here, I'll take your pack," he said, and slipped the straps off her shoulders. "This way – you're nearly there."

He led her around the rock.

"Oh, how lovely!" she exclaimed.

Water was trickling down the rock-face into the stone cup of a pool. Opals and rubies, washed by the running water, sparkled from the rock. Others glimmered up from the floor of the pool. The lip of the cup was covered by moss, which had managed to spread some distance over the floor of the grotto.

"Sit down here," invited Thorn. "It's quite dry – and really soft."

It was too. The mossy surface positively invited sleep. She yawned again.

"You ought to eat something," he said.

"I'm not hungry," she answered.

But she managed a little food, then climbed into her sleeping bag and closed her eyes. Now she was still, all her fresh grazes and scrapes made their tingling presence known. To deflect her mind from them, she thought of the beautiful things they'd come across in the last four caverns. Querne Rasp, their creator, was herself beautiful . . . But her beauty was skin-deep. Under the beauty, the enchantment, lay murk and murderousness. Querne – the black crystal at the centre of the star . . .

Jewel stooped, cupped her hands and dipped them into the pool. How cold the water was! As droplets spilled and fell splashing back, she lifted her hands and drank, and felt the liquid burn her mouth and throat like freshly melted ice.

Some impulse prompted her to turn. From the top of a nearby rock, a man was leering down at her. He was exceptionally ugly. He had one functioning eye: the other was hooded with wrinkled skin. His mouth was a crooked slit. His ears were misshapen flaps, and hair like a hedgehog's prickles stood spikily up from his skull. The corner of his mouth twitched, then he ducked down out of sight.

Jewel turned to where Thorn was sleeping, his bag close to her own. A giant hand squeezed her heart. Thorn was there, asleep still, but from Jewel's own bag a dark head was poking out. Someone must have crept into it after she slipped out for a drink! Angry now, she moved closer, then stared in disbelief. The sleep-drugged face in the rumpled bag was her own . . .

She started awake, looked wildly up: but no second self was there, standing gawping down at her. She turned her head towards the rock from which the watcher had leered down: but no one was there either.

Thorn was still asleep. Their packs were where they'd left them, Thorn's bow within reach of his arm. Her boots waited behind her head. Everything looked the way it had looked when she'd crawled into her bag.

A dream, she thought, nothing more than a dream . . .

But so vivid . . . The touch of the water, the *taste* of it, then the shock of that second self . . .

More than a dream, then: a sending. That was what it had to be. Her gift of sight had flashed her a warning: beware of a man with one eye. And maybe he really *had* been up there, in the flesh, leering at her.

She got herself out of her bag and padded across to the pool. Its water-mirror was limpid, and a familiar face returned her downward stare. She broke the image with her hands, brought water to her lips and sucked it up thirstily. The water was dream-cold, ice-fiery in her throat.

She splashed water on her face and felt it swill away the last vestiges of sleep. Her tiredness of the day before had gone, she felt fit and well.

"Jewel!"

Thorn was sitting up, rubbing the sleep from his eyes.

"Come and try this water," she said. "It will really wake you up!"

He did.

"Hey, that's cold!" He too splashed water on his face. "Hungry?" he asked.

She was, she realised.

They sat cross-legged on their sleeping bags, breaking their fast. Neither spoke for some time. Then Thorn said: "Jewel, do you think we're getting close to Querne now?"

"I wish I knew," she answered. "The whole point of labyrinths is to keep you going round and round without getting anywhere."

"But we seem to be somewhere now. This cavern and the last – she must have put a lot of effort into making them what she wanted. That boat, the mist . . . all these gems, this beautiful pool. She must come here from time to time."

"I'm sure she does. She likes beautiful things, and she likes mystery too."

"So why aren't they enough for her? Why does she want power too – to control people's lives? You and I don't want those things."

"No . . ." But even as she uttered the word, Jewel felt a curious kind of prickling inside her skull, as if some hitherto slumbering portion of her brain had woken up. To be Querne, to have her power – what would that be like? To be able to reshape the world in your image. Surely that would be wonderful, it would make you a sort of god. Very few people had the ability, you had to be exceptional. But then, she thought, I *am* exceptional, *I'm* a Magian too . . . Don't I have it in myself to be as great as Querne is? Maybe greater, in the end, for while she'd turn the world to evil, I would turn it to good. I'd get rid of all those people whose only notion is to destroy, like Deacon Brace and the Spetch brothers and the boatmen who attacked us on the dam and the Woodmen, and I'd reward all the people who do good, Sybs for instance. That would make for a better world, and it would all be down to me.

A vision of herself in a splendid gilded chair hoisted high on men's shoulders and getting cheered by huge crowds sprang up in her mind, and her imagination thrilled to her own magnificence.

Well, why not? Why should Querne be the one to rule the world? Why not she, Jewel Ranson, the no-account trader's daughter?

She snatched a look at Thorn, who was staring at the water as it dribbled into the pool, his jaw moving up and down as he chewed thoughtlessly. All at once it struck her just how ordinary he was – and worse than that, how young! Good grief, he was still a child! What could someone like Thorn know of power and greatness? How could he hope to understand her? Why did she need him anyway? Whatever she had to do she could do without his help. Let the lad go back to Norgreen and marry a girl from his settlement . . . As for herself, Jewel Ranson, well, *she* should only marry someone truly exceptional – or maybe no one at all, for where in her new-made world would she find a man to match her?

She got to her feet. It would be best to tell him now, before they went any farther. But when their eyes met, she found herself saying instead, "I never told you what I saw through the crystal, did I?"

"No. What *did* you see?"

She told him. When she'd finished, he looked pensive.

"So Makepeace is a murderer . . . What a hypocrite he is! We make a habit of meeting people who are not what they seem."

"Well here's someone to look out for – a one-eyed man with spiky hair. I have a feeling he'll turn out to be *exactly* what he seems."

"A one-eyed man?" Thorn exclaimed.

"That's what I said. I saw him in a dream just before I woke up."

"Jewel, you're having me on."

"See that rock?" She pointed. "He was up there, spying on us. It was Spine Wrench, I'm sure, though I've never seen him in the flesh. "

"Jewel, you're scaring me."

She grimaced. "I'm scaring myself. Is there any good reason why *you* shouldn't be scared too?"

She's in an odd mood this morning, he thought, and smiled uncertainly.

They packed their bags, then clambered back over the rock-ridge and went on down the path. It wound about till it reached a door.

The next cavern was dimly lit, with a mere scatter of gem-lights on its visible walls and low-hung ceiling. Jewel and Thorn paused to let their eyes get used to the light. When they had, they saw that a lush carpet of grass stretched out ahead. The grass wasn't green but mauve, and so short that it gave the impression of having been recently tailored. Here and there grew flowers a couple of inches in height. From their strong stalks, fretted yellowy leaves grew in pairs, and each was topped off by a crimson, globular blossom.

"There are no footprints here," Thorn complained. "I can't even see a path."

"There isn't one," said Jewel.

"So what do we do? Hunt for a door?"

She sighed. Why couldn't the stupid boy work it out for himself? "We'll have to follow the wall round. Otherwise we may blunder about and not find anything."

"So which way? Left or right?"

She shrugged. "Left?"

"OK."

They set off. After a time they reached a corner – a right-hander – and turned with it. Not long after, the same again. The cavern was narrow here. They continued along the wall, following its vagaries as it dipped in or bulged out, doing what caverns do. Underfoot the grass was springy; they steered around occasional plants.

Then they halted, frowning. A mass of the strange flowers was blocking the way ahead. Shoulder to shoulder they grew (if plants can be said to have shoulders), several rows of them.

"That's funny," said Thorn, "they weren't so close anywhere else . . ."

"No . . ." Jewel agreed. She felt oddly uncomfortable.

As if in response to the same impulse, they twisted to look behind them; then their glances turned to stares. Plants were moving towards them, edging slowly across the grass.

As Thorn stared at the impossible, he felt something touch his foot. He looked down and saw a plant clamber up onto his boot. There it clung by its snaky roots.

Then he let out a yell. The thing had bitten him! He could feel teeth in his leg! Seizing hold of the red globe, he yanked it free of his leg. The cloth of his trews tore, the blossom snapped off its stalk and he flung it away from him. The plant dropped off his foot.

"Run!" he shouted. "Jump over them!"

Jewel, who had seen everything, needed no second bidding. Together they ran at the plant barrier and launched themselves upwards. Over the bulk of them they sailed before landing on the rearmost and squashing them flat. Without pausing they ran on, keeping in sight of the wall. Plants came scuttling out of the twilight on nimble, rooty feet to throw themselves at the fleeing pair, who beat them off with swinging arms. Thorn crashed his fist into one blossom and, as its crimson petals squashed beneath the blow, he caught a glimpse of a toothed red mouth. Man-eating plants!

On they ran. Wall and more wall loomed before them out of the gloom. Just how far could the exit be?

Rounding a sharp left-hand corner they spotted a door further along. But the plants were aware of it too. Twenty or thirty deep, they clustered thickly around it, blockading the escape-route.

Jewel groaned. This was a nightmare. Perhaps she was still asleep . . . Please let me wake up, she thought . . .

Thorn drew his knife. "We'll have to fight our way through."

"We need the crystal," said Jewel. "Hold them off while I get it out."

Slipping her pack off her shoulder, she began to unfasten the straps. But quickly as she was moving, the plants were quicker still. Detaching themselves from the crowd, a number came hopping towards them.

Thorn swung his knife in a slow arc, slicing off the nearest blooms. This had an unexpected effect: undamaged plants behind the beheaded ones bent their leafy stalks and sank their teeth in the chopped-off globes. Sounds of chomping and slavering.

Cannibal plants! But more were coming at them, and Thorn had to jump forward to stop a couple getting at Jewel as she pulled the green crystal in its wrapping from her pack. As his knife slashed into a crimson head, he felt teeth fasten on his free arm. Ouch! He tried to pull his arm away, but the blossom clung grimly on, its roots dragging along the ground. Mindful of the danger that he might easily stab himself, he brought his weapon up into its head. He felt the teeth let go: the plant dropped limply to the grass.

Next moment a gout of green fire came spurting from the crystal, and the nearest flowers combusted in red and yellow flames, their blooms blackening and hissing angrily.

Jewel advanced on the crowd, throwing out fiery gusts. Plants that were not incinerated fell back, clearing a path. Thorn gathered up Jewel's pack and followed after her. Their boots crunched on smoky ruins.

When their way to the door lay open, Jewel turned to protect their backs and swung the crystal in a blazing arc. But the plants had backed well off, and none were caught in this parting shot. Pulling the door open, Thorn motioned Jewel through. Then he followed and shut it behind him.

They were safe.

18

FIRE AND ICE

They leant on the tunnel wall.

"You were bitten, Thorn," said Jewel, when they'd got their breath back.

"Yes – but it's nothing."

"Nothing? Let me see."

The plants' pointy teeth had left semi-circular punctures in his arm and in his leg. The wounds were oozing blood. Jewel went to work, swiftly closing them.

Thorn said, "Just as well you're a Magian. How many deaths would I have died on our travels if you weren't?"

"Don't go speaking too soon," she counselled wryly. "There's plenty of time still for dying. We haven't found Querne yet."

And talking of dying, she thought, without Thorn to hold those plants at bay while I got the crystal out, I'd never have made it back there. They'd have been on me in their hordes. I could have killed a lot of them, but they'd have had me in the end: they'd have torn me to shreds. How could I have imagined I could do without Thorn? And those fantasies about replacing Querne and ruling the world. I wasn't thinking straight this morning. This place does weird things to your head. I'm going to have to watch myself.

Thorn said, "Do you get the feeling that we've gone wrong somewhere – missed a short cut, I mean? I can't imagine Racky walking all this way underground."

"I think you're right," Jewel replied. "There has to be a short cut we simply haven't found."

"So what of the footprints we followed? A trick to bring us this way?"

"Yes. To take us into the cavern of the cannibal plants."

"But we survived them."

"We did. But I suspect Querne is still only playing with us."

The terrain of the next cavern contrasted with the last. There were more gem-lights, no grass and not a plant was to be seen. The landscape was craggy and rich in outcrops, but on a much bigger scale than in the cave of many grottos. A rough pathway wound away to disappear between two stones humped like the backs of lake-monsters.

Again there were no footprints. Were they on the right track? There was no way they could be sure. But if the new level of danger they'd just encountered meant anything . . .

Jewel donned her pack but kept her crystal, swaddled in its cloth, in her hands. She didn't intend to get caught again. Off they set down the track.

It meandered amongst the rock forms, looping and twisting and doubling back, sometimes narrow, sometimes wide. Nothing seemed to grow here, and they neither saw nor heard sounds of insects or animals. Hemmed about as they were, they caught few glimpses of the walls, and the full extent of the cavern stayed undisclosed.

"Hey, it's warm in here," said Thorn.

It was, too. And, as they moved deeper into the cave, the heat increased.

Sweat was beading on Thorn's forehead. He wiped it away with the back of his hand and undid a button on his shirt. But he kept his jacket on: if they should be attacked again, he wanted to have his hands free . . .

The track took them into a deep-cut defile. Here they'd be vulnerable to attack from above. But no attack came, and as they rounded a rock, they sighted a yellow glow beyond the crags ahead of them. Now, as they advanced, the number of gem-lights decreased; the glow was compensation enough. Soon there were none of the pinpoint lights, just the glow – strengthening. The path was climbing now. Their boots scraped on the rock floor as they warily advanced.

The defile twisted again. Light flickered high on the wall, playing across its cracks and fissures.

Fire, thought Thorn. There's fire somewhere up ahead.

A final turn; then, as they crested the rise, the enclosing outcrops fell away. Away to left and right the cavern walls were visible. The source of the glow was very near. A dozen paces and they could see it.

They were standing on the high lip of a circular concavity, a scooped-out bowl of stone. Down in the centre gaped a vent, and from the vent leapt yellow flames, their tips forking and flickering and casting a restless play of forms on the slopes of the bowl and the cavern walls. Glancing at Jewel, Thorn saw flames in her eyes, as if a fire was burning there. She looked changed, sinister, and her otherness struck him with the force of a mental fist.

Magians may *look* human, he thought, but they're a different order of beings to us ordinary folk . . .

It never occurred to him to think that Jewel would see flames in *his* eyes.

There appeared to be no pathway round the lip of the bowl: they'd have to go down, past the fire-vent, then climb the opposite slope. Reluctantly, Jewel returned the crystal to her pack. Then they started to descend, edging carefully down the rock. Waves of heat beat up towards them. Sweat sprang from their glistening faces, running into their eyes and mouths. Again and again they smeared it away.

At the bottom of the bowl the air was hot and somehow thick, like a sweltering summer's day. The ground beneath their boots was warm. Flames curled and spat from the vent, as if to snare the travellers. The closer they came to it, the hotter the ground got. Their clothes clung to their bodies, sticking at armpit and groin. Flames crackled above their heads, restless and sinuous as snakes. Then the fire-pit was behind them, and they were grateful to begin the climb up the other side of the bowl.

Once at the top, where the ground was level, they sat down with their backs against a rock and drank some water. The terrain on this side of the bowl was much as that on the other had been: a little way below the lip, a second defile slipped away amongst the crags.

Hot and sticky still, but somewhat restored, they got moving once more. Downhill now, they walked more quickly. High above their heads, flame-tongues flickered on the rocks, but, as their influence waned, gem-lights began to reappear, shining like glow-worms. The path ducked under an archway, then a second, then a third.

Still the path took them downwards. The lights multiplied in number. But now the cavern opened out and the ceiling lifted, receding. Up ahead, a second mouth yawned in the floor, an almost circular opening. But there were no flames here.

Beyond the pit, the cavern ended. And there, at last, in the right-hand corner, they saw a door. Circling around the pit, they made their way towards it.

What next? they wondered. What next?

The tunnel beyond the door was the longest one so far. Beyond the door that marked its end lay a vision of whiteness. Their eyes struggled to adjust. Then the chill hit their faces, and they grasped what the white was. Snow! Snow blanketing the floor. Snow thick on boulder and crag.

Snow below ground? Impossible . . .

But for the Magian they sought, impossible things seemed possible.

Thorn stooped, scooped up whiteness and brought a fistful to his lips. It burnt with cold.

"Snow," he confirmed. "The real thing. I'll be damned!"

"Extreme heat, extreme cold. First you roast, then you freeze. Querne's idea of a joke?" Jewel did not seem amused.

"That's odd," Thorn observed. "I can't see any lights . . . It ought to be dark in here, but it isn't."

This was true. No gem-lights were visible in the ceiling of the cavern, but Jewel and Thorn were able to see a fair distance into the cave. The atmosphere seemed luminous – as if the snow itself was giving off a gentle glow. Beyond the immediate boulders and crags, each capped with white, lay a dim region where shape merged into shape. You couldn't tell how deep or shallow the cavern might turn out to be.

But the footprints were back – and with a teasing difference from the ones they'd seen before. Two sets appeared on the snow: one set coming, one set going.

Thorn took a few steps forward and squatted down to examine the tracks.

"These sets of prints were made by the same boots," he declared. "And the set moving away from us is the later of the two: you can see where some footmarks press down on top of others." He looked up at Jewel. "Another trick to lead us on into danger?"

"Quite possibly," said Jewel. "But I wonder . . . did I really see Spine Wrench in the gem cave, not dream him like I thought?"

"If Spine *did* see us, he's probably gone to report the fact to Querne. So if she didn't know already we were here, she may now." He poked at the snow with the toe of a boot. "I don't like this," he went on. "We aren't geared up for these conditions. We could end up frozen stiff, a pair of permanent snowmen."

"One snowman, one snowgirl." Jewel returned Thorn's smile. "Well, no point in standing around. Let's move."

They got going again. Their boots crumped on the snow, inscribing fresh signatures. The trail wound among juts and crags. Where the ground was level, the footing remained sure, but where it sloped, rising or falling, they had to step more carefully, for the rock was slippery under its soft covering.

Now, on their left, the cavern wall bent in towards them.

From a series of inverted shelves hung rows of icicles, the longest of them several times the height of a man or woman.

Further along, an arm of rock reached out from the wall to form an overhang of sorts with a neighbouring crag. From its underside, more sharp spikes stuck glassily down. This gave the overhang the look of some rock-monster's upper jaw, crowded with needle-teeth and poised to bite. Both sets of tracks led underneath.

"Are we walking *under* that!" Thorn's exclamation expressed a distinct lack of enthusiasm.

"One-eye did – twice," Jewel replied.

"If those icicles should fall . . ."

"They look firm enough to me."

"Famous last words . . ." he muttered.

They went forward, stepping with exaggerated delicacy like people forced to cross a pond thinly sheeted with ice.

But none of the spikes fell, and they were through to the other side.

Soon the landscape changed again. Up from the ground, filling the region directly ahead, rose a number of glassy cones. Broad at the base, they tapered to points some four feet above the ground. The trail dived in amongst them.

Thorn and Jewel went forward, bending and turning with the footmarks, rounding one spire only to find others rearing ahead. Opaque, these curving surfaces offered little by way of reflection – only elusive, flitting smudges as the humans moved among them.

The air was icy against their faces, their breath rose in clouds, and the cold seemed to penetrate their clothes and the soles of their boots. Thorn slipped his hands into his pockets; if your fingers became numb and you needed to use your bow, then you really were in trouble. Out came the green crystal again. Jewel activated it just enough to keep her hands warm. She could make it blaze, she knew, but would call on that resource only in an emergency. Thorn looked ruefully at the stone: if only *he* could hold the thing . . .

As they rounded one more spire, a different scene confronted them.

Trees. Not one or two, but a whole thicket of them – even, perhaps, a small wood. *Small* in both senses, for the trees were miniature versions of the trees in Judy Wood. Two to three feet in height, they were perfect in every detail. They had trunks, branches and leaves. But every knot and gnarl on the trunks, every last forked twig, every finely veined leaf had been sculpted out of ice.

On went the footprints, straight between two of the trees.

Jewel and Thorn moved forward, and the trees closed ranks around them. They were exquisite, but unnerving. No breeze disturbed their leaves; they stood utterly motionless, a band of crystal martyrs doomed to pose here forever.

Thorn and Jewel padded on. As if in deference to the trees, their feet made no sound. They might have been walking on air.

Thorn blew out a cloud of white. "I don't like this silence. Where are the birds? Surely there ought to be a few?"

If this was an attempt at a jest, it fell flat. Jewel said nothing. She was thinking about Querne, ice-sculptress extraordinary, and this cold, bloodless beauty almost no one would ever see.

They heard the sounds at the same time, exchanged looks and came to a halt.

"What is it?" whispered Thorn.

Jewel's answer was a question. "What does it sound like to you?"

"Like – well . . ." Thorn faltered. "Like a number of people scraping knife-blades against glass."

She nodded. "Couldn't have put it better myself."

For a moment neither spoke. The distant sound continued.

Then Thorn said, "Perhaps it's nothing. A breeze among the trees." But even as he said this, he didn't believe it.

Jewel shrugged, and on they went. Above their heads, the delicate ice-leaves did not so much as twitch, the glass-sleek branches made no sound. Still higher overhead loured a sky made of stone.

The scraping noise intensified. Either it was coming towards them, or they were going towards it. Invading Thorn's ears, it seemed to spread through his body, scratching away at his nerves as if to rub them red-raw.

Then, up ahead between two trees, something moved. Thorn and Jewel stopped again and stood peering through the trunks, trying to make out what it was. But whatever was moving there was made of the same stuff as the trees, so this was no easy task.

Jewel twisted to look left.

"That noise!" she exclaimed. "It's coming from over there too!"

"Not just from that way," said Thorn, uneasily. "To our right, as well . . ."

It was true: the noise was coming from all sides except behind them.

They peered again . . . and seemed to see rods of glass with lumps on top, moving toward them!

Robbed for a time, or so it seemed, of the will or ability to move, they held their ground, eyes locked on the shapes moving among the trees.

Then they came into view.

Thorn groaned. The rods were legs, and the legs were walking – or crawling. These were creatures of some sort, creatures twice a human's height, creatures out of Querne's dreams or anyone else's nightmare. Each crawler had eight legs and each leg was jointed. In amongst the legs was slung a nugget of diamond. Out of this body protruded a head, and out of the head a pair of silver threads – the creatures' feelers. On they came, scraping and scratching, immune to the cavern's climate because they too were made of ice.

Jewel and Thorn stood unbelieving.

Ice-spiders?

Ice-spiders!

They didn't look in the least friendly.

Thorn slipped his bow off his shoulder and reached behind him for an arrow. He nocked it and fired. The arrow flew between the trees, glanced off the foremost spider's head and buried itself in the snow. Thorn drew and shot again. This time his aim was better. The shaft struck its head full on.

And shattered, harmlessly. The spider didn't even pause.

"It's no good," Thorn shouted. "We can't fight them. Run!"

He turned to go, but saw Jewel hesitate.

The crystal was warm in her grasp. Thorn can't fight them, she thought, but maybe *I* can . . .

What's she waiting for? he wondered.

"Come on, Jewel!" he urged.

Discretion overcame valour, and the pair took to their heels. They ran back the way they'd come, kicking the snow up in their flight.

The trail was easy enough to follow. But now, away on each side, they saw movement among the tree-trunks. The same spindle-swing of legs, relentless and mechanical. The same scritching of knife-blades. More spiders, closing in.

And the spiders were not slow. They might have been walking when first sighted, but now they too were hastening. And, blessed with eight legs, they were quick.

The spiders were closing on three sides.

"Faster!" cried Thorn.

"I can't go any faster!" she gasped.

The trail rounded a tree, then took off at a new angle. Thorn swerved to stay with it, but when Jewel, who was a few paces behind him, twisted to follow, she slipped and fell full length. The snow sheet cushioned her fall, but the breath was knocked from her lungs and the green crystal went spinning. The girl lay winded and gasping.

Thorn had run two dozen steps before he registered what had happened. He stopped and, turning, saw an ice-spider poised above the girl. It lifted a shining leg and seemed about to stab down at her, but Jewel rolled over and grabbed the leg close to its end. There was a flash of energy and the spider blazed like a star. Then it melted. Its rod-like limbs buckled and it collapsed onto the snow, its body molten and runny, its feelers waving feebly as they drooped and liquefied.

She looked wildly round for the crystal, but was unable to locate it.

Then more spiders were around her.

"Run, Thorn!" she shouted. "Save yourself!"

Another spider lifted to strike, and again she seized the threatening limb. The spider flared up like the first and it too began to melt. For a moment, its nearer allies fell back, but then on they came again.

Jewel was on her feet now.

"Run, Thorn!" she shouted. "Run!"

Thorn watched, powerless, as a third spider jabbed at her, catching her in the back. Twisting, she grasped the attacking limb, and again the spider flared and collapsed.

But more of the creatures struck at Jewel and he saw her body sag. Even so, gamely, she managed to grab a fourth limb, but this time could do no more than cause its lower part to melt.

Then she fell back on the ground and was lost to Thorn's view.

He turned and fled through the silent trees.

19

SPINE WRENCH JANGLES
HIS BELL

Surrounded by ice-spiders, Jewel lay on the snow. She had
known that she was doomed when the first one stung her. A
fierce chill had invaded her body, sapping her physical energies.
For a while she'd fought on, but, as more spiders added their
stings, numbness had spread through her limbs until she could
no longer resist.

A spider dipped its head above her. Multi-faceted, its eyes
flashed – two intricate emeralds. It opened its mandibles, a pair
of glittering pincers with hooked points like ice-thorns. If it
should sink them into her body . . .

She tried to open her mouth to shout defiance at the monster,
but her muscles were paralysed. She was so cold, so tired . . . Her
eyelids kept drooping . . . She had to fight to keep them open.

This is a wretched end, she thought. Please let Thorn at least
escape . . .

Her eyes closed, her mind shut down and she did not hear
the bell.

It rang harshly through the clear air: *jangle-jangle-jangle*. A
man held it by the handle, and he shook it up and down as he
came limping through the snow.

The ice-spider heard the bell and closed its jaws obediently.

Warmly clad in a fur-lined jacket and leather over-trews, half-mittens that covered his hands but left his fingers free, and with a furry cap on his head, the man threaded his way through the crowd of spiders. Not one moved to harm him. In fact, none moved at all: they might have been frozen where they stood — ice-statues, cunningly carved.

The bell was a curious object. Cast in brass and much polished, it gleamed like new gold. Its upper half was a perfect sphere incised with obscure symbols; its lower half was divided into six clawlike prongs. These stopped short of meeting, leaving a hole big enough for a couple of fingers to push through. Inside this metal cage dangled the jangling clapper-ball.

The clangour abruptly ceased: the man had inverted the instrument, transferring his grip from its knoblike handle to its clapper, which he now held captive between finger and thumb. Bending over the girl, he studied her with a crooked grin.

He was a sight for sore eyes, though he had only one of his own — a leering, bloodshot orb. The gap its partner might have occupied was hooded with wrinkled skin.

He *tsk-tsked*, and blobs of slaver squirted from his mouth.

"Silly missy! Silly miss!" Was he talking to himself or was he speaking to the spiders? Either. Or both, perhaps . . . "Thought she could fool old Spine again? Nobody does it twice and lives. *Now* just look at her! Cold as a fresh corpse's toes!" He produced a gruesome chunter somewhere between a croak and a giggle. "Slippery Spine was too many for *she*! *And* her a Magian too!" He patted the nearest spider's leg with every appearance of affection. "With a bit of help from his friends."

So saying, he squatted and, by dint of raising Jewel's upper body from the snow, unhooked her pack from the girl's shoulders. Then he let her flop back.

"Now: let's see if it's in here . . ."

Unfastening the straps of the pack, he peered inside suspiciously, then began to remove the contents and drop them one by one on the snow. He proceeded slowly, with much sucking in of lips and frequent gurns and grimaces, as if he feared there might be something hiding inside that would bite. At length he frowned, turned the pack upside down and gave it a shake, then dashed it to the ground.

"It's not here," he muttered. "But it must be . . . Did missy drop it?"

He stepped back and, turning, began to peer about, scanning the ground near Jewel's body.

But not for long. Tiring of his fruitless search, he tapped his bell against one of the foremost spider's legs. As he was still gripping the clapper, only a dull *thang* resulted, but this seemed to be enough. The spider cocked its head to gaze down at the one-eyed man.

"Corryn!" Spine Wrench commanded the largest of the spiders. "Green crystal! Find!"

Raising two of its forelegs, Corryn began to rub them together. This produced the scratching sound that Jewel and Thorn had heard earlier. The rest of the spiders came to life and backed off in an orderly manner, leaving a space where the snow was pocked and scuffed from their feet. Corryn now set off at a slow walk, circling Jewel's body and moving its head from side to side. Its silvery feelers twitched as if it expected to pick up an odour or tremor in the air. Nearly two circuits were complete, the second wider than the first, when it stopped, raised a foreleg and pointed at the ground.

With a grunt of anticipation, Spine Wrench teetered across to the indicated spot and started scrabbling in the snow.

There came a blinding green flash.

"Owww!" yelled Spine as he flew spectacularly backwards, dropping his bell, and measured his length in the snow. The nearest spiders peered down at him, their eyes expressionless. They might have been examining a rock or a squashed louse.

"Bloody baubles!" cursed Spine, beating the snow with an angry fist. "Damn and blast the lot of them!" Then, muttering, "Poor old Spine, the indignities you put up with . . ." together with a selection of imprecations, he struggled to his feet, retrieved his bell, and, pulling a grubby rag from his pocket to wrap round his right hand, cleared the snow around the crystal.

Now, seemingly forgetting his curses, he murmured, "Look at you, you beauty! Oh she'll be pleased, she'll be pleased, and old Spine will get a treat!" An expression of glee brightened his features; then they went sour again. "But not the treat he wants most, not the thing he most craves: Racky Jagger out on his neck and old Spine top rat! Oh, wouldn't it be lovely if she gave Racky the boot? Better still, if she handed Racky over to the spiders – that would make Spine's day! That would make his ears waggle!"

And, to give himself a foretaste of this treat, he slipped his hat off and waggled his ears.

"That's the way, that's the way, that's the way old Spine does it, and any scab who doesn't like it gets a tickle of Spine's knife!"

Unfastening the straps of the half-pack he wore on his hip, he put the wrapped crystal inside and re-secured the thongs. Then, taking up his bell, which he'd set down on the snow in order to deal with the crystal, he rang the instrument vigorously, but this time with a different rhythm.

"Wakey wakey, sleepy spiders! There's busy business to be about!"

The spiders stirred from their lethargy, flexing legs and twitching feelers.

Spine tapped the same spider as before on the same leg. Corryn scrutinised him coolly, eyes lustrous, all-judging.

"Come on, roll-a-ball, roll-a-ball!" commanded Spine belligerently, illustrating his order with an energetic gesture.

Had the spider felt so inclined, it could have bitten off his head with a single snap of its pincer-jaws. But it did nothing of the kind.

Out from its body across Jewel's waist it spun a cable of silver, then kicked the girl onto her back, rolling her over in the snow and wrapping loop after loop around her until she was well and truly trussed.

Now, wondered Spine, should I wait till the other spiders come back with the lad? Or get this stone straight to Querne?

He peered through the trees. There was no sign of movement there.

Well, they'll bring him along, thought Spine. He'll be dead meat by now. I might as well get off back . . .

He rang his bell again. Corryn turned and stalked off, dragging feet-first after it the girl in her silvery cocoon. Beside her limped the bellman, threatening to fall at every step but somehow staying on his feet.

The other spiders fell in behind, bubbles of glass mounted on stilts, their bodies wobbling as they walked. With them, through the ice-wood, went the scritching of knife-blades drawn across glass; also, intermittently, the jangling of the bell.

Querne Rasp sat in her chair, her eyes fixed on nothing. Her pallid skin seemed stretched too tightly over her high cheek-bones, and the lights glimmering from the walls accented the planes of her face, creating pools of darkness in the hollows beneath her eyes and shadows under her cheekbones. Her long, chestnut hair at this moment seemed black – as did as her eye-brows. Hers was a tense and strained beauty.

By her side on top of a table lay a large four-pointed star cunningly wrought from spun metal. Set in each point was a pocket, as was the area at the centre. Four pockets were occupied: the central one by the black crystal, the others by the smaller red, blue and yellow stones. The Magian's right arm rested along the tabletop, close to the crystals.

The room was a place of fascination – of lacquered cabinets with silver-handled, tantalising drawers, elegant tables with marbled tops and straight or curving legs, gilt chairs richly upholstered. On the cabinets and tables stood many curios and knick-knacks – glass, pottery or wood. The tapestries hanging on the walls showed strange animals and birds that might have lived in other worlds or originated in vivid dreams and fever-ridden nightmares. The room was L-shaped, with the foot of the L out of sight. Querne's bed was in that part. It had snake-headed bedposts and rested on heavy, taloned feet: the snakes – viridian-scaled and fork-tongued – possessed ruby eyes that seemed to burn out of their heads and threaten to lock you up in a trance. Mole-fur throws, soft and smoky-black, lay strewn across the bed.

The chair Querne sat in was made of black wood and elaborately carved. The life-size head of a feral rat topped off its high back, jaws bared to show savage teeth.

On the rock walls between the tapestries hung a number of gilded mirrors. These, oval or rectangular and of various sizes – the longest taller than Querne herself – held reflections of the room that enhanced its dimensions, multiplying its contents and emphasising its extravagance, and when Querne sauntered about she would pass from mirror to mirror, not one woman but many women, distributed – fractured – among the dizzying surfaces.

There came a knocking at the door: two strokes, pause; one stroke, pause; then two strokes again.

Querne turned her head to one side and examined her face in the nearest mirror. Now, as it stared back at her, her reflection began to soften: its cheekbones lost their sharpness, its smudges and shadows receding, its sense of strain dissolving away. Her image was ten years younger, flawlessly beautiful once more.

"Come in," she called.

The door opened and Spine Wrench came lurch-limping in. He'd shed his outdoor clothes in favour of comfortable indoor garb, and carried his hip-pack in one hand. Closing the door behind him, he advanced towards the menacingly double-headed chair – rat above, woman below. He halted a couple of paces short and – stoop-shouldered, head lolling, a lopsided, self-satisfied smile plastered across his face – stood waiting for Querne to speak.

"Well?" she prompted after a time.

"Got it!" he announced, lifting his pack and shaking it, his features radiant with triumph.

"Give it to me," commanded Querne.

Wrench took out the wrapped crystal and passed it to the Magian, who set it on her lap and threw back the folds of the cloth. The jagged edges of the stone caught fractions of light from the mirrors and answered with opalescent gleams.

"Five!" said Querne Rasp with a mixture of awe and avarice. "Five crystals – *I have them all!*" And feasted her eyes on the green stone.

Her faithful servant said nothing. He knew when to keep his mouth shut.

Watching, he saw Querne's right hand go creeping towards the stone. Her fingers, he noticed, were trembling. But just as woman and crystal were about to make contact, she drew her hand back and drew in an audible breath.

She's properly hooked, he thought. Can't keep her hands off them, and they're slowly eating her up. Perversely, he found the notion exciting as well as worrisome.

Querne looked up at Wrench. If she read in his expression what was passing through his mind, she gave no sign of doing so.

"What of the girl?" she enquired.

"The spiders have her," said Wrench. "All trussed up and frozen stiff. She won't be going anywhere."

"She did well to get so far. She has more lives than a king rat. She ought to have died in the ironworks – *would* have died there but for Racky."

"Why? What did Jagger do there?" asked Spine.

"Of course, you don't know, do you . . .?"

"You told me you left the girl for the blue rats when you took the black crystal from her. You said you didn't know she'd survived until I came to you this morning and told you I'd seen her in—"

"Don't tell me what I know," Querne snapped at her minion. "When my brains turn to snow, you'll be the first to feel the freeze."

Spine looked down at the floor and shuffled nervously on the spot. "Yes, mistress," he mumbled.

"So, then," said Querne, mollified by this show of abjection, "when you'd gone, I took the black crystal and looked into it. It was Racky and the girl's friend, Thorn Jack, who saved her skin. But Racky paid for it with his life."

Spine looked up from the floor. "Jagger's dead?" he said, as if he couldn't believe his ears.

"Yes . . . and I have to admit that he surprised me at the last."

This was an understatement. It wasn't just that Racky's desertion had taken Querne by surprise, but that he'd died to save Thorn. To Querne, the notion of giving up your life for another person was inconceivable. But then, she'd told herself, I have no children, Racky did. A child does strange things to your head . . .

Well now, thought Spine. This is the best news I've had since I heard of Gummer's death.

"What shall I do with the lass?" he asked.

"Leave her where she is while I decide what to do with her; as you so rightly say, she won't be going anywhere." Querne grinned a sinister grin. "Perhaps I'll keep her on ice for evermore, as a trophy. What of her friend – Thorn Jack? He's almost as much a pest as the girl is – or should I say, *was*?"

"He ran away," Spine admitted, "with the spiders at his heels. He's likely dead meat by now. Even if by some freak he got out of the ice-cavern alive, his days are numbered. With the cannibal plants on one side and the spiders on the other, he can't go forward, can't go back."

Querne frowned. "I don't like loose ends. Go and check if the spiders have brought his body in. If they haven't, track him down yourself and send him to his maker. Bring me his head as proof."

Spine's eyes glittered. "That will be my pleasure, mistress!" He fingered the hilt of the long knife sheathed on his belt. He'd never cut off a head before; it ought to prove interesting, all those bones and tubes and sinews. A bit of blood wouldn't bother him. He would smear his tongue with it: that was the way you took your enemy's powers into yourself – as long, of course, as he was dead.

"Good. You've done well. Now: about your business, man!"

But Wrench didn't move. He stared nervously at the Magian.

"Er, mistress . . ." he began.

"Yes, Spine?"

He pointed to his ravelled eye. "You said . . . umm – you might sort this out for me . . ."

Querne smiled. "So I did. And so I might. I'm still thinking about it. I'm not sure I don't prefer you as the handsome man you are. Still, get rid of Thorn Jack: then we'll see."

Spine grinned uncertainly.

"But . . ." he began. Then, thinking better of it, "Yes mistress," he finished.

His lower shoulder drooped still further. He turned and shuffled towards the door.

As he closed it behind him, anger flared in his eye and he choked off a curse. The woman can hear through rock walls . . .

Promises, he thought, that's all old Spine gets out of her. And where would she be without him to cook and do for her? Running here and running there, keeping things hunky-dory. Who else would do that, who else would work with those scary spiders, who else would ring that bell? One fine day Spine'll up and sling his hook, see if he doesn't. Then she'll be sorry.

But then he remembered that Jagger was dead. That was reason to celebrate. And if – no, *when* – this Thorn Jack was dead too, perhaps Querne *would* relent and give him his eye back again. After all, he, Spine, was her right-hand man now. Surely she would, she *must* . . .

With a vigour that belied his ravaged looks and rolling walk, he made his way back to his room.

When Spine had gone, Querne turned her attention to the crystal on her lap. She knew no greater thrill than contact with a new stone. And now she had all five of them!

Originally she'd thought of the crystals as separate entities, things to be used one at a time. But when she acquired her second stone, it was immediately clear that they were linked in sympathy. Awaken one with the other near, and the untouched stone would start to glow. Wielding two at the same time increased the pleasure she got from them. But the real breakthrough came with the third crystal's arrival. How surprised she'd been when the triangle shape that seemed the most natural arrangement began, first to slowly revolve, then to spin faster and faster, creating, at its centre, a kind of vortex.

Querne had put the yellow crystal to work in one of two ways. When she was in an active mood, she would search through the images it contained of worlds past and present; when she fancied being passive, she would surrender herself to the sensations it aroused. Her discovery of the vortex effect changed everything. She could project herself through it into the worlds of the crystals and move about in those worlds, also attract things with it – as she'd drawn Jewel to her before exploring the ironworks. What was more, the vortex effect was reversible: she could draw things *out* of it.

What might she not be capable of with a five-crystal vortex? The possibilities seemed endless.

Except it hadn't proved that simple. The previous evening, back from the ironworks with the crystal she'd taken from the girl, she'd made her first – and so far only – attempt to wield four stones at once. She began by arranging them in a square – but they refused to revolve. Only when she placed the black stone at the centre did they move and start to spin, creating the vortex effect that she desired. But now, to her surprise, the black crystal disappeared and the vortex began to dilate, exerting a terrific force. Suddenly things were difficult. She felt fear prickling her skin. The three-stone vortex had been stable; this one was not, it threatened to leap away and go zooming around the room, perhaps vanish through a wall – anything seemed possible. She was relieved when, without mishap, she got it shut down. Perhaps with the fifth stone it would work properly. Yet she wasn't convinced of this. Her sixth sense told her that the black stone was flawed. Had the Magian who'd created it in this world or some other – who but a Magian could it be? – made a mistake?

I was right to be wary of this stone, she told herself. But I'm Querne Rasp, aren't I? I can overcome this problem. Practice makes perfect. I shan't attempt five crystals till I've mastered control of four. That will be the best thing.

Single crystals, of course, were easy, and the green crystal was calling. What sensation would she experience when she gave herself up to it? What sensuous excitements, what mental visions would it produce? Each stone, she'd found, was subtly different from the rest, though all were addictive.

She grasped the stone with both hands and green fire flared at its heart. For a few moments she stared straight out in front of her; then her eyeballs rolled in their sockets, showing slightly bloodshot whites, and her body relaxed in its chair.

The Magian sank into the depths of the stone.

Wearing his furry jacket, over-trews and fur cap, and toting his bell, Spine Wrench entered the ice-cavern, the second largest in the labyrinth (the largest was the lake cave). Because of its shape and due to the columns that rose in places from floor to ceiling, you could, if you were inclined to, think of this cavern as a group of linked caves: eight, to be exact. As the ice-spiders' domain, it was Spine's favourite of all those in the labyrinth, and towards its denizens Spine bore a paternal air. For if anyone might claim to have fathered the spiders, it was Spine.

He, like Gummer his elder brother, one-time master of Roydsal, had been born in Lowmoor. "Circumstances drove us apart," so Gummer would say to Spine when by accident they met, scarcely able to wait for the two of them to be driven apart again. Their paths through life had reached an early parting of ways. While Gummer made himself rich through various dodgy enterprises, Spine languished in the Belly, eking out a smelly existence through the carting of night soil. Taking its cue from Spine's family, Lowmoor had never cared for him, regarding him as an error – or worse, a disease – of nature: something best shunned lest you catch it yourself. Only Querne Rasp had shown any interest in him: quite possibly, he reckoned, because no one else did. Querne was contrary, and not afraid to do unpopular and contrary things. Obliging Spine made himself useful to her, became a servant of sorts and, when Lowmoor decided it had had enough of Querne, announced his determination to go into exile with her. He looked forward to her revenge with a keen sense of complicity.

Spine knew a lot about Querne – more even than Racky Jagger. Jagger might have been Querne's lover, but it was Spine in whom the Magian tended to confide. He knew, for instance, the history of her connection with the church. Before her banishment, Querne's practice of her skills had often taken her from Lowmoor. It was on one such outing that she'd stumbled across the church. At that time, it was untenanted: viewed, on account of its beetling spire and extensive graveyard, as a place to be avoided. But Querne was untouched by superstition and found the notion of a god or gods an absurd proposition – a fact that failed to endear her to Lowmoor's many pious folk.

Exploring the church fearlessly, she discovered underneath it the seven six-sided chambers that the giants had built as a novel kind of crypt. There they had stopped, seeing no use for the extensive network of caves that lay beyond. But, penetrating this, Querne was struck by its extent and physical variety. In the biggest cavern of all she found an accumulation of water: a sizeable pool to a giant, a small lake to a human. The potential of the place as refuge and base were obvious, so when she was banished from Lowmoor she and Spine moved in and set to to develop it into a huge labyrinth: should enemies seek her out, not only would they have to strive to find a way through, they'd have to contend with the devious defences she installed. Its fancy grottos and galleries had taken her years to perfect, but she had the yellow crystal to boost her natural powers and provide her with ideas, and she got there in the end. From time to time she still tinkered with this cavern or that, adding, refining or subtracting as whim directed.

When the two wanderers arrived – Stephen Peters, a mystic and sculptor, and Higgins Makepeace, an unstable visionary obsessed by death and dreams of power – Querne watched the pair for a time before revealing herself to them. Absorbed in creating the Iron Angel, Peters paid her little attention, but Makepeace proved receptive, and she set to work on him. He told her of his dream – to found a religious sect with himself at its head, a self-styled Grand Ranter. Makepeace, Querne saw, had some power of rhetoric, but a limited imagination: the construction of a persuasive myth was way beyond him. It was not beyond Querne, however, and it amused her to think it up and lay it out for him. Her influence over him grew, and when she observed that Peters was beginning to question the way the Angel was turning out, she began to hint to Makepeace that the sculptor would soon be a problem. What if the effigy's maker should decide to unmake it? Perhaps he was surplus to requirements . . . To begin with, Makepeace shrank from the notion of murder, but Querne persisted in pouring her poison into his ears, and his resistance weakened. And surprise, surprise: no sooner was the Angel finished than its maker fell from his scaffolding and broke – *snap!* – his neck. Makepeace was Querne's creature now. As long as he kept his disciples out of her hair (as he did, having other fish to fry), she was content his group should occupy the church above ground. They kept other wanderers away. Meanwhile it amused her, as a sort of human experiment, to shape the way the cult developed and the end towards which it grew. Spine himself, however, had little interest in the cultists. As for the Iron Angel, it gave him the willies and he steered clear of it.

Spine had his own art objects. Here, in a part of the ice-cavern denied to the spiders, was a grove of ice-sculptures – strange animals and birds that Querne had once fashioned for him. Her inspiration came from the source that produced her tapestries. At one time she'd told him the names of all these creatures, but he remembered only a few: the trinculum, a spiny, hard-shelled creature with nine mouths and as many spiralling tongues; the woolly mammoth, with its lumbering body, great ears and upswept tusks; the gryphon, winged, hook-beaked and four-pawed; the octosaurus, which ran on eight whippy tentacles and had a triangular head full of teeth; and the squell, a three-horned snail-like tree-crawler that immobilised its prey – birds – by emitting a piercing scream, then sucked them into its maw.

But the ice-spiders were Spine Wrench's joy. Whenever he was with them, their beauty would fill him with pride and a sense of achievement – for, although Querne had created the spiders, it was Spine who'd suggested spiders as a mobile defence force. This prompting was the product of a long enthusiasm, for his liking for spiders dated from early childhood. He could remember quite clearly his first sighting of the tribe. Happening one day as a small boy on a web in one corner of the bedroom he shared with Gummer, he'd marvelled at its intricacy and formal perfection. The web's maker sat at its centre, leggy and motionless, an object lesson to human beings in patience. Then a half-witted midge had flown smack into the network, gluing itself to the strands. Straightaway the spider went about its spidery business: administering a poisonous bite to keep its prey subdued and smartly roping the insect up. So great was Spine's pleasure in observing all this that he hurried to share his discovery with his brother, three years older than himself. A mistake. Gummer's response was to screw up his face and utter an *ugh!* of disgust. That would have been bearable, had Gummer left it there. But Gummer did not. Fetching a thick stick, he knocked the web to the ground, beat the spider to a pulp and jumped up and down on it, shrieking with glee.

A second object lesson. Thereafter, Spine kept his new enthusiasm to himself. If he found a spider in the house, he never mentioned it. If its web was in a spot which made it liable to be found, and the spider was small enough, he would catch it, carry it outside and set it free. If the spider was too big or too quick to be caught, he'd drive it off and wreck its web, reasoning that for the creature to be unhoused but alive (it could build a new web) was in every way preferable to being (*bash! crash!*) dead. When in settlement school one of the teachers asked the children to name their favourite creatures, Spine showed his cunning: "Rats," he declared. Hardly original, but the lie served its purpose.

As time went on and Spine became more and more isolated, more and more a loner, he came to see the spiders as his natural allies. They too were unloved, they too were persecuted. If he could only have had a spider for a brother instead of Gummer! *Then* he would have had someone to stand up for him. *Then* people wouldn't dare to treat him the way they did. A spider of human size or bigger, majestic, perfect and deadly – not crookbacked and one-eyed, as he himself had been since birth . . .

Nearing the ice-webs now, Spine pictured them in his mind – stretching from crag to crag, hanging in crannies and outjutments, rigid grids of air and crystal, lattices of ice-cables . . . the spiders sitting at their centres or lurking in handy nooks of rock. Not, of course, awaiting victims to fly into their traps. Ice-spiders do not eat, although their ice-jaws can chew. They need nothing to sustain them. In fact they don't need to have cobwebs at all: they could park themselves anywhere. But Spine had wanted them to make webs – for make webs is what spiders do – and Querne had humoured her servant's fancy. And there was always the chance that one day someone would trespass into their realm to end up coldly cocooned, suspended in ice-limbo.

Well, today was that day. Earlier, Spine had stood and

watched as the spiders hung Jewel, tightly trussed, just above the ground in the place designated for storage of prey. Chipping away the odd ice-thread that encircled her head, he'd gloated over his captive. Ice-beads stuck to her hair and eyebrows, her lips were a bloodless pink, her skin as white as fresh snow. After which, he'd left to give Querne the green crystal and make his report. And by now, he expected, as he neared the holding-place, jangling his bell to announce himself, Thorn Jack would have joined her, and Spine would have *two* hapless danglers to lord it over.

Surprise? Astonishment? No: shock. Shock was the word for what Spine felt as his unbelieving eyes took in not only that Thorn Jack wasn't there, as trussed and iced out as his female friend was, but that Jewel's body had gone – whisked away by God knew what – out of old Spine's grasp.

Only then did he realise a still stranger thing: not one spider had answered his bell. What's more, not one could be seen. None lurked on a rock, sat quietly in its web, or dangled by a silver cable – not even the sentinel charged to stay here on watch when all the others left the cave.

Whatever had whisked the bodies away had made the spiders vanish, too.

Then he noticed on the ground a puddle of freshly frozen water – where, when he left earlier, no such puddle had been . . .

And here were tracks. Imprints of boots not his own, they led up to the spot where the girl's body had hung, and led away. Where she'd hung, the snow was scuffed.

She hadn't walked, she'd been taken.

305

Yes, taken. And Spine knew by whom. Thorn Jack was the only candidate. But if Jack had taken her, the spiders couldn't have captured him.

Puzzlement showed on Spine's face. How in the name of fiery Hell could the lad have escaped them? And where were his beautiful spiders now? The frozen puddle might have been *one* spider, but no more than that . . .

There was, of course, only one way to find out. Spine at once set off to track this mortal enemy down.

20

THORN JACK GETS LUCKY

If he hadn't been so preoccupied with running, Thorn would have wept, wept for Jewel.

She's dead, he thought as he careered along: dead. Or if she isn't yet, soon will be. And there's nothing I can do . . .

But nobody can run fast and weep at the same time. And Thorn was running for his life. Through the ice-forest he ran, his feet pounding down the snow. With, behind him always, that sound – a sound that threatened to freeze his heart – the scraping of knife-blades on glass as the spiders came after him.

He threw a glance over his shoulder. His nearest pursuer was only a few feet behind. It seemed to bound over the snow as if its legs were sprung, a nightmare conjured from glass.

Thorn swerved sharply to the left, skidding round the trunk of a tree, and the spider, swerving to follow, side-swiped the tree. There was a sound of splintering and a leg joint came flying past Thorn's head and went cartwheeling over the snow.

One down – great! But still the spiders came after him. The scratching sound was in his ears, inside his head, echoing there. It might be the last sound he'd hear . . .

Then something caught his leg and sent him tumbling across the snow. He ended lying on his back. A spider loomed over him. Deliberately it lifted a leg to stab down at him. Yet the stab never came. The leg remained poised above Thorn, as if frozen in the air. Why doesn't it strike? he asked himself.

The spiders were all around him now. Emerald eyes looked down at him from opaque glassy heads, remote and inhuman, without a spark of feeling. Ice-machines doing their job . . . Yet none of them made the slightest move to attack him.

Only now did a ticking sound register on his ear. It was coming from somewhere close. The spiders? No, not the spiders: it was closer still than that. The sound was coming from Thorn himself!

From one of his pockets, to be precise.

But how could that be?

Pushing a hand into the pocket, he drew out the slim silver case that Racky had given him. Without a doubt, this was the source. It ticked with a steady pulse as if it had a mechanical heart. Yet it lay motionless on his palm.

Then, as he manoeuvred the little case in his hand, his thumb brushed the red button set in one end of it. The spider poised above him twitched.

Coincidence? He pressed the button firmly. The spider began to shake. But not just the nearest spider: the others were shaking too.

He took his thumb off the button; the shaking stopped immediately.

He stared at the little case. "I – I," Racky had said. Of course! Racky had wanted to say *ice – ice-spiders* probably – except the words were beyond him. The gift wasn't a parting whim. When Racky grasped that Thorn and Jewel meant to enter the labyrinth, he'd given Thorn the object as a defence against the

308

spiders. It could only, Thorn realised, have been made by
Querne herself – like the whistle he'd got from Minny. Racky
couldn't have trusted the spiders; he must have asked Querne
for something to use against them if they attacked. The object
became active if the spiders got too close; the ticking stopped
them from touching you. And if you pressed the button, they
shook!

I wonder, he thought . . .

He pressed the button and held it down. At once, every
spider in the party began to shake. The shaking began gently,
but slowly intensified. Soon the spiders began to rattle, as if
their joints were in danger of shaking themselves apart. Not
only that: something was happening to the limb the nearest
spider had lifted to strike. A drop of water rolled down it and
splashed to the snow; then another, and another.

The spider was melting: *all* the spiders were melting!

Thorn rolled clear of the spider – not a moment too late. The
monster buckled and came crashing to earth only inches away.
Then, one after another, the rest of them collapsed. Amidst the
wreckage of their limbs, their chunky bodies were caving in, dissolving like snowballs rolled too near a scorching fire. Propped
on his good elbow, Thorn lapped up the spectacle.

All around, the ice-trees stood like mute sentinels.

He took his thumb off the red button and kissed the silver
case. You little beauty, he thought. First the whistle; now this.
Querne couldn't have foreseen how her creations would be
used – or, rather, by whom. So – she wasn't all-seeing, she made
mistakes. And people who make mistakes are not invulnerable.

Thorn got to his feet and slipped the case back into his

pocket. Around him, the spiders merrily bubbled in their puddles.

Everything was different now. He had a weapon to fight them with. Pausing only to pick up his bow, which had slipped from his shoulder just before he hit the ground, he set off at a steady jog through the silent ice-trees. The trail was easy enough to follow. Forty-eight spider legs had left their prints on the crisp snow. Soon Thorn reached the spot where Jewel had battled impossible odds. There was no sign of the green crystal, but here lay Jewel's pack, its contents strewn about the snow. Quickly he gathered up her stuff and shoved it back in the bag, propped the bag against the nearest ice-tree and continued on. The pack would be cumbersome to carry. Soon, clear of the battleground, he made out, amongst the pock-marks made by many spidery feet, a continuous broad furrow. A body being dragged? The thought of Jewel, cold and helpless, dragged along by an ice-spider . . . Thorn strove to control his anger: I must be cool, deliberate. Please let her still be alive, he petitioned the glistening trees . . .

Here and there he made out bootprints, one set coming, one set going. They looked identical to the prints he'd trailed from the start of the ice-cavern. So the spiders had a keeper – Spine Wrench, it had to be. When Wrench had crept into Jewel's room at Rotten Pavilion, he'd put a spider in her bed . . . Spiders again! How dearly Thorn yearned to meet this one-eyed spider lover. From that encounter, he vowed, only one man will walk away . . .

He came to the edge of the ice-forest. Ahead, across an open space, rose more of the cone-shaped spires. Most likely they

310

completely encircled the wood. He started across and was halfway when he heard it: that telltale scratch-scrape of knife-blades on glass.

More ice-spiders were coming. They must have sensed his approach.

Well, this was as good a place as any to confront them. Here he could clearly see what he was up against.

Keeping an eye on the ice-towers, he hurried back to the frozen trees and, choosing a trunk, slipped behind it.

The spider-sound became louder. Then the creatures themselves appeared, stepping out from among the spires. On they came across the clearing – five, ten, fifteen of them: ice-blooded and emerald-eyed.

Come on you beauties, he thought, I want every last one of you . . .

When they were no more than a couple of feet away, he stepped out from hiding, the silver case concealed in his hand.

As Corryn, the chief ice-spider came right up to Thorn, the object began to tick. Corryn halted, bringing the rest of the party to a stop, then stared down at Thorn as if sizing up this human who seemed unafraid. Its eyes were expressionless. Did it know it was in trouble?

Pointing the silver case at Corryn, Thorn thumbed the button down.

The spiders promptly began to shiver, as if suffering from the cold. Their legs tinkled and chimed, like a host of suspended rods surprised by a flurry of wind. Then they began to turn to water. Droplets beaded and dripped from their limbs and from the underside of their bodies. One by one, in a crunching of joints, the spiders subsided onto the ground. Their bodies lost their chiselled contours and became jellylike lumps; then the lumps in turn dissolved. A great pool of melt-water fizzed and steamed in the clearing. Soon it would freeze once again.

Were those the last of Querne's spiders? That remained to be seen.

Avoiding the gleaming spider-pool, Thorn crossed the clearing and entered the region of ice-spires.

Once again it was child's play to follow the trail left by the spiders. Jogging through the towers, Thorn kept a sharp watch about him: there might be more spiders lurking.

He'd met none, however, by the time he emerged from the spires. In front of him now was a rock wall with an archway wide enough to allow the spiders to march through two abreast, with room to spare. Passing quickly through this, he halted, stunned.

Everywhere, vertically strung between rocky knolls, he saw ice-spiders' webs – lattices of filigree, precise and geometrical. The smallest was as big as the biggest house-front in Norgreen.

The spiders' den – would he find Jewel here? Or had Spine Wrench or Querne taken her body somewhere else? If Jewel *was* here, he had to hope she'd be within reach – not dangling high in the air as he himself had been when Jewel had rescued him from the crazy twins' trapeze-room.

He moved warily through the white-clad tumble of rocks. Underfoot, the powdered snow was much marked by spiders' feet. Yet still, here and there, he made out the print of a boot. The spiders' keeper had come this way. Gem-lights, studding the crags and walls, lit the scene with a ghostly light, but where they caught the hanging traceries the meshwork sparkled. The taut ice-cables put him in mind of spun silver, but to support a spider's weight each must have terrific strength. The cavern was beautiful but uncanny.

Many webs were at ground level and he moved in amongst them. The nets trembled as he passed, subtly responding to the disturbance his body made in the air. The atmosphere was oppressive, and a sense of unease grew in him.

Snow crunched under his boots, the sounds alien in the chamber.

On an impulse he jerked about. No one was there.

But someone's watching me, he thought . . . Some*one* or some*thing* . . .

Rounding the next rock, he caught sight of Jewel's body. Trussed with ice-threads, only her head and feet free, she hung by a loop from a metal hook hammered into the face of a crag. Her feet barely cleared the ground. It wouldn't be difficult to unhook her. He started towards her.

Then some instinct, honed by experience, made him glance up.

Directly towards him, down from above, an ice-spider was hurtling. There was no time to move.

But right at the last moment, as if the creature had rammed an invisible barrier, it stopped. There it hung, swinging a little, its legs inches above his head. Thorn moved out from underneath it, pointed his ticking case at the spider and pressed the button.

It began to shake where it dangled. Beads of moisture erupted all over its glassy body. As it stared blankly at him, emerald tears budded on the surface of its eyes. Then the spider was dripping water, drops splashing onto the snow. At length, its cable melted through, it went crashing to the ground. Its feelers twitched weakly, then simply dissolved away.

Thorn looked warily about, but could see no more spiders. That must have been the last one – Jewel's guard holding its post. Circling the dribbling hulk, he went quickly to the girl. His heart trembled at her deathlike appearance. Her skin was ice-pale; frost clung to her stiffened hair, scurfing her eyebrows and lips.

"Jewel!" he hissed, "Jewel!"

He might have been talking to a corpse.

As he wrapped his arms about her, he almost recoiled from the chill of the bonds that bound her round. Then she was down off the hook. Kneeling, he tried to lay her on the floor, but found her wrappings sticking to him and had to tear himself free. Then he took out his knife and began to hack away at the loops. They weren't easy to break, but by dint of sawing and chipping he managed to strip them all away.

Jewel lay inertly before him. Still kneeling, ignoring the cold that was assailing his joints, he took hold of her wrist and tried to find her pulse with his fingers. For quite some time he could feel nothing until – the faintest of throbs? Hope leapt in his heart. Or had he imagined it? He waited . . . and felt a second throb, as feeble as the first. She was alive, she had to be. Yet the beats were widely spaced.

I've got to warm her up, he thought.

But I can't do that here. Stay too long, I'll freeze too.

Hoisting her up, he slung her over his right shoulder. She was

314

lighter than he'd expected, but he had a long way to go. And she was cold, oh so cold! He set off at a slow jog.

First, through the ice-cavern, with its spires and still trees. Nothing appeared to threaten him, but – Hell! – the going was tough! Twice he halted, laid his burden down and massaged his numb shoulders, begrudging each instant that this added to his journey. Soon his whole body had turned to a mass of shrieking aches; neck, shoulders, arms, back and as for his poor legs, he had to force them to keep moving, battling on step after step.

Jewel got heavier by the yard until at last he began to fancy that it wasn't a slim girl he was toting on his back but the Church of the Iron Angel, every piled-up block of stone. And he was cold, oh so cold! He clenched his teeth but they rebelled, starting up an insane chatter as if they belonged to someone else, a traitor lodged inside his head intent on mocking his puny efforts.

Still he kept going, he'd die before he gave up.

Near the end of the ice-cavern, he wanted to weep with fatigue. He wanted to lie down and sleep. But he fought his way to the door, wrenched it open and struggled through.

At last, the ice was behind him. As he struggled on past the empty pit, he felt the first intimations of heat drifting towards him, wave in welcoming wave.

Stopping to lay Jewel down, he found he was so stiff that he could barely bend his back. His hands shook as he brushed a cap of frost-rime from his hair, then rubbed them against each other.

But he couldn't stop here, he needed intenser heat than this.

Hauling up Jewel once again (how heavy she was!), he stumbled on.

Next stretch: the climb to the lip of the fire-vent.

This was utter agony. Every step he took he was convinced must be his last: his knees would give way and he'd go rolling back down the slope. His wrenched and punished muscles screamed: Not a step further! Not a step! But he forced them to take that step, he forced them to go further.

Until at last, bone-weary, feeling more dead than alive, he'd put the stone arches behind him; he crested the rise.

He paused, sucking in air. After the ice-chill, the fire. The flames were licking from the rift in the rocky bowl below, rich with heat, and already he was sweating. Over his shoulder, Jewel hung limply, an apparently lifeless sack, arms dangling, long black hair clear now of frost-rime. Thorn's jacket was soaked with water.

He began to descend the slope, one arm wrapped around her legs, the other keeping contact with the rock to steady himself. A slip now could prove disastrous.

Then he was safely down. Heat came blasting up from the earth, drifting in waves from the fiery vent. How close ought he to take her? As near as he dared . . . He laid her tenderly on the ground. Then he unslung his bow and pack and pushed the pack beneath her head. Along the way he'd thought of dumping it, not once but ten times; but there were food and water inside, and he'd not abandoned it.

She seemed as pallid as before. He felt again for her pulse and in a while located it: faint still, but undoubtedly there. He stood, knees creaking, and took a step away from her.

316

Stretched out on the ground, she looked uncomfortable, forlorn. Having carried her for so long, it seemed cruel to let her lie there, separate and alone.

So Thorn lay down beside her. Slipping an arm beneath her body, he pulled it to him. Her head settled on his shoulder. This seemed better, this seemed right.

He stroked her hair and cheeks, and whispered her name like an incantation.

"Wake up, Jewel, wake up!" he implored her. "Wake up – *please.*"

He touched her lips with his. They were soft, but cold still. What if she'd gone too far to return, too far into the limbo brought on by the spiders' stings?

His voice grew thick with emotion. "Wake up, Jewel, come back to me. I need you – *need* you. I can't do this alone." And, finally pushed to the point of admission: "Wake up! You *must* wake up . . . Come back, Jewel: *I love you.*"

But she gave no sign of hearing. Murmuring endearments, he rocked her body to and fro until, exhausted in body and spirit, he fell silent – and then asleep, still clutching the girl to him.

Spine Wrench moved through the ice-spires. He was not an experienced tracker, but he'd encountered little difficulty in following Thorn Jack's trail. Where the snow lay a little thicker, the young man's feet had come down hard, and it was obvious that he still carried the girl. This was good: it would weaken Spine's adversary. Spider-tracks, too many to count, indicated that groups had come and gone in both directions. But, as yet, Spine hadn't sighted any of them.

Emerging from the spires, he saw the clearing ahead with the ice-wood on its far side.

Then he saw something else – something that oughtn't to have been there.

He set off across the clearing, stopped and stared at the ground. A sheet of fresh ice glimmered, stretching almost to the trees.

Ice. He remembered the little pool in the web-cave and knew where the ice had come from. It was all that was left of his spiders – his beautiful brainchildren, his perfect ice-machines. Somehow Jack had destroyed them.

A sense of loss the like of which he'd never felt before struck Spine like a leaden fist and he reeled from the blow. Then anger flared up in him, and a hatred so intense it threatened to burn his heart away. Yet the organ went on beating: scorched, but beating, beating still. Wrench gave vent to a stream of curses, the filthiest he knew, and kicked at the snow in his fury. Then his hand went to the hilt of the knife sheathed at his belt. Pulling it out, he laid it flat against his cheek. It was as cold as an ice-blade.

Thorn Jack, he vowed, you'll never again see the sun.

Then, grim-faced and limp-lurching even more fantastically, he skirted the spider-pool and vanished among the frozen trees.

21

A CLASH OF KNIVES

"Fleck," said Manningham Sparks, "will you do something for me?"

The ratman was sitting on a chair by the rattery door. Soon, saddle-rats and carriages and rat-carts would arrive, bringing cultists from all over to this afternoon's great meeting, and he'd have his hands full.

"Of course," he replied. Then, detecting a look he'd seen before in the Ranter's eyes, he added, "As long as it doesn't conflict with my commitment to the Church."

"I'm afraid it does, Fleck. What I'm asking you is this: not to go to the meeting today."

Fleck Dewhurst got to his feet and looked the Ranter full in the face.

"I have to go, as you well know. The Grand Ranter wants *everyone* to be present this afternoon. It means leaving the animals unattended for a time, but my duty to God comes before my duty to rats."

"Your duty to God, Fleck – or your duty to Higgins Makepeace?"

"What's the difference, Manningham?"

"There's all the difference in the world. I don't believe Makepeace is a man of God at all."

"*Not a man of God?*" The young man was scandalised. Manningham had criticised Higgins Makepeace before, but he'd never before expressed such an extreme opinion – not in Fleck's hearing, at least.

"He's of the Devil's party, Fleck. All that interests him is having power and dominance. He'll drive the Church to ruin, and you with it – if you let him."

"I don't believe that, Manningham. And what you say is blasphemy. An attack on the Grand Ranter is an attack on God Himself: he's told us so many times. I ought to report you – straightaway."

"Then report me, if it's your duty."

"You'll be excluded from services. He's never cared much for you."

"The feeling's mutual. Well, go on then: do your duty."

But Fleck stayed where he was, looking distinctly uncomfortable. He'd always liked the Reverend, esteemed him as the good man he knew him to be. And when the Ranter stepped closer and laid a hand on his arm, Fleck didn't move to shrug it off.

"Listen to me, Fleck. I'm no Syb, that's plain enough, but I have a very bad feeling about what's going to happen today. There's evil in this place – there's been evil here for years – and it's centred in Makepeace and that iron abomination. He's going to demand something sinful, something monstrous, from you all, and I fear his influence is such that you may all agree to it."

Fleck looked down at the ground, and didn't reply for a time. When he spoke, it was to repeat a precept that had been drummed into him. "*Obedience is the first virtue: obedience to the will of God and His ministers on this earth.*"

320

"But are you sure that Higgins Makepeace is a minister you can trust?"

"Yes, I'm sure," said Fleck.

"Then God help you," said the Ranter. "And God help *me*, too."

Through the stifling veils of a dream, the scrabble of boot-soles on rock.

Thorn dragged himself awake and saw – Spine Wrench, it had to be! – half-climbing, half-sliding down the near rocky slope, a long knife gripped in his hand.

Quickly withdrawing his arm from under Jewel's motionless head, he rolled away and sprang to his feet.

His body shrieked. He was a mass of aches and pains, worst of all in the thighs and shoulders, and as stiff as a plank of wood. And his head – how it ached! It was hot here – so hot . . . and now he had to fight for his life.

Wrench was down the rock slope. He'd shed his protective clothing after leaving the ice-cavern so that his movements would be free; also his beloved bell. You couldn't kill a man with a bell, not if you had no ice-spiders, but you could do it with a knife. Back in his Lowmoor days, he'd killed two men in knife-fights who'd crossed him in the Belly. He relished the simplicity of the world at such a time: you knew exactly where you were. There was you, there was your enemy, and there was your destiny. But your destiny wasn't fixed, it was yours to decide by judgement, skill and perhaps a touch of luck. He'd always had these things, and he would have them again today. Kill this pest of a lad, and Querne would give him a second eye.

Thorn unsheathed his own knife. It was shorter than his opponent's. Well, that couldn't be helped. Then Wrench was moving towards him, half crouching, shoulders forward in the manner of a practised knife-fighter, knife-hand weaving to and fro like a restless adder's head.

Never before had Thorn fought hand-to-hand with knives – not seriously, at any rate. Sure he'd practised with dummy blades and knew moves and counter-moves. With his physique and physical strength, he'd been better than any other lad in Norgreen of his age, and not inferior to many older. But now, sidling towards him, was the real, deadly thing. Reality had a way of being different from play.

The men edged around each other.

Spine Wrench grinned and spat.

"I'm going to cut you to shreds, Jack. You're going to wish you'd never been born."

Thorn made no response. He'd been taught to ignore taunts. *Your opponent may try to distract you, but you must NOT be distracted.* Norgreen's fighting instructor was a man named Skim Diamond. Diamond never boasted; Diamond didn't need to boast; his scars bore eloquent witness to the fights he'd survived. More of his precepts now ran through Thorn's head. *Watch your opponent's slightest action, note how he stands and holds himself, try to pinpoint any weakness or eccentricity in his style . . . Keep in mind always that he may be out to trick you, lure you into a foolish move . . . Above all, never sell yourself – most fighters who die in battle are killed with counter-thrusts . . .*

Like Thorn, Wrench was right-handed. That was something, at least. Left-handed opponents could be awkward. Wrench had only one eye – the right. That would cut down his field of vision, impairing his leftward range. To take advantage of this, Thorn ought therefore to move right, away from Wrench's bad side. But Wrench had set their terms of motion, and Thorn was presently moving left. He had to try to change that. Also Wrench had a gammy leg – unless of course he was faking it. In spite of that he seemed surprisingly light on his feet.

He was dangerous – no mistake. And Thorn was way below par, with his stiffness and his pains. There was an ache in his left temple and he could feel the blood throbbing under his over-heated skin. He'd have preferred to lie down again and go back to sleep.

Wrench gestured towards Jewel. "Girlfriend sleepy, is she, lad? Doesn't want to wake up? That's because there's no coming back from where *she's* gone! But I wouldn't worry yourself: *you'll* soon be sleeping too – for good!"

Again Thorn did not respond, not even glancing at Jewel. Wrench was creeping in closer. Their knife-tips could almost touch.

Feinting right, Wrench swept his blade in an arc towards Thorn, but Thorn merely stepped to the right – then kept on moving that way.

Turning to follow him, Wrench grinned, revealing a battery of chipped and yellowed teeth.

He made a forward lunge. This time Thorn stepped back. As he did so, sweat trickled down his face.

"You look hot and bothered, boy. Quite a way you carried the girl. Bet you're proper knackered." Wrench grinned maliciously. "Waste of effort, sad to say. Couple of passes of my magic wand —" he gestured with his knife "— and you'll be rat-meat, son."

He jumped forward and thrust again. Thorn parried and their blades clashed. Wrench was first to recover; ducking low, he struck upwards. Thorn swayed to one side, but he wasn't quick enough. The blade caught him midway between armpit and waist and he felt a sharp pain. Instinctively he counter-thrust, but Wrench already was slipping away, and Thorn's knife sliced through air.

"You're slow, lad. *Dead* slow!" Wrench sniffed his weapon. "Don't you love the smell of blood — just so long it's not your own!"

Blood came welling from Thorn's cut, staining his jacket a dark red. It badly needed staunching, but there was nothing he could do.

Crouching and grinning, Wrench moved towards Thorn again . . . who found himself backing off. Not a bright idea at all.

The heat behind him was intense. How far was he from the fire-vent? Very close, he had to be. The leaping flames threw shifting patterns on Wrench's battered features, giving him the look of a devil out of some Ranter's vision of Hell.

Then Wrench feinted again and swung his knife at Thorn's head. Thorn blocked with his left arm and felt the shock of bone on bone as their forearms collided. Blood slopped from his side, sizzling and bubbling on the rock. Wrench tried to stamp on Thorn's foot but Thorn read the move. Quickly step-ping to one side, he grabbed Wrench's knife-wrist, counter-thrust and felt his blade bury itself, glancing a rib as it drove home. With a bellow Wrench butted the youth. Thorn toppled over backwards. But he still gripped Wrench's wrist and the man was dragged after him. Drawing up his knees, Thorn got them under his opponent's chest and, with a powerful upward thrust that ripped pain from his leg muscles, threw him clean over his head.

Wrench registered his fate moments before it claimed him. As his momentum took him flailing over the brink of the vent, a hideous scream ripped from his mouth. Then he was gone.

Thorn, twisting, saw the flame-tongues spring up to double their height, crackling wildly, then start to settle back again. He didn't suppose they were gifted such a mouthful every day . . .

As he got to his feet, faintness washed through his head and he tottered a couple of steps. His thigh muscles felt torn. His side seared where it was cut. Speedily wiping his blade on his sleeve, he sheathed the knife and clamped his hand on the wound. His cheekbone was aching. He would have a black eye, too.

It was then that a familiar voice spoke his name: "Thorn!"

Jewel lay propped on one elbow, palely smiling at him.

"Jewel!" he cried. "You're back!"

All at once the world was fine.

". . . And then, well, you saw with your own eyes what happened to Wrench. So now you know the whole of it."

Thorn fell silent, his story finished. The two of them had sat with their backs against a rock while he'd filled her in on what had happened after the spiders defeated her. Jewel, who'd been nibbling an oatcake, swallowed; then said: "Wrench brothers make a habit of coming to bad ends, don't they? Gummer chokes on a pearl, Spine falls in a fiery pit . . ."

"I blame their parents." Thorn grinned. "No discipline, that generation."

"Haven't I heard that somewhere before?" Jewel squeezed his hand. "Ouch!" he exclaimed, making no effort to reclaim it. "*You're* getting your strength back."

Jewel laughed. "*You're* exaggerating. But yes, I think I am."

In fact considering, she thought, that I expected to be dead, I'm feeling pretty good. The freezing numbness that had claimed her after the ice-spiders had stung her had almost entirely gone, its only sign now a slight tingling in her toes. Perhaps, after all, their touch wasn't meant to kill; or perhaps her Magian's powers had served to preserve her. Either way, she was alive, and recuperating fast.

No, *more* than alive. I feel reborn, she thought. Like someone granted a second life.

She said, "I'll look at that wound now."

"Are you sure?" asked Thorn. "You mustn't exhaust your strength when it's just coming back."

She laughed again. "Yes, I'm sure!"

She'd inspected the wound earlier and bandaged it for him with a strip of cloth torn from a spare shirt in his pack. The gash was clean, she'd declared. Wrench's knife hadn't been dipped in poison as they'd feared. But, apart from stopping the bleeding, she'd attempted nothing more. Now, exposing the wound, she pinched the lips of the gash together and set her mind to knitting them up.

As he watched her at work, Thorn's mind began to drift. Pictures of people came into his thoughts, to be quickly replaced by others: Minny Pickles, Racky Jagger, Manningham Sparks, Emmy Wood, Burner May, the Spetch Brothers, Roper Tuckett, Deacon Brace, Briar Spurr and, last and certainly least, Spine Wrench. So many different people, so many contrary beliefs, so many ways of doing things. And then, with a sense of seizing an ultimate truth: It's not what you *believe* that matters, he thought, but what you *do*. It's your actions that tell the world what sort of man or woman you are.

He ought to tell Jewel this, but didn't want to break her concentration. He would tell her another time.

"You'll do," said Jewel at last. "One good turn deserves another."

"I was trying to save my skin: I didn't have time to think about you."

"But you carried me here," she said. "All that way through the ice-wood. That was something tremendous. And then you fought Wrench and won. I think you're wonderful. I don't know how I could have thought—"

She shut her mouth abruptly.

"Thought what?" asked Thorn, puzzled.

"Oh . . . nothing."

"I think you're wonderful too," he said. "In fact —" she saw him blush "— I was terrified by the thought you might be dead – frozen for ever. I honestly don't know . . ." He ground to a halt, looked away, chewed his lip, looked back, then drew a deep breath. "I didn't know how I was going to live without you, Jewel. I – I *love* you!"

There, he'd said it, blurted it out. Now just watch her laugh at him. Deserve him right for baring his soul.

But Jewel didn't laugh. Instead she stared at him intently with her grey Magian's eyes – eyes that stripped you right down. But Thorn had stripped himself down, there were no layers left to peel.

She said quietly, "I love you too, Thorn. I'd be a fool *not* to love you. I've realised something, too. I need you to anchor me, to keep my feet on the ground when I'm in danger of floating away."

He thought he knew what she meant. Being a Magian must be a sort of running temptation – just look at Querne Rasp. As long as Thorn stayed with Jewel, she meant he could exert a steadying influence on her. What sort of influence? The influence, he thought, of my ordinariness.

Jewel smiled. "You're not ordinary, Thorn. You're one in a thousand. Isn't that what your friend Manningham Sparks said of you?"

"Damn it!" he mock-complained. "You're reading my mind!"

"No, reading your expression: that said it all."

Thorn returned the smile. I ought to kiss her, he thought.

Next moment, he did. Or was it Jewel who kissed him? Whichever way it was, they were in one another's arms and their mouths met, to lock and cling. Her lips were moist and warm, no longer cold as they had been, and he didn't want the kiss to end.

It was Jewel who drew away.

"That was nice," she said simply.

"Then let's do it again," he said.

"We will – but not now." She rose to her feet. "We've got to go."

"*Go? Now?* But you're still recovering—"

"I feel fine. Look, Querne thinks I'm out of the picture, trussed up in the ice-cavern. You've just killed Spine Wrench and eliminated the spiders. But we have to assume that Wrench found the green crystal and took it to Querne before he came looking for you. Four quincells were bad enough, but now she has all five she can create the full star, set the complete vortex spinning. For all her amazing abilities, I don't believe she can control it. What if it explodes again? We've got to try to forestall her. We need to move while we've the advantage of surprise."

Actually, she wasn't sure if it was much of an advantage. Querne was fiendishly powerful. But it was better than nothing.

He nodded. "That makes sense."

But the lack of enthusiasm in his voice was obvious. She saw him glance at the slope of the bowl and knew exactly what he was thinking. *Now I've got to drag myself back up there again.*

"Give me your hands, Thorn," she ordered.

He held them out and she clasped them. Then she closed her eyes. Moments later, he felt a surge of energy run through his body, rippling along his sinews and muscles and coursing through his veins. It washed his many aches and general weariness away, leaving him fit and renewed.

She opened her eyes. "Better?"

"Better!" he affirmed. Then his face became serious. "Jewel, what are you going to do when you get to Querne?"

It was the question she'd been asking herself since they'd penetrated the labyrinth. And she still had little idea. Something, she'd kept on telling herself, will occur to me. But, as yet, nothing had.

"I'll think of something," she said, with as much conviction as she could muster. "Let's get going."

He swung his pack onto his back and picked up his bow. Habit, of course: bows and arrows would be no use whatsoever against Querne. But the feel of the bow's metal shaft, so expertly tempered by his friend Roper Tuckett, was comforting, the touch of a friend.

They started to climb the rocky slope.

Their journey to the end of the fire-cavern proved uneventful. Everything looked the same as before. But, a little way inside the door that led to the ice-caves, they spotted a heap of clothes topped off by a strange bell.

Jewel picked up the bell and rang it. A harsh jangle.

"That horrible man used this to control the ice-spiders."

"Not any more," said Thorn. He took hold of a fur cap, but quickly threw it down again. "Ugh! It stinks of Spine Wrench!"

As Jewel surveyed the garments, an idea popped into her head. I wonder, she thought. If Querne can, why can't I? After all, I learnt to mask myself in the cloak of secrecy.

"Do you remember," she said, "what I told you Querne said to me at Rotten Pavilion – that moral people were all too easy to second-guess?"

"I remember."

Jewel smiled. "It's high time," she said, "that I tried to second-guess Querne."

Picking up the discarded over-trews, she began to pull them on.

Thorn watched, puzzled.

"What on earth are you doing, Jewel?"

"Dressing up," she joked.

"But that stuff stinks!"

"There are worse things than stinks."

After the trews she donned Wrench's furry jacket and cap and pulled on his half-mittens.

"How do I look?" she asked, striking poses in front of him.

Unwilling to tell her, he replied, "I will say this: you won't be cold in the ice-cavern."

"Bad as that, is it? Just as well, then, I'm not modelling these at a fair. Now, Thorn: I'm going to turn my back on you. Stay exactly where you are until I turn round again."

"Whatever you say," he agreed. As he knew well by this time, Jewel did nothing without a reason – even when what she did seemed eccentric, to say the least.

She turned away from him and closed her eyes to concentrate, then summoned an image into her mind. This she tested minutely, refining it, honing it as near as she could to perfection.

But this was the easy part. Next came the difficult bit . . .

Thorn waited, intrigued. Jewel was full of surprises. To go through life with her – what an adventure that would be!

If, that is, they got out of this labyrinth alive.

Time stretched, and stretched some more.

At last, Jewel turned round.

"How do I look?" she asked.

Except that the face and voice weren't Jewel Ranson's at all.

22

ABOUT-FACE

Thorn was too stunned to speak. If he hadn't known better, he'd have sworn that the person standing there was the knife-fighter — resurrected from the fire-pit, alive and unroasted. Those battered features, that empty eye-socket with its ravelled skin . . . the face was unmistakable. Jewel even had Wrench's stance, seeming to teeter as she stood. When she'd turned round, she'd limped.

Now she grinned — or Wrench grinned — showing sparse yellow teeth, then spat on the ground at Thorn's feet.

"Who are you, young whippersnapper?" she growled in Wrench's voice, or a good imitation of it, and when she suddenly lurched forward, Thorn took a step back before he realised what he'd done.

"God in Heaven, Jewel!" he cried.

Seizing Wrench's bell, Jewel shook it up and down, sending peal after peal bell-echoing through the cavern. "Where are my spiders, my beautiful spiders?" she demanded, goggling alarmingly with her good eye.

Unable to help himself, Thorn burst into laughter.

Jewel silenced the clapper. "If you've so much as *tickled* one of my spiders," she said accusingly, "I'll cut your scrawny heart out and feed you to the cannibal plants!"

With difficulty, Thorn regained control of himself. "You look as though you would, too, Jewel Wrench!" he managed

"So I look convincing, do I?" Still she spoke in Spine's voice. "Spine couldn't do himself better."

"Hmm . . . I don't imagine I can fool Querne for long, but there's a chance the disguise will buy me enough time to mount an attack on her. Here's what I have in mind . . ."

They got going and, as they walked along, she laid out her plan.

"Sounds good to me," he said when she'd finished. "Let's hope it works. But how did you manage to change your face like that?"

"Remember me telling you that when I met Querne at Rotten Pavilion *she* was wearing a different face and called herself Moira Black?"

"I remember."

"Well, anything Querne can do . . . I had to conjure up a mental picture of him, as accurate as I could make it, then *think* my own features into a likeness of his. After all, I've transformed stuff that *isn't* myself, such as metal and wood: why not the stuff that's me? But it wasn't easy. I had to alter my bone structure, then the texture of my skin. It's all a question of technique — like the cloak of secrecy."

"Hope you can change yourself back again. The thought of kissing one-eyed Spine —" Thorn gave a pretend shudder.

Jewel/Wrench pouted. "I'm not *that* ugly, am I?"

"No uglier than that toad we saw back in the churchyard."

"I think toads are rather sweet."

"There we differ: I've always thought them scabby things.

And whenever I pulled faces as a child, Morry would warn me: 'Watch out! Your face will stick!'"

Jewel appraised him thoughtfully. "How do I know it didn't?"

Thorn grinned. "You're in a feisty mood. Perhaps you should get yourself frozen more often!"

"Kissed more often," she replied.

They reached the outer edge of the ice-wood without incident, but no sooner were they in amongst the trees than it started to snow. At first the fall was sparse, and they could almost count the flakes as they came drifting to earth in the spaces between the trees. So slowly did they move, that you might have thought them loth to add their number to the whiteness that already quilted the ground. They were as big as your thumbnail and as white as daisy petals. And here was a strange thing: the snowflakes failed to linger on the branches of the trees to build up a covering there: as each flake struck a leaf or branch, it would flash like a diamond and immediately dissolve: vanish, that is, not melt. The ice-trees remained snow-free, receding into the snowfall like a congregation of wraiths.

As the fall thickened, visibility closed in. If the tracks made previously by the ice-spiders, Spine Wrench, and Jewel and Thorn themselves hadn't been so well marked, the two young people might have lost their way. Jewel was glad of Wrench's furs, which compensated for their pong by keeping her snug and warm. Poor Thorn, she thought: the cold was clearly getting to him. Still, at least he wasn't stuck with having to limp, like she was. She'd considered dropping the limp until they were out of the ice-cavern, but had decided it was better if she stayed in character: that way, being Spine might become second nature to her.

334

As she trudge-lurched along, she began to wonder how Querne had created this underground climate. It shouldn't have been possible. Well: how, for that matter, had she created the fire-vent? It didn't seem likely that there'd always been one there. It snowed *above* ground, of course, and somewhere in the world (of which she knew so little, and yet, on account of the crystals, more than anyone else alive with the exception of Querne herself) there might be actual fire-pits. But why think only of *this* world? Querne had access to other worlds through the agency of the crystals. Had she discovered another world where it snowed underground, and decided to copy it? That seemed the likeliest explanation, though it only got her so far. Why oh why, with all her power, couldn't Querne have done good? But then into Jewel's mind came a memory of the Norgreen Syb and her parable of the two moons. Querne had made her choice long ago – the invisible moon, the moon you cannot see in the sky. But perhaps the parable simplified things. Perhaps it wasn't about making a once-for-all choice you never went back on, but of choosing afresh each day when a moral decision had to be made. How difficult life was! Jewel thought of the chain Minny Pickles had given her, and the twofold nature of the moon that it symbolised. She still wore it round her neck. Concentrating, she could feel the disc pressing against her skin; it was hard and round and warm. The virtues of iron, Minny had said, were strength and subtlety. Well, she'd have need of both when it came to confronting Querne.

"There's your pack," said Thorn when they came to the place where Jewel had fought the spiders.

"It can stay there," she said. Wrench had left it behind once:

why would he retrieve it now? "You should leave yours, too. It will free you up for action. We can collect it when we come back this way."

If we come back this way, her mind traitorously corrected.

Thorn dumped his pack beside hers. It went against his grain to abandon his bow and quiver of arrows, but down they went too.

When the pair reached the edge of the wood, Thorn pointed ahead into the steadily falling snow. "Most of the ice-spiders are under there – in a flat sheet of ice. It's bound to be slippery. Best give it a wide berth."

They set out across the space, their feet crunching on snow. Inside twenty paces they were totally cloaked in the fall, but as they pushed on, first one, then two, then three of the ice-spires showed dimly through the veil of flakes like a trio of conical ghosts.

They reached the far side of the clearing, but snow had obliterated the trail that Thorn had followed earlier. Could he navigate by memory? He'd have to give it a try. Besides, his toes were half frozen.

"This way," he announced, sounding – he was surprised to find – full of a confidence he didn't at all feel.

They went on through the ice-spires. The snow-quilt was knee-height now, making progress difficult. If it got much deeper . . .

Then, abruptly, the fall stopped. One moment flakes were coming down, the next they were not. It was as if some giant hand had pulled a lever high above and closed the vents out of which the snow dropped.

A couple more turnings, and they saw ahead the cavern wall in the gap between two spires. And, soon after that and still better news, the archway into the spiders' lair. Thorn had navigated well.

Though she'd been a captive here, this was new territory to Jewel. Forgetting for a moment the disguise she was wearing, she exclaimed at the astonishing sight of the ice-webs. They hung glistening as before, survivals that had outlived their outlandish creators. How long before they in turn crumbled to ice-dust?

Here the snow lay no thicker than it had when Thorn had passed this way with Jewel over his shoulder. Walking was easy once again. Thorn pointed out the spot where Jewel had dangled in her cocoon and the frozen puddle which was all that remained of the sentinel. But this was as far as Thorn had come: now they would have to find their way. Surely, however, they couldn't be far from Querne's lair . . .

"Right, Thorn," said Jewel. "Sorry about this, but it's time to turn you into a captive."

Thorn grinned wryly. "You think you've killed a man, but hey presto! He bounces back, large as life, and ties up you! Life isn't fair."

"Who promised you it would be?"

Thorn slipped his knife-sheath off his belt and Jewel attached it to her own. Then, taking a short length of cord from Thorn's pack, she tied his hands behind his back: not too tight, but not so slack that the knot would appear suspicious.

"From now on," she pronounced, "you walk in front of me."

Then they went forward again and soon found themselves

climbing, as the rock sloped upwards. Now they came to a second archway with, beyond, some smaller caverns. In these the meagre snow-sheet was unpitted by spider-tracks. They passed through a large-scale grouping of ice-carvings – strange beasts that didn't exist in their world, if they ever had. Soon after that, the snow disappeared, and Wrench's prints lost themselves among the bare crags.

They kicked the snow off their boots. Moments later, they were climbing the steepest slope yet, the ceiling dropping ever lower.

One final turning, and a door presented itself in the rock face. It gave onto a tunnel that was, if anything, longer than the one that had brought them into the ice-cavern. But at last they reached the door that marked its end and went through. Ah! For the first time in what seemed an age, they were out from under a rocky roof and back beneath a smooth ceiling of giant-laid flagstones.

Thorn pointed upwards. "See what I see?"

"Yes," said Jewel. "It looks as though we've gone round in a huge circle: we're under the church floor again."

At length they came to a rocky wall with a human-sized door in it. This time the tunnel was comparatively short. Squatting by the next door, Jewel took off a mitten and set her palm to the rock floor. She remained there for a time. When she straightened up, she announced,

"The room's empty. Let's go in."

This room was Spine's, by the look of it. They saw a table, a couple of chairs, a chest of drawers against one wall and an ancient truckle bed, its castors wedged with bits of wood to stop it rolling about. A number of garments hung on hooks, including a spare set of furs. On top of the chest of drawers stood a jug of water, a razor, a shaving bowl and a cake of soap. One notable absentee was a mirror on the wall. But maybe Spine hadn't been terribly keen on his own reflection, and shaved by touch. His appeared a diminished existence, though perhaps he wouldn't have thought so, with his beloved ice-spiders dwelling in the next cavern – though now he would never see them again, or they him.

Jewel set down Spine's bell. This chamber seemed warm after the caves, and it now occurred to her that she needed to swap the furs for less bulky clothing. Querne would be suspicious if Spine turned up in outdoor garb. So, doffing the furs, she dressed in a coarse shirt, coarser trews and a lighter, hide jerkin, and loosely knotted a blue neckerchief around her throat. That was a whole lot better: she felt freer in these clothes – though they too gave out a strong whiff of Spine.

Set in the wall opposite the door through which they'd entered was a second, matching door. The room it led to contained a cupboard, inside which they found food, utensils and cutlery, also a water-barrel. Close by was a hearth full of ashes, beside it a grid on which sat a kettle and two pans. A little further off was a pile of firewood. Here Spine must have cooked. Directly overhead in the ceiling was a dark chimney-shaft that would allow the smoke to escape.

In addition to the doorway through which they'd entered the room, three others could be seen. The leftmost led to a cavern unsuitable for habitation: its furthest reaches couldn't be seen. The central door gave entry to a room much like the one were in – down to having four doors. The door on the right gave access to a comfortably furnished room, but one of masculine character. Racky Jagger's, when he'd been here? Jewel and Thorn didn't go in: the room had just one other exit, whose position matched that of one of the doors in the central cavern.

So into the central cavern they went.

As they crossed the floor, Jewel felt a disturbing sensation in her feet. Vibrations were flowing towards her through the solid rock. She reached out towards Thorn's hands, tied behind his back, and grasped his left forearm, bringing him to a halt. Twisting about, he favoured her with a questioning look.

"It's Querne Rasp," Jewel breathed. "She's in the room directly ahead. And she's using one of the crystals."

Approaching the rattery after his walk (he'd needed to think, and walking had always helped him in that), Manningham Sparks saw that the yard had almost filled up with rat-carts and carriages. He'd never seen so many there, and here were a couple more to add to the colour and the bustle. A dozen or more saddle-rats were tied up to hitching-rails. Plainly he'd underestimated the Church's popularity, and not for the first time he wondered how it was that Higgins Makepeace had managed to bring so many sensible people under his sway. But perhaps people weren't sensible. Did gullibility know no bounds?

Fleck had stationed himself at the entry, where, as they arrived, he issued instructions to drivers and riders as to where to park their vehicles or tie up their rats. No point in trying to speak to him right now, thought the Ranter. In fact, no point in trying to warn him off again: his mind is fixed.

Spotting a man from Lowmoor he knew, a pompous tanner whose wife had died the year before, he walked up to him.

"Hello, Walter," he said. "I didn't expect to see you here. How are things in Lowmoor?"

Walter Kershaw started. "Oh, it's you, Ranter Sparks. I can't say I'd expected to see *you* here, either."

"Where else would I be on such a momentous day as this promises to be?"

"Where indeed," Kershaw replied, deaf to the Ranter's irony.

Walter Kershaw was a short, balding man with a skin as brown as the hides he tanned and a talent for drowning his sorrows in the ale he brewed himself. Today, however, he seemed eminently sober.

"So – how *are* things in Lowmoor?" the Ranter repeated. "People up in arms, are they?"

"Up in arms? Why should they be? We have a new Council now, and strong and sensible men they are."

"Tyler Mabbutt? Loman Slack?"

"The very men. They've created a force of men to give the settlement full protection."

"Protection from whom?"

"From those bent on undermining our community, of course: those who murdered the Councillors and members of their families."

"That's good to know," said the Ranter. "You must be relieved to be in such safe hands."

"So most people think – though we have a few misfits."

"Misfits?" queried the Ranter.

Kershaw leant toward the preacher. "Best not to talk about

341

them. It doesn't do to know people of that ilk, if you see what I mean."

Manningham did indeed. If he went back to the settlement, he'd be "of that ilk" himself.

"And I'll tell you something else," Kershaw confided. "We now know exactly who was responsible for the attack."

"Oh? Who was it?" The Ranter was genuinely interested now.

"Some lowlifes from the Belly. They were traitors in Wyke's pay – agents of the Headman there. They were found with incriminating materials in their possession."

"What will Lowmoor do with them?"

"It's done already. They were killed resisting arrest."

"You must be pleased. And what about Wyke?"

"Rumour has it," Kershaw whispered, "that our foundry has developed a new type of weapon – something the like of which has never been seen in the world before. The word goes it will be used against Wyke." He smiled smugly. "*That'll* teach the devils – killing our children in their beds."

"I bet it will," the Ranter agreed, grim-voiced. Clearly things had moved fast since he'd left the settlement.

"Well, time to go in," Kershaw said. "Don't want to miss anything, do we?"

Manningham Sparks failed to reply. Missing this meeting, he thought, would be best for everybody. But what was the point of telling this idiot anything?

They joined a few stragglers and went into the church. Thomas and Josy were standing just inside the great door and gave the Ranter a disapproving look as he nodded and walked by.

"Not the most popular man here, eh?" said Kershaw humor-
ously.

"So it would seem," said Manningham. Hmm . . . perhaps
Kershaw wasn't completely impervious . . .

Moments later, they passed out of the transept into the body
of the church, and Walter Kershaw was forgotten. The size of
the gathering was beyond anything the Ranter could have pre-
dicted. There had to be well in excess of a hundred souls
present – men, women and children.

Pray God, thought Manningham Sparks, they're not all
mindless disciples, like the resident cult members; pray God
they can still think and reason like free beings. Yet even as he
prayed, he felt a deep sense of misgiving. What if the congregation turned out to be putty in Makepeace's hands?

The importance of the occasion was marked in the physical
arrangements that met the eye. The damaged pulpit had been
removed, to be replaced by a modest dais just four steps high.
Its platform was big enough to accommodate six or seven per-
sons. Directly behind reared the riveting spectacle of the Iron
Angel, so close the effigy seemed to cast a brooding, spiky
shadow. On either side of the platform an arc of chairs radiated,
additional wings for the Angel, the number of seats that of the
inner circle of resident cult-members. At present these were
empty.

No great gap divided dais and congregation. The number of
people who'd turned up outnumbered the seats available. Little
over half of them had managed to grab chairs; the remainder
had positioned themselves at the rear or to the side. Children sat
on the floor at the front.

To say there was a buzz of expectation in the dusty air would be to sell the scene short. The cultists were in a ferment, like a vat of yeasty ale, and Higgins Makepeace himself had yet to make his appearance.

Bad, bad, thought the Ranter: people as individuals might well be intelligent, but drop them in amongst a mass and you might easily conclude that they've left their brains at home.

But now a bell began to toll and the congregation hushed. Then there was movement on either flank. From the north transept came the Grand Ranter followed by half his acolytes; from the south transept came the other half with Fleck Dewhurst at the rear. He was the one tolling the bell.

Impressively in step, these wings converged upon the centre. The Grand Ranter mounted his dais, the resident cultists lined up in front of their chairs.

Fleck's bell ceased to toll. The Grand Ranter scanned his flock, his gaze passing from face to face, allowing the silence to stretch until each separate dust-mote riding lightly on the air seemed to sparkle with significance. Manningham Sparks could hear his heart beating (*thump . . . thump . . .*) and the church seemed to press down on him and the other humans gathered at the nub of its hollow cross like an intolerable weight.

Then Higgins Makepeace began to speak.

23

RITES OF PASSAGE

Jewel halted at Querne's door. Beyond it was the woman who had almost killed her twice.

Yet her mind was oddly calm, so clear it seemed to Jewel to be almost emptied out. Where was the fear she'd felt before? Had she somehow gone beyond it? She tried summoning up an image of her father, but nothing came. As if to remind herself of the stubborn, hard reality of the world, she thrust out a hand, grazing her knuckles against the wall. *Pain*, that was real.

Behind her, Thorn was trying to banish thoughts of death – and failing. What was being dead like: absence of feeling, nothingness? Could be there really be Heaven, or Hell, as the Ranters maintained? He conjured up his sister's face. Never to see Haw again, after they'd parted as they had, only made matters worse. He tried telling himself that Jewel was bound to get the better of Querne, but the truth was that Jewel's plan had failed to convince him, though he hadn't said as much.

Jewel's contact with the wall brought her a sudden realisation. This part of the labyrinth lay directly beneath the nave. She sent exploratory filaments into the rock and upwards. Overhead lay the open space between pews and chancel. Here the cultists had gathered for the assembly the Ranter had mentioned. But how could this knowledge help Jewel's coming struggle with Querne?

Breaking contact, she straightened, turned Spine's face towards Thorn, smiled faintly and crookedly, and rapped on the wood.

There was no answer from within.

The two exchanged uneasy looks. Jewel rapped a second time.

Still no answer came. She was about to knock a third time when a voice called, "Come in!"

Opening the door, Jewel shoved Thorn into the room. He took a few stumbling steps, then checked himself. Jewel/Wrench limped in after him and closed the door.

The room was a blaze of light and colour, and it took Jewel a few moments to sort out what she was seeing through her single eye. For, here and there, mirrors – one of them taller than a man – hung on the walls, each adding its quota to the stew of competing shapes.

Then forms and images settled down, and she saw what was to be seen. Across the rug-strewn floor, amidst a clutter of furniture, the Magian occupied an elaborately carved chair topped off by a rat's head, its teeth bared as if to bite. On a table to her right the five quincells sat in a rack, with the black crystal at the centre. Dressed in a long-sleeved robe, sapphire blue with crimson trimmings, her fingers crusted with gems and wearing a necklet of gold, Querne Rasp looked superb. Would Querne fall for the younger Magian's ploy?

But Querne's anger seemed genuine. "Spine! I told you to kill the boy, not to bring him to my room. What the hell are you playing at?"

Jewel/Wrench cast down her eyes. "I'm sorry mistress," she grated, "but the situation has changed."

"Changed? How has it changed?"

"The girl – the girl, yes, well . . ."

"Get a grip, you goggling gargoyle! Spit it out, Wrench!"

"The girl, mistress, she's escaped—"

"*Escaped!*" cried Querne. "Impossible!"

Jewel, staring at the floor, nodded like a glove puppet.

Down her body into her feet and out through her boot-soles she sent filaments of consciousness that snaked into the rock, to slip away down fissures and veins. She would outflank Querne, come to her chair from behind, spring tough cords out of its wood, rope her down before she knew it, then seize the green quincell and destroy her enemy.

But the projection was difficult, for at the same time it was necessary to maintain her disguise, act the part of Spine Wrench *and* keep talking lucidly. "I went to the ice-cavern, mistress, but the girl's body had gone . . ."

"*Gone!*" thundered Querne.

"Yes, gone . . . What's more, all the spiders had vanished too."

"But the girl was spider-stung and trussed! Even a Magian couldn't escape from those bonds."

"Well, somehow she did . . ."

The Magian stared at her minion.

Jewel's exploratory filaments were pincering in now; soon they'd reach the legs of the chair.

"But you captured the lad?"

"As you see. The spiders caught him among the trees in the ice-cavern."

"Why didn't you kill him there and then? I told you to bring me his head."

Oh, thought Jewel. I couldn't have known that. Now she'd have to improvise.

"With the girl at large again, I thought he'd be a useful hostage. And he might know where she is."

"Did you ask him?"

"Yes – but he wouldn't answer me. Even when I applied, well, a little bit of pressure. So I thought I'd bring him to you. You'll soon worm it out of him."

The filaments reached the legs of the chair and now began to climb.

"Worm it out of *him*! I'd rather worm it out of *you*!"

And Querne began to laugh – not in the deep-voiced, masculine manner that Moira Black had done, but lightly, even sweetly, like water tinkling along a stream. And at precisely that moment Jewel's attack was rebuffed. Powerful counter-thrusts beat her advance forces away, pushing them down the legs of the chair. She fought back, striving to hold her bridgehead, but was driven out of the wood and halfway back across the floor. At which point the pressure relented. Jewel mounted a second assault, but was unable to make ground: she might just as well have tried to knock a wall down with her head. Querne, she sensed, could easily have forced her further back, but seemed content with the ground she'd won.

The battle was over. Jewel straightened her body. Relaxing her hold on her facial mask, she let her features flow back to their natural state.

Querne's laughter had abated. She remained in her chair,

regarding Jewel with an expression of amusement.

Reaching out, Jewel broke Thorn's bonds with the touch of a finger.

Curious, she asked, "When did you know that it was me?"

"When you knocked on the door," said Querne.

"As soon as that?"

Querne heard dismay in the girl's voice. "Wrench used a coded knock," she said. "You weren't to know that. It was a pretty good disguise – with the exception of your boots. Wrench has clodhoppers for feet. Or ought I to say, *had*?"

"*Had* is right," said Thorn, rubbing a chafed wrist. "Sadly, he slipped and tumbled into the fire-vent."

"How clumsy of him," said Querne.

"That's what we thought," said Thorn.

"You two seem bent on being a nuisance. Wrench was a useful tool. Now I need a new servant. *You* perhaps, Thorn Jack, when your tiresome friend is dead?"

"Never!" declared Thorn.

"Never say never," said Querne. "A little tinkering with your brain and you'll do anything I ask."

"If *we're* nuisances," said Jewel, "*you* are a much bigger one. We know what you're planning – the gunpowder, the cannon, attacking peaceful settlements, killing innocent children. Why can't you leave people alone?"

"I wasn't made for a quiet life. Neither were *you*, Jewel Ranson – or you wouldn't be here today." Querne smiled sweetly. "I must say, I prefer it when you're wearing your own face. Spine's battered old mug did nothing at all for you. And it wouldn't do to die looking completely ridiculous."

"What makes you think I'm going to die?"

Querne emitted a peal of laughter. "What makes you think you're not? You've got guts, I'll give you that. But if the attack I just parried is the best you can do . . ."

Thorn said, "Querne Rasp, will you answer me a question?"

"Trying to buy time, Thorn Jack? It won't do you any good."

"Will you or won't you?"

"Depends what the question is."

"What was your hold over Racky Jagger? He claimed to be my father, yet he still betrayed me."

"So he didn't tell you . . . Watch, then, and you'll understand."

The Magian's face began to change — the planes of her underlying bones, the shade and shape of her eyes, the delicate bow of her lips. With her face changed her hair, going from chestnut to black, acquiring waves and falling so as almost to cover one eye. At last, the change stilled.

"My mother!" breathed Thorn. He was entranced and appalled. "You became my mother for him!"

Querne/Briar smiled and tossed a tress away from her eyes. "Love makes fools of people," she said. "It was Racky's one weakness. As long as I gave him what he wanted, he'd do anything for me — even betray you, his son. Until sentiment got the better of him." A hint of cunning came into her face. "What I was for him I can be for you, Thorn. Wouldn't you like your mother back?"

Rising from her chair, she held her arms out to him.

The Grand Ranter was holding forth. He'd begun by recounting the myth of God's original angel and his murder by evil men. He was aware of the power of stories and knew that, of all stories, myths were the most powerful. It didn't matter if you'd heard them before; so much the better if you had, for then the narrative unrolled with the inevitability of fate. As he moved on to speak of the Iron Angel, he felt his body quiver and his mind expand, and he exulted in his potency. He sensed the force of the tormented effigy inside him, as if he too was made of iron: these people were clay in his hands, he could make them do anything . . .

He paused to savour the moment and let expectation build. Every eye was riveted on him; the dusty air glimmered; the very stones of the edifice seemed to tremble at the imminence of some great revelation.

Now to move in for the kill.

"Five years have passed," resumed Makepeace in his most sonorous voice, "five years to the day that I first walked into this building, five years to the day that I first set eyes on our Angel, five years since the vision that led to the founding of our Church. And now the circle has closed, the adder has swallowed its tail: for last night as I knelt here, praying for God's guidance, a second vision was granted to me."

At this news, a murmuring arose among the cultists; but he silenced them with a hand.

"Listen and understand: what I have to tell you is fearful and wondrous, awesome and glorious. First you must know that the end of the world is near – the end God signified when He sent his second angel, the end I have prophesied so often over the years. And not next year, not next week, not tomorrow – but *today*!"

At that last, terrible word, a fresh buzz arose; people glanced fearfully about, as if expecting to see signs that disaster was under way.

But all was as before: the massive pillars leaping to the vaulted roof of the church, the illuminated windows, dust drifting in the air.

The Grand Ranter silenced the murmurs, and when he spoke his voice was thrilling, as if a spirit were speaking through him.

"The end will be fearful, but dear friends do not fear, for *you* are the chosen ones, *you* are God's elect. Only have faith, have the courage to obey and do His most sacred bidding and you will be saved, you will fly, and all the joys and all the beauties of Heaven will be yours! What is this frail, brief life against the promise of life eternal?"

Standing to one side of the congregation, Manningham Sparks was sweating. He shifted his feet nervously, clenching and unclenching his fists in his agitation. Makepeace had often preached about the end of the world, but never before today had he had the gall to name the day. But now he had – and that day *was* today! Makepeace was insane. But Manningham sensed that more was coming – something still more terrible.

The buzzing died away. All eyes were locked upon the Iron Angel's prophet, masterful in his robes and effortlessly eloquent.

I have them, Makepeace thought; I have them, they are mine.

"Listen, and I will tell of the vision that came to me. As I knelt on this floor before the figure of the Angel, my knees cold against the stone, it was not this church I saw, nor its shadowy presences. It seemed I stood upon a cloud, looking down at the living Earth. And lo! The ground shook with earthquakes, cracks and fissures split its surface, the end of all things had begun! Mountains crumbled, rivers burst, great forests crashed to the ground. Everywhere, settlements collapsed in rubble and ruin. People fled, howling and wailing over the surface of the Earth, but they could not escape judgement. The ground opened and devoured them with a host of hungry mouths.

"But here in this church I saw that many people had gathered. Those people are the people that I now see before me. And a voice spoke to them, the voice of God through His vessel — the humble man who stands before you. The people hearkened to God's words. And sitting among them was a family — husband and wife, daughter and son. They rose and came forward and trod the steps to where I stand. They looked on one another with expressions of utmost love. Then as she smiled upon him, the husband took his knife and with one thrust killed his son. Likewise his daughter. Likewise his wife. Then he smote himself dead. And all four died smiling, sure and certain in their faith."

Anger and dread vied in Manningham Sparks for dominance. He saw now what Makepeace would say, and it was even worse than he'd feared. That a professed man of God could preach such a twisted faith . . . it flew in the face of everything that Manningham Sparks believed.

The Grand Ranter flung up his arms.

"Then an angel came flying in through the great window yonder, smashing the glass to smithereens with the blast of his coming. And he had eyes of diamond and wings of gold and raiment of silver. And in his strong shining arms he caught this little family up, and carried them off to Heaven, for they were the first of his chosen ones. Then, one after another, all those present in the congregation did likewise, bravely taking their knives and releasing their souls. And in flew angel after angel, bearing them all swiftly away. And last of all died their prophet, satisfied in his mission, and he too was borne away to the future that is promised.

"Then came the end of all things. This great church collapsed, and winds howled about the world, and humanity was no more.

"And this was my vision. And thus the future was foretold – the future that comes to us today, *yes, today*!"

Even as the Grand Ranter spoke, the ground trembled. Chairs rattled and the Iron Angel himself seemed to shiver. People looked wildly about and clutched at one another in fear.

"See, it begins!" cried Higgins Makepeace. "There is no time to be lost! To defeat death, all must die – there is no other way! Which among you will be first to seize the certainty of glory?"

Glory? thought Manningham Sparks: damnation, more like.

Scanning the congregation, he sought to read the strange mixture of emotions on people's faces. There was fear there, certainly, but hope and *joy* – how could that be? What was wrong with these people's souls? If this madman's call was answered, there could be mass suicide. But surely no one would be crazy enough to volunteer to die? Surely God wouldn't let this happen. The moment would come when the Grand Ranter's spell would snap, the cultists return to their proper senses and rebel.

"I ask again," cried Higgins Makepeace: "which among you

will be first to claim the glory that is promised?"

Tingling silence. Then, in the front row, two people rose to their feet: a husband and wife. Every eye fixed on them. Next, two children – a boy and a girl – got up from the floor: exactly as the Grand Ranter's vision had foretold. All at once reality was mimicking prophecy.

"We will be first," said the father in a deep, firm voice, and led his family to the dais and up the steps.

Manningham Sparks was consumed with horror. The little family formed a line, then stood waiting for instruction. For a long moment, Manningham's tongue seemed locked up in his mouth. Then it loosened – God had not deserted him in his time of need.

"No, no! This is wrong!" he cried out, and ran forward.

Thorn stared at his mother. There was such a profound expression of love in her eyes that he took a step forward – two – before he checked himself.

This was *not* his mother. This was an impostor, trying to cast over him the dark spell of her presence. He recalled parting from the real Briar on the edge of the ironworks; how, in her stiff fighting clothes, she'd hugged him to her breast, so that he felt her hardness even as she embraced him. *That* was my mother, he thought, not this caricature.

"You're wasting your time, Querne Rasp. You're not my mother, and you never could be. You may have mesmerised Racky, but he rejected you at the end, and instead chose me. Now that Spine Wrench is dead, you're alone and pathetic. And that's how you too will die."

Briar's mask melted away, to be replaced by Querne's own features.

"That's where you're wrong, boy," she declared angrily. "I shall make the world my plaything, and men and women will worship me. And perhaps I shall never die. Perhaps I shall discover the secret of immortality. But the girl there will die and you shall become my slave. I shall crush you both like ants."

As Querne pronounced the word *crush*, Jewel was granted a sending. Vivid images flashed across the screen of her mind. The vision's intensity almost stunned her, but now everything made sense. She understood what she had to do.

"That may be so," she conceded, speaking with a calmness that belied the excitement she felt. "After all, it's you that controls the five quincells; Thorn and I have none of them."

"*Quincells?*" said Querne. "What sort of a name is that? My *crystals*, do you mean?"

"Call them what you like," said Jewel. "It doesn't make any difference."

But it made all the difference. If Querne didn't know their name, she couldn't know who had made them and why they'd been made. *Names are things and things are names.* Querne might have extracted from the quincells some of the knowledge they contained, but she knew nothing of James Mayfield and his ill-fated experiment.

"So," she went on in a calculatingly scornful voice, "you haven't yet dared to wield all five crystals."

"Haven't wielded all five? Of course I have!" blustered Querne.

Jewel laughed. "No you haven't, not all five together. You

tried earlier today to operate four, didn't you, and it was all you could do to keep the vortex under control. You were relieved to shut it down."

"Stuff and nonsense, girl!" Querne's cheeks were a furious red.

Jewel decided to turn the knife. "I think you're *afraid* of the black crystal. I think you're afraid of finding that your powers are limited. For all powers are limited, or human beings would be gods."

"Listen who's talking! I could crush you, Jewel Ranson, with no more than my little finger—"

"Perhaps you could. But it doesn't alter the fact that the crystal star, the five-fold vortex, is beyond you. And it will always be beyond you, no matter how long you live."

"Stuff and nonsense, girl!"

"You're repeating yourself, Querne. That's what old people do. If you dare wield the five, prove it to me – here, now. Then I shall be the first to bow down and worship you."

"Why should I care what you think?"

"Because like you I'm a Magian, the only person who can understand what a feat it would be."

Thorn had become increasingly confused by this exchange. What was Jewel doing? Had she taken leave of her senses? She seemed bent on provoking the very thing they'd come to prevent. But he kept his mouth shut. Jewel did nothing without a purpose. She must know something he didn't.

"Of course," Jewel added with an impudent smirk, "if *you* daren't wield the crystals, give them to me. *I'll* do it."

Querne snorted. "What sort of a fool do you take me for?"

"No one who could wield the five crystals could be a fool."

Querne sank back into her chair. It was hard to decide whose look – the Magian's or the carved rat's directly above her – was the more malignant. If Querne could have killed with a look, Jewel would have given up the ghost then and there. But, reaching out, the Magian moved her hand over the quincells, touching one after the other: the black crystal first, then the other four in turn. As her fingertips touched them, the stones sprang into life, shooting out their separate light-rays towards the ceiling, where they played upon the rock like an impossible rainbow.

Querne bent back her hand so that her fingers pointed up. The quincells rose from their rack, shifting into the vertical plane. The crystal star bathed the rock walls in a brilliant light show.

"Do you see," said Querne triumphantly, "how powerful I am? And what a little fool you were – *are*, ever to doubt me?"

Closing her fist, she snapped her fingers. The crystal star began to revolve. While it still moved slowly, the five stones remained separate. But as the star's speed increased, they merged into greeny-blue. The black crystal vanished to leave a black hole in the centre, and this seemed to dilate like a sinister alien eye. Around the spinning stones, a kind of nimbus appeared.

The whole chamber was vibrating, dislodging dust and small fragments of rock from roof and walls. Querne paid no heed to this, instead fixing her eyes on Jewel.

Abruptly out of the vortex leapt a tongue of yellow flame. It was aimed at Jewel and Thorn, but the girl had foreseen it. An instant before the eruption, she threw herself at Thorn. The pair went sprawling on the floor and the flame splashed the wall behind them, scorching the rock black.

Querne grinned. Next time, she thought – next time for sure I'll have the girl!

But, in a quick, fluid movement, Jewel tore the Lowmoor Syb's moon-chain from her neck and threw it across the room. *Like the wire that conducts the charge of lightning to earth.* Except that the chain didn't touch the floor . . . The iron disc flew straight and true and disappeared into the vortex. There was a high-pitched hiss and the eye blazed out violet. The flare rebounded off walls and ceiling, and the whole chamber shook. Querne was thrown backwards, and as she hit the floor hard she lost control of the quincells. They jumped away from her and drifted spinning into the air.

Querne tried to get to her feet, but could not. A sharp pain was in her hip. It's broken, she thought. Gritting her teeth against the pain, she propped herself on her left elbow and, reaching up with her right hand, directed an impulse at the vortex to bring it back down under control. She frowned with the effort, and lines of strain crawled over her face. The vortex wobbled, spitting out mauve and amber sparks. The drain on the Magian was terrible. Her features tightened, the skin shrinking back to the bone, aging her. Then the vortex seemed to steady and dip back towards Querne.

"I have it again!" she cried. There was triumph in her voice.

Jewel and Thorn were on their feet now, but when Thorn made a move to cross the floor to Querne, Jewel held him back.

Doubts pressed in on the girl. What if the sending I had was wrong? What if what I saw was only one possible future? If it doesn't come about, disaster will strike again, just like it did in the Dark Time.

The vortex rose through the air, pulling Querne up after it. Astonishment showed on her face as her feet left the ground. She kicked out, struggling madly, and must have done so to some effect, for the spinning quincells slipped back and she fell to the floor with a thump. She shrieked with pain. The vortex crackled and yawed and spat a jet of black particles out. The ceiling melted at their touch and the jet passed through and out of sight.

There came a screech of tormented metal. Peering up at the smoking hole directly above her head, the prostrate Magian screamed.

The Grand Ranter watched as Manningham Sparks came charging towards him, then waved a languid hand. The resident cultists on his left jumped up out of their chairs and formed a human barrier. All but one: Fleck Dewhurst remained seated, a look of concern upon his face. He seemed uncertain what to do.

The cultists closed around the preacher.

"God is Love!" he was shouting, "Love! Not suicide! Not murder! Not death! It's death you're worshipping here!"

Then he was writhing in their grasp. A hand clamped itself to his mouth, reducing his protest to a gurgle.

Higgins Makepeace glared at Sparks from his place of elevation.

"Ranter Sparks, since you cannot remain silent," he said, "you compel us to silence you."

Manningham stared at the cultists holding him, then beyond them at the waiting congregation. Surely they would be with him. Surely they understood the madness of mass suicide, the monstrous nature of the thing the Grand Ranter had proposed?

Every face expressed censure, true, but not of Higgins Makepeace. Of *me*, thought Manningham Sparks. They would rather die than live.

Closing his eyes, he prayed: God, help us in our need. Come to us with Your infinite love and mercy, touch us now . . .

But the voice of God did not reply. Instead, inside the Ranter's head, a laconic traitor drawled: *God helps those who help themselves.*

But what if you *can't* help yourself?

His silent prayer faltered. His body sagged. He was beaten.

Higgins Makepeace turned to the family lined up in front of the dais.

"This is a great thing you do," he informed them floridly. "Your names will be written in gold on the cloudy walls of Heaven."

Has he forgotten, thought the Ranter, that none of them can read?

"Have you a knife?" Higgins Makepeace asked the father.

"I have," said the man, speaking as if he was in a trance. He drew a knife from the sheath at his belt and held it up. Flakes of light deflected from it.

"Are you desirous of glory? Are you desirous of entry into the life that is promised – both for yourself and your loved ones?"

"I am," said the man.

"Are you ready to do God's will?"

"I am," said the man.

"Then take courage," cried Higgins Makepeace, "and kill your first-born!"

The father turned to his son and kissed him tenderly on the forehead.

Manningham struggled against his captors, but he couldn't break free.

The father raised his knife to strike.

The church floor trembled . . . then, with a *whoosh* like an outbreath of God, black particles fountained up directly beneath the Iron Angel. Shooting into the air, they opened like the blossom of a purple, impossible flower, peppering pillars, walls and roof, passing through wood and stone as if they hadn't been there. Sunrays gaily stoppered the gaps.

The Grand Ranter swung round to see what was happening. Time hung fire in the stunned silence, then the effigy, which the surge of particles seemed not to have affected, began to slide into the hole.

Crying "No!" Higgins Makepeace bounded down the steps of the dais and threw his arms out as if to grasp the statue and drag it back. But, as the Angel's baleful face, haloed with spikes, dropped towards him, a prominent tine snagged his clothing. Makepeace tried to pull away, but now another prong caught him. In an anguished screeching of metal, the Iron Angel slid into the hole, taking the prophet down with him. Makepeace squealed like a shot rabbit; then he and his icon were lost to sight.

The building creaked and groaned. Crackings and rendings were heard.

Manningham Sparks wrenched himself free of his captors.

"The roof is going to collapse!" he shouted. "Run, run for your lives!"

People needed no further bidding. Chairs were thrown aside as worshippers leapt to their feet. Then everyone was running — men, women and children — elbowing and barging in their eagerness to escape. The congregation, the resident cultists, the little family of four who'd came so near to sacrifice — people who moments before had been eager to die — had collectively discovered that they wanted to live. The myth of the Iron Angel, the Grand Ranter's influence, the torn shreds of a dead cult — were abandoned in the rush to escape the end of the world.

Detaching itself from the ruined vault, a beam came plunging to the ground and smashed into the wormy pews.

Amidst the frenzy of flight, only two men held back — Manningham Sparks and Fleck Dewhurst. The Ranter had spotted a couple of children left behind in the rush — a small boy bewildered, a tiny girl crying — and now he hastened towards them. Fleck saw and went after him. More beams came hurtling down. As each hit the ground with a deafening report, the doomed edifice shuddered and shook.

"Get the boy!" shouted Sparks.

Fleck needed no second bidding. Reaching the child, he caught him up and turned and ran for the south transept.

As Manningham reached the little girl, one of the pillars fell sideways and went crashing to the ground, releasing billows of filth. Then the Ranter too was running, puffing and blowing comically, the girl tucked beneath an arm. Above the drifts of dust and cobwebs, a window of blue sky yawned as a section of rib-vaulting sagged.

Then Fleck and the Ranter were under the arch and into the transept, hurrying on towards the door.

There was chaos outside the church. Some people had fled along the pathway and were already lost to sight; others had vaulted into the saddle; others had mounted carts and carriages and whipped up their rats. Two of the vehicles had collided and a cart had overturned, and as Manningham glanced about, hoping to spot someone who might claim the child he carried, he saw the dazed driver crawling away from the trap.

Behind them, a chunk of vaulting dropped with an ear-rending roar into the church, and the ground shook like water.

"Is this the end of the world?" Fleck yelled in Manningham's ear.

A man and a woman came running up.

"What are you doing with our children – trying to kidnap them?" The man snatched the girl from the Ranter, while the woman grabbed the boy. Both children howled as their parents scuttled off.

Fleck and Manningham exchanged puzzled shrugs.

"Let's get out of here," said the Ranter. "The church walls may go next!"

He led the way down one of the tracks that he frequented in his walks. Splinterings and detonations sounded to the rear.

It's as if, Manningham fantasised, the church *wants* to die . . . But how can that be? *Now* who's crazy? he asked himself.

In a wail of strangled metal, the Iron Angel slid out of the hole the black atoms had drilled in the rock and dropped towards the spinning vortex and the hapless Magian on the floor. When the effigy struck the crystals there was an ear-splitting *BANG*! and the vortex exploded. Mirrors shattered, showering glass. Five fiery nuggets launched on separate trajectories, the quincells fired themselves through the flagstones of the ceiling as if nothing was in their way.

Querne didn't stand a chance. The Iron Angel crashed down on her, killing her instantly.

Chance kept the effigy in an upright position. Impaled on its metal spikes, crushed in the descent, the Grand Ranter dangled limply, an abandoned doll. Blood dripped from his boots.

Deafened and stunned, it took Jewel and Thorn a few moments to gather their wits. As they stared at the wrecked room, trying to take in what had happened, the chamber shuddered under some terrific impact.

"It's the church," said Jewel grimly. "That jet of particles – the roof's beginning to collapse."

"We've got to get out of here!" cried Thorn. "But the labyrinth . . . !" He frowned. "It's too far – we'll never make it . . ."

Jewel seized his arm and pointed at the wall. "Look!" she exclaimed.

Where the full-length mirror had been, to the right of Querne's chair, an egg-shaped opening gaped in the rock.

"A passageway!"

"Come on!"

They hurried across the room, their boots crackling on shards of glass, and into the mouth of the passageway. Roughly nine inches in height, it had been tunnelled through solid rock and was lit at intervals by the same gem-lights that studded the labyrinth.

It drove straight ahead, its floor neither rising nor falling. As Jewel and Thorn sped on, they felt more impacts above. The hugest threw them to the floor, where they lay bruised and gasping. Fragments of rock drizzled on them.

If the roof should collapse!

But no, somehow it held. They got to their feet and hurried on.

Still the floor continued level. Then, all at once, they came out from under the stone. Now the tunnel ran through clay. At regular intervals, walls and ceiling had been shored up with planks, and more had been laid underfoot. But in places, where the walls had been left exposed, slides had occurred, and Jewel and Thorn had to scramble over the falls. The clay stuck to their boots, making the soles slippery and slowing their progress. Thorn was leading when a tremendous impact bulged out one wall, springing a plank across his path to smash into the opposite side.

A shout came from behind, and he turned to see a clay slide devouring Jewel's legs. He took the few steps back, grabbed her out-thrust hands and heaved. There was a reluctant sucking sound and Jewel popped free. Thorn's feet slid from under him and she landed on his chest.

Then she was on her feet again and pulling him up. On they ran.

The end of the passageway took them both by surprise. One moment they were in a tunnel, the next they were standing at the bottom of a shaft. They craned upwards. The sides of the shaft were lined with planks and cross-braced, and every so often there appeared a gem-light. The nearer lights burnt brightly, but the more distant glimmered like stars in a dark well. Attached to one side of the well was a metal ladder.

"You go first," said Thorn.

Jewel was about to comply, when an impulse held her back.

"No, you," she said firmly.

"But—"

"Go!" she commanded him.

Thorn shrugged and began to climb.

Despite the clay on their boots and hands, they made reasonable progress. The shaft was deep, but at last Thorn announced,

"I can see the top, Jewel! We'll soon be out!"

The shaft was capped by a wooden lid hinged on one side. Thorn gave a heave. It lifted, teetered, then flipped over with a thump onto the ground. Sunlight poured into the shaft.

At the very same instant, from somewhere not far distant, there came a terrific crash as of falling masonry. The ground shook beneath the impact, rattling their teeth in their heads. A crack! sounded from below. The ladder quivered as the planking twitched nervously; next moment, planking and ladder began to slide down the well, baring a coarse tangle of roots. Thorn made a grab at this as the rim of the shaft receded from him.

Coarse fibres were in his fists. For a moment the slide stopped.

"I can hold us!" Thorn shouted. "Climb up beside me!"

Thorn squeezed to one side and Jewel began to climb, edging

up alongside. But her head had reached a point no higher than Thorn's knees when ladder and planking together slipped out from under them both. As the rung she was standing on slid away from her, Jewel grabbed hold of Thorn's legs.

Moments later, the ladder was gone, leaving the two of them dangling there.

"Hold on, Jewel!" Thorn called down. "I'll try to pull us up!"

But he couldn't, not with Jewel's weight dragging on him.

Then the root he held with his left hand tore from its moorings. Tossing it away, he shifted his grip to a neighbouring growth.

"Help!" he shouted. "Help! Help!"

Up above only a circle of sky was visible, cool, blue and implacable. And now the root he held with his right hand was also pulling free. He quickly switched that hand too. A clot of soil fell from the wall, hit his shoulder and dropped away. His arms were weakening now, his body protesting at Jewel's weight.

"Help!" he shouted out again. "Anyone up there – help!"

Jewel sensed Thorn's strength ebbing. If only Magians could fly! Perhaps if I let go, she thought, he can climb to the top . . .

"Don't let go!" Thorn cried. "Don't you dare let go! Either we both escape, or—" He let the sentence hang.

Now who's reading minds? thought Jewel.

Minds . . . *Minds!* Why hadn't she thought of that before? Shutting her eyes, she cried out silently: *Help! Help us! Help! Over here, in this hole! Please help us! Help! Help!* Beaming out the message with all the strength at her command.

Soil was crumbling fast. The roots were barely holding on . . .

A strong hand grasped Thorn's wrist.

"Hang on there, you two!"

Thorn looked up. Manningham Sparks, by all that was impossible! Beside the Ranter's head appeared a second: the ratman Fleck's.

Thorn's other wrist was grasped. As soil crumbled and fell away, Thorn and Jewel were hauled up.

No sooner were they clear, than the edge of the shaft collapsed and tumbled into the well, taking with it the wooden lid.

The four humans lay panting amidst a patch of primroses. They were outside the churchyard. Jewel and Thorn stared at the church. The whole of the roof had gone and parts of the upper walls too. Where the steeple had stood jutted a broken jaw of stone.

Manningham Sparks grinned at Thorn.

"We're even now, you and me." The Ranter was pleased with himself. "You see, Thorn, how God works? He sees and weighs everything. You saved my life at Brokenbanks so I could save your life here."

Thorn smiled and nodded. He wasn't sure the Ranter was right, but if Manningham saw it that way, who was he, Thorn, to object?

"Did you hear my cries for help?"

Preacher and ratman exchanged looks.

"We heard *something*," said Fleck, "but whether the voice came from *outside* our heads or *inside* it . . ."

Jewel smiled, but said nothing.

The four got to their feet. Jewel looked ruefully at her clothes and boots. They – like Thorn's – were smeared with yellow clay and stuck about with bits of grass.

"I need a bath," she observed.

Manningham Sparks grinned. "I know the very place you need."

The place in question was an inn on the Lowmoor-Wyke road. The four travelled there together, saying little as they walked, minds preoccupied with the whirl of events they'd lived through. After they'd cleaned themselves up (drawing on all the landlord's patience and many pans of hot water), they met before dinner for a turn in the inn garden – a patch of short-clipped lawn hedged around by taller growths.

"Where will you go next?" asked the Ranter.

"I—" Thorn began, then stopped and looked at Jewel.

"*We*," she said, "are going to Wyke, then on to Norgreen. We must warn the settlements against Mabbutt and Slack. They have weapons from the Dark Time that have to be destroyed. But if the settlements join together, they can defeat the ironmasters."

In her mind's eye she saw herself, wrapped in her cloak of secrecy, creeping into the enemy camp, laying a gunpowder trail away from the barrels and blowing them up.

"Iron," the preacher murmured. "Why is every bad thing iron?"

It isn't, Jewel thought. Iron shattered the crystal vortex, iron crushed Querne Rasp. Nothing's either black or white.

Black or white – the two moons. She thought of the Syb's iron chain. How much had Minny Pickles seen? More than Jewel herself had done? And when had Minny had her opening – even before the pair met? I'd love to talk to that canny old woman again, Jewel told herself.

"What about you?" Thorn asked the Ranter.

"Norgreen, I'm thinking," Sparks replied. "From what you once told me, the place is badly in need of a preacher. One who *really* knows his stuff!"

Thorn smiled. You just couldn't keep the plump Ranter down. "What about you, Fleck?" he said.

"Could Norgeen use a ratman?"

"I'm certain it could."

"Then it's Norgreen for me, too."

Just then, in the thick grass beyond the lawn's edge, something glinting in the late-afternoon sun caught Jewel's eye. She pushed in amongst the tall blades to take a look.

There lay the black crystal, a purple glimmer at its heart. Of the other quincells, no sign.

They're scattered again, she thought, much as they were by the great disaster.

She knelt down and peered at the stone. It had passed through solid rock, yet it appeared none the worse. Was it indestructible?

The quincell's heart flickered violet. It had destroyed Querne Rasp . . . Yet how beautiful it was. Was it waiting here for her, as it had in the Great Nest? Was her destiny tied to it? With it she'd be able to explore the wave function, travel to unimagined worlds.

Thorn came up beside her and saw what she was looking at.

"Don't touch it!" he said sharply. "Leave the damned thing where it is!"

"I can't do that," she replied. "Someone else will find it here."

"Only a Magian can wield it. What other Magians do we know?"

None, thought Jewel, but I can't be the only one. And who knows, as I do, how dangerous it is?

She reached for the stone—

Then hesitated.

JEWEL AND THORN by Richard Poole

When Jewel Ranson's father is attacked and killed, Jewel vows to avenge his murder. Befriended by Rainy Gill, a travelling juggler, she sets off in pursuit of his killers.

Returning with a stolen crystal from a ritual test to mark his coming of age, Thorn Jack discovers his younger sister has been abducted. With the enigmatic Racky Jagger as his guide, Thorn trails her kidnappers through the heart of the mysterious Judy Wood...

As Jewel and Thorn move towards a momentous meeting, dark forces gather around them. And the ruby crystal stolen by Thorn begins to take on a significance he couldn't possibly have imagined...

ISBN 0-689-87290-9

THE BRASS KEY by Richard Poole

Blackmailed by the sinister Spetch twins, Jewel and
Thorn must journey across land and water to retrieve
the mysterious brass key. Until they find it and return it
to the Spetches, Thorn's sister Haw is at the cruel mercy
of the twins.

But Jewel and Thorn encounter unexpected, malevolent
forces along the way and discover a new and even more
dangerous opponent lurking in the shadows...

ISBN 0-689-87290-9